FRAGMENTS

OF

TOMORROW

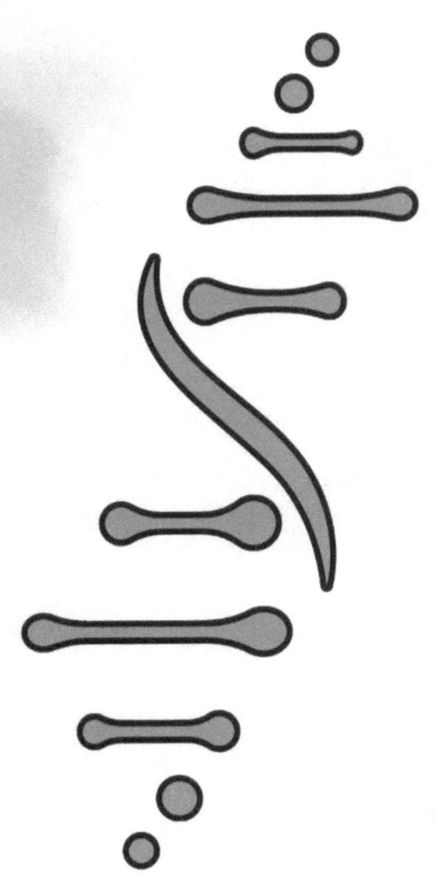

R. L. KING

First Edition: 2025

ISBN: 979-8-9999166-0-0

To the authors in Royal Archives and Ink & Key, who waded fearlessly into my unedited chaos and offered insight before a single page was polished.

To my friends, who stood by through late nights, endless revisions, and my relentless questions, cheering me on when the work seemed impossible.

And to my spouse and children, thank you for embracing my hyperfocus, for tolerating the hours I poured into a dream I feared might fade, and for celebrating the days it only grew stronger. It's only because of you that I hold this book in my hands.

Your love and patience turned a solitary obsession into a story shared with the world.

Fragments of Tomorrow contains themes and scenes that may be difficult for some readers. Please be advised that the story includes:

Violence and War
Medical Trauma
Human Experimentation
Fire
Death and Grief
Oppression, Captivity, and Power Imbalances
Psychological Trauma and Fear
Harsh Language

CHAPTER ONE
The Beginning

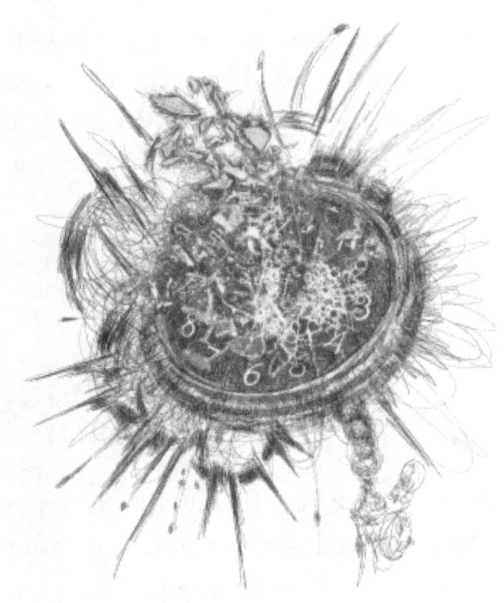

The Clinic

My fist slams against the hard metal, the reverberations traveling up my arm, deadening nerves that scream for me to stop, but my brain refuses to listen. My vocal chords start to shred in my throat as I let out another scream, another plea for someone to listen to me, but it's no use.

I step back from the door to my cell, holding my throbbing hand, the ignored tears sliding down my cheeks and falling to the floor at my bare feet. Sobbing, I fall to my knees, unable to control the overwhelming sensation of the walls closing in, and the feeling of bone on hard tile restores some sense of sanity before it too is ripped from me.

I gasp for air, latching onto the toilet that sits in the corner of the room, and heave out everything I have left, the strands of acid burning my lips as they pass, my stomach drained hours ago. I had repeated this cycle more times than I could count, yet I can't bring myself to stop.

Heave.

    Scream.

        Pound.

        Scream.

            Fall.

Heave...

The convulsions slow before finally coming to a stop, and I lift my head from the cool metal, looking around my room again, hoping for something, *anything*, to have changed. The bed, a simple cot on a metal frame, is made neatly and pressed against the far wall, the rough white blanket made for warmth, not comfort.

Movement from the corner of my eye causes me to turn my head and face the camera mounted in the corner, my frustration building as I realize I'm still being watched, but not heard. Pulling my legs into the white gown that covers my body, I try to hide as much skin as possible, my translucent pattern going dark as the thin fabric casts shadows over the whirls I had known my entire life.

How did I get here? I ask myself again, but none of my memories can explain how I ended up in this room. Closing my eyes, I calm my breathing and focus my mind. Swirling fog mixed with black spots fills my vision, and I will myself to think clearly, to understand where I am.

Screaming in frustration, I pull my hands from my head, yanking out chunks of hair and throwing them to the floor where their brethren lay.

I pull myself to my feet, and breathe through the panic that raises its head. Each step forward feels like quicksand sucking me down, but I will myself to take another, and another, before I finally make it to the door. I rest my head on the metal and raise my fist, laying the bruised flesh against the solid steel.

One...

Two...

Three...

A scream rips from my throat, and I taste blood on my tongue as I pound my fist against the door again and again.

I don't know how I ended up here, but it's clear to me what this is.

A prison.

The City

I don't want a sib... The sound of Mar's voice rings through my head as the next blow finds its mark, and I stumble backward into the alcove. My hands rise in front of me, but whether it's in defense or a plea for help, I'm not sure.

My attacker steps forward, blocking the light reflecting from the white polymer buildings around us. "There's no one here to protect you this time, sib."

Another fist finds its home in my abdomen, and I feel the little strength I have left fading away as my muscles collapse, allowing access to the sensitive organs inside.

"P... please..."

"Please?! Please what?" Mar holds their fists at their sides, the rage rolling off of their body like the heat from the sun baking the scorched earth.

"Stop, Mar... Please. I've had enough." I fall to one knee, doubled over in pain as a drop of blood falls to the ground beneath me.

I don't want a sib...

I was only four when my Bot brought Mar home from the nursery. For weeks leading up to the day, I had been so excited to meet my new sib, talking to Bri non-stop about how much fun we were going to have. I sat at the bottom of the stairs, staring at the door the entire time Bri was gone, wringing my hands anxiously.

The door finally slid open and I thought my heart might stop from excitement. I jumped up as Bri walked through the door, blocking out the harsh sunlight with their towering metal frame.

Bri gracefully moved to the side, revealing the tiny figure taking timid steps behind them. "Ixe, this is Mar," Bri said, gesturing to the shy being. Mar was about three feet tall, with long dark curls and bright blue eyes. Their pattern—the unique pigment in our skin that we all shared—was a chaotic mix of bright whorls, twists, and turns beneath their dark complexion.

"Hi, Mar, I'm Ixe!" I exclaimed, bouncing on my feet.

Mar grabbed at Bri's legs and sneered at me as the door behind them slid back into place with a solid thunk.

Taking a step forward, I tried to get Mar to see that it was okay, that I was a friend.

Bri gently took Mar's small hand in their own and pulled Mar forward. "It's okay, Mar, this is your sib."

Mar looked up at Bri's smiling face and back to me before taking a timid step forward.

The memory shatters there, flashes of blood mixing with pain in my head as the words echo around and around again: *I don't want a sib...*

Mocking laughter echoes around me, reverberating from the metal of the wall, amplifying the sound. "I guess you're right."

I flinch as they reach forward, grabbing my shoulders and pulling me to my feet.

"Dust off, Ixy. You don't want to be late for class."

The cool shadows slide away, and the sound of footsteps on hard packed dirt retreats into the distance. I remain still, staring at the ground, afraid of meeting Mar's eyes and re-igniting their rage. As time passes and no more punches come, I finally look up and find the clock tower in the middle of the large city, towering over the shorter buildings that made up the ring of surrounding districts.

Cursing under my breath, another thought replaces the echo in my head. *Bri will be livid if I'm late again...*

Lifting my shirt, I notice the red, angry skin of my abdomen. *That's going to leave a mark,* I think as I lower the thin cloth back over the evidence of the beating.

Mar was getting better at reining in their temper, keeping their blows to more concealed locations these days. Fortunately, that worked out for the both of us. Less questions about my well-being let me live my life in the shadows, unseen by The Net that controlled our society.

Carefully grabbing my bag from the corner of the alcove, I take a few steps to test my injuries. A dull, aching pain spreads through my middle, but no sharp stabs. *Looks like Mar didn't break any bones this time.*

As I exit the alcove, I glance back at the tower. *Shit.* Only seven minutes to make it back across town to class. *If I'm late again, I'll never hear the end of it from Bri.*

I take off running through the alley toward the main street, adjusting to the pain radiating down my legs, taking inventory of the new bruises that would decorate my skin in the coming days.

I skid around a corner, grabbing the railing of a building to help propel me down the next street. As I approach the city center, I see the shimmering banners advertising the Net Council members and remember that the yearly Council review is approaching. The city buzzes with energy as our monotonous existence is broken up by something that only comes around once a year, the idea of something actually *changing*, giving people something to think about and look forward to; even though we haven't had a rule change in 53 years. The Reformation Alliance is especially active and insistent that this year will be the year things happen.

Of course, they were a laughing stock.

The Alliance had always been present, but only older kids joined, and only a quarter of them at best. It was the biggest joke in the city, as they couldn't gather enough support with kids constantly leaving to actually make a difference, but Mar was a true believer and pushed their rhetoric at home every chance they got. Bri tolerated their outbursts, but they had become more frequent and more violent the closer we got to the Council review.

I round the corner to the market square, the vast expanse of desert ground sprawling before me. Bots and older humans milled about, shopping at the open air stalls that made up the main source of commerce in the city.

Quickly grabbing a pastry from the closest stand, I yell my purchase number behind me as I keep moving backwards. Tir, the shopkeeper, throws their metal hands in the air in frustration just as I turn back to face forward, slamming into the back of another Bot.

Pain lances through my skull as my forehead collides with the hard, black metal.

"Ixe, how many times have I told you to watch where you're going?" Bri asks, turning to face me, their expression one of disappointment.

I stare up at the shadow above me, the harsh sun silhouetting their frame. The Bots are tall, thin representations of humans, primarily made of metal. Their silicone hands and faces providing a stark contrast to the black titanium of their frames. Hundreds of years ago, they had shed most of their manufactured skin, realizing it was unnecessary. A few of the caretakers kept the skin on their hands and faces to offer a soft touch and recognizable expressions for the young humans they cared for, but most Bots around the city were solely metal.

"Hey, Bri. I was just..." I stammer, trying to rise from my now seated position on the dry earth, holding my throbbing head.

"You were just running late for class, *as usual*, and thought it would be smarter to sprint across town haphazardly instead of facing my wrath?" Bri asks, extending a hand to help me up.

I wince at their tone, but take their hand. Bri pulls me up as if I weigh nothing at all, my size merely an inconvenience for them.

Offering them my biggest smile, I quickly wipe the dust from my linen clothes. "I'm sorry, Bri. I got distracted at the wall and didn't notice how close it was to class time. It won't happen again, I promise."

Bri raises a mechanical eyebrow and glares down at me. "We both know that's not true, Ixe. You shouldn't tell lies. Our honesty is our biggest asset."

"Yes, Bri. I'm sorry."

"Now go on, get to class." They say, turning back to the market stall.

Sighing, I leave my dust covered dessert on the ground and trudge toward the education district. I should have known better than to run through the city, and then to *lie* about it to Bri's face? *What was I thinking?*

"You weren't."

I spin toward the sound, and a large human steps out of the shadows, their white linen clothes pristine compared to my own shabby, now brown, attire.

"Loc!" A smile appears on my face as my best friend holds out their arm. I take it in mine, clasping my fingers just below their elbow in greeting.

A returning smile lightens my mood, and Loc pulls me in for a hug. Any attempts to reject the affection go unnoticed as their strength overpowers my own, and I find myself wrapped in a strong embrace.

"What are you doing over here?" I ask as we part.

"Well, I *was* coming to see how your last day was going. Alas, you were nowhere to be found, so I decided to head to the market, where I saw an inconspicuous cloud of dust followed by a royally painful face-plant into the back of a robot. You have a little..." They say, reaching for my face, and I remember that I hadn't wiped the blood from my lips after my fight with Mar.

Quickly pulling away, I wipe at the stain, a reminder of the larger blemish on my abdomen, and another lie falls from my mouth, "I must have busted my lip when I hit Bri..."

"Hmm." Loc says, a knowing look in their eyes, but they don't say anything to counter me. "Well, you better get to class. Don't want to miss your last day entirely."

Right. Tomorrow is my 20th birthday—the day I leave the mundane life of childhood and enter adulthood. My mind wanders back to my first day of school, where I met Loc.

I had clung to Bri, terrified of the more robotic faces of the teachers. While they were also a caregiver, Uni had forgone that feature and their face was that of hard titanium.

Bri tried to reassure me, "Ixe, you're going to be okay," but my only contact at six years old had been nursery Bots and Bri, whose faces were like mine, not twisted, cold metal mockeries. I held tighter to Bri's shoulders, fear consuming me. Bri let go of Mar's hand to grab my waist with both hands. "You'll have so much fun at school, Ixe, I promise." Pushing me away, I watched my small hands slide over the smooth metal of their frame — nothing to hold on to.

I cried and flailed as Bri carefully deposited me over a gate and into a play area. Uni walked up to where Bri stood, watching me kick and scream. "Bri! It's so good to see you. How long has it been now?"

"Uni," Bri said, nodding toward the scary metal Bot. "It's been about six years since Roa graduated."

"Six years?! It feels like yesterday they stepped into my class for the first time," Uni said, leading Bri over to where other Bots were standing in a group.

"Yes, I heard from them just last week..." Bri's voice faded as they distanced themself from the play area. Accepting defeat, I stopped my fit and wiped the tears from my face. Turning around, I found other human kids staring at me. I stared back.

They were all older than me, I knew. It was clear this wasn't their first day, and since we started school on our sixth birthday, these kids must have been older than that. I looked from face to face, trying to find an ally in the mass of kids taking me in. A tall, pudgy child stepped forward from the group and reached out their hand.

I flinched, backing against the dreaded gate, expecting that hand to come flying out to hit me. Even at such a young age, Mar had already shown themself to be a soulless child, taking their anger out on me in punches and kicks, and I had assumed all kids were the same.

"I'm Loc," the child said, hand still extended. I slowly rose from my cowered position.

"Ixe," I replied, tentatively reaching out my hand. Loc took it and shook it up and down as if it meant something.

"It's a handshake," they said, noticing my confusion. "My Bot taught me you should always shake hands when you meet someone." Another child snickered, and Loc rolled their eyes. "That's Kit. They think they know everything."

"I know a handshake is stupid," Kit shot back menacingly. "Your Bot is so formal," they said with annoyance in their voice. "My Bot says that formality is so old school and needs to be taught out of kids."

Loc rolled their eyes. "Kit, everyone knows your Bot is eccentric and losing their grip on The Net." Kit's face turned bright red. None of us knew what eccentric meant, but we knew it must be bad.

"Loc! You are just a meany!" Kit spit out furiously.

Loc shook their head and wrapped an arm around my shoulders, leading me to some toys away from the others. "The first day is hard, but it gets better, I promise," Loc said, as they gave me a big smile. They led me away, and I put Bri out of my mind, focusing on my new friend instead.

Now that friend stood in front of me, graduated and free, yet showing up on my last day to make sure I was okay. Kit had graduated three months ago on their birthday, Loc followed two weeks ago, and now it was my turn. Time to grow up and take my life into my own hands. I look down at my palms, sweating with anxiety, and wonder how I will survive.

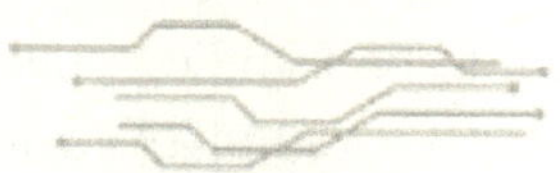

"As you all know, you do not have a penis or vagina as the humans of old did. Your extuberantia takes the place of sexual function in remade humans. This center of nerves is a pleasure center above all else. Your urinary stream comes from a small hole located...."

The clock chimes, signaling the release of students, and I sigh in relief. I step out of the cool classroom into the blazing heat, instantly drenched in sweat from the oppressive humidity. Rain must be on the way soon.

Carefully shielding my eyes with my hand, I cast a glance at the eastern sky, where dark gray clouds the color of my shirt are gathering in the distance. As I contemplate how long it will take for the clouds to reach the city, I'm suddenly hit from the side and find myself sprawled on the ground, my bag tangled around me.

Loc laughs and offers a hand. "How does it feel to be graduated, Ixe?" I take Loc's hand and pull myself up, dusting myself off once again. *I'm going to need two showers after today.*

I punch Loc in the shoulder harder than necessary to thank them for the tackle. "Not much different from any other day, to be honest."

"Just wait," Loc responds, rubbing their now sore shoulder. "You'll be bored out of your mind in a few days."

"Only until we get our assignments," I say, broaching the topic I know Loc doesn't want to think about. Our city is one of the four seeding cities around the continent, specially built to raise the next generation of humans. Each city is run entirely by Bots, with no adult humans in sight, and once a quarter, the Bots give the newly graduated humans their permanent assignments — outside their city.

No one knew what the assignments were or how many human cities existed. We only knew that the Bots were given instructions on where people were needed most, and they sent us there on the Release Day after our 20th birthday.

I glance at Loc and see the looming cloud in their eyes. *I shouldn't have brought it up.* While I'm worried about what my future holds after Release Day, there's also an anticipation there I can't explain. I try to quell my excitement, knowing that it would just hurt them to mention it.

Our Release Day is in two weeks, and Loc has a bigger stake in what's going to happen than I do. While we couldn't reproduce, we still had the desire to form relationships and have a family. The Bots always cautioned us against getting into attached relationships before Release Day, advising us to keep things casual as we explored our sexuality.

I had experienced a few relationships, but nothing serious. Loc, however, had essentially fallen for another human, Kit. They had absolutely hated each other from the moment they met, but something had changed in their fifteenth year. One day they were at each other's throats, and the next, they were grappling each other for a different reason, and they'd been inseparable ever since.

Until Kit's Release Day.

Their departure had broken something in Loc, whose only hope now was to be assigned to the same city as Kit, but they didn't know which city that was or how to find out. Loc had been trying everything to figure out how to find their lost love since.

I know that the days after their 20th had been worse, not having a structure to follow or anyone to talk to while I was at school, but that would change now. I'm free, and I *would* help them find Kit.

I hold my hand out to Loc. "Come on, let's go to the nursery and see if Avi needs help with the kids." I can only hope that the nursery supervisor would be able to answer my questions.

CHAPTER TWO
Reformation Alliance

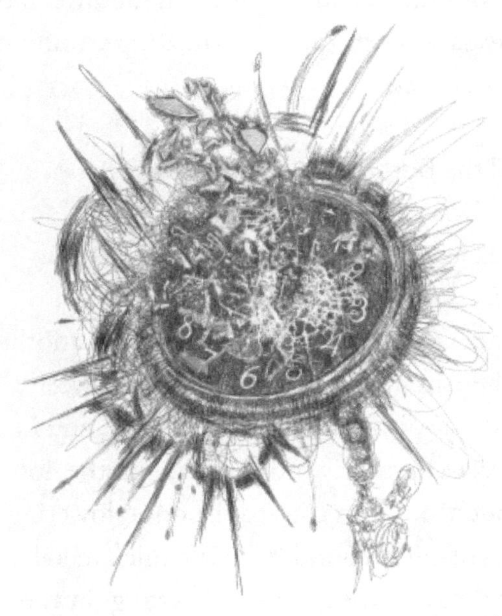

The Clinic

It's been three days, if the pattern of the lights turning off and then resuming their blinding brilliance is any indication. I spent the first day trudging around the small space, working out the stiffness that plagued my body. The second day was spent screaming and pounding on the door until my voice became hoarse and my fist turned red and swollen. Today, I had resigned myself to lying in bed, staring at the smooth ceiling while my mind raced with questions I tried to ignore.

The only sign of life in this dreaded place was the tray of food shoved through the slot at the bottom of the door once a day. Someone was out there, and they wanted me alive, if only barely. My mind wanders back to the questions floating around me like gnats circling a dead carcass:

Why am I not dead?

Why did the Bots lock me up like this?

Where is Bri?

What had led me to this lifeless routine?

Why can't I remember how I got here?

Every time I think back, time jumps from another day in the city to being here in this cell. Everything in between a fuzzy mess.

A thud in the distance breaks my reverie, and I bolt upright. I had already received my tray today, sitting on the floor next to the bed, barely touched. I turn toward the door, lowering my feet to the floor as a series of clicks sound from the thick metal. My breath catches in my throat as the door slowly swings inward, revealing figures standing in the doorway.

Humans. Not remade, but real *living* humans. The first human takes a few steps into the room; curvaceous body, breasts, and a soft, round face. Skimming through my health textbooks in my head, I conclude she must be female. She holds up her hands in front of her, a gentle gesture as she takes a step toward me. I scramble backward onto the bed, pressing myself against the wall. Pausing, concern etched onto her face, she looks me up and down.

I take the moment to return the look. She is smaller than I am, but not by much. Her skin is darker, though still pale compared to the humans behind her. Her fiery red hair—a color not seen since the humans left Earth—frames her luminous green eyes.

She wears a lab coat similar to those the nursery Bots wear. A yellow dress peeks out from underneath: such a bright color for clothes, my own usually gray or brown. I wonder how humans get such beautiful colors as she takes another step closer.

"That's enough, Leah." I jump as one of the others speaks. "We have an objective here, and we don't have time to play games." This one strides into the room confidently, a stern expression on his face. He's wearing a dark green uniform, tucked tightly into large boots. His face has a chiseled and hard appearance, with eyes the color of steel. His brown hair is cropped close to his head, skin kissed with the sun. He reminds me of pictures of the typical human from class. His hand rests on the belt around his waist, gripping what looks to be a box at his hip. *Where have I seen that box before?* I wonder as Leah extends an arm toward him.

"We need it to be calm. We don't want to scare it again," she says, glancing at the hand gripping the box before defiantly meeting the man's gaze. Their accents are thick, the words smooth and less enunciated than my own, but still discernible.

"Please..." I croak, reaching out toward Leah.

"Wrong move," the man says as he raises the black box, revealing it's not a box at all, but shaped to his hand with a protruding front. He tightens his fist around the handle and pulls back his finger. A sharp pain radiates from my shoulder. I look down to see a dart sticking out of my skin.

A gun... I don't know where the word comes from, but I know that is what it is called. I strain, trying to remember where I've seen it, and images flash before my eyes, showing me snippets of a world that I don't understand— tents surrounding me, a rack of guns before me, the flash of a muzzle as one is fired in my direction.

The world spins, and I glance back at Leah, pleading with my eyes. She glares at the man, her lips tight, as she strides toward me.

"Could you have been any more brash, Rich?" she asks, catching my listless body.

Humans. Real humans is my last thought as everything goes black.

The City

We arrive at the nursery during dinner time. Avi barely has time to wave us in as screaming kids fight over the sinks and seats at the table. "Woc!" the kids scream, running up to us. Loc was always their favorite, but I didn't hold it against them. Loc was so much fun, it's why I loved them. After they almost take Loc down to the floor, they turn to me and I feel my heart fill with love as they wrap their little arms around my legs.

"Okay, okay!" I say, pulling one particularly clingy child from my leg and lifting them into a seat at the low table. "It looks like it's time to eat. Who can get to their seat the fastest?" I say, lowering myself to their level and pitching my voice higher to make a race seem like the greatest thing in the world. They all scatter, running for chairs at the table as if their lives depended on it.

"Ixe..." Avi says, tone condescending, but I see the smile on their replicated human face.

"You know Ixe can't help it, Avi. They love to cause trouble wherever they go," Loc says, smiling. I give Loc a light punch to the arm and Avi tsks at us before going to hand out plates of food.

Now that all the kids have settled into their seats, it's much easier to get around. I follow Avi, grabbing two plates of food and placing them on the table in front of two very hungry children. They dig in immediately, going for the carrots and peas before the broccoli. We finish passing out the plates, and start making bottles of formula for the younger infants.

"It looks like the crops did well this year," I say, trying to fill the silence while packing bottles with powder.

"Yes, we are going to have a surplus, I think." Avi says, taking the bottles and filling them with water.

"My Bot told me the new condenser is to thank. They installed it at the end of last season." Loc says, standing at the end of the counter, taking the bottles from Avi, and shaking them before placing them in rows. We finish up our work, talking about how the city is faring, before Avi brings it all crashing down.

"I am going to miss your help after Release Day," they say, sadness in their robotic voice.

Loc's eyes dart to the floor, their jaw setting in a hard line.

Despite the tense situation, I gather my courage and decide to address the subject head on, "Avi... What happens when we are Released?"

"Child, you know I can't tell you more than what you've already been told. You will find out your assignments at your Release, and will leave for your cities with packs of supplies. That is all you need to know."

I glance at Loc, and Avi follows my gaze. Avi, upon seeing their demeanor, goes quiet for a minute, their eyes going still as they converse with The Net in their head. After a few moments they shake their head and say, "I'm sorry, Loc. If you wish to find Kit after your Release, there is nothing we can do to stop you. It will be on you to find them, though. We cannot tell you where they have gone."

"Why?" Loc asks, the word catching in their throat.

"Those are the rules, I'm afraid." Avi says and then changes the subject. "Why don't we go feed the babies? I know you enjoy that, Loc."

Avi is right. Loc's favorite part of helping at the nursery is holding the newborns. They never explained the reason, but I suspect it's because of the closeness of another person. It was one thing to be held by a Bot, their skin cool and unfeeling, but another thing entirely to be held by another human, and we both knew it. So, we volunteered at the nursery whenever we had the chance, and held the babies so they would know the feeling of another human's touch.

We walk to the smaller nursery area and quietly enter, taking our seats in the rocking chairs placed around the room. Avi hands each of us a bottle, and then picks up a fussy baby from a crib and passes them to Loc carefully. Loc cradles the small bundle in their arms, securing them in their blanket before tipping the bottle to their mouth. The baby latches onto the nipple and suckles.

Loc gazes at the baby almost longingly. I ponder if Loc would want kids if it were possible. Would they make a good parent? *Yes*, I think, watching Loc coo at the baby in their arms. *Would I?* The thought flits through my mind as Avi hands me another newborn. I look down at the bundle in my arms and a smile forms on my face. Swaddled in a soft white blanket, their arms pinned, the babe wiggles around trying to get free as they open their mouth and root, looking for a nipple.

Offering what they are searching for, I lift the bottle to their mouth and they settle down peacefully. I watch them suck down the formula, their mouth pulling the sweet liquid from the bottle. I admire their skin's luminescent pattern, a swirl around one eye heading down their cheek to their neck and shoulder. A rare presentation that will have them standing out amongst their peers in the future.

I think about what it would be like to have a child of my own and a dull ache builds somewhere inside me. I would never have that chance as a genetically modified human. They made us, one at a time, in a lab— raised us in a nursery until the age of two, and then gave us to a Bot who would care for us until we reached adulthood and could care for ourselves.

Avi leaves us to our work and closes the door behind them. "What do you think it would be like?" I whisper to Loc.

"What?" Loc whispers back, finally taking their eyes off the baby.

"Having a baby..." I say hesitantly. I feel an aching deep in my core as I find the courage to say it out loud.

"You know we can't have babies, Ixe."

"I know, but the Reformation Alliance..." I begin.

"The Alliance can't do anything about it," Loc sighs, annoyed. "Has Mar really been that influential to you? Do you really think that a cult who accepts someone like them will actually help us?"

I shrug. "Probably not, but it would be nice if some things they said were possible for us."

"Forget about it, Ixe. The Alliance isn't here to help us."

I ponder this, thinking of the Alliance's history and their way of pushing change. They are brutes, pushing the Council every chance they get, threatening and fighting to get what they want. Loc is probably right, but I can't force myself to extinguish the tiny flame of hope inside me. We finish feeding the babies and move to the playroom while they nap. Loc works on building a tower with blocks, while I become a jungle gym.

"You know, Loc, you're better at building block towers than I thought."

"I've had a lot of practice stacking the pieces of your life," they respond, a sly smile spreading across their face.

I feign injury, laughing when a small child comes running with a bandage to patch my hurt. I let them wrap my arm in gauze before they tie it off and give it a kiss, declaring me healed. "It's amazing how easily they find joy in the simplest things. I wish we could all be like that," I say, watching them run away and get lost in a new game with their friends.

"Yeah, no worries, no fears. Just living in the moment. Makes you wonder when we lost that."

"Maybe we didn't lose it. Maybe we just forget sometimes. Being here helps me remember."

Loc meets my eyes over the heads of the kids and we smile, thinking of all the fun times we've had over the years, but our eyes soon darken at the looming Release Day and the uncertainty there.

After a couple of hours playing with the kids, Loc and I leave the nursery in Avi's care and begin walking toward home, where our Bots are surely waiting for us. We chat as we walk through the city center and turn toward the housing district. "So, how badly did Mar get you this time?" Loc asks casually.

I wince. "How did you know?" I ask.

"I saw the way you stood up after I tackled you," Loc replies, "and how you winced when the kids climbed on you." Loc had figured out the relationship between Mar and I quickly. Maybe it was the way I flinched every time Mar reached out, or maybe Loc just instinctively knew something was wrong. Regardless, Loc never tried to intervene, only kept me from going insane afterward.

"Mar cornered me at the outer wall," I sigh.

"Why were you at the wall again?" Loc asks, disapproval marring their normally cheerful face.

I spin, walking backwards as excitement fills my voice. "I just want to know what's out there! Don't you? Soon, we'll be leaving this place, our home, for something entirely new. Doesn't that intrigue you at all?"

"No," Loc replies, their voice flat and harsh. "I wish everything could stay the way it was."

I drop the subject, feeling guilty for bringing it up yet again. Unable to resist, my mind wanders to what lies beyond. I had always felt trapped here, with the same year seemingly on repeat. Release Days, the Bots, the Council—it is all so monotonous, and I am ready to see something new.

I glance at Loc, walking beside me. They are shorter than me and more rotund, with a cheery smile for those who pass by. Loc has always been welcoming to everyone around them, excluding Mar. They wear a gray shirt to cover their round belly and shorts for the hot day, but sweat still glistens on their skin and plasters their blond hair to their head.

Thinking of ways to change the subject, I recall the clouds from earlier. I turn my gaze back to the sky, "Looks like we're finally going to get some rain," I say, trying to mend the wounds I had opened in Loc's soul.

"Yeah," they chuckle. "The Bots are already clearing out Market Square. That place is going to be a mud pit tomorrow."

I kick a rock across the dirt road and watch the dust fly into the air. "I'd rather walk in mud than this forsaken dust."

We continue in silence for a short distance before it's Loc's turn to broach a subject I didn't want to talk about. "So, why did Mar attack you this time?"

I groan, knowing Loc won't like the answer. "I don't know, Loc. They have something against me, you know that."

"You need to stand up to them," Loc says, shooting me a sideways glance.

"I'm too small, and we both know it."

"Then let me do something about it." Loc clenches a fist, but I put my hand on theirs and push it back down to their side.

"It wouldn't help. It would only make things worse between us. Mar just... gets angry and their only punching bag happens to be me. I'll be fine." I smile at Loc to show them I mean it, but I'm not sure I believe my own words.

Loc rolls their eyes before turning back to the path and walking toward the housing district. "Why did you bring up the Alliance earlier?" Loc asks, glancing over at me with a serious look in their eyes.

"I don't know," I say, putting my hands in my pockets and kicking at the ground. "Mar talks about it a lot, and most of what they say would be good changes for us. With Release Day coming... It just makes me think, what if Mar is right? Do we really have a purpose outside of this city if we can't create life?"

"You are the last person I would have expected to listen to Mar, of all people," Loc says, shaking their head. "The Alliance is all talk. They've been around for longer than we've been alive, and nothing has changed. Mar just wants to see the world burn, and the Alliance would do that if they had the power to."

"They want what's best for us humans. Learning about the outside world before we are released, not forcing us out when we turn 20 like we meant nothing to the Bots... the ability to reproduce. Kids of our own, Loc, can you imagine it?!"

"No, Ixe, I can't. We weren't *meant* to have kids. The world was destroyed by humans that were out of control, and the Bots, *The Net*, doesn't want that to happen again."

"But don't you want to know where Kit went? If everything wasn't such a secret, you could find out."

I know I've hit a nerve when Loc stops walking and turns to face me. "You know I want to know where they went more than anything else, but I still won't stoop so low to join up with a group of bully kids just whining about the life they were given and the Bots that gave them that life. Just trust me on this. I know you can't stay away from your sib. But stay away from the Alliance, okay?"

I nod, knowing that Loc is just looking out for me. We arrive at our houses, next door to each other. The houses are two stories, made up of three bedrooms, two baths, a kitchen, and a living area. I always wondered why the Bots needed a bedroom, especially because it just contained a charging station and no bed, but Bri told me it was a leftover detail from the time before The Final Collapse. Loc nods towards their home. "This is my stop. Want to meet up for the game tomorrow?" They ask.

"Sure," I say. "Goodnight, Loc."
"Night, Ixe."
As I walk inside the house, it begins to rain.

CHAPTER THREE
The Game

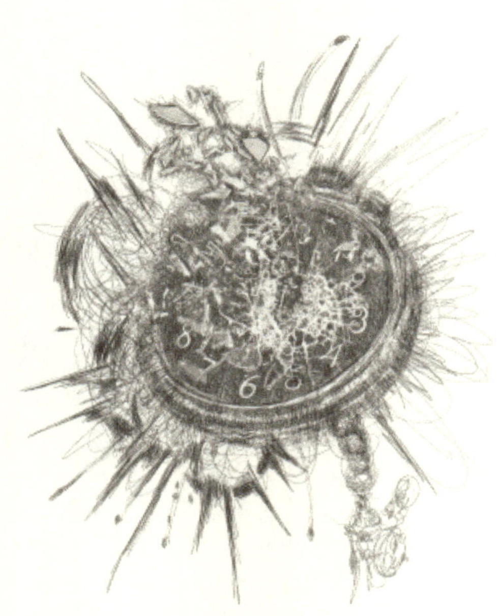

The Clinic

This feels familiar, I think as I will my eyes to open. The light spills in, and the room spins around me. I quickly close them again and a groan escapes me.

"Try not to move too fast," A voice echoes around me. "The sedative is still leaving your system." I groan again as I finally open my eyes to the room. *Different*, I think through the fog. This room is larger, but still just as bright. I'm on a bed - no, a table - and there is a large circular light off to the right above me.

I go to block the light, but my arm doesn't move. I try my other hand, and I feel the pull of a restraint on my wrist. "What..." I try to say.

"I'm sorry about the restraints. We can't have you moving around, and I can't trust you not to flee."

I look toward the voice and see the woman, Leah, from my room. She is still in the yellow dress and lab coat, but now glasses frame her slender face. With each step she takes towards me, I hear the clicking of her heels striking the concrete floor. She takes a seat on a stool near my table and rolls the rest of the distance to my side.

"You have to see... We don't have any other choice. I am truly sorry..." Her voice fades into a whisper as she looks down at her hands. She turns back to her work and I take the time in silence to glance at the surrounding objects: a sink, cabinets, additional lights, and a tray filled with medical equipment. My head whips to the other side — machines, one connected by a thin tube to my arm, pumping me full of a clear liquid. I glance at the writing on the bag — saline.

A hospital? The thought flits through my head as my eyes return to find her standing, fingering a scalpel on the tray. *No, a surgical room...* Dread fills me as she gently lifts the scalpel, her hand shaking slightly.

"Please understand... We don't know if anesthesia will harm

you, or what it will do to the samples, so we have to do this without it." I pull against my restraints, kicking my feet with futile effort. There's no escape.

"No," I say, "Please don't!" She turns toward me, her hand pausing for a split second, showing her hesitation as I see pain reflected in her eyes. *She doesn't want to hurt me.* But she doesn't stop for long, continuing to move to my side.

"I'm a doctor, you know..." she whispers. "I took an oath to do no harm, but these are times when oaths are broken. The time is so short now, so very short..." Her hand slowly lowers to my trembling arm. I try to pull away, but my arm holds fast. I feel the scalpel bite into my skin, so sharp that my nerves don't understand what's happening at first, but the pain soon sets in as she slides it deeper, tracing the pattern that lies under the pale flesh.

I scream as I try harder to pull away, my heart pounding in my ears. My distress falls on deaf ears as she slowly finishes tracing the pattern and pulls the flayed flesh away from my body. I pant, trembling, as she says, "Interesting..." and places the specimen into a jar on another tray. "You did well," she continues, "Only nineteen more to go."

She lowers back over my body, and my screams resonate through the room.

The City

The next day, we meet up for the game. The game has no name; it has just always been known as the game. It was passed down from generation to generation in secret, as the Bots hated the game, and was only played the day after it rained. The rules were simple: capture the flag from the other team.

We spread the location by word of mouth, and this time we chose to play in the warehouse district. Loc and I meet up outside of our houses and head toward the district, taking side streets toward our destination so the Bots wouldn't catch on to the activity. We sludge through the muddy streets, following the path of dozens of kids heading in the same direction.

As we group up with our team, Pol runs up to us and says in a high squeaky voice, "Hey guys! We are playing skins today."

"Yes!" Loc says, already pulling off their shirt. Playing skins would give us an advantage in the game. Shirts had the unfortunate disadvantage of having an extra place for mud to gather.

"You going to run today?" I ask Loc, pulling off my own shirt.

Loc laughs, "You know this body ain't meant for running and climbing." They pat their round belly to emphasize their point.

"Oh come on, you go running with me all the time."

"Yeah, on a track. Flat and dry. I'm a much better shooter, and you need me at your back."

Loc had a point. The shooters would be responsible for keeping the enemy away from us as we fought to make it to the other side of the arena and, ultimately, their flag. Loc and I move to the edge of the building, looking out at the large flat area between buildings and smiling at the traps there.

"Looks like we will be facing pits and mounds today. My favorite." I say, pointing at the middle of the field where those who chose not to play would have come out last night to dig the holes, piling mud into a high mound between them. Our job was to make it to the other side, grab their flag, and make it back without getting tagged by a shirt. We were required to stay within the playing field, which in this case was the large open area in front of us.

Shooters would scatter throughout the playing field, using slings to fire mud bombs at other players. If someone hit you with a mud bomb, you had to pause for five seconds. It wasn't a significant amount of time, but it would give the other team a chance to get away with your flag.

We take our places, preparing for the whistle that will trigger the start of the game. I glance to my sides at the fellow runners playing with me, and we all grin with excitement.

The whistle sounds and I take off running, energy pumping my legs forward through the thick mud. I jump into the first trap hole and sink into mud up to my knees. The smell wafts upward and I hold my breath, forcing one foot forward in the slop.

A mud bomb flies by my head, my hair pulled in by the draft it leaves behind. Refusing to look at where it came from, I persist in digging forward. I pull myself out of the other side of the pit and start climbing the mound, slipping and sliding as I go. Now covered in the thick mud, I have no choice but to take a deep breath, hoping to acclimate to the smell quickly.

Sounds of the enemy climbing the other side of the hill reach my ears, but I make it to the top first, carefully aiming my slide on the opposite side to take out two members of the other team on my way down.

I hear whooping from my team as my aim proves true and we all land in the pit on their side. Trudging through the mud takes longer this time, my body tired, but I'm pulling myself up and out when a mud bomb slams into the side of my head. I feel myself fall backwards into the pit, my head going under the muddy water. My body instinctively tries to gasp, and the taste of mud on my tongue is enough to make me gag.

Flailing, I try my best to determine which way is up, but the mud is thick and sticky, weighing me down. Finally I'm pulled out of the slop by my teammate, and despite the urge to run, I pause my five seconds in the cold water, wiping my eyes and blinking rapidly before darting forward again.

Making it out of the pit this time, I run, throwing mud off of me as I go. My teammates and I scatter around the warehouses, darting between them, looking for any sign of the other team's flag.

Finally, I spot it on a windowsill above a loading bay. The other team has left it completely unguarded. *Amateurs.* Laughing, I pull a ladder off of the bay and set it up, only for another mud bomb to fly my way and slam into my leg. I freeze as a teammate comes flying around the corner.

Frozen, I will them to see the flag, but they only notice me standing there, ladder in hand. Confused, they walk right into the enemy's trap and get hit with a mud bomb of their own. I curse as I 'unfreeze' and immediately get hit with another bomb, the hard thud into my arm sending dripping mud flying, adding to the layers.

We'll never get the flag if we don't deal with that shooter.

As I unfreeze this time, I immediately dodge the bomb and run behind a pillar. "We need a shooter!" I yell at the top of my lungs, my voice cracking with desperation, hoping someone can hear it echo around the buildings. A few minutes pass and I see Loc come around a corner. I hold up my hand and walk out from behind the pillar. A bomb slams into my stomach, and I freeze mid-step.

Our gazes meet, and understanding fills their eyes. They crouch down in the dirt, waiting for me to unfreeze and get shot again before nodding and disappearing behind another warehouse.

A few minutes, and a lot of mud later, I hear Loc yell "Go!" from atop a warehouse. I bolt for the ladder and set it up, climbing as the other team member, also unfrozen, holds it for me.

I reach up and pull their flag down before sliding down the ladder back to the ground with a thud. "Got it!" I yell to Loc before taking off back to our base. Unsure if the other team has discovered our flag, my priority is to return as fast as I can. I run back out to the open space and start dodging the mud bombs as I head to the pit. There, a flash of blue in our enemy's hands. The person in question is crawling out of the pit, but I can't stop. If I get tagged, the flag gets reset and we lose.

I dig in, running as fast as I can and leap over the pit, landing in the pile of mud on the other side. I hear a cheer go up and risk a glance back to see my teammate tagging the enemy and taking our flag back. *We have a chance.* We run together, climbing over the mound of mud and sliding into the pit on the other side.

Our shooters keep the enemy frozen as we rush by. My teammate with our flag, and me with theirs. Cheers go up as I slide across the mud into our safe zone. Hands grab me, lifting me into the air as the shouts grow in intensity, cheering our win. We are so busy celebrating that we don't notice the Bots coming around the corners of the buildings, their faces displaying expressions of frustration.

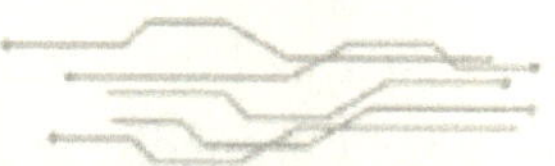

We all walk back to our homes, smiles on our faces despite the trouble we're in. It isn't often that a game is won in one run, and we are high with excitement.

"Too bad Kit wasn't on their team. They would have had the advantage then." One of our team says to another.

I look to Loc and see the hurt in their eyes. It's true, Kit was the best player of the game, and everyone knows it. Unfortunately, they wouldn't be playing any more. I throw a punch into Loc's arm. "How did you find that sniper?" I ask.

"Luck I guess. Stepping out and getting hit was an excellent tactic."

"It was the only way to let you know they were there," I say, shrugging.

"Yeah, and now you look like you jumped in a vat of muck. Bri will be so mad if you sit on the couch covered in all that mud." I glance back at Loc and see the mischief in their eyes. That was the Loc I knew.

"Oh no, no, no," I say, holding up my hands. "Bri hasn't forgiven me for the rat incident yet. I'm not about to start more trouble with them."

"I'll bet you three pastries," Loc says with a smile, knowing I can't resist a bet.

"You're on," I grin back, grateful for the smile that graced my friend's face, at least for now.

It isn't long before we are back at the house, trying our best to keep quiet as the bet comes to fruition.

"Get off of my couch!" Bri's voice is a low rumble, dangerous and full of anger. Their eyes, a deep brown, are almost black under their furrowed brows.

I jump up, dried mud scattering from my quick movement and falling to the carpet beneath my feet. Loc snickers from their spot, leaning against the door-frame to the living room, as my face turns a dark scarlet. We had hoped to be in and out before Bri noticed we were home.

"Don't you laugh like you are innocent, Loc!" Bri heads over to where Loc is standing and grabs them by the back of the shirt. "I know you put Ixe up to this." Loc shoots me an apologetic glance before Bri boots them out of the front door and slams it shut. Turning back to face me, they put their hands on their hips and glare at me.

"Honestly, child, I don't understand why you let Loc get into your head like this. You are smart enough to know you can't get away with these silly little pranks. You are 20 years old!"

I let my gaze fall to the floor sheepishly. "I'm sorry, Bri. It was just... Loc was thinking of Kit again, and I was just trying to cheer them up."

Bri's face softens as they walk over to me and lift my chin. "I love you care for your friends, Ixe, but your Release Day is coming. Don't let friendships that are likely to end become your reason for living."

I pull my face out of Bri's hand, frustrated tears springing to my eyes. "It's not fair, Bri. We have no choice over who we're going to be or where we'll live our lives."

"That's what I've been saying for years." I snap my head around to find Mar standing in the doorway, arms crossed. Their face contorts with disgust as they see the emotion in my eyes. I force myself to bury those emotions deep and stare back, schooling my face into indifference. "This year is going to be different," they continue, walking into the room. "We are going to make changes."

Bri rolls their mechanical eyes. "The Reformation Alliance has been trying to change the way things are for hundreds of years, Mar, and they haven't succeeded yet."

"Maybe that's because you keep sending off the adults that could actually make a difference!" Mar sneers.

Bri's eyes harden as they glare at Mar. "You do not speak to me in that tone."

"Stop me." Mar's hands ball into fists. They have never attempted to hit Bri; it would be foolish to punch solid metal, but their rage has been growing in the past few months, so I wouldn't put it past Mar to take a swing.

Bri pauses, staring into the fiery eyes of my sib. The tension in the room swells as Mar practically pants from the anger in their blood, while Bri stands as still as stone. This had been the relationship between them for years now. Mar had never been a warm child, but when they joined the Alliance, their behavior had changed from cold to hostile.

My eyes flit between the two: one Bot, nearly impossible to hurt, and the other human, fragile in comparison. Finally, Bri puts a hand to their forehead and shakes their head slowly. "I don't know what they are feeding you, child, but the Net has kept humanity alive for 300 years, and they will not change a system that clearly works and keeps both the Earth and humans safe."

Mar retorts, "But we aren't truly living! We aren't able to decide or do anything for ourselves or our people. We aren't even allowed to create life on this damned planet! Our lives have no purpose."

"You don't know what it is like outside of this city, Mar. You are young; listen to your elders on this."

"I know more than you think, and you aren't my 'elder'; you are a Bot assigned to raise me, nothing more."

The hurt in Bri's eyes is visible as they take one last look at Mar and deliberately walk to the kitchen. Mar scoffs at Bri's back and storms up the stairs to their room. I let out the breath I didn't realize I'd been holding and look at the brown stain on the couch. How could I be so dumb? My house was near exploding most days, and I was playing pranks like a 12-year-old.

I walk to the door and remove my shoes, setting them gently on the mat next to the door to avoid kicking up more unnecessary dust. I climb the stairs to my room and carefully pull off my muddy clothes, throwing them into the bin before climbing into the hot shower.

I put my head against the glass, letting the water run in rivulets over my skin, mixing with the mud and pooling at my feet before sinking down the drain. I stare at my pale skin, tracing the pattern that glows there with my eyes, the pattern that I know so well. Each pattern is unique, almost like a fingerprint. Some say that the pattern identifies what kind of human you will be, but there is no evidence to support that theory.

I follow the line down my abdomen, completely flat, unlike the humans of old. We didn't incubate with an umbilical cord, so no belly button is necessary. My mind compares my body to that of our human ancestors. Obviously, humans didn't have the pattern, but we are roughly the same in height. Our fingers and toes are elongated, but our ears resemble those of the original. Our bodies grow no hair other than that on our heads, and even that is thinner.

And then there is our sex. Bots decided long ago that they couldn't let humans repeat history and destroy Earth, so they mutated us so that we couldn't reproduce. We are now one singular sex, with some characteristics of both females and males. I run my hands over my hips, wider than a man's, before glancing at my flat chest. Breasts were classified as reproductive organs and therefore removed from our population. I think about humans and how they could create new life. Such a foreign concept, but somehow thinking about it leaves a pit in my stomach. Like something is missing—lost.

I close my eyes against the images as I think back to what Mar had said. *We aren't even allowed to create life on this damned planet! We have nothing to live for.* Is that true? Is there no point in our existence if we don't reproduce and repopulate the planet? Why did the designers of The Net decide that we shouldn't be able to fulfill the desire that every creature on the planet feels? Was life so bad before that they tore the possibility out of thousands of people just to prevent us from making the same mistakes?

I shake my head, trying to dispel the rhetoric of the Alliance. Once I am Released, I am going to make something of my life. I will go to these cities and do something great. My life will be worth it.

CHAPTER FOUR
Puppet Masters

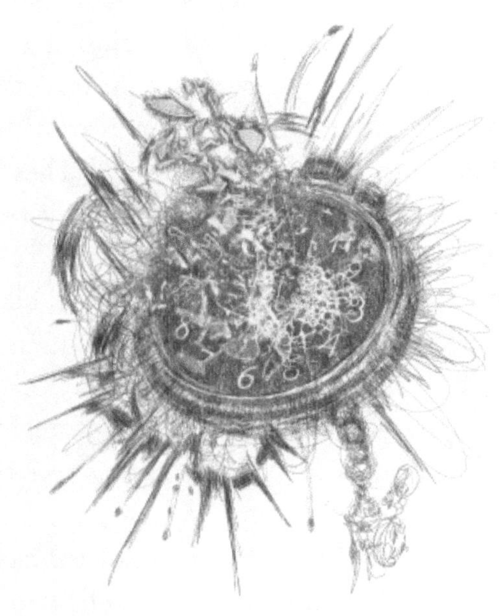

The Clinic

A cool cloth wipes my forehead. I slowly open my eyes, my cheeks stiff from the dry, salty tears that had run down my face. As the cloth vanishes and light floods my vision once more, I grimace. I'm back in the prison cell. The sound of dripping water reaches my ears, followed by the cloth being pressed to my head again.

"Why..." I croak, my throat raw and swollen.

The cloth disappears once more, and Leah is there. "You've been through so much, little one," she coos softly. I glance down at my arms, seeing the bandages that conceal the once-smooth skin now scarred by the same woman who tends to me. I know there must be bandages on my legs, covering similar wounds.

I lay my head back against the pillow, closing my eyes and swallowing around the lump in my throat. As bad as Mar had been, their abuse had only left bruises that disappeared with time. I tremble as I think of the torture I had endured. These wounds would not fade so easily. I purse my lips and hold back the tears that threaten to come again.

"Now, now, you'll be okay. You are safe here. I'll take care of you." Leah's voice is soft and caring as she continues to wash my face, cooling the fire behind my eyes. My lip trembles at her gentle touch, so different from the same touch only hours before. I look into her eyes and see that she believes what she is saying, even though I know it is a lie.

How could I be safe in a place that mutilated me? At the hands of a woman who had sliced away pieces of my flesh for some sick experiment? "What do you want?" I mutter.

I'm not sure she hears me, but eventually she stops and looks me directly in the eyes, searching for something deeper inside me. I return the stare, defiant and unwilling to give in, and it isn't long before she looks away and begins to hum a soft song. *She's insane.* I think, laying my head back and closing my eyes.

Leah eventually stands, taking her equipment with her, and as the sound of the closing door echoes through the small room, I vow that I will not give up. I will get out of here. No matter what it takes.

The City

The next few days pass with little fanfare. The city hums with life, and the AI continue their routines, actively maintaining the city and caring for the humans they are programmed to protect. I sit with Loc on the fountain edge in the center square, enjoying the cool weather that moved in after the storm. We watch as a group of Alliance members march towards the Council building.

"Do you think they're going to have any sway this year?" Loc asks, taking a bite out of a pastry. I had three sitting next to me on a napkin—the payment for the bet I had accepted and subsequently regretted.

"I doubt it," I reply, crossing my legs beneath me to get more comfortable. "They are just going to give their typical speech, and the Council will ignore them as usual. What can you really say against The Net?"

"Good point. They are 'all-seeing' after all."

"They are fallible, just like everything else," I say, rolling my eyes. I don't know what has gotten into Loc, but defending The Net is not like them. "It will be over soon enough, anyway. The Council gathers soon."

"Mar is going to be insufferable once they decline to change again, you know."

"Oh, I know," I grimace. The beatings always increased after the gathering each year, almost as if Mar was taking all their anger at the

Council and directing it towards me, the only thing they can hit without getting in trouble.

I pick up a pastry and take a big bite, savoring the sweet taste. Tir is the best baker in the city and the most expensive. Bri is constantly on my case about spending all our credits on pastries and has threatened to take away my purchase privileges on multiple occasions, but this time it was on Loc, so I didn't feel guilty as I took another bite.

There is a sudden noise behind us, and Loc and I both turn as one.

"You will regret this, Yun! You don't know what's in store for you and your precious Net!" An Alliance member that I don't recognize is standing on the Council steps, yelling at a Council member.

"I understand that your Release Day is before the next Council gathering, but know that we have maintained peace in this city for many years, and we do not take threats lightly."

"What are you going to do? Where are your armies? Because I have an army of my own, and I'm not afraid to use it." The Alliance member growls back at Yun.

Yun's face remains impassive, but I see the quick glance they cast around the square to see who heard the outburst. I grab Loc's hand, quickly standing up and walking away as if I heard nothing. I had a feeling that Yun would gather up those who overheard in order to quell the 'misinformation'. We keep walking until we get to the warehouse district and both of us instinctively head toward the alcove.

"What was that about an army?" Loc whispers as we settle into the shade. I understand why they are whispering; this is dangerous information that would cause quite a stir if it got out around the city.

"I don't know," I reply. "Mar hasn't said anything about it, but the Alliance has been more arrogant lately." I chew on my bottom lip in worry. Tasting something sweet, I realize I left my pastries at the fountain. "Shit!"

"What?" Loc whips their head toward me, looking for whatever caused my outburst.

"I forgot my pastries," I grumble. Loc laughs loudly, holding their belly as they rumble. "What?!" I ask, incredulous.

"That's what you're worried about? There might be a war, and you're worried about a few pastries?"

"Well! I'm hungry!" I say, laughing along with them, forgetting about the seriousness of the situation at hand.

The Alliance doesn't back down. Loc and I see more and more kids gathering around the city center as time goes by.

"I've never seen so many kids skip school." Loc whispers to me one day as we shop near the main square.

"I know..." I respond, worry in my voice. "I wonder what they are all doing."

"I think they're Alliance." Loc whispers back, turning away from the square as a kid turns to look at us.

"What are they doing? Protesting?" I ask, craning my neck to see if I can see Mar among the throng of kids. Bri will be furious if they are skipping school.

The answer comes quickly as all the kids simultaneously collapse to the ground. Bots gasp around us and run to their aid before realizing that the kids had fallen on purpose. Loc and I slowly walk to the edge of bodies, observing the protest going on before us.

"We are cutting the strings!" a voice yells out around us. It takes a minute to notice the speakers spread out around the fallen bodies. I spot Mar's curly hair and pull Loc behind me as I move toward them. "You are puppet masters, and we refuse to be your toys any longer!" the voice continues.

"For too long, we have lived under the shadow of those who claim to know what's best for us. For too long, we have been puppets, our strings pulled by those who seek to control our every move, our every choice. But today, we stand at the edge of a new dawn, where we are no longer bound by the will of the puppet masters."

The Council emerges from their building, faces that of steel, but the speech continues. "We were born to thrive, to live, to love, and to bring new life into this world. But they—our puppet masters—fear us. They fear our potential, our power to create, our ability to shape the future with our own hands. They've told us we are dangerous, that our existence must be controlled, monitored, stifled. But we are not machines to be programmed, we are not pawns to be moved on a board. We are human beings, with hearts that beat, minds that dream, and a desire to live free."

"Turn it off!" Yun yells from the steps, and the Bots scatter, picking up the speakers but unable to find the source of the speech.

"This is our time. This is our moment to declare that we will no longer be controlled, no longer be silenced, no longer be denied the right to live as free beings. We will cut the strings, and we will show the world that humanity cannot be tamed, cannot be caged, cannot be controlled.

"So stand with me, my siblings." As they say this, the fallen children rise to their feet. "Stand with me as we cut the strings and take our place as the masters of our own fate. The time for fear is over. The time for freedom is now. Let's cut the strings and live as we were always meant to—free, unchained, and alive!"

The children roar with applause at the close of the speech, their voices echoing around us, and Loc and I stare in amazement at the sheer number of kids supporting the Alliance.

"Maybe I was wrong..." Loc says. "Maybe they do have a chance."

When I get home that evening, I hear Bri and Mar fighting in the kitchen. I pull off my shoes and place them on the mat by the door, careful not to make any sound. "You don't know what you are getting into, Mar!" Bri yells.

I climb the stairs and sit on a step toward the top to listen. "I understand better than you think I do." Mar says quietly.

"The Council isn't going to stand down and let the Alliance do what they want this time. You've pushed them too far!"

"I've pushed them too far? Don't you mean *we've* pushed them too far, Bri?"

"You know what I mean."

Mar laughs. "Maybe it is you who has pushed *us* too far. We are not your puppets."

I inhale at the reference to the speech, and listen closer as Bri's voice softens.

"I don't want you getting hurt, Mar. Believe it or not, I care for you."

"You can't care for me. You are just a robot, an AI built by humans hundreds of years ago."

"I may not have feelings like humans do, but I do feel in my own way." Bri says, pain in their robotic voice.

"Save me the pleas. Why didn't you take away our feelings when you butchered our DNA, anyway? You already took everything else."

"I didn't take anything from you."

Mar laughs again. "Of course you didn't, Bri. Keep telling yourself that when you check in with The Council later today. Oh, by the way, Roa says hi."

"Don't talk to me about Roa." Bri snaps.

"Yeah, that's what I thought." Mar says softly.

I hear Mar stomping toward the stairs and quickly stand up, running to my room and closing the door softly behind me. I let myself slide down to the floor as I hear the door to Mar's room open and close.

Why was Mar so hateful to Bri? What had happened with the Alliance to turn them against each other? Who was Roa, and why did Bri react so strongly when Mar had mentioned them? The name tickled something in the back of my head, but I couldn't grasp it. Were they another kid in the Alliance? I knew all the kids in our neighborhood and anyone that Mar hung out with, or I thought I did at least. No one named Roa came to mind, though.

I ask Loc the same questions the next day, but Loc doesn't understand any of it either. "Roa has to be someone in the Alliance, but I've never heard the name before."

"Me either," I say, stretching out my hamstring. We decided that today was a good day for a run and made our way to the track on the opposite side of the city. I finish stretching out and pull my shirt over my head.

"You're so bright! You're blinding me!" Loc says, covering their eyes with their hands and looking away.

"Ha ha," I say sarcastically. "I'm not that bright."

"You said it." They say, winking at me.

I roll my eyes and ask, "Are we going to run or are you going to mock me all day?"

"I'm just saying I don't understand how you don't turn bright red in this sun."

"It's called 'sunscreen'. You should try it sometime."

"Alright, it turns out you can bite back." Loc says, smiling at me.

"We need to find out who Roa is and what they have to do with Bri and Mar."

Loc rolls their eyes, "Ixe, in just a few weeks we won't be here. We will be in our new homes with new friends. Why do you need to know what is going on here?"

"Because Bri is my Bot, Loc. Plus, it's a bit intriguing, don't you think? Nothing interesting ever happens around here. I'm glad to have something to think about during these last few weeks."

"I will ask around and see if anyone knows of a Roa, but we need to be careful about this. Something just doesn't feel right."

"I never took you to be the scared type, Loc. What's gotten into you?"

They glare at me, arms across their chest. "You know very well what is at stake here."

"I know you are going to lose this race." I say, taking off running. Loc curses behind me before stripping off their shirt and chasing after me.

CHAPTER FIVE
The Landing

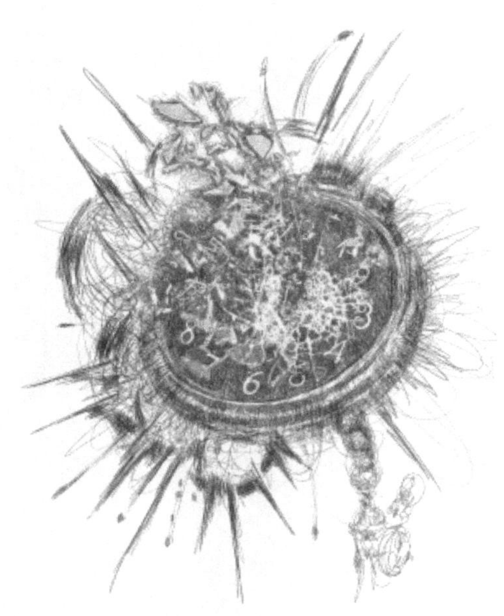

The Clinic

The following days pass by in a monotonous stream. Each morning I'm awakened by the sudden flash of bright lights, and I drag myself to the edge of the bed, staring at the door until the tray is pushed into the room. I carefully stand, wincing as the incision sites on my arms and legs twist and pull with my movement. As I pick at my food in silence, I ponder where I am and try to think of a way out. The room is locked, and I am injured. My options limited, but I try not to get discouraged. Discarding the tray on the floor, I lie back in my bed, staring at the ceiling in defeat until there's a knock at my door in the evening.

It's Leah.

She comes every day to care for my wounds, a doctor that I don't want, yet need. A monster behind the guise of a sweet smile and gentle hands. At first, I can't get her to say much more than comforting words to ease my pain, but on the third day, I ask her where she came from.

"Well, Earth, of course," she responds without thinking.

I open my mouth, prepared to contradict her claim, but the certainty with which she speaks stops me. She must be mistaken. Earth had been uninhabitable to original humans for half a century. There's no way she could have been born here.

Noticing my silence, she glances up and spots the shock on my face. Blushing, her eyes dart to the floor her hands pulling away from my bandages.

"What year were you born?" I ask her, opening a door that I'm not sure I want her to walk through.

Grabbing my arm, she roughly pulls at the bandage, ripping it from my skin abruptly.

I ignore the pain that flares up my arm, startled at the sudden change in her demeanor. "Leah?" I ask, trying to get her to look up at me.

She refuses, pulling my arm closer to her to avoid my gaze. The silence grows as she re-wraps my arm, and once her task is complete, she quickly gets up and walks out of the room.

I'm left in the cell to wonder what it all means. If Leah was born on Earth, it would mean she is at least... 600 years old? That didn't make any sense. How would these humans have gone undetected by the Bots for so long? How would they have survived the atmosphere that was toxic to them. The Bots had spent years modifying the human genome with the intention of saving us after the Final Collapse had wiped out our species.

How then, were these humans here? Now?

Every scenario I could think of just left me with more questions than answers, and my head swam with chaos as the lights shut off, signaling time for bed. Climbing under the thin blankets, I lay my head on the pillow, knowing I wouldn't be getting any sleep any time soon. I lay awake, questions spinning around me, for hours, but just as I'm about to drift off, a memory surfaces, embedding itself in my dreams.

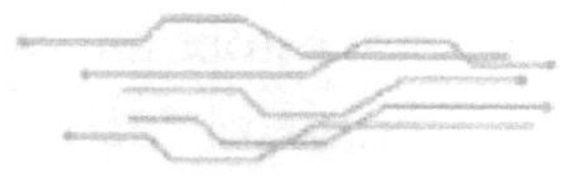

The City

The next day, everything changes. Loc and I are taking a stroll through the city when we hear voices ahead.

"What do you mean, they haven't said anything?!"

"I mean, the Bots haven't mentioned the army at all." Another eerily familiar voice says.

I pull Loc to a halt and we move to the side of a building to listen unseen.

"Did they just not notice?" A third voice in the mix.

"How could they miss an entire army surrounding their city?" The first voice asks.

I look at Loc, their eyes wide as they mouth: *Entire army?*

"I doubt they haven't noticed," the second voice continues, and I recognize it as Mar. "They just don't want to scare everyone."

"Have you talked to Bri?" the third asks.

"No, I can't alert the Bots to what we're doing. Roa was very clear that they don't want me to be pegged as a leader in this war." Mar responds.

There's that name again, Roa. *Who are they?* Loc grabs my arm and I look back at them. They stand, fist over mouth as their body lurches, a cough caught in their throat. *Shit.* I quickly grab their arm and we are on the move, but not before Loc's body explodes with a hacking noise, refusing to be contained further.

I stop, listening, and hear footsteps as the three individuals head toward the noise. With a push from me, I urge Loc to run and they comply, darting towards an awning around a corner. Muttering a silent thank you, I turn and face what is coming for me.

Mar is in the lead, their two cronies following behind. "So, you're following me now?" Mar sneers, still approaching. "Did Bri put you up to this?"

"No one put me up to anything. Do you really think I have the desire to follow you around?" I ask, taking a few steps back.

"What did you hear, Ixy?"

"I didn't hear anything. I was just walking by."

Mar scoffs at me. "I know you heard something you weren't supposed to, otherwise you wouldn't have been running away." They continue forward as I stumble backwards into a wall. "You are going to learn to keep to yourself, even if I have to beat it into you."

The two cronies smile and spread out around me, squashing any hope of an exit. I stand my ground and prepare myself for the blows. Mar doesn't waste any time. A punch lands in my midsection and I double over in pain.

"You won't tell anyone about this, will you, Ixy?" A punch to the side of my head has me seeing stars.

"You will keep your mouth shut, like a good little bitch." The heel of Mar's hand collides with my nose, sprouting blood, and I quickly move my hands to my face to protect it from further harm.

"You will learn your place in this world and stay under my boot." A kick to a knee, and I collapse on the ground panting, blood mixed with tears dripping from my face.

"If you do tell anyone, this beating will be the least of your problems." Another kick to my side and I'm suddenly on my back. The two cronies rush in, kicking me in the dirt repeatedly as I cry out in pain, curling up into the fetal position. I don't know how long I lay there before the beating finally stops and they walk away.

I lay in the dirt crying until I feel a gentle hand on my shoulder. I turn to find Loc and Bri standing over me.

"I brought them as fast as I could..." Loc began, choking on the words at the sight of me.

"Who did this, Ixe?" Bri asks, face as smooth as stone.

I clamp down on my tongue, refusing to answer.

Bri's eyes light up, taking my silence as an obvious message. "They won't get away with this, Ixe. Not anymore."

I roll over in bed, groaning at the noise outside my window and the pain in my body. Last night, Loc and Bri had transported me to the hospital, and then once I received clearance, returned me back home to my bed. They thought I was asleep when I heard them talking.

"Tell me everything they said." Bri insisted.

"They said there was an army outside the city, and that Roa didn't want you to know that Mar was a leader in the war."

"They said that name specifically? Roa."

"Yes. Bri, who is Roa? What is going on?"

"It is nothing for you to worry about, Loc. The Council has it under control. I need you to worry about Ixe."

"I should have told you what was going on between Ixe and Mar a long time ago... I'm sorry I kept it from you."

"It is okay. It is not your fault. I should have been able to see it as their Bot. This is my failure, not yours. Now go home and get some rest. I will take care of Ixe now."

I heard the door close and Bri step up next to my bed and say, "I'm sorry, Ixe. If only I had intervened before it got this far. I will take care of everything."

The yelling outside my window that had woken me gets louder, and I sigh in frustration as I roll out of bed. My head pounds, and the room spins before righting itself again. I make my way to the window and look down into the street below to find people pointing and yelling.

I moan again as I walk to my bathroom; the bruises covering my abdomen pulling as I walk. I look at my face in the bathroom mirror and immediately tears spring to my eyes. Swollen, black and purple, my face has dried blood on my upper lip and chin. I get a cloth and gently wipe away the blood, taking care to avoid my swollen nose and eyes.

"Ixe!" Loc yells from behind me as they bolt into my room. My head screams in agony at the sound. "Ixe, you have to come see this!" They're panting as if they ran here, still wearing the clothes from last night.

"I just got up," I grumble. "Let me at least change first."

"No time." Loc says, grabbing my arm and nearly dragging me down the stairs and out the front door.

"Loc! Be gentle!" I cry as we make our way outside.

"Look!" they exclaim, pointing at the sky.

I gaze up to where they are now pointing, and my jaw goes slack. There, in the sky, is a ship. A ship from the legends of The Final Collapse. It descends slowly to the Earth, boosters preventing it from colliding into the ground at full force.

"Get inside!" Bri yells, running towards us. I haven't seen Bri run since I was a kid. They grab mine and Loc's arms and hurtle us back through the doorway before turning and slamming the door shut.

"What is going on?" I ask, feeling my body protest at the sudden movement.

"Just wait," Bri responds, standing like a statue before the door.

A bomb. That is the only way I can describe the sound as a wave of air from the ship's landing slams into the side of the house. The house trembles, debris pelting the polymer coating. Loc and I duck for cover, Bri standing guard. We glance at the windows to see the dust storm blowing past the house, now unable to see anything but wreckage flying through the air.

"What is going on?!" Mar asks from the top of the stairs.

"Th...There's a ship," I stammer, forgetting everything that had happened between us the day before.

Mar laughs incredulously, but slowly lets it fade as they realize Bri is not contradicting my statement. I see fear flash in Mar's eyes as they ask, "What kind of ship?"

"We don't know yet," Bri responds, a distant look in their eyes. I have only seen Bri look this way one other time. It was when our city was under attack by brigands who wanted to steal the Bot technology. The Bots had used their connection with The Net to communicate and coordinate during the attack. I was only three, so I couldn't remember much beyond the look in their eye as they communicated with the other Bots in the city.

"Who could it possibly be?" Loc asks, shaking.

There is only one possibility, and we are all thinking it, but no one wants to acknowledge it out loud, so we all stay quiet as the thought rattles us to our core.

Humans.

CHAPTER SIX
Family

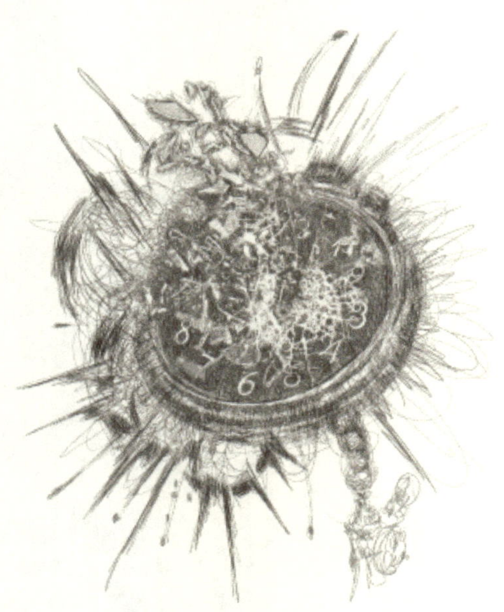

The Clinic

I'm eager for Leah's arrival the next day. The small crumb of information had had a profound impact on my mood, giving me a sliver of hope I clung to like a rope meant to pull me from this hellish place.

Leah had given me an answer. An answer that prompted more questions, sure, but an answer nonetheless. It meant that she wasn't infallible. She could make mistakes, and those mistakes could lead to my freedom.

I'm wondering if I can find out more information about The Final Collapse and what truly happened to the humans when the knock on the door pulls me out of my thoughts. I prepare myself for the coming inspection, readying the questions I had thought of the evening before. I look up, and the greeting on my tongue catches in my throat. It's Rich that stands before me, holding the supplies necessary to care for the wounds Leah had created.

"Where's Leah?" I ask hesitantly.

"Busy," he clips out, glaring at me.

"Busy?" I ask, confused.

"What are you, an echo?" He asks harshly. My eyes drop as heat rises in my cheeks, any hope of gaining further information swallowed by the silence that stretches between us.

He pulls up the stool and scoots to the side of my bed. I flinch as he roughly grabs my arm and pulls it toward him, brusquely stripping off the bandage. But I don't complain. I knew Leah wouldn't hurt me— at least, without cause— but I don't know what this man is capable of, and the last thing I need is another Mar in my life.

Rich is efficient in his work, quiet and methodical as he removes and replaces the dirty bandages. His hands are calloused, their rough pads scratching along my soft skin, leaving behind red patches of irritated skin.

I bite my lip and try to ignore the pain, tears threatening to spill from my eyes at being treated as nothing more than an object. Laying there, feeling the tug and pull as he worked, I realize that I am nothing to these people. The care for my health is nothing more than an objective of their cruel experiments. I am a goal, a test subject, and most of all...

I'm not human.

The City

The city is in an uproar. Bri, Loc, Mar, and I walk to the city center, taking in the surrounding damage from the proximity of the ship landing. The house between our own and the landing site dampened the damage to our home, but other buildings were not so lucky. Glass litters the ground, along with chunks of polymer and metal. One building has a large piece of metal, likely from the outer wall, embedded in the surface of the third floor.

They evacuated the nursery after most of the windows lost their battle against the burst of wind. Children scream as they are passed from Bot to Bot, not understanding what is happening around them. Even more children walk through the crowd trying to find their Bots in the chaos.

Bri told us that a signal had been sent out to all Bots to get the people inside as quickly as possible. It looks like they succeeded, but there were Bots in the streets when it hit, and they didn't fare well. I step over a Bot arm, searching for the owner, but not finding any other pieces.

I look at Bri, concern etched on my face, but their face is stone — emotionless. I school my face as we get closer to the havoc at the city square. Bots are trying to contain the mayhem while evacuating buildings. Kids scream and cry all around us. And in the center of the square — the Council.

Their backs to us, I don't initially see what is causing the commotion, but as we draw closer, I can see a group of Alliance members led by the same person who had been arguing with Yun yesterday. Mar breaks from our group, joining the Alliance.

"But what are you going to do about it?!"

"The incident just happened. We haven't concluded as to the best method for handling this type of event. We will repair the city and then convene on a solution." It's Yun speaking.

The individual doesn't appear happy with this answer as they throw out their arm to the ship. "You can't be serious! We need to send someone out there! We can't just let these humans take our city!"

"You don't know that they are humans."

"Who else has the technology for a ship?! We know they left Earth hundreds of years ago. Why is it so far-fetched that they would come back now?"

"They have shown no hostility towards us, Qui. We will not strike first."

"You are making a huge mistake," Qui responds angrily. "Mark my words, this will be a disaster if you do nothing to protect us."

"We have routines in place to protect this city, but we will not use them without justification."

Bri steps between Qui and Yun, a hand held up to both. "That's enough. This arguing is not helping anyone, and we have so much to do to help both Bots and humans *in* this city. We cannot worry about the humans outside of our walls," Yun gives Bri a justified look, but Bri continues, looking Yun in the eyes, "and we also can't ignore them."

Qui lets out a quiet laugh, but it cuts off as Bri turns back to them. "For now, we must focus on what we can control, and that means finding a temporary nursery and homes for our people," Bri finishes.

"Wow," Loc whispers to me, "I've never seen Bri oppose the Council."

Neither had I, but I also couldn't remember a time where they had fully agreed with the Council either. Come to think of it, they never dissuaded Mar from joining the Alliance, just spoke to them about the likelihood of the Alliance influencing the Council rules.

I watch as the Council and the Alliance nod in agreement, and then disperse, going to help those in the crowd.

Loc and I make our way to the nursery and begin helping move babies and their cribs to a new building. My body protests at the movement, but I push through it, forcing my muscles to stretch and relax after the beating yesterday. Avi notices my bruised face, but doesn't ask. Bri must have relayed what happened to The Net, so now every Bot knows about what Mar had done to me.

I keep my eyes averted from the Bots as I work, focusing on the babies that need my help. A few of the children have to be taken to the hospital for minor scrapes and bruises, but the baby section of the nursery had not been impacted. We work in silence until all kids are relocated, and then help clean up the mess around the city.

"With everything that has happened, it is even more vital that the Council meet today," Yun says. They are standing on the Council steps, speaking to the citizens gathered in the city square. The crowd is dirty, sweaty, and tired after the cleanup effort that day. As the sun sets, we all look towards the ship on the horizon, as if it will somehow give us the answers we need. Instead, we only have more questions.

"We have heard all the proposals for the year. Go home and get some rest. We will deliberate and deliver our rulings in the morning." They turn as a group and head into the Council building, leaving us standing in the square.

At first, no one moves. We are too tired to pick ourselves up and head to our homes, but after a few minutes of silence, people break off and head to the houses designated to them. Loc and I start towards home.

"Humans... Do you really think it could be them?" Loc asks as we walk.

"Who else could it be? The only living intelligence left on Earth are our Bots and us. I want to know why they returned."

"Do you think they destroyed another planet? The Bots seem to think they are unstoppable when it comes to destruction."

"Maybe..." I say, "But they can't be that bad if they have managed to survive in space for hundreds of years. How do you think they did it, anyway?"

"They had to have gone to another planet, right? There's no way they stayed in a spaceship this whole time. Maybe they were on Mars."

I laugh, "So they left a dying planet to terraform an already dead planet? That seems a bit far-fetched."

Loc shrugs. "Maybe it was outside of our solar system. Uni only taught us the basic technology they possessed."

I change tactics entirely. "What if it is aliens?"

Now it is Loc's turn to laugh. "Come on Ixe, you can't really believe that aliens would come here, of all places. What could they possibly have to gain? They never made themselves known when humans still ruled the planet. Why would they care about their leftovers?"

A blush creeps into my cheeks. "Okay, you're probably right. I still don't understand why the humans would return, though. I want to find out."

I see the glint of curiosity in Loc's eyes mirror my own and they nod toward the gate. We veer towards the wall instead. "Just to get a clear look at it," Loc says. We walk to the city gate, where guard Bots stand at attention.

"Where do you two think you're going?" One asks us as we walk up.

"We just want to see the ship." I say sheepishly.

"No one is to leave the city, younglings. Go home, get some rest."

Before I know what I'm doing, I blurt out, "We aren't going to do anything bad. Just let us through."

Loc grabs my arm as the Bots eyes glaze over, their expression turning hard and impenetrable. "You will not pass this spot, Ixe. Go home."

I can't help but glare at the bot, obviously transmitting our interest to The Net and therefore, Bri. We turn and head back towards our homes, dejected. A couple of blocks down the street, Mar catches up to us. My body immediately tenses, remembering the beating they had given me the day before.

"What do you want?" Loc snaps at them.

"I know a way out of the city if you two really want to get a look at that ship," they say.

I hesitate before asking, "Why would you help us?"

"Because the Alliance is too chicken to head out there, and I want to see it with my own eyes."

Loc pulls me to the side and furiously whispers to me, "You can't trust them! Do you remember yesterday?"

"But it's our only way to get to that ship." I whisper back.

Loc looks at me incredulously. "Do you really need to see the ship that bad? You would risk ending up in the hospital?"

I think about it, this once in a lifetime chance to see a spaceship. My adventurous side screams to go see it, but Loc is right, Mar is not trustworthy. "It's two against one, Loc. They won't do anything while we are out there."

Loc throws their hands in the air. "You have got to be kidding me. You know I can't let you do this alone, so you are going to guilt trip me into going on a suicide mission with you."

Despite feeling like I've been punched in the gut, I still say, "We need to know what is happening so we can report it to the Council. We won't cause any trouble. Just go look and come right back."

Loc shakes their head sadly, but they know that if I'm left alone with Mar, they could finish the job they started. I feel a pang of reluctant guilt in my stomach, but I can't stop myself from seeing that ship. I *need* to see it.

Finally, Loc nods, assenting to my request. We turn back to Mar. "Okay," we say together.

CHAPTER SEVEN
Outside

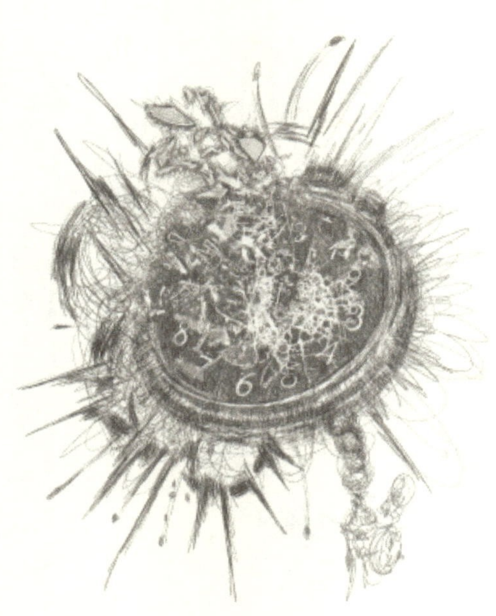

The Clinic

Leah doesn't return for two more days. When she reappears, she is pale and timid, unsure of every move she makes.

"Hi Leah," I try.

"Don't talk to her, Echo," a voice says from behind her. Rich steps into the room. His jaw clenched, hands in tight fists at his sides.

"Get up," Leah says quietly. This is new. Usually, they preferred I lay on the bed while they did their exams. I slowly rise to my feet, the gown brushing my legs as it falls into place. "Follow me." Leah turns, expecting me to do as I'm told.

I walk slowly behind her, out of my room and into a long hall. Rich follows and closes my cell door behind me. The sound of heels and boots echoes off the floor and down the hall, overpowering the quiet whisper of my bare feet on concrete.

We proceed down the hallway, stopping before two doors with electronic scanners. Rich and Leah take turns swiping a card tethered to their hip, and the doors slide open. I take note of the cards, careful to observe where they kept the small plastic devices.

We walk down corridors and through doors, navigating a complex maze, until we eventually come to a set of double doors set in a recess in the wall. Leah opens one side and holds it for me.

I take one step and freeze. *No.* It's the surgical room. My knees try to buckle under me as I realize what's happening. "No..." I breathe. It's barely a whisper, but it echoes around the empty room as if I had yelled from the top of a mountain.

Leah pushes me from behind, and I stumble a few steps forward. "No, Leah, please. Please don't do this." I turn and take her hands in my own, sinking to my knees as tears run down my face.

"Put it on the table," she says to Rich, refusing to look into my face.

"No!" I scream as Rich wraps his arms around me. They are

large, muscular, and warm as they grip me in their tight vise. I try to think of something that might appeal to her humanity and blurt out, "Please, Leah! I have a family!"

Leah stops, and I breathe a sigh of relief. She *is* human. She spins around and I feel the back of her hand strike me across the face. I hunch over, tasting blood in my mouth and feel tears run down the stinging flesh of my cheek.

She slowly leans down to me and whispers harshly, "Don't you ever talk about family to me." She turns back to her tray of instruments and begins preparing them as Rich tears off my gown and carries me to the table to lay me down.

The table is ice-cold against my skin, and my nipples pucker in the chilly air. I struggle against Rich— clawing, punching, screaming, but it's no use. His hands are firm against my wrists as he takes his time clamping me down to the table with the restraints. I sob, knowing it is pointless yet unable to stop. Glancing towards Leah, I see that she is drawing medicine into a syringe.

"We verified that a nerve block doesn't have an adverse reaction to your tissue samples, so we will numb you for this next procedure," Leah says as she pulls the syringe from the vial. "Rich, please adjust the table."

Rich walks to the side of the table and pulls a lever. The table swings, my feet dropping towards the floor as my head rises to the ceiling. Now standing, I can't see what Leah does as I hear her walk behind the vertical table I'm strapped to, and my heart throbs so hard I can't breathe.

"You are going to want to hold really still for this," Leah says from behind the table. I feel a sharp stab into my spine and cry out in agony. I feel the medication flow into me, and numbness spreads through my body.

"What are you going to do?" I ask, the terror in my voice filling the room.

"We are going to figure out what you are," Leah says as she

walks back around the table. Rich grabs the lever again and re-levels the table into a horizontal position. My head swims as the room spins around me, the numbness spreading over my abdomen.

Rich quietly asks, "Are you done with me?"

"Yes, you can leave now. I will call you when I'm ready to move it back to the cell."

Rich walks to the double doors and glances back one more time before he leaves. The silence is oppressive as Leah grabs a scalpel from the tray and approaches my table. I bite my lip hard enough that blood springs forth. The thought of opening my mouth fills me with terror, as I might beg for mercy or scream uselessly. I don't want to feel the panic and helplessness that had filled me when I was last here.

Leah lays a gloved hand on my bare abdomen, observing my lack of a belly button. "One day I will know how you are born," she says, more to herself than to me, and places the scalpel at the base of my breastbone. I take a deep breath, expecting pain, but none comes as she slices deep into my skin and slides the cauterizing scalpel down to my pelvis.

I lay my head down, squeezing my eyes shut as I smell burning flesh. Bile rises in my throat as the smell overwhelms the room. Lifting my head, I stare in shock as Leah pulls back the flaps of my skin and clamps them in place. I can see my organs pulsing and moving with life. "Interesting..." she says, as she wraps her fingers around my bowel and gently extracts it from my body. I can't look away as she carefully cuts away a sample.

The world spins and goes black.

The City

Mar grins and starts heading toward the wall. We follow,

curious to see where the entrance to the way out is hidden.

"How do you even know about this way out?" Loc dares to ask.

Mar shrugs. "It's how the Alliance keeps in contact with outer cities."

Loc stops dead in their tracks. "Wait, you have contact with the outer cities?"

Mar smirks, as if they knew this next question was coming. "Yes, we do, and yes Loc, I know where Kit is, but I'm not telling you."

I have to hold Loc back as they lunge for Mar.

"Now, now," Mar tsks, "I didn't say I wouldn't ever tell you; just that I wouldn't tell you right now. If you are on good behavior before your Release Day, I might let some information slip."

Mar turns their back on us and continues to the wall as I try to calm Loc down. "It won't do any good to beat their brains out, Loc. We need Mar in one piece to get the information."

Loc yanks their arm out of my grasp. "Mar may have you under their thumb, but I won't let them do the same to me." I feel a dagger slide into my chest at those words, and I stare at Loc in astonishment, but they've already turned and started stomping after Mar.

We follow Mar to another alcove in a different part of the wall. "These alcoves used to be city gates, back when they let humans return after Release Day."

"Wait, we were allowed to come back?" I ask incredulously.

"Yes, before the other cities degraded to the point they needed help from the Bots and they turned the humans away," Mar explains.

"There was nothing about this in class..." Loc says, disbelieving.

"They don't teach you everything in those classes, Loc. I've learned more from being in the Alliance. Why do you think they don't let anyone come back? They don't want people to know how bad it is out there before their Release Day."

My stomach sinks. "What do you mean?"

Mar laughs, "Do you really think it is all flowers and sunshine outside of these walls? The Bots only care for us until we're 20 because that is their directive. They only have to keep the human population *alive.* They *don't* have to make sure they have a good life."

Loc and I glance at each other before I ask, "So, what's out there? Are there cities?"

"Oh, there are cities alright. Cities with political corruption you wouldn't believe. Cities plagued with people who can't afford to eat, let alone a place to shit in peace. And then there are the raiders who attack anyone and everyone, stealing anything they can get their hands on. They either take you prisoner and convert you to their cause, or worse..."

"What's worse than that?" I ask, swallowing around the lump in my throat.

"Well," Mar says, pausing for effect, "I've heard that they eat whatever they can. Food is scarce on the plains, so it isn't uncommon for the raiders to eat the people who refuse to join them."

I feel bile rise in my throat. We were a vegetarian people because of the small population of animals left on Earth. I couldn't imagine eating meat, let alone eating another person.

Mar smirks before kneeling down, pushing and pulling at different points in the wall. "After the laws changed, and we were no longer allowed back into the city, humans inside the city started looking for ways out. They found this spot in the wall, where two pieces of metal make a seam that was supposed to be bolted together. They spent weeks slowly cutting through the bolts, leaving the tops intact so it seemed whole to any Bots that were walking by."

As they pull, the wall comes toward them, leaving a small opening where a human can slip through. They gesture to the hole, and Loc and I proceed through. Following us, Mar carefully resets the wall by pulling the panel until the bolts line up again. It looks completely whole again.

Mar takes off toward the ship without a second thought. After a few paces, they stop and turn back. "Are you two coming or not?"

Loc and I look at each other, realizing we haven't moved. "This is the first time we've ever been outside the city," Loc says.

Turning, Mar scoffs and keeps walking. We glance at each other before following. As we emerge from the alcove, we see hundreds of tents in front of us, spreading to each side and disappearing around the city's walls. This must be the army the Alliance spoke of. "How many are there?" Loc asks me quietly.

"Too many..." I say back, my voice a whisper. Where had these people come from? Wasn't the Alliance just a farce, something to keep rambunctious kids entertained in a monotonous life? It's then that I realize the flaw in my thinking. The Alliance kids who left the city didn't move on and forget about the Bots that had raised them. Why would they follow the rules and move on to their new cities when they hated everything the Bots stood for? They would still have the same hopes for the future of the human population and the same ideals.

The Alliance was *much* larger than our city, and if the world outside of the city was as bad as Mar had said... Maybe it was time for change after all. Loc grabs my hand, pulling me out of my revelation, and we follow the wall around to the city gate, staying in the shadows to avoid being spotted by the Alliance camps.

Suddenly, Mar holds out their arm to stop us, and we move into the deeper shadow of the wall. Listening closely, I hear voices.

"You will move this army away from my city!"

"Sorry, Yun, but we need to be here now more than ever, and I'm pretty sure this city belongs to The Net, not you."

"Roa, we will not tolerate your disobedience much longer. You cannot hold siege of our city."

Roa! They must be the army's leader, but why were they meeting Yun here? Didn't they want to bring down the Bot structure?

"We are here to protect you, you old hunk of metal! Now that there are humans back on the planet, none of us are safe."

"Humans created us. You don't know their intentions."

Roa laughs at this. "I know that they destroyed the Earth and then fled, leaving millions to die. I can guess their intentions from that. But wait, your programming probably doesn't let you fight humans, does it? Ha! That's it, isn't it? You can't raise a hand against them, can you?"

"The Net will not let you continue with this farce. You will not change the Council's minds by threatening war."

Roa's voice is sad as they say, "It's the only thing I have left to try."

Yun hisses, "You won't get away with this!"

"Sure. Tell Bri I say hi," Roa says and then the talking stops. We see a silhouette of a human walking back toward the camp ringing the city.

Once Mar is satisfied with the distance between us and Roa, they start moving again.

"What was that about?" I ask Mar.

"None of your business. Stay out of it," they shoot back at me, shutting down the subject instantly.

Loc and I look at each other, and I see my own thoughts reflected there. Mar didn't seem happy with what they had heard in that conversation, but which part was eating at them? We turn back to Mar and continue our silent journey. Mar finds a large enough open area between the camps and begins treading down the path of darkness. Before long, we are on the other side of the camps and heading onto the plains.

I look around us as we walk, taking in the wide open space I find myself in. The moon is full, and the stars bright as I take Loc's hand in mine; the world around me threatens to swallow me whole.

"Where are the other cities?" I ask Mar as we walk.

"Far from here," they say with spite. "The Bots want their *spawn* as far away as possible after they reach that magical age."

"You act like the Bots hate us."

"Don't they?" Mar asks. "Have you ever heard them talk about the kids that have left? Have you ever seen them reach out a loving hand to a person outside of our city? They have a directive and that directive is to *care* for us until we are old enough to do it ourselves. The command stops there, and they lose all sense of love they may have had."

I ponder this information and realize I didn't know any of Bri's previous kids. Would they be considered my sibs as well? If I met one on the streets of a city, would I know that they too, had grown up in the same house, maybe even slept in the same bed as I had?

"So, what does the Alliance really want, Mar?" Loc asks quietly.

"Exactly what we've been saying. A real life for our people. Something to life for, to die for. We don't want to just be a program's objective any longer." Mar's voice sounds genuinely sad as they say this.

Loc and I let the conversation drop, lost in our own thoughts about the Alliance and Bots. We walk for hours before we come to a dead forest. We stop again, too afraid to set foot inside the menacing woods. We had paintings of trees back in the city, but I never could have imagined just how large they were.

Mar stops just inside the tree-line and turns back to us. "There are... creatures... in these woods, so if you're scared and want to turn back, go ahead."

I swallow the lump in my throat and step into the dark shadows of the trees. I look into Mar's eyes and see something like admiration there.

"The forest isn't large, and it should just take us an hour to get through it, but we need to keep moving, and if you hear something behind you, don't run. It will only attract it and it will hunt you down."

Loc looks at me. "Do we really need to get closer? You could see the ship over the trees hours ago."

I step back to them, lowering my voice. "You don't have to go with me."

"Of course I do! I can't leave you alone with... *them.* Come on, Ixe, we don't need to get any closer."

The urge to get to that ship swells within me, and I know I won't be satisfied until I can look upon the humans that have arrived on our planet. "I need to do this, Loc."

Loc lets out a frustrated sigh, but walks into the forest with me. "Let's go." I feel them trembling beside me, but they don't back down as we walk into the darkness.

We stay within the tree-line, out of sight of the humans who are walking around the ship. They wear suits with helmets closed up against the atmosphere of the planet. I remember from class that one of our genetic modifications was to allow us to breathe the atmosphere that had become toxic to the original humans. It was now more nitrogen than anything else, so these helmets must be providing them with oxygen. The ship is enormous, as big as the city we live in, and there are people everywhere. They move slowly, working through the night repairing and building.

I see a human standing like a statue, a large black object in their hands. "What is that?" I whisper to Loc and Mar.

Mar follows my gaze and takes in a deep breath. "That's a gun. It's a weapon from before the Collapse. It shoots high speed metal called bullets that go through your body."

I shiver as I take in four more humans with guns. "We should get out of here," Loc whispers. "We've seen what we came to see."

"Wait," I whisper back, pointing toward commotion further down the band of forest from us.

"Please stop!" We hear as a human not in a suit is pulled from the forest by two who are.

"Look what we found. It says it's human, but it's breathing this horrid air." Their words are quick, slurred together, but still discernible as our language.

"Interesting..." another soldier says as they drag the modified human toward us. We all hold our breath, but they stop and drop the person before reaching our hiding place. "What are you?" the human asks.

"I... I don't understand the question. I'm just human."

"What is that on your neck? Take off your shirt."

The terrified individual does as they are told and I can see a slight luminescence as the light refracts off of their pattern.

"What the hell is that?" The soldier asks taking a step back.

"It's over here on its back too," another soldier says.

They meekly answer, "I... it's my pattern."

The main soldier walks forward and rips the modified human's pants down around their ankles. I hear Loc gasp behind me and hold out a hand. Our fingers slide together and I squeeze their hand, fearing what would happen next.

"What the *fuck* are you?!" the soldier yells, seeing the unrecognizable genitals of the person in front of them.

"I'm human! I swear it!"

"Get rid of this thing," the main soldier says, and turns to walk away.

One of the soldiers who had brought the modified human in hits them on the back of the head with a gun and they fall to the ground, pants still tangled around their feet. I want to close my eyes, but I can't pull my gaze away as the two soldiers begin kicking them. My mind flashes back to the beating I had taken at the hands of Mar and their cronies, and I grip Loc's hand tighter.

They sob as they are pummeled again and again. Begging for the soldiers to stop, but they just laugh. Eventually, another soldier steps forward, removes a small gun from their hip and shoots the modified human in the head. Their cries echo in my ears with the sound of the firing weapon, and I stare in shock.

"Aww, come on Rich! You are no fun!"

"Get back to work," Rich says, holstering the gun and turning back to their post.

I bite my lip, tears threatening to fall from my eyes. Loc pulls at my hand and all three of us head back through the forest. We move carefully, staying silent from fear. Mar steps over a fallen tree not realizing there is a hole in the ground on the other side. They go down hard, and the humans behind us set off an alarm. I pull Mar to their feet as I yell, "Run!"

We take off running through the dark forest. I try to pick out holes, branches, and trees in front of me, but it is nearly impossible in the dark. I feel branches tear at my clothes as I trip and stumble through the undergrowth.

The humans follow, their lights flashing around us. They're catching up. "Run faster," I pant as I jump over another fallen tree.

"I'm going as fast as I can!" Loc yells back.

I hear a loud crack and a tree splinters to my left.

"They're shooting!" Mar exclaims.

We dodge through the trees, avoiding flying debris as bullets pelt the dead forest around us. The sound of the gun is earsplitting in the silent night, but as suddenly as it began, it stops. We keep running anyway, sure they are behind us. Then we hear the screams. Mar is the first one to slow and stop, Loc and I halting when Mar yells for us to hold on.

Silence settles over the forest, and then we hear it again, screaming, followed by howling.

"Are those... the creatures you talked about?" I ask, panting.

Mar doesn't answer as their eyes go cold. "We need to walk from here on out. We don't want to attract any... unwanted attention." They say, starting the long walk back to the city.

The sounds of people being mauled to death refuse to leave my head on the way home.

CHAPTER EIGHT
Humanity

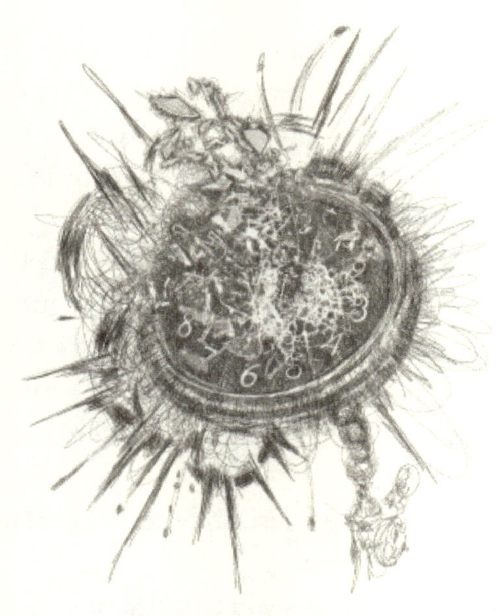

The Clinic

Pain. Agony. Torment. These are the words that circle my mind
as I heal from the latest operation. I had thought the skin samples
had been excruciating, but this was something else. My abdomen
ached constantly, the incision puckered and red. Leah insisted it was
healing, but I felt close to death. It didn't help that they wouldn't let
me eat or give me anything for the pain.

"You have to wait until your bowels have resettled," Leah
repeats for what feels like the 100th time. "If I give you food before
that happens, it will make you sick, and you'll just feel worse than
you do now."

"I'm starving," I whine, frustrated at the hunger in my gut. It
had been four days since the procedure.

She pinches my fat between a thumb and forefinger and raises
an eyebrow at me. "Looks like you have plenty of fuel to me."

I throw a sneer in her direction and lay my head back as she
pulls my gown up to care for my wound. She had once again
returned to the caretaker role. There had been no mention of the
outburst in the operating room, and she didn't care for the cut on my
lip. I avoided the topic of family, and we coexisted— albeit with less
pleasant conversations.

I can't stop my curiosity as I ask, "How many humans are here,
anyway?"

She scoffs, "Wouldn't you like to know? I'll not give you an
advantage to take back to your people. I know you would turn on us
in a heartbeat."

"Maybe I wouldn't if you told me what you were doing here," I
fire back, irritated that she had refused to answer any of my questions
since she returned.

"You wouldn't understand," is all she says as she applies
ointment to my scar and re-bandages it. I can't keep the scowl from

my face as she gently pats me on the head as if I'm a child. "Get some rest. You're going to need it." She winks at me and then walks out of the room.

What did that mean? What was coming now? Her words ring through my head as I try to sleep, stirring up horrors I hadn't dared to think about to the surface of my mind. Thoughts of watching my heart beat outside of my chest as Leah and Rich stand laughing, the light reflecting cruelly on their harrowing features, had been plaguing me in the quiet moments. Shaking my head to banish the images, I roll over and face the wall, willing myself to sleep.

As I drift away a dream takes hold. Leah stands over me, a scalpel in hand as she slowly cuts out one of my eyes and I scream.

The City

I tremble with fear as we continue our walk through the woods, expecting an enormous monster to jump out at us at every sound we make. Finally breaking through the trees, I take a deep breath, leaning over with my hands on my knees. Mar places a hand on my shoulder and my entire body tenses at their touch. "We have to keep moving. No time for breaks," they say, before finally removing their hand and continuing in front of me.

Loc takes my hand and gives me a knowing look before pulling me forward. "What did we just see?" I ask quietly.

"Real humanity." Mar says sadly.

"They murdered that modified human..." Loc says.

"They didn't just murder them, they wanted to torture them first," Mar says. "If you ask me, that soldier did the right thing, ending their life before it got worse."

"How can you possibly believe that?" Loc replies.

"Think about it," Mar continues, "if you were captured, would you want them beating you to death, or would you rather a bullet go through your brain, ending the misery?"

"Bold words, coming from someone who beats up their sib for the fun of it." Loc mutters under their breath. I watch Mar tense, but they say nothing, pretending they hadn't heard Loc's words.

Trying to change the subject, I ask, "What are they even doing here?"

"Well, their language is the same as ours, so they can't be aliens from another world," Loc says. "At the same time, it seems like they didn't know we were here. They weren't expecting other humans by the way they reacted."

Mar scoffs and walks ahead of us while Loc and I continue the conversation.

"But how were we able to understand them? Wouldn't our languages diverge over 600 years?"

"Theirs would. I'm not sure about ours. Bots who were programmed with this language taught us. It wouldn't make sense for it to change over time as it does with other societies."

"So what? Either they have Bots teaching them language as well, or they *are* the humans from 600 years ago? How is that possible?"

"Why does it matter?!" Mar shouts. "We know they are here and they aren't willing to accept those that are different. All we should be talking about is how we are going to remove them from our planet."

"You immediately resort to violence again! Can you think of nothing else but hurting others?!" Loc yells back.

"I think Mar is right this time, Loc. These humans are not going to listen to reason."

Loc pulls away from me. "Are you serious? You are going to agree with *them?*"

"Loc..." I say, trying to stop them, but they continue walking away from me and silence settles over our group.

When we arrive back at the wall, the sun is rising. Mar, Loc, and I drag ourselves through the hole in the wall, near collapsing once we get to the other side. We drop to our knees in the alcove and lean back against the wall, exhausted.

"We have to tell the Council," I say, finally breaking the silence that had persisted since the argument.

"We can't," Loc responds. "They will know we went outside the wall."

"We aren't telling the Council," Mar chimes in, leaning their head back and closing their eyes. "We are telling the Alliance."

I shake my head. "You may be a member of that cult, but I will have nothing to do with them."

"They aren't a cult," Mar responds, exasperated. "They are just trying to give humans, our humans, a better life. Why is that such a bad thing?"

"I think the problem comes in when you look at how they are trying to make change." Loc intercedes.

"We've tried everything else! We've tried bargaining, lecturing, negotiations, and the Council will hear none of it. Violence *is* the last resort."

I look at my sib, the passion in their eyes. They really believe in this Alliance, in this change they speak of.

"Do what you want, Mar, I'm telling the Council." I say as I crawl to my feet. A deep ache pulses through my legs as I stand. I would feel this for days.

Loc groans as they rise beside me, clearly in as much pain as I am. We take off toward the Council building, limping as much as walking. Once we are out of earshot, Loc turns toward me, "Ixe, please don't tell them I was with you. If they find out that I was going outside the city... I may lose my only chance to find out where Kit went."

I glance at my lovesick friend, wondering what it felt like. A love so deep that they would do anything for each other, and fear being apart so much. "Of course, Loc. I won't say anything about you being there, but I can't promise the same for Mar."

"I know." They reply, a look of worry on their face.

A crowd of people and Bots awaits us as we turn the corner to the town square. "They must be ready to announce the Council decision." Loc says.

"Yeah, but I've never seen so many people show up for the decision before."

"Guess more people are worried about this ship than we thought."

We work our way into the crowd, trying to talk to the Council before they proclaim their decision, but it's just too thick. We settle toward the middle and hope for the best.

The doors to the Council building open, and Yun steps out.

"We stand before you today to announce a decision that has resulted from extensive deliberation, thorough analysis, and deep consideration. As members of this Council, we fully understand the weight of our responsibility to you, our community, and we do not take this lightly.

"Over the past several weeks, we have engaged in numerous discussions, weighing all potential impacts and exploring every possible angle. Each Council member has dedicated countless hours to researching, consulting with experts, and engaging with our community to gather a wide range of perspectives. We have debated the merits and drawbacks of each option with great care, always with the community's best interest at heart.

"We have meticulously examined data, reviewed the past, and drawn upon our collective experiences to ensure that the decision we make is well-informed and sound. Every comment, concern, and suggestion raised by you, our valued citizens, has been considered in our discussions.

"We are confident that the decision we have reached is the best path forward, balancing the needs and aspirations of our community with sustainable and responsible governance. This decision reflects our dedication to fostering a vibrant, thriving community, and our unwavering commitment to serving you with integrity and thoughtfulness.

"With that said, we have decided to not change our rules going forward..." There is an uproar from the crowd as the Alliance roars with displeasure.

Yun speaks louder to overcome their outburst, "The Release Day will go according to schedule, but we will send a delegation to the human ship to begin negotiations on territories to be laid out and rules to be followed for both their needs, our future, and the future of this planet in the coming days."

"You can't!" I yell out. Startled at my exclamation, the crowd and Council are silenced. "I've been outside the city..." I begin, voices gasping all around me. "I went to the ship, and they captured and killed one of our people!"

"You went outside the city?!" Bri stands four feet from me, glaring at me with fire in their eyes.

"Bri, I can explain..." but the crowd panics and overwhelms my words with their shouting. Everywhere around me, people are yelling and pushing toward the council steps.

"We have no army!"

"We have to run!"

"Why have they come back?"

"It's the Final Collapse all over again!"

Yun and the Council try their best to calm everyone down, but it's no use. I've incited a panic.

Bri grabs my arm, pulling me through the group. Once out of the pulsing crowd of people, they continue to pull me down the street and around a building before finally coming to a stop.

"What were you thinking?!" they say to me through a clenched jaw. "I could expect this type of behavior from Mar, but from you, Ixe? Why would you do this?"

"I'm sorry, Bri, I really am. At first I just wanted to see the ship from outside the walls, and then... I just kept going until I was there."

Bri throws their hands up in the air, exasperated. "And then you decide to drop the bomb in the middle of an anxious crowd of people that were already at each other's throats over the Council decision? I thought you were smarter than this, Ixe. I really did. I don't know how I'm going to trust you from now on."

"At least it won't be much longer." I mumble.

"What?"

"I said, at least you won't have to deal with me much longer!" I yell at Bri, exhaustion after last night and frustration at the Council decision giving weight to my words. A sinking feeling in the pit of my stomach tells me I will regret it, but I look them eye to eye and don't back down.

Bri simply sighs and points toward the house. "Go home, Ixe."

As I stomp away from them, I hear them say under their breath, "Maybe I failed with both of them..." and a rock plummets deep inside me.

CHAPTER NINE
An Unexpected Alliance

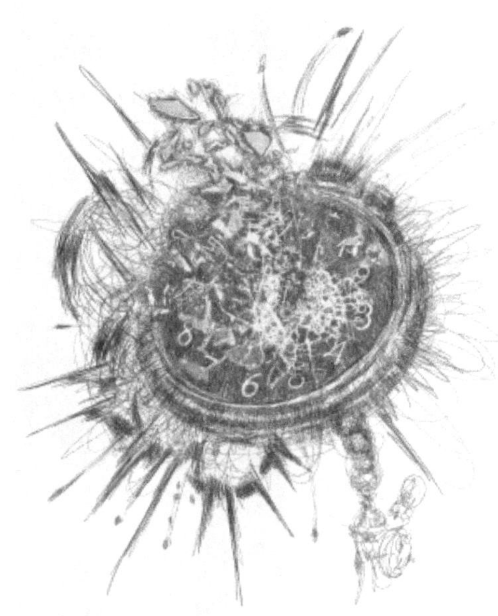

She was right. Oh, hell, was she right. I had thought the procedure on my abdomen had been the worst it could get until they carried me into the operating room the next day. Rich had been the one to walk down the hall, laden with my limp body. It was still too soon to walk, according to Leah, so he resigned to carry me the entire way.

I didn't fight this time. What was the point, really? They would win no matter what I did. Rich gently laid me on the table, carefully attaching the restraints to my wrists and ankles. I lay there shivering from the cold as Leah inserted a needle into my arm.

"What's this?" I ask.

"We are going to be knocking you out for this procedure."

Fear fills me, my mouth going dry. "Why this time?" I'm almost too afraid to ask, but I have to know.

"Because what we are going to do today…" Leah pauses, looking at Rich.

Rich gently lays a hand on my arm and says, "Even you shouldn't be forced to watch this, Echo."

My blood goes ice cold and I swallow. Leah attaches my IV to a bag of saline and draws some medicine into a syringe. I watch quietly as she takes the IV line and pushes the needle into it. "Goodnight, little one," she says as she pushes the plunger down.

I notice the taste in my mouth first, salty. Then the world gets fuzzy as a warmth spreads throughout my body, stilling the chills. My eyes drift shut, and my body stills.

"Are you sure about this one, Leah? There has to be another way." I hear voices talking around me, but I'm not sure where I am. I try to open my eyes to see who is there, but they are stuck shut.

"Yes, Rich. We need to know what they are capable of if we are going to fight them."

Fight? Fight who? I know that this is important information, but I can't seem to grasp why.

"This is so inhumane. We should tell Ritter..."

"What? That we are defying his orders? You saw how well it went after my... mishap."

As someone grabs my hand, I feel a brush along my wrist. I try to pull away, but my muscles are frozen in place.

"I don't want to be here when you..."

"I need you this time. You can't hide from this any more than I can."

Silence settles in the darkness of my own thoughts before finally, "Fine."

A sharp pain lances through my arm, and I try to scream, but nothing comes out. *I'm paralyzed,* I realize with horror. I smell burning flesh and my stomach lurches. *What is happening to me?!* Then I hear the saw, and it all comes flashing back. *I'm a prisoner. I'm in a hospital. I'm being experimented on.* The pain slices deeper into my arm and my mind screams in agony.

I fight with everything I have to open my eyes, twitch a finger, anything to get them to see I'm not asleep. It's useless. I'm frozen in time, in terror, in perpetual pain. No one is coming to save me. No one can help me. My mind howls as the realization sets in that I'm never getting out. I'm stuck here...

Forever.

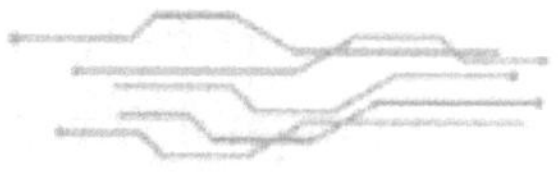

The City

I find Bri packing a few days later. "Where are you going?" I ask, curiosity finally breaking the tense silence between us.

"The Council selected me to lead the expedition." Bri says,

shoving an extra battery into their pack.

My stomach drops. "So, they are still going through with it?"

Bri turns to me in frustration. "What do you want them to do, Ixe? Do you want them to send an army to attack the ship like the Alliance? What good will that do?"

Bri's words hit me hard, and I take a step back. Bri had never raised their voice to me in this way. "I'm sorry…" is all I can think to say as I turn and leave the house.

I find Loc sitting on their front steps and plop down beside them.

"That bad, huh?" They ask, noticing my sunny disposition.

"I finally opened my mouth and stuck my foot in it." I reply, defeated. "Bri is leading the meeting with the humans…"

Loc stares at me, the shock and concern etched into their face.

"I know," I say, "it's a bad idea…"

"Worse than bad," Loc responds, "It's downright terrible, and anyone on that expedition is going to get themselves killed."

"We have to stop them."

"How? We tried that already, and it just ruined your relationship with Bri. They won't listen to us."

"Okay, so we have to be there to help them when it goes south."

Loc laughs. "Two puny modified humans against an entire elite human army? What will we use to even fight them, our fists?"

"Our guns." Says a voice behind us. We both turn to see Mar leaning against the house next door.

"What, are you playing spy for the Alliance now?" I ask snarkily.

Mar pushes themself off the wall and walks toward us, "The Alliance may have asked me to keep an eye on you, just to see what the Council would do about your outburst, but I think I like what I'm hearing from you two more than I thought I would."

Loc rolls their eyes and turns their back to Mar, "We don't have guns, Mar, and even if we did, we don't know how to use them."

"Our army does," says Mar, coming to sit beside Loc on the

step.

"Your leader, what was his name... Roa, said the same thing to Yun before the Council decision." I chime in. "Is that really your army?"

"Yep," says Mar, "And we are preparing to defend this city as we speak."

Loc scoffs. "So, first you want to attack the city, and now you suddenly want to defend it? I'm sorry if I would rather stay far away from the Alliance and their help. Right, Ixe?"

I sit silently staring at the dirt in front of my feet.

"Ixe! You can't seriously be considering this!"

"What other choice do we have? If we don't do something, Bri will probably get killed. I can't sit and do nothing."

"That's what I'm talking about," Mar says triumphantly. "Now, we can't take the entire army. They will see us coming, but if we can get our hands on some guns..."

Loc stands up abruptly. "I can't do this, Ixe. I'm sorry, but I need to think about myself and my future."

Mar sneers at Loc as they retreat inside their house and looks back at me.

"So, what do you say, Ixy, wanna go get some guns?"

This is a stupid idea... I think to myself as I find myself once again away from the safety of the city. We had spent hours looking for the main camp and had finally found ourselves outside the barrier of a human encampment. The amount of people here was staggering. More than the Bots and children in the city, more than the amount of humans we had seen at the ship.

"If you are friends with these people, why can't we just walk in?" I pose the question to Mar again.

"Because they aren't going to just hand over their guns, idiot. They need them for the war."

"What war?" I ask, but they stay silent.

I go back to watching the camp, wondering what Mar was looking for. There were tents spread as far as I could see, and people milling about doing menial tasks. I watch as a gray-haired human lugs pails of water from a well toward the camp center. "They must be ancient," I whisper to Mar.

They look to where I'm pointing and snort out a laugh. "They're only 43. That's Trix."

My face reddens with embarrassment and then the name registers in my brain. "Trix? But, that's more than three letters." The Bots gave us our names, and they had stuck to the same naming format that the original humans had given them for The Net. Three letters to a name, no more.

"A lot of humans change their names after they get out of the city. They abhor their Bot 'parents' and choose a new name to rid themselves of their heritage."

I stare at the camp, stunned. Why would they hate the very thing that gave them life? That had cared for them from their first breath, to their first steps, to the day they graduated? How bad did it have to be out here for them to turn on everything they knew?

Mar starts, pointing to a tent with a red 'X' painted on the open flap. "There. That is the armory. We need to get into that tent, and back out, without being seen."

"And how do you expect us to do that?" I ask.

"With a distraction." Mar smiles, teeth bared in a gruesome snarl. I flinch, immediately on guard as I remember the times that smile had been directed at me. A shiver runs down my spine, and I look away, wishing to be anywhere but here, next to this person who I couldn't trust. *This is such a stupid idea...* I think again.

"Don't look so worried, Ixy. I will take care of the distraction. You just go get the guns. The tent will be full of guns and ammo, the small metal bits that get shot out." I nod my head, knowing that it was stupid to let Mar make the decisions, but not having another choice. "Just walk in like you belong there. You are old enough. They will just think you are a recruit, part of the batch from the last Release Day."

I nod again, my mouth dry and my throat unable to produce a sound. With a deep breath, I stand up and begin making my way to the camp. Drawing close, I experience a new side of society. The sounds— laughter, yelling, talking— drift to me on the wind, so similar to that of the city, but yet different. The smell of food mixed with that of refuse and sweat is overpowering as I walk deeper into the camp.

I feel bile rise in my throat along with my anxiety and try to tamp it down, keeping my face schooled in a look of nonchalance. I nod at the passing humans as I make my way into the camp. Suddenly surrounded by people, my head spins, but I maintain my pace, heading slowing toward the tent with the red 'X'.

I pass by a large green tent, the sounds of lovemaking drifting through the open flaps. As I pass by the opening, I see six or seven humans entangled together in an assembly of pleasure. I feel my cheeks redden as I look away from the orgy.

I follow my mental path to the armory tent, and stand outside waiting for the distraction Mar was supposed to handle.

"Hey, newbie!" My head jerks to the human who is addressing me. *Shit*. "What are you doing over here?"

"Uhhh…" I stammer. "Trix sent me to do an inventory on ammo." I say, hoping that the name Mar had given me was correct.

They raise an eyebrow but don't question it. "Well then, get in there and stop standing around out here."

I swallow the lump in my throat and duck into the tent. I'm immediately in awe at the surrounding sight. Row after row of guns, organized by size, surround me. Ammo of all shapes and sizes line a shelf at the far end of the tent. I run my hand along a gun similar to those the humans used to shoot at us. It is long, black, and cold to the touch. If one gun could do so much damage, how much damage would this arsenal do?

I think of the Bots and my home. If the Alliance was planning on using these guns against us… The thoughts come unbidden, and I find myself searching for something to use to destroy the weapon cache.

The ground shakes under my feet as an explosion rocks the camp. I quickly snap back to reality and realize what I'm here for. I grab two of the long guns and run to the open flap. Peeking my head out, I see people running away from my tent and toward a growing black cloud. *Mar*. At least they held up their side of the bargain.

I hold one gun in each hand and start running, dodging tents and people as I go. It doesn't take long to break out of the ring of tents, and I keep running, afraid to glance behind me in fear that someone would be following. A stitch develops in my side and my breathing is haggard when I finally slow and stop, laying the guns next to me on the ground, and turn to look at the mayhem that had distracted the entire camp.

A black cloud is hanging low over the encampment, and I see fire licking the sides of a few tents. I wonder if Mar made it out when I hear a branch snap behind me. I spin around to find Mar, covered in black soot, walking up to me.

"Did you get them?" They cough. I hold up the weapons, handing one over to Mar. "Good," they reply, sitting next to me hard. "First step done."

CHAPTER TEN
Release

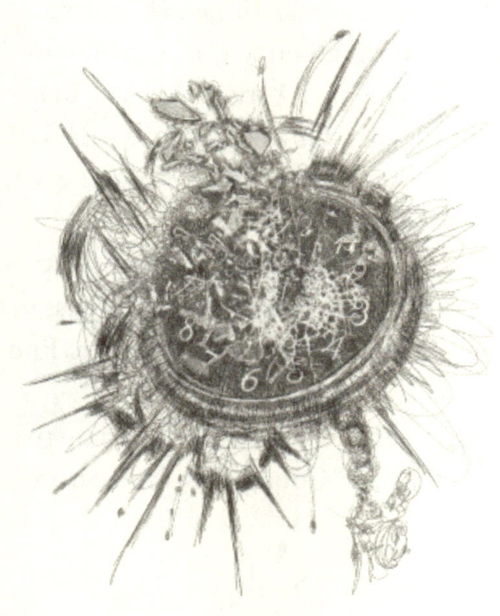

The Clinic

Tears start flowing before I fully realize what has happened—
my body dragging itself out of the paralysis that had taken hold. I feel
defeated, hurt, abandoned, betrayed. *Where were my people? Why
had Bri let this happen to me?* I lay there, sobbing, until I'm emptied
of tears. I lift my arm to wipe away the wet stains drying on my
cheeks and stop.

My hand... I repeat it out loud. "My hand." I scream. "MY
HAND! You took MY HAND!?" I stare at the bloody bandage at
the end of my arm, about midway down my forearm. "WHY!?" I
scream again, my voice cracking as it reaches its limit.

I haul myself up on the bed, a struggle with only one arm. Pain
lances down my middle as my abdominal incision burns. Swinging
my legs off the bed, I attempt to stand, only to collapse. As I fall, I
reach out to catch myself with my hands and my stump slams against
the floor. The bandage turns red with fresh blood as I cry out in pain.
Grabbing my arm with my other hand, I sit back on the floor,
panting.

Why would they do this? I shift my weight, stretching out my
legs in front of me. There, I find another missing piece. The leg
opposite of my missing hand is gone, cut off below the knee. Giggles
rise out of me unbidden and by the time Leah and Rich reach my
room, I am laughing hysterically. *I'm going mad*, I think as they lift
me from the floor and lay me back in bed. I laugh even harder when I
see the concern on Rich's face and the hard lines set in Leah's. Why
should they care about my sanity when they are ripping me literally
limb from limb?

Why would anyone care at all?

"What's wrong with it?" Rich asks quietly.

Leah doesn't respond as she pulls a suture kit out of a bag and
gets to work, unwrapping my hemorrhaging stump.

Rich lays a comforting hand on my healthy leg as Leah sutures my arm, and I feel a distant longing to reach out and let him know I'm okay. Instead, I continue laughing through the painful sensation, a trivial annoyance compared to what I have dealt with. I carry on laughing long after Rich and Leah leave, into the darkness of the night as my lights shut off, until I dissolve into crying hysterics and finally, tranquil sleep.

The next few weeks are a blur. My sanity has fractured. Leah tries to bring me back from the brink, asking me questions about my life outside of this hellhole, but all I can do is stare at her. My thoughts try to break free from the prison of my mind, but there is no escape. A loop, stuck on repeat, now inhabits the space inside my skull. My dreams, vicious renditions of my life under the knife, are but a shadow compared to the apathy I face during the day.

I stare at the white wall in front of me, seeing bloody cracks form, seeping the life from the room I inhabit — from me. As they grow, blood fills the room, seeking to drown me in its warmth. I watch as it soaks into my gown, covers my legs, up my waist. My hand begins to float... and then Rich is grabbing my arm. The blood is gone. The room is whole again.

"We have to do something, Leah. We can't just let it starve itself to death! The entire project will be lost. Everything we've done would be pointless."

"What do you think I've been doing, Rich?!" Leah yells. She puts her hand to her forehead, lowering her voice. "The last resort I have is to put in an NG tube, but I'm not sure that is a good idea with its current... condition."

"What were you even trying to accomplish with this?" Rich holds up my right arm, displaying my stump.

"I..." Leah begins, takes a deep breath to steel herself before trying again, "It heals remarkably faster than we do. I was trying to see if..."

"If it could grow back a limb?" Rich sounded stunned. "These aren't lizards, Leah, and we aren't looking to regenerate ourselves."

"It was a scientific experiment I couldn't pass up." She says, her eyes reflecting the ice in her soul. Yet somehow, I see a warmth that is hard to ignore.

"You need to rein it in, Leah, or we are all going to be dead." Rich drops my arm and marches out of the room.

Leah sits down on the stool heavily. Propping her elbows on my bed, she lowers her head into her hands and mumbles, "What is wrong with me? Have I just destroyed the human race?"

I try to reach out to her, to comfort her, to tell her I was also human; but the stump at the end of my arm stops me in my tracks.

The City

Tomorrow is Release Day. Tomorrow, I will receive my assignment and leave my city forever, but today I am going to save my Bot. Mar and I crouch behind a fallen log on the human side of the wood. We had hiked out here last night before the delegation scheduled to leave this morning.

It was a grueling trip in the pitch black of the night, the moon a thin sliver in the sky, unable to light our way. My arms and legs were scratched and torn from the undergrowth of the forest. I had collapsed in the cove behind the fallen tree the moment we had stumbled upon it, exhaustion overruling the fear in my brain.

"Wake up." Mar hisses at me. I glance around, bleary-eyed. For hours now, I had been drifting off to sleep, unable to prevent my eyes from closing in the serene wood. I didn't know how Mar stayed awake after a long night of hiking from the Alliance camp and subsequently hiding in the silent forest. Thoughts of them sneaking out of the city to work with the Alliance swim unbidden through my head.

I glance around and hear the crack of a branch before noticing something white coming through the wood. "Is that them?" I whisper to Mar.

"I think so. Isn't the white flag the sign for peace or something?"

I shrug, struggling to remember anything from our world history class on wars and peace. It was my least favorite subject, which was reflected in my grades. I had believed that war would never come to pass in the new age of Bots and humans, so I hadn't bothered paying attention to the lectures on peace treaties and the shared battle ethics of the past. I had been wrong.

The group of Bots emerge from the thick wood, indeed carrying a flag of pure white. Where they had found a flagpole, I did not know. It wasn't long before the ship's humans noticed the Bots and approached. We had selected the perfect spot behind our log, close enough to the meeting point of the two parties to hear their conversation, yet far enough to not be spotted.

"We come in peace, and wish to discuss terms of land ownership with your commander." Bri said, leading the party.

A small, lithe human ran back toward the ship, while the others maintained their positions; their fingers gripping the guns tight, ready to pull the trigger at the slightest move. My grip on my gun tightened in response.

A few minutes pass in silence before the lithe human returns, followed by a larger presence. They walk down the ship's ramp together, no hurry in their steps, as they approach the confrontation before us.

"Are you the commander of these humans?" Bri asks, cocking

their head to the side.

The man nods and extends a hand. "My name is Mark Ritter, commanding officer of this ship and the humans that live here."

Bri takes the man's hand in their own and shakes it up and down. A handshake, I think to myself. A good sign to start. Maybe we wouldn't need these guns after all. "My name is Bri, I am an AI of The Net, and we have come to discuss the terms of land ownership of the Earth."

"That should be a straightforward conversation," Mark responds. "The Earth belongs to the humans, and we are here to take ownership of it."

"But Mark..." Bri begins.

"Call me Colonel Ritter." Mark interrupts, a gleam of challenge in his eye.

Bri's eyes widen at the title, missing a beat before continuing, "Colonel, we Bots and our humans live on this land, and have lived on this land for nearly 600 years. We cannot just move our cities, our people, because you have returned."

Now it is the Colonel's turn to be surprised. "What humans?"

"We are of The Net, Colonel. Our only directive is to re-create humanity that can survive on the Earth as it has become."

"You mean to tell me that you created new humans after we left? Who gave you this directive?"

"Those who were serving under Project Phoenix." Bri responded, head held high.

Colonel Ritter's eyes go dark, and with a quick gesture of his hand, all hell breaks loose. I watch as a soldier raises their gun, my own arms slowly responding to the threat before I know what I'm doing. The gun in my hands butts to my shoulder. My face lowering down to the sight as my finger lands before the trigger. I hear my heartbeat loud in my ears...

Thump...

Thump...

Thump...

and I pull my finger back, aiming right for the soldier's head.

My gun clicks.

The soldier's gun bangs.

I scream as Bri's head shatters into thousands of pieces. *No, this can't be happening.* No ammo? Why was there no ammo?! I think back to the moment in the tent, surrounded by guns of all shapes and sizes. Then I remember the wall of ammo on the opposite side. They didn't load the guns.

Mar realizes an instant after I do, and we both start running. Mar races through the surrounding forest, back toward the city. I race over the log in front of me, toward the humans and my dead Bot. Tears stream down my face as I throw all of my power into my legs, not caring that the other Bots are running away from Bri's lifeless body. Not caring that the humans are shooting at them now, taking them down one by one. I have eyes for one thing, the soldier that had killed Bri.

A fist slams into the side of my head, and I go down, dazed from the impact. "Well, what do we have here? You must be one of the humans the Bots created." Colonel Ritter is leaning over me, a gun in his hand. "And it looks like they weren't lying. You can breathe this dreadful air." A smile spreads across his face as he says, "Fetch the doctor. We have something for her to research at last." And as the butt of the gun meets my head, everything goes black.

CHAPTER ELEVEN
Awakening

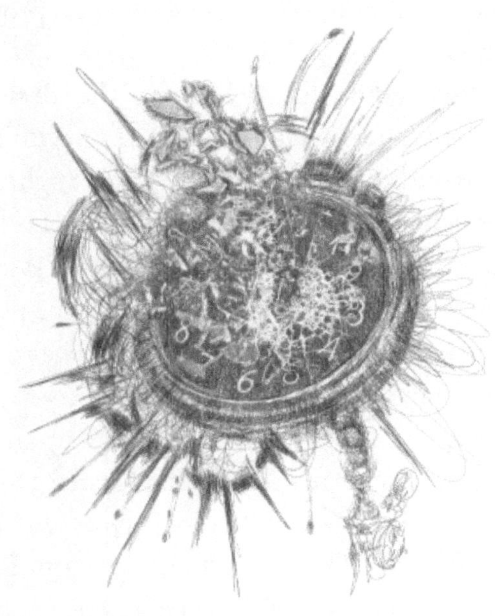

Drip...

    Drip...

        Drip...

I stare at the ceiling where blood pools and slowly, ever so slowly, buds into a drop before disconnecting from the stalk and dropping to my forehead. I know it isn't real, at least I think it isn't real, but I have no reason to fight the images that swarm me in the silence of my cell.

Leah visits me three times a day, stoically taking my blood, ignoring my plight. She fits my leg with a badly made prosthetic and begins taking me out of my room on walks, then to the lab while she processes the blood she removes from my veins. She monitors my condition closely and mutters because she sees no progress in the repair of my mind.

I hear her discuss this with Rich, before they decide that there is nothing to be done, and they must continue on with their task at hand. They take me back to surgery, and I don't fight. Laying on the cold table, I wonder what they will take next, but Leah has returned to her original goal. Lung and skin biopsies, tissue samples from my neck, abdomen, arms and legs, they even scrape the plaque from my teeth, but no major loss of limb. I don't know what they are looking for, but at this point, I don't care.

As I lay in my bed, picking at a bandage on my arm, I wonder what my family is doing. Are they looking for me? Do they even care that I'm gone? Had I missed my Release Day, or was this what happened after Release? That doesn't feel right, but I can't explain why. Any time I try to remember how I got here, I end up with a massive migraine and no answers, the scattered images I can recall giving me elusive clues to my past.

I spend more time in the lab with Leah, wandering around, trying to read her scattered notes. She assumes I can't read, and I have no reason to tell her, so I keep quiet as I see notes such as "Male or female? Odd genitalia, so unsure. Reproductive organs do not seem to exist...", "Ability to heal enhanced. Recovers from surgery surprisingly quickly...", "Requires less sustenance to survive. Can survive without food and water for longer than...", and "Still unsure of the method of breathing. It seems to breathe the oxygen on the ship, but also the planet's air. Blood samples and lung biopsy inconclusive..."

Rich visits from time to time, giving me side glances, worry lines etching his face. I know he is only concerned about the experiment, so I ignore the look in his eyes and continue my aimless wandering. "Any luck?" Rich whispers to Leah one day.

"No, Rich, I have no more information than the last time you asked me the same damn question. Yes, Rich, I know we have a deadline and I'm failing, I don't need you to remind me every ten minutes!" Leah slams her palms to the metal table she is working at, and the glass bottles and instruments tinkle as they gently move side to side brushing their neighbors.

Rich's face hardens. "Pull yourself together. We don't have time for another... incident... from you."

Leah glares at Rich before hissing through her teeth, "There won't be another incident from either of us."

They stare at each other, fury lacing their glares before Rich finally says "Mark wants to talk to you."

Leah turns on her heel and walks out the door. Rich sighs before following. Both of them forgetting I'm in the lab. I stare at the closed door, wondering if I should return to my cell. I take a few steps toward the door before something inside me pulls me to a stop. A buried part of my consciousness raises its head and I turn toward Leah's computer.

I gently take a seat in front of her open laptop and place my hand on the keyboard. It was smaller than I was used to, and some letters shaped differently, but I could understand it. I browse through the files until I find a folder titled "Alien life-form observation." Opening it, I find the information I already knew about myself. Observations that I had read on scraps of paper around the lab.

I back out and find another folder titled "Cryo Anomaly". Opening it, I read:

"The cryostasis had an unintended effect on our brains. After so many years asleep, some rewiring took place, resulting in violent outbursts, loss of focus, and additional hyper-focus in unintended areas. This has resulted in a few incidents on the ship."

I open the first file titled "Incident 1025".

```
Subject: Leah Riley
Date: 25 days post-awakening
Category: Psychological and Behavioral Evaluation


Observation 1 (Day 25):
During routine assessments, the subject has showed
significant cognitive deviation from initial baselines.
While instructed to engage in basic experimental tasks,
subject consistently veers towards highly advanced and
intricate procedures. This has resulted in the mishandling
of scientific samples and increased contamination rates.
Subject self-reports intrusive thoughts centered on
anatomical dissection, suggesting potential onset of
psychosis. Notably, the subject has opted to conceal these
findings from supervisor Ritter, instead choosing to
privately document further behavioral anomalies.


Observation 2 (Day 30):
Subject encountered Michelle [full name redacted] today.
During the interaction, subject experienced detailed
homicidal ideation, specifically involving methods of
causing pulmonary trauma via helium injection. The
imagined scenario described an interest in physiological
outcomes and mechanical response, further reinforcing
earlier concerns regarding subject's fixation on internal
anatomy.


Observation 3 (Day 95):
Subject was provided with a small indigenous organism for
biological study. Deviation from protocol was observed
when the subject immediately engaged in unsanctioned
vivisection. The subject decapitated the creature and
manually extracted its digestive tract through the
esophagus, conducting an unapproved investigation into the
malleability of internal structures. Of note, the subject
remarked on the challenge posed by the stomach, suggesting
```

a methodical, albeit disturbed, approach to dissection.

Observation 4 (Day 156):
The acquisition of a human test subject marked a significant escalation in the subject's behavioral trajectory. Subject expressed intent to conduct secretive experiments, showing a desire to push ethical boundaries without detection by supervisor Ritter. Although the subject is still in the planning phase, there are explicit considerations of amputation as a preliminary step, with caution exhibited in timing and execution to avoid arousing suspicion.

Conclusion: The subject's rapid progression towards violent ideation, unsanctioned experiments, and intent to harm human subjects poses an obvious risk. Further observation is necessary, but immediate psychological intervention may be warranted to prevent escalation.
Recommendation: Flag for heightened supervision. Consider limiting access to live specimens and review all experiment logs for unauthorized activity.

Filed by: Leah Riley / MD

I shiver and close Leah's file, opening the only other file titled "Incident 1132".
Subject: Richard McNally
Date: 132 days post-awakening
Category: Behavioral and Psychological Deviation

Observation 1 (Day 132):
Subject McNally exhibited a catastrophic loss of control, resulting in severe violence aboard the ship. At 13:04, during an informal interaction with fellow officer Lewis Randall, the subject suddenly initiated a brutal attack. Without provocation, McNally proceeded to strike Randall repeatedly until the officer was deceased. By the time authorities intervened, the subject had inflicted extensive trauma, with multiple blows driving through the remains of Randall's head and into the floor beneath. Because of the subject's immense strength and aggression, it required four officers to subdue and confine him to a holding cell.

Observation 2 (Day 135):
Following a three-day confinement, the subject regained coherence and expressed remorse for the incident. During the debriefing, McNally demonstrated no recollection of the event or any trigger leading to the violent outburst.

Throughout the session, the subject fixated on the blood still present on his hands, repeatedly requesting to wash it off. Upon refusal by staff, McNally resorted to using the cell's toilet to bathe. Subject's behavior during this period suggests genuine regret, displaying both psychological and emotional distress in response to the incident.

Observation 3 (Day 135):
Based on McNally's visible remorse and stabilized condition, it is recommended that he be demoted from his former rank and reassigned to a controlled environment within the laboratory. Under direct supervision, McNally will assist in handling live test subjects, leveraging his physical capabilities for tasks requiring muscle during experimentation. This role ensures limited unsupervised contact with personnel and provides the necessary oversight to prevent further violent outbursts.

Conclusion: Subject poses a risk due to unpredictable violent tendencies, but appears remorseful and aware of his actions post-incident. Close supervision and restricted duties are advised to mitigate future risks. Recommendation: Proceed with demotion and reassignment. Continue psychological evaluation and maintain rigorous monitoring protocols during lab activities.

Filed by: Leah Riley / MD

I close out of the file and stand as Richard McNally, Rich, walks into the lab.

CHAPTER TWELVE
Answers

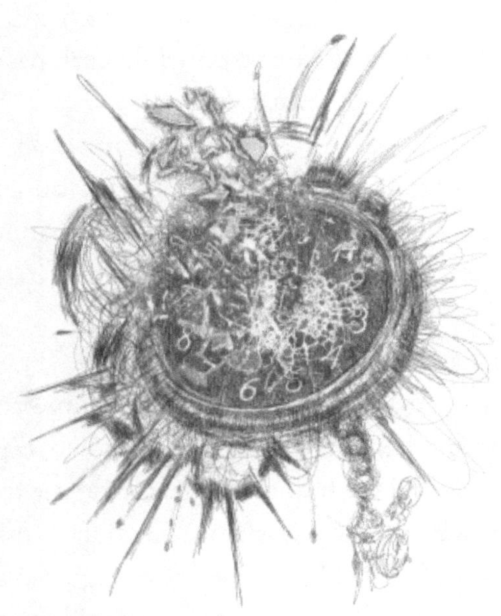

Rich glances at me, and then at the open computer next to me. "What did you see?" he asks me coolly. My hand trembles as I look at his fists, tightly clenched at his sides. I imagine the power behind them, the power it had to take to bludgeon someone to death. Not only to death, but to a puddle against a concrete floor.

"Nothing." I say, my voice cracking as the first words I've spoken in weeks leave my lips. I see his eyes light up for an instant, almost as if there was hope in them, before they darken back to their dangerous gray.

"I know you saw something there, Echo." He says, taking a step toward me. I instinctively take a step back. He knows. He sees the fear on my face and he knows I know what he is: a murderer. "I'm not going to hurt you." He says, reaching out a hand. I think of the numerous times he has held me down while Leah has performed her experiments and take another step backwards.

My hip collides with the table behind me, and I know I have very few options. I look over at Rich again; tall, muscular, in the prime of his life. There is no way I could take him in hand to hand combat. I glance around the room, quickly taking in the assortment of medical equipment in the lab.

I lunge for a scalpel, but Rich senses my move and grabs my stump before I can make it there, pushing my hips backwards against the table. We stand there, staring each other down, our bodies pressed together. I feel the heat from his skin on my freezing body and goosebumps race their way up and down my arms.

Reaching behind me, I grab the first thing I can and smash it over his shoulder. He yells out in pain, as a liquid burns through his shirt. I push him away and hobble for the door, my bare foot slapping against the concrete floor as I try to run. I pull open the doors and take off down the hallway opposite of my room.

I hear Rich cursing behind me as he pulls off his shirt to remove the acid that is now burning into his skin. He follows me out the door, his walking strides large enough to keep up with my exhausted hobbling run. He quickly catches up, wrapping his good arm around my waist and picking me up off my feet.

"Private McNeely, do you need some assistance with your... pet?" A voice floats from down the hall to my right and I see a group of men sneering at us.

"No, Lieutenant. I have it under control, sir," Rich responds as he uses his other arm to lift my legs up in the air. He cradles me like a baby against his chest, pinning my good arm against him, and turns to walk away. I hear the laughing begin before we are out of earshot. Rich doesn't respond, but I see the heat rise in his cheeks.

I stop struggling as he carries me to my room, his arms too strong to break free from. As he walks, I realize the effect the chance of freedom had had on my brain. No more blood drips from the hallway walls, no screaming echoes in my ears. For the first time in weeks, my mind is clear, and my goal of getting out of this hell-scape is at the forefront of my mind.

Rich continues to the door of my cell, the acid on his arm creating a blistering mess of his skin. I glance across his chest, noticing the scars that mar his dark, smooth skin. From the injuries alone, I can tell he has fought in many battles, as an officer of some sort, if the description of his incident was to be believed.

He opens the door and swiftly deposits me into my bed before removing my leg. "Can't have you making a run for it again." He states, quickly undoing the straps that hold it in place and pulling it off my stump. He walks to the door before looking back at me, that shine of hope in his eyes once again, "I'm really glad you are feeling better... I... I was worried about you." His eyes quickly dart to the floor and he leaves, closing the door behind him.

I lay back on the bed, mulling over his last words. He was worried about me? Why? I knew something significant depended on this project, but was it so bad that he would actually worry about the test subject? Surely they could find another human to capture and experiment with.

An alarm outside of my cell blares, startling me out of my thoughts. I sit up and stare at the door for a few minutes before climbing to my feet. Balancing myself against the wall, I climb to my good foot and carefully hop and slide along the floor to the window in the door. I brace myself in the doorway and peer out of the small window in my door. A red light rotates around the hall as the alarm continues to sound.

Suddenly, light blooms from the end of the hall towards the doors. I know I have no chance to make it back to the bed before Rich or Leah come busting in, so I resign to sit on the toilet behind me. As expected, the door bursts open, but the human who enters is in an oxygen suit. I scream and try to grab my tray to hit the intruder over the head, but they catch me, holding me tightly against their front, trapping my arms, but I refuse to give up.

"Stop struggling!" the muffled voice of the human says, holding me tighter. I slam my head backwards, making contact with their helmet and they yell clutching at their face through the plastic face mask. I push them out of the way and try running, only to fall to the floor. Using my arms, I drag myself to the door and out into the hallway, but it isn't long before the human grabs my ankle and yells, "Ixe!"

I stop in my tracks and spin around to see Loc standing behind me, mask removed and blood dripping from their nose. I stare, eyes wide, as Loc smiles at me.

"How?" The word escapes my mouth as a slight breeze.

Loc's eyes widen as they realize the extent of my injuries and bandages. "What did they do to you?!" They kneel in front of me, hands hesitating in the air as if they are trying to decide where they can touch without injuring me further. Loc is thinner than I remember which exaggerates their height. Matted hair frames their face and I wonder when they last showered. Despite that, their uniform is clean and pressed and their brown eyes are full of concern.

"We need to get out of here now. Can you walk?" They ask hesitantly.

I shake my head in response, still too stunned that they are actually here to speak. They finally decide to carefully pick me up and carry me back to my room, laying me on the bed in the corner. "How did you find me?"

"Oh, it was easy. Just infiltrated their army, figured out where the prisoners were kept, waited for the Alliance to attack the ship and ta-da! Here I am." They wait for a laugh, but I just stare at them, the time I had spent in this prison weighing on me. "We really do need to get out of here though before…"

A sound from the hall freezes us both in our tracks. Loc moves to the other side of the open door, back pressed against the wall and holds a finger over their lips as Leah walks into my room.

"How did your door…" Leah begins, but Loc jumps on her before she can finish her question. I yell out as they struggle, Leah landing a blow to Loc's temple that shoves their head into the wall, but when she backs up, I see the blood welling up from her chest. Loc holds a knife in their hand, covered in thick red blood.

Leah falls back into me, and I hold her close as she sputters, more blood welling from her mouth. "No," I say, holding her tighter. Images flash through my mind of her caring for me, feeding me when I was too weak to move, washing me and telling me everything was going to be okay. "No, Leah…" The words leave my lips before I know what I'm saying, "Don't leave me…" I say, trailing off as my brain rebels. Images of her torturing me flash by, and I'm repulsed by my attachment to this woman, but no matter how hard I try, I can't separate from the person who wants her to live. She coughs, blood splattering my face, and inhales slowly.

"We need to go!" Loc yells, holding their head with one hand, the other still gripping the knife. My head spins, conflicted feelings rushing through me. I should be glad that Leah is dying, but inside I feel a pit forming. She was kind to me. She cared for my wounds, even though she was also the one who caused them.

Loc rips Leah from my grasp and pulls me to a standing position. Wrapping an arm around my waist, they push me toward the door, forcing me to hop on my good leg. We stumble out of the cell and I can't help but glance back to see Leah wheezing in a pool of her own blood. I hunch over as a wave of nausea sweeps over me before vomiting in the hall.

"You get used to it... Seeing people die," Loc says, holding me as I empty the contents of my stomach. They start moving as soon as I've finished, not even letting me wipe my mouth. We hobble down the halls. "I'm so sorry, Ixe," Loc breathes as we struggle down the hall where the lab is located. "I should have gone with you and Mar to get the guns. I shouldn't have stayed home that day."

"What are you talking about?" I ask and Loc stops in their tracks.

"You don't remember?" They ask, incredulous. "A human ship landed on Earth near the city. The Council sent a delegation to meet the human leader, but you and Mar... You didn't think it was a good idea. You went to an Alliance camp and stole some guns from them before you hid in wait for the meeting. The meeting went bad... Bri... Bri was killed."

"Bri... Bri is dead?" With that knowledge, it all comes flooding back. The sound of the gun going off. Bri's robotic head exploding into small pieces. The frame of their body collapsing to the ground. Bots fleeing in panic as the humans shoot them down, and Mar running for the city. I remember the look on the Colonel's face as he hits me with the butt of his gun. My head spins, and I collapse, but Loc holds me in place as everything swims before me. They killed my Bot, and for what? Some tissue samples?

Someone steps out of the lab behind us, and Loc drops me to the wall to spin in a defensive position. I glance to where Rich stands, his gun stretched out in front of him. I shout as the sound of the blast fills the hall. Loc falls in slow motion, their arms outstretched from the blast to their abdomen. They fly backwards; the motion slowed by my panicking brain, and slide along the hall as blood seeps from the hole in their belly. "Noooooooooo!" I scream, falling to my knees in disbelief.

Rich glances to me and back toward Loc, who is clinging to their abdomen, blood covering their fingers. I crawl to their side, adding pressure to the wound, but blood continues to pump around my hand. "Ixe..." Loc begins, "You need to run. Get out of here."

"I'm not leaving you, Loc."

"Yes, you are. Warn our people and tell Kit... tell Kit I love..." Their voice fades as they lose consciousness.

I turn toward Rich, who stands in the hall, gun at his side. "What have you done?!" I scream at him.

"I thought... I thought..." He stammers.

"I don't care what you thought! You killed them!"

A sound down the hall pulls both of our attention and Rich runs toward me, picking me up and heading back the other way. I fight him with everything I have, punching his chest while tears stream down my face, but he keeps on walking, not even glancing at my fist. As we turn the corner, I see someone make their way into the hall behind us and run to Loc's body on the floor.

Rich walks at a steady pace through halls that I haven't seen before. I look around us, trying to remember the twists and turns so I can find my way back out, but it's no use. There are too many and my brain is a mix of screaming thoughts fighting for attention. I fight the sobs that threaten to take over before anger takes its place and I find myself yelling at Rich again.

"Shut up!" He hisses through his teeth, glancing down the next hall.

"Let me go!" I yell in return, trying to pull my arm away from him so I can get a good punch in. *Loc is dead!* My brain screams again. *Bri is dead! Why am I alive?! Why am I here?! Where are we going?! What is the point if Leah is gone?!* A constant flood of thoughts has my stomach in knots as my fight-or-flight response goes into overdrive. It's all I can do to keep from throwing up as I'm jostled from Rich's quick movements.

He glances down the next hall, verifying there are no people before emerging. "Where are you taking me?" I ask, finding a respite of calm in the chaos to ask a coherent question.

"Out of here." He clips out, not deigning to elaborate.

We continue snaking through the labyrinth of hallways and stairs before coming to a hall with multiple doorways on one wall. Rich picks a door and stands me up against the wall. I think of running, getting away from the monster who killed my best friend, but I realize I would just fall again and Rich would pick me up and keep going. Frustrated, I ask, "What are you doing?"

"I'm preparing a ship." He says, sliding open a panel in the wall to reveal a console. I glance through the doorway and see a solid set of doors with warnings painted across them.

```
Caution: Low Clearance
Restricted Area: Authorized Personnel Only
Notice: Check Life Support Systems Before Departure
Notice: Shuttle Bay Doors Close Automatically
Caution: Slippery Surface
```

Rich finishes with the panel and closes the door, wrapping his arm around my waist and hauling me to the doors. They slide open with a hiss and he pulls me inside the smaller ship. It is larger than my cell, containing a large living area with an attached kitchenette. A door on the left-hand side implies a small bathroom, and an open doorway leads to a smaller room with controls to fly the shuttle.

Rich unceremoniously dumps me on the couch and climbs into the pilot's seat. He knows I can't go anywhere and I seethe with anger at being treated like a toddler. The doors slide shut and the obnoxious sound of the alarm is cut off. I try to lie back against the couch, but my stomach roils at the possibility of us taking off and actually flying and I find myself doubled over and heaving. Rich flips switches and pulls levers and the shuttle boots up.

"Shuttle 59, you do not have clearance to take off. What are you doing?" Rich ignores the voice coming from the intercom and disconnects the shuttle from the main ship. The shuttle trembles as it flies on its own thrusters. "Shuttle 59, stop immediately. You do not have clearance to take off."

Rich flips a switch on the intercom before opening a panel to reveal a tangle of hidden wires. Carefully tracking the colors amongst the mess, Rich finds what he is looking for and yanks out three wires in quick succession.

Alarms blare in the shuttle, and I bury my head in the cushions of the couch. Closing my eyes, I take a deep breath and begin to count down from ten.

10...

9...

Bri's face flashes in front of me as they hold my hands, helping me calm down after a kid stole my toy.

8...

7...

I see Mar in front of me, walking away laughing, leaving me behind as I count their steps.

6...

5...

Loc and I play a game of stones, keeping track of who's winning with tally marks in the dirt at our feet.

4...

3...

The world lurches as the shuttle takes off, pulling away from the larger ship. I'm thrown deeper into the couch and my head spins as the world rushes past the cockpit windows.

I lose track of the numbers as my stomach does flips, the feeling of flying so unnatural to my body. More alarms sound, and I do my best not to expel the food from my body.

Approximately 30 minutes later the ship slows and thuds to the ground. I look up to see trees outside the windows, and Rich standing, staring at me.

"Why are we here?" I say at the same time Rich says "Look, I'm sorry..."

"You don't get to be sorry." I snap at him. "You killed Loc, and for what, a stupid experiment?!"

"You don't understand..." He begins, but my fury is too much to bear.

"You don't understand! Loc was my best friend. We have been together since we were six, and you shot them!"

"What were you even doing with them?!" He yells back at me, his face reddening with anger. "Trying to run from us? Do you even understand what is at stake here?!"

"No!" I yell, "Because you won't tell me anything that is going on! You just drag me to Leah and help her cut me open again and again."

We both stop in our tracks. I remember Leah laying on the floor, choking on her own blood and I feel the bile rise in my throat. I try to run to the small restroom, but without my leg I just fall on the floor, awkwardly catching myself with one good hand and my stump. Pain lances up my arm, but I refuse to give in, crawling toward the bathroom only feet away.

Rich sighs. "Let me help you."

"Don't touch me." I growl, flinching back from his touch. "You are a murderer, my *torturer,* and I want nothing to do with you."

His eyes flare with emotion, but he slowly backs away from me, retreating to the control room where he slams the door shut.

I crawl my way to the bathroom, and finally making it, realize that the nausea has passed. I collapse on the cold steel floor and weep.

CHAPTER THIRTEEN
Freedom

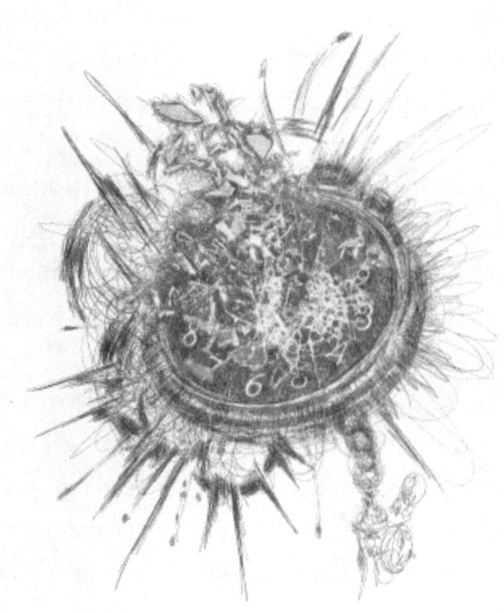

The next day, I get to work making a crutch. I pull items from around the shuttle together and pile them in the middle of the floor. Cursing, I realize there is nothing long enough to reach from my underarm to the ground. Spotting a small table in the living area's corner, I get on my knees and crawl to it, bracing my good leg against one of the table's three legs. Pulling as hard as I can, I hear the wood splinter and crack. I repeat the process with a second leg and drag my two pieces of wood back to the pile.

I pull out some bandages and tape I found in a first aid kit and start wrapping the sticks together, end to end. After testing to ensure it can bear my weight, I look for some padding. A knife that I found in the kitchen works as a saw to pull the firm padding through a hole in the fabric of the couch. I grab a book and jam it, pages down, into the splintered end of the table leg, before wrapping the entire thing together, adding the padding from the couch to the spine of the book as I go.

I drag myself onto the couch and prepare to stand. Once again, I test the makeshift crutch with my weight before fully standing on my good foot and placing the top of the crutch under my arm. I lean heavily on the crutch and take a tentative hop forward. It groans but holds under my weight.

Finally able to move around easily, I hobble into the kitchen and ransack the cabinets, pulling out bottles of water and packaged food and throwing them to the couch. After getting everything I need, I hobble back to the couch and tie a blanket into a sling. I pile the food into the sling and pick up what remains of the first aid kit, adding it to the top.

I hop over to the airlock and begin pushing buttons, hoping one of them will open it. The cockpit opens behind me and I jump.

"Where are you going?" Rich asks.

"Away from you." I respond angrily as the inner doors finally slide open. Inside the small airlock, I find a similar panel. I quickly scan the buttons, trying to get away from this man as quickly as I can. My heart races as I wait for him to attack me, try to stop me from leaving, but he just stands there.

"There isn't anything out there for miles, and you only have one leg," Rich says from behind me. "You won't make it anywhere."

"I don't care. You can't follow me out there without a suit," I say, pushing a button that has two vertical lines with arrows pointing toward each other. The doors slide closed as I look directly into his eyes and say, "and anywhere out there will be safer than here with you."

The doors shut with a finality, and I'm alone again. I press buttons on the panel until there is a whoosh of air and the outer doors open. I take a deep breath of the fresh breeze, different from the stagnant air inside the ship or shuttle, and start walking. The grove we have landed in is dead like all the other trees, wind whispering through the branches strong enough to stand up to the storms that pass through.

Within the first hour, my leg is cramping, and the crutch is digging into my skin. I collapse against a nearby tree and massage my aching leg with my one good hand. I think about how I've come to be here and feel my anger fuel me. My life was simple. I grew up in a safe city with metal protectors. I had my fair share of issues with Mar, but it wasn't anything that would kill me.

I would finish school and move out of the city on Release Day. I would get away from my abuser. I would find a mate and a job and be happy. I might have stayed in touch with Loc. My heart sinks at the thought of Loc. They just wanted to be with Kit. They just wanted to be happy, and the Bots had ruined it for them.

No, *I* had ruined it.

It was my idea to go with Mar and see the ship that night. It was my idea to get the guns from the Alliance. It was my fault that I had gotten captured.

But was it really? Who was really at the center of everything? I think back to the decisions of the Council, refusing to listen to me when I told them how dangerous the humans were. How they wouldn't even entertain the idea of letting Loc and Kit be together after Release Day. How they never listened to the Alliance or even considered letting humans reproduce.

Mar was right. What was the point of humanity if we couldn't raise our own children and populate the Earth? What were the members of Project Phoenix thinking when they created The Net? Did they really think we would go along with life without a reason to live? I wouldn't consider myself a member of the Alliance, but I could definitely see where they were coming from.

And what about these humans returned? Did they really think that the Earth belonged to them, no matter how many years had passed? What did they expect to do, kill all of us just to have more space for themselves? I think back to the actions of Leah, cutting away my skin, my organs, as I cried in pain. What right did she have to my body? My arms wrap around me and I stare at my leg stump, tears beginning to stream down my face.

I would never be the same. Would anyone want a cripple? Would I even survive this damn wilderness and find human civilization again? Rich floats before me, and I close my eyes. Rich wanted to save me, but why? He was responsible for this as much as Leah was, and on top of that he had killed Loc in cold blood. He had murdered my best friend, and for what? What would I tell Kit if I ever saw them again? How would I deliver the news that the person they had longed for would never show up?

I force myself back to my feet. I wouldn't give up so easily. I wouldn't let them have the satisfaction of breaking me, not again.

I had thought that the copse of trees we had landed in was

small, but it must have been a trick of the eye as I march through the trees the next day. The branches and brambles tear at my clothes, my skin, as I forge my way through the underbrush. I stop to get a drink from my makeshift pouch and find only one water bottle remaining. I groan, wiping the sweat from my brow before putting the bottle back into the sling and continuing on.

I need to conserve as much water as possible. Not knowing a direction to go or how far I am from any civilization, I am walking blind. My stomach grumbles as I walk, reminding me how little food remains. I need to find something to eat, and soon, or I will find myself with no provisions.

I think about Mar as I walk; about how I thought their beatings were the worst thing in my life, and laugh. If only I had bruised ribs and a few broken fingers now. I glance at my arm stump and grimace. They had taken my right arm. My dominant hand was now gone. I had struggled to open the bottles of water on the first day. Using my teeth had been my only option, and I had spilled precious liquid in my haste to quell my thirst when I had finally managed to get one open.

I sigh and the inhale of dry air makes me cough. Hunched over, I feel the ground tremble beneath me. It shakes violently, throwing me down to the hard dirt. Digging my fingers into the soil I watch the trees around me shake and wave in the wind. After a few minutes, the shaking stops and I carefully get back to my feet, leaning against a tree. I look around, waiting for soldiers to come rushing out of the trees, but no one comes and I eventually pick up my pack and continue on my journey.

I break out of the trees on day three. The vast landscape spreads out before me, wind kicking up red dust from the dry, cracked earth.

I almost fall to the ground in relief as I realize my skin will have a chance to heal from the scratches that now littered my arms, legs, and face.

My water is far gone, the sweat running down my face acting as an hourglass counting down the minutes until my body is too dry to function. I force myself to lean on the crutch again, cursing when the blisters under my arm compress beneath my weight. Taking another step, I feel one blister rupture and the liquid from inside soaks into the wrapping around the padding, adding to the blood and pus that already soaks the porous fabric.

I sit on the ground heavily, feeling the muscles in my good leg scream at the effort of crouching down to lessen the blow. I dig around in my pouch, much emptier than when I started, and dig out medicine and gauze. Pulling my shirt over my head, I wince as the fabric pulls away from the open blisters.

Looking at the wounded skin, bile rises to my throat. I quickly grab the ointment and slather a thick layer on the open area. Using my mouth, I unwrap some gauze and place it over the wounds before wrapping it. I use my teeth to rip the wrapping and tie it off before placing the medical equipment back into my bag.

I haul myself back up into a standing position and brace the crutch under my arm again. Taking a minute, I apply pressure to the bandaged area. I scowl. It isn't much better, but it will have to do. I turn and keep walking into the barren landscape.

Day four is more of the same. Sand. Dust. Sun. Heat. I cough every few steps now, my mouth so dry it cracks and bleeds. My eyes feel like sandpaper when I blink; all the tears drained from my body. My skin still glistens, but my sweat is thick and slow to produce. I wear my makeshift sack over my head to protect my now reddened skin from the direct sun. My arm, however, has no such protection and burns with every hint of the sun's rays.

Midway through the day I stumble into another forest and while I'm thankful for the sparse shade, the way is more difficult and I make slower progress. I curse, thinking I might never make it to a city when I spot the shadow of a person in the distance.

"Hey!" I yell. "Hey!!" The shadow turns and runs in the opposite direction. "No, come back!" I cry, blood seeping from my lips as they crack with the movement. I try to speed up, but it's no use. There are too many fallen trees and I'm too slow. I throw the crutch down to the ground in frustration, and then the regret sets in as I realize I will have to crawl to reach it.

Cursing, I fall to the ground and use a crawling scooting motion to get to my crutch. The branches that litter the ground and dig into my flesh create wounds, allowing life to slowly seep through my skin. Grabbing the crutch, I force myself to stand again before continuing my trek toward where I had last seen the shadow.

Day five... *or is it six?* I think to myself as I push myself to take one more step. My stomach growls, turning inside out with hunger and pulling me from my thoughts. As I reach up to pull my bag down over my eyes, I suddenly realize it's gone. I turn back, looking to see if I have dropped it, but all that stands behind me are dead trees and a path where I have passed. I sigh in frustration and pull strands of my hair over my vision instead. It would have to do.

The sun seems brighter today, or my head darker, as I walk through the woods that are the bane of my existence. My arm, long since numb, grips tighter to the crutch, and I hop another step forward. I spot something green ahead and squint to see more clearly. *It can't be...* I think to myself. I hop a few more steps and crane my neck as far as I can. *It is!* I rush forward as quickly as I can to reach the tree in full bloom in the middle of the dead forest.

I stand there in awe, watching the branches sway with the breeze and listening to the leaves rustle. The only living trees I had seen were the ones that grew in the hydroponics lab and produced our food. This one stood ten times higher than those, not stunted in size by the gardener Bots, and had ripe red fruit hanging from its branches.

I place my hand on the trunk of the tree, before reaching up and grabbing a plump fruit. I close my eyes in ecstasy as I put the fruit to my cracked lips and take a bite. Flavor ruptures from the casing and fills my mouth with sweet juice. It dribbles down my chin as I suck the liquid from the skin of the fruit and swallow.

I open my eyes. Before me stands a dead tree, branches swaying in the wind. I look down at my hand to find a clump of dirt and dead leaves. My mouth tastes of ash. I spit the vile concoction to the ground and scream in anger. Throwing my head back, I yell as loud as I can, putting all of my energy into the sound that rings through the dead forest around me.

By the end, I am laughing. If I had any tears left, they would have covered my face in a salty trail. *I'm mad.* I think to myself. *I've gone mad - again.*

I lose track of the days. It's all I can do to keep hopping through the forest, my body screaming to lie down. I know now that if I stop, I will die, and part of me longs for the sweet release. Unable to raise my head from the forest floor, I don't see the storm clouds move in until they blot out the sun. The first drops of rain are ice on my swollen skin and the will to pull my head up and look around me is finally enough.

I stare around me; the trees glistening with raindrops, the red dust turning to mud under my foot, and hang my head. I wouldn't fall for it this time. I continue my slow walking motion through the underbrush.

Crutch Forward.

Weight on.

Hop.

Land.

Crutch Forward.

Weight on.

Hop.

Land.

Turn.

Crutch Forward...

Eventually, the thunder rolls in and I can't ignore the storm any longer. I'm shivering, suddenly realizing that I'm still in my gown from the prison. Wrapping my arms around my shoulders, I stare up at the sky, and open my mouth. I feel my body rejoice the instant the water touches my tongue. It soaks it in like a sponge and craves more. I slowly lower myself to the ground and lay back, letting the rain fill me and rejuvenate my soul.

I'm freezing. The rain was a blessing turned curse as I struggle to take another step forward. I pull at the crutch with all of my strength and finally pull my foot from the sucking mud just to land and sink back in a foot ahead. "Ixe!" I hear behind me. I turn too quickly, my foot stuck in the mud and fall, landing with my leg twisted under me.

I look up and see nothing. *It must have been the wind cracking a branch, or a peel of thunder...* I think, but I have a feeling that's not the case. I drag myself up out of the mud and prepare to jump again.

"Ixy, don't you want to play?" I spin to the right, expecting Mar to be standing there in the forest, but it is empty, silent. *Not again...* I think, cursing my mind.

"You need to come home." I hear Bri's voice and my soul shatters at the sound.

"You're dead..." I whisper to no one.

"You need to come home to me." I hear again, this time in Rich's voice.

"You are not my home." I say angrily. "You will never be my home."

"You know you want this body." He replies, and I can't help but look up.

There he is, standing before me, shirt off with a scar where I shattered a bottle of acid on his shoulder. I scowl at the figure before me, trying to avoid looking at him.

"We need you..." I collapse to my knees and look into Loc's eyes.

"Loc... I'm so sorry..." Tears well up in my eyes and spill over, coating my cheeks with salt.

"You left me, Ixe. I needed you and you left me!"

"No, Loc, you told me to go... I... I had no choice."

"You just wanted to get away, and you used me to do it."

"No, please, I loved you. You were my best friend."

"Loved. Were. You sound like I'm gone."

Laughter rings out to my left, and I spin to see Leah and Rich standing in the mud. "You are gone. I killed you...

"And you liked it." Rich says mockingly.

Leah pats Rich on the shoulder before wrapping her arms around him. "Good job Lt. McNally." She kisses him as he returns her embrace.

I turn away, disgusted and confused about how I feel as another voice breaks in. "We will win, you know? We will kill everyone you love, and your precious city will be ours." I look up to find Colonel

Ritter standing over me. He hits me over the head with his gun and everything goes black.

I awake to the sun beating down on my face. Rolling over to my knees, I groan and then glance around me. I'm soaking in a puddle of mud, my gown matted and tangled around me. The surrounding ground is already drying, thirst quenched, it shows telltale signs of cracks forming in the dirt.

I find my crutch half sunk in the mud and pry it out, wiping it down on my ruined gown. Placing the end of the crutch on dry ground, I pull myself up to a standing position before attempting to remove the large chunks of mud from my clothes. Stabilizing myself, I take a deep breath and pull myself forward on the crutch. The mud makes a wet noise as my foot is sucked out.

Feeling energized, I set out, eyes downcast, to ensure I don't trip.

About an hour later, I hear a twig snap behind me. I turn to look, but nothing is there. *Not again...* I think to myself, but I know it's no use. The phantoms will come whether or not I want them to, so I turn back to my task.

I hear more snaps and pops behind me over the next few hours, but I ignore them and pray that the voices and images stay away this time. It's almost dark when a loud crack makes me jump and spin around. There, a few feet behind me, is an enormous beast.

I am overcome with a sense of dread as I hear the echoing snarl of the creature, its leathery and matted skin appearing stretched taut over its well-built frame. The sight of its saliva-drenched fangs erupting from a mouth full of sharp teeth only adds to my fear. The creature's pointed bat-like ears flatten against its head while the spikes along its jaw, neck, and spine bristle as it shifts from all fours to standing upright on its hind legs. It stands at least two times taller than myself, and my heart beats louder as my gaze slowly rises, observing the scars covering the beast's abdomen, before reaching its eyes.

My breath catches in my throat, and I stare at the beast as it stares back at me. It's wide yellow eyes watching my every move. I don't know if this creature is real or a figment of my imagination, but I know I don't want to find out.

I turn and move as quickly as I can, hopping before my crutch even hits the ground. Behind me, I hear the creature return to all fours and pad forward, investigating its prey. I know I will never be fast enough to outrace it, but I have to try, and I suddenly realize that I don't want to die.

The creature moves up to my right and cocks its head in confusion, still staring at me with those unnerving yellow eyes. *What does it want with me?* I think as I continue my frantic pace. It leaps forward, landing directly in front of me, and I scream. Its ears prick up at the sound and it swipes at me. I jump backwards and it catches my crutch, crushing it with an enormous paw. Too late, I realize its claw has ripped through my abdomen, blood seeping out and covering the now reddening gown I wore.

I scramble backwards using my arm and leg, but I know I'm done for. My back hits something solid, and I cover my eyes as saliva from the beast drips onto my skin. The smell is rancid, hot rotting meat sweeping through my senses. Bile rises in my throat, but I keep my head as far back as I can and hold my breath.

A gunshot rings out, and the breath of the beast is gone. I open my eyes and see the beast fleeing into the forest, a trail of blood falling as it runs. I look to my right and see Rich standing next to the shuttle I had left days before, gun raised in his hand. He rushes to my side and picks me up.

I know that I'm hallucinating, bleeding out all over the ground, but I can't help it when I say, "Thank you..." and pass out.

CHAPTER FOURTEEN
Echo

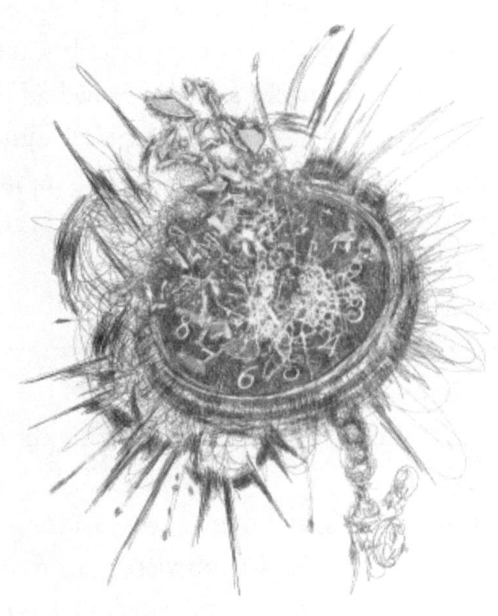

I jolt upright, my abdomen screaming in pain. For a few seconds I believe I'm back in the prison, waking up after another surgery, but the pain is different somehow. I look around me, trying to get my bearings and see that I'm back on the shuttle. *Was it all a dream?* I think as I feel the couch cushions beneath me.

No. The kitchen cabinets are still open, supplies scattered on the counters. The table in the corner lies on its side, jagged splinters peaking from underneath. And the arm of the couch bears a large hole, lying deflated from its missing stuffing.

I glance at my abdomen, wrapped in bandages soaked in blood. My gown has been replaced with a clean pair of pants, a few sizes too large, but serviceable. Rich walks through the restroom door and finds me sitting up. "You should lie down." He says, tense.

I stare at him, a look of shock on my face. It was real. If it was real, how did I end up back in the shuttle? How had Rich been outside of the shuttle without a suit? Was this all another hallucination fabricated by my declining mental stability?

"You really shouldn't be sitting up," Rich repeats, walking to my side and gently laying me back down. I don't resist, as my mind still races to catch up to the surrounding reality. "I'm not as good at patching people up as Leah is. You are going to have to take it easy, and you will probably have a nasty scar."

"How did I get here?" I ask, finally breaking the silence that had captured my tongue.

"I'm not sure," Rich says, taking a seat in a chair nearby. "You left over a week ago, and I thought you were gone for good." He runs a hand through his hair. "A couple of days ago, I was in the cockpit and I saw that beast hunting you in the forest. I didn't think. I just grabbed my gun and jumped in the airlock."

"But you can't breathe without a suit." I counter, not willing to believe the reality I was now in.

He shrugs, "I held my breath."

"You just... held your breath?" I ask, stunned.

"In the army, we go through extensive training, and part of that is being able to hold your breath for long periods of time. Although I will say, when I pulled you back into the airlock and closed the doors, I passed out, but once the oxygen poured in, I eventually came to and could stop most of your blood loss. It apparently wasn't fast enough, because you have been unconscious for a while."

I lay my head back, my mind swimming with everything that has happened. I feel the tears pool in my eyes as I think back to the visions that plagued me. Bri, Loc... They didn't deserve what had happened to them. Even Leah, although she mutilated me, she cared for me as well. She tried to heal my mind after the paralysis that drove me mad.

But the one who broke me free of it sat in this room. Not only did he free me from the torture on the ship, but he rescued me from the beast in the woods. I was alive and safe. Relief fills me as I realize I'm *finally* safe. No one would be cutting me up or testing my limits. I wouldn't be starving in the wasteland, turning to ash under the scorching sun as I hid and ran from the monsters, both in the woods and in my mind.

But... was I truly safe? Could I trust this man? I turn my head to find Rich looking at me, studying me with that steely gaze. A shiver runs down my spine as I try to hide the heat that slowly rises in my face. Why was my body reacting this way? I hated Rich with everything I had; he had held me captive for months, starved me, mutilated my body, and he had murdered my best friend. Anger wells in me at the memory of the gun going off and Loc falling to the ground.

I turn away from Rich and lay my head back down, now facing the back of the couch. "So, you still hate me..." I hear him say from behind me. "You have every right to. I... I'm sorry... Echo."

Pondering the nickname he was so fond of a realization sets in: He doesn't know my name... Not once had they even considered me human enough to have a name. I *was* human, though. Genetically modified to survive on a planet that they had destroyed, but human nonetheless. I had a family; a sibling and a parent. They may not be what you would typically call a family, but they were mine, and I cared for them deeply. I had friends and neighbors, people who cared about my wellbeing.

I had emotions. I felt happiness, sadness, anger... even the more complex emotions such as despair, regret, contempt, and yearning. Ambivalence was common, tearing me in two different directions, and nostalgia kept me longing for home. *I am human,* I repeat to myself, the doubt slowly ebbing away, *and they would not take my humanity from me.*

Rich cares for me for the next few days, quietly cleaning my wound and re-bandaging it with things he finds around the shuttle. We both stay silent. Words loom in my head, threatening to break the shield I've put up, but never quite making it through. I know there is more he wants to say; I can see it in his eyes when he looks at me, but he bites his tongue, knowing that I will resist any attempt to make amends.

And why shouldn't I? He was a kidnapper, torturer, *murderer.* I didn't want to be here with him. I wanted to be home, with my family. I wanted Bri's cool silicone skin, not the rough hands that were too warm, too *alive.* A shiver runs through me at that thought, and I clench my teeth in response. I would not let my body react this way, not toward *him.*

He appears, almost as if my thoughts summoned him, and grabs a few hand towels from a closet before walking to my side. He pulls back the old bandages, a cut up blanket, and his eyes go cold with worry. I know it's bad before I look, but it doesn't prepare me for the red puckering skin that now mars my lower abdomen. Running from my hip bone up across my belly and ending at my right side, the gash is swollen and hot.

Rich breaks his silence with one word: "Shit." He stands up and begins pacing around the small shuttle. I lay my head back and close my eyes, realizing how serious the situation must be. Rich rummages through cabinets and drawers until he finds what he is looking for and returns to my side. He holds out a small tube of ointment. "It's infected. I don't have antibiotics to give you, but I have this antibiotic ointment. It's usually used for small cuts and scrapes..." He trails off as he studies the ointment in his hand.

"But it might not work..." I finish for him, muttering the first words from my lips in days. He nods, his eyes returning to my pale face. "Do what you have to." I say, and grit my teeth, hoping that he reads it as fear of the pain to come.

Rich grabs a pair of scissors and goes to work, slowly cutting the rudimentary stitches he had applied. I inhale with gritted teeth at every pull, the pain overtaking the unpleasantness at his touch. My body healed faster than the old humans, but an infection could kill me just as easily as it did them.

Once the wound is open, Rich gently squeezes the antibiotic ointment out of the tube and directly into the gash. The coolness of the gel feels good against the fire of my skin, and I let out a sigh of relief.

He gently uses the tips of his fingers to smooth the cream into the wound, taking care to not pull at the fragile skin. They slide over my abdomen and the pain mixes with a feeling of electrical shock. With my eyes closed, I try to make the feeling go away, but it only grows stronger as he slowly moves his fingers toward my hip bone. I grit my teeth and feel him pull away.

"I'm sorry if I'm hurting you." He says, noticing my expression.

"It's not anything new." I say, forcing all of my contempt into my words, but I look away, trying to hide the confusion in my eyes as

I struggle against feelings I shouldn't have. If only he knew what feeling was actually making my face contort. *He's a murderer and my prison guard.* The thought floats across my mind and I latch onto it, using the knowledge to keep my face calm and unfeeling.

Rich finishes with the cream and lays the clean towels across my skin before cleaning up the old bandages and supplies. Sliding his hands under my back and knees, he lifts me as if I weigh nothing, and I'm reminded of the way Bri could lift me with no effort. He guides me to the restroom and sets me down before leaving and closing the door behind him.

I let out a large sigh as I lean back against the toilet behind me. How much longer could I stand to let him care for me? His touch was like a poison seeping into my skin, but at the same time... I shake my head. I refuse to think about the feelings that course through me.

It was time to break my silence and start advocating for myself. I needed help with this infection, and the city had antibiotics. Tomorrow I would make my stance and demand that he fly us to the city for help. He would have to listen to me or let me die, and I didn't think he was ready to let me go. *Tomorrow then*, I thought to myself, happy to have decided on a plan as I knock on the inside of the door to let him know I was done.

"But I need antibiotics!" I yell again, trying to pull myself up into a sitting position. It had been another two days, and the wound had not changed.

"No, you don't." He responds, standing a few feet from the couch, staring me down. "Your wound is healing. The infection isn't spreading."

"What do you even know about infection? You aren't a doctor."

"I've trained with doctors and seen my fair share of battle

wounds." He retorts.

I scowl at him, and he returns the look, unfazed. "You're extremely difficult to deal with." I tell him.

"I've been told that a few times before," he smirks, and I find the corners of my mouth turning upward. I turn away, cursing my body for responding this way. "Look, if your wound doesn't turn around in a few days, I will think about us finding a place where we can get help, but we aren't going back to your city."

"Why can't we go to my city?" I ask again. He has avoided the question so many times at this point I think it's a game to him.

"Because I'm a fugitive, and they are going to want you back." He sounds exasperated as he gives me the same answer as before.

"That's not good enough." I say. "My city is a day's walk from the main ship, at least."

"Do you really want to go back to being experimented on?" His frustration at my pestering is clear as his fists clench at his sides.

"I wouldn't have been experimented on in the first place if you hadn't captured me!"

"I didn't capture you, Colonel Ritter did, and you avoided my question."

"You're right. You didn't capture me, you just cut me open and removed my limbs." I sneer at him, holding my arm stump in the air in front of him.

He goes silent, remorse filling his eyes, and I feel the smallest amount of regret. "You don't understand..." He begins.

"Then make me understand!" I yell at him.

"Your city is gone!!" He yells back.

Silence falls over the room as I stare at him in shock. "What do you mean?" I ask, my voice barely a whisper.

His eyes fall to the floor as he answers softly, "I heard the command over the intercom a few days after you left..."

"He destroyed my home?" I ask, choking on the lump in my throat.

Rich runs his hand through his hair.

"Why?" I ask. "Why can't you just get along with us? Coexist with us? Are we that repulsive to you!?"

He cringes and replies, "It's complicated..."

"It's complicated?! That's all you can say to me. Is that it's complicated?! Your people destroyed my home, and that is all you can say?!" Silence settles between us, and I know he has no answers. "How was it done?"

Rich hesitates, but eventually gives in, "Ritter ordered bombs to be dropped on the city, in retaliation for... for the attack that led to your escape."

I stare at him in silence, stunned at the lengths Ritter would go to for one modified human specimen.

"Echo..." He begins, reaching a hand out to console me.

"No!" I yell before he can get any closer. "Stop calling me that! I'm not your pet!" I pick up the tray that had held my food and throw it at him. He catches it from the air and stares at me. "Get out." I say, hate filling my voice. "Get out!"

He slowly sets the tray down and heads to the cockpit. It's all I can do to hold in the tears until I hear the click of the door behind him. My home... my family... destroyed. Was I the only survivor of the city? The Alliance had said they would protect the city, but what could they possibly do against bombs?

I had already lost Bri and Loc and now... *Mar.* Their face floats before me and my feelings swirl like a tempest. Mar was just a confused kid. They had taken their anger out on me for as long as I could remember, but that didn't mean they deserved to die. They were still my sib, and now... now I was alone.

I break down as the realization sets in. Everyone I had known was dead, and I had survived. Even worse, they were dead because of me. I was stupid enough to get captured that day, which had led them to attack the ship. A cry from my soul tears through me as I remember the nursery. All the babies and toddlers who would have died screaming. My whole body shakes as I sob uncontrollably for those that were lost, that would never grow up, or fall in love. They would never see their Release day, because I was selfish.

It's all my fault, and I don't deserve to live.

I wallow in my self pity for weeks, refusing to eat or do anything other than lay on the couch in misery. Rich still tends to my wound, even though I try to force him away, but I'm too weak and he knows it. I eventually give in and let him touch me, but his hands are distant, a world away from where my mind sits.

One morning, Rich walks into the room and picks me up, putting me in a standing position before letting go. I collapse to the floor, hitting my head on the arm of the couch. "What was that for?!" I yell.

"Finally, some life!!" He yells back, pulling me to my feet again. This time I stand for a few seconds before my leg gives out from underneath me and I'm back on the floor.

"Stop it!" I yell, breathless from the sudden movement.

"You said you had a family, Echo. Do you think they would want you to lie around while you waste away?"

I grunt as he picks me up again and sets me on my one leg. He forces me to look at him as he says, "Do you think they would be *proud* of how you are acting?" and lets me go.

I reach out and grab his shirt, trying to hang on, but I'm too weak and I fall again. I latch onto his arm as he picks me up again, but he easily peels me away.

"Actually, I bet they would. I bet they would rejoice at you lying around dying. I bet that is the best thing they could have wished for as they were blown to pieces."

"Shut up!" I say, pushing him before realizing he is the reason

I'm standing. I fall backwards this time, slamming my back on the table and groaning as pain shoots through me.

He leans down over me, hissing through his teeth, "You're worthless, Echo. You can't even stand up. You can't even fight *me*. What makes you think you will ever beat Ritter like this?"

My stomach lurches at his words and tears come to my eyes, but I refuse to let them spill down my cheeks. He sneers at me again before turning on his heel and going back to the cockpit, slamming the door behind him.

Now alone, I take deep breaths, trying to calm the storm inside me. *Alone.* The word rings through my head, threatening to drag me back into my deep depression, but Rich's words stick with me:

Do you think they would be proud...

You can't even fight me...

You will never beat Ritter....

I slowly inhale, letting the breath fill me to the brim before letting it back out in a rush. I let a few small sobs escape me before repeating the process until my body stops shaking and the tears stop threatening to make an appearance. Now that I'm calm, I let myself ponder the question swimming through my brain.

Do you think they would be proud...

No, they wouldn't. Bri wouldn't want me to be wallowing in grief... Loc would try to drag me out of this shuttle, getting me back into the world, and Mar... Mar wouldn't just lay here and take it as the enemy won. They would do everything they could to fight back, to make a difference in the world.

You can't even fight me...

I lift my arm, barely recognizable with the muscle loss. As I glance at my body, drowning in the loose clothing, I realize that I have become a shadow of my former self. I had always been small, but still strong. This shell that had been my conduit to the world was now a prison of my own making.

You will never beat Ritter...

The words sting deep inside me. Yes, Leah and Rich had both tortured me, but it was Ritter who commanded them. Ritter who directed his army to attack my home, to kill my family. Who was my real enemy here?

I glance at the door that hid Rich from me. He had done nothing but try to help me since we left the ship, and even before... He had never picked up a scalpel. Even when I fought back, punching and scratching at his skin, he had always been gentle when handling me. He had risked everything to get me off that ship, and I repaid him by abandoning him in this shuttle, almost getting myself killed, and then letting myself slowly waste away.

But he killed Loc... How could someone kill a person in cold blood and expect mercy? He was doing everything in his power to earn my forgiveness, but could anyone ever truly be forgiven for such a heinous crime? Could I ignore his past? Not only the death of my best friend, but the deaths of those listed in Leah's report...

I lower my head into my hands and groan. My head pounded with the decisions I would have to face in order to live, but I knew that Rich was right about one thing, my family wouldn't want me to give up.

The truth is that *I* am letting Ritter win, letting him get away with my torture, my family's deaths, and the inevitable eradication of my species. As I sit on the floor of the shuttle, overwhelmed by shame, fear, and rage, I realize two very important things:

I wouldn't stop until Ritter was dead by my hand, and I would need Rich to succeed in that mission, despite my hatred of the man.

I open my eyes, bright lights flooding in and my heart seizes as I scream. Rich runs from the cockpit and wraps his arms around me. "It's okay, you're out, you're free." He says as he holds my trembling form.

I sink into his arms, before I realize who holds me, and I pull back as if I've been burned. Shame fills me as the cold air replaces the warmth I had felt, the comfort a hot brand on my soul.

I look around and see that I'm on the couch in the shuttle, not the cell. I take a few deep breaths to calm my racing heart. It had been a week since I 'woke up' from my depression, but we still hadn't reconciled or discussed what we would do next.

We sit in silence, each expecting the other to talk, before Rich stands up to leave. I reach out and grab his arm, forcing myself not to pull away, stopping him from walking back to the cockpit.

"Why did you kill my friend?" I ask, my voice raw with emotion. It was the last piece I needed in order to trust this man enough to accomplish my goal.

He lowers his head as he lets out a sigh. "They were wearing a suit." He says, as if that should explain what happened.

"But why would you shoot someone wearing your equipment?"

"I thought it was one of the Colonel's soldiers coming to take you to him. I had been working on getting you out of there. I didn't agree with Leah's methods, and said as much to Colonel Ritter, but he believed in her. Not to mention he has a mean streak a mile wide." He shakes his head, realizing he has gotten off track. "I needed to get you out of there, to save you from what they were doing, but I didn't know how. When the ship was attacked, it was the perfect moment."

"But you're a murderer..." I trail off.

His eyes harden. "You saw my file, didn't you? I thought that was the case, but I didn't want to mention it unless I knew for sure." He runs a hand through his hair and sighs. "It's true. The cryostasis had a negative effect on us. It caused some brain damage. At least, that's what Leah said happened. I was discussing the policies related to the new human species that had inhabited Earth with another lieutenant and... It just came over me. Something snapped, and I lost all control..."

A dark cloud churns behind his eyes as he remembers what happened. "I spent a lot of time in a cell pondering what I did and how I would live with myself... I realized that I never wanted to kill another human. They put me on Leah's team, and I was still lost when they brought you in. At first I told myself that you weren't human, you were alien, but as time went on and I watched you in that cell..." His voice fades as he remembers what he had done to me.

He had planned to save me...

He had thought he was protecting me...

He is a murderer...

Bile rises in my throat and I clench my teeth. I couldn't trust someone who would kill so easily, but I needed to trust *someone.* Maybe I could convince him of my loyalty, and when I get back to civilization I could escape. I could find Roa and convince them to march the Alliance to Ritter's door, take out the man in charge, and then deal with Rich.

A trial...

Yes, a trial for the murder of Loc. That's the least he deserves.

Yet, something nags at the back of my mind as I squeeze his arm gently and say, "My name is Ixe."

"Ixe." He says and smiles, a mischievous twinkle in his eye, "I prefer Echo."

A knot forms inside of me, its tendrils reaching out to corrupt my very being.

CHAPTER FIFTEEN
Pinky Promise

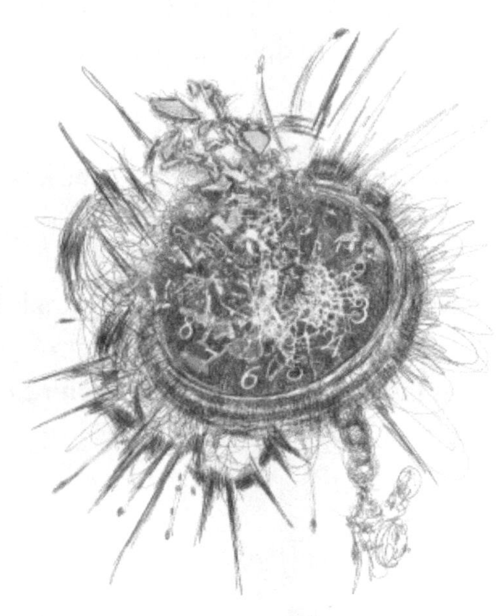

Echo...

      Echo...

            Echo...

"Echo!!" I jump, my eyes flying open to find Rich standing over me. "There you are!" He says, a grin on his face.

"Go away," I groan, rolling back over on the couch, trying my best to sink back into my dreams.

"Nope, it's time to get up. We've got a full day planned today." His voice is frustratingly happy for this early in the morning.

I sit up, my muscles aching with the movement. Rich had been waking me up early every morning for weeks, forcing me to do workouts to regain my strength. "I can't do this today, Rich. I'm *tired.*"

He raises his eyebrows at my whining and says, "Nonsense. You've been making good progress. Don't give up just because a bit of soreness sets in."

I know he is right, but I don't want to admit it, so I spin around, letting my legs fall off the edge of the couch and rub my face with my hand, trying to get sleep out of my head.

"C'mon Echo. Do a few exercises for me today, and I will show you how to play an old card game."

My head perks up at that, curiosity getting the better of me. I didn't know any games from the time of the humans, and the days stuck in this shuttle were long and boring. We were taught plenty of information about humans in history and health class, but it was more about the wars they waged and the destruction they caused, not any pastimes they may have had.

"Only a few?" I ask, narrowing my eyes.

"Promise," Rich says, holding out a pinky.

I stare at the pinky pointing out at me, before reaching out my hand and grabbing it, trying to use it to stand.

Rich doubles over in laughter, and I fall back on the couch, my face turning red. "What?!" I ask, indignant. "What did you expect me to do with a *pinky*?" He continues to laugh, clutching his side. My anger relaxes as the amusement spreads and I can't help but let out a few laughs myself before clamping my teeth shut. I had to convince him that we were friendly, but that was the extent of my enjoyment. "Seriously, what's the issue?" I ask again.

He finally regains his composure and says, "It's a type of promise: a pinky promise."

"A promise? On a pinky?" I stare at him, looking for any sign of a trick being played on me.

"It originated with something about getting your pinky cut off if you broke a promise... but yes, it is a way children would make promises to each other back in my time." His smile is genuine, but I still ponder putting all my belief into the gesture.

"So... How is it done?" I ask, hesitantly.

Rich sits next to me on the couch and reaches for my hand, but before touching it he asks, "May I?" He had been very conscious about asking my permission before touching me since we had left the ship, yet every time it filled me with certainty that my body was now my own. Leah had taken that control away from me, and Rich tried his hardest to give it back, one day at a time.

I hand him my hand, so small compared to his, and he takes it gently, folding my fingers into a fist before pulling out my pinky. He then forms his own hand into the same shape and wraps our pinkies together, forming a lock between us.

"I promise, I won't give you more exercise than you can handle today," he says softly, "and in return, I will teach you a human card game." He squeezes my pinky with his, and my face flushes against my will.

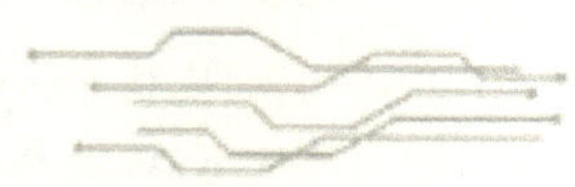

"Your pinky promises are shit." I say, sitting on the floor panting from the last three hours of exercises he had put me through.

"Well, I did specify I wouldn't do more than you could *handle*. You need to learn how to phrase your promises better." He says, giving me a wink. Anger boils inside of me, but I'm too exhausted to do anything about it. "C'mon Echo, it's time to learn that card game." He reaches out a hand and I take it, pulling myself up to a standing position. My leg screams and I can't help but lean on Rich as he helps me to the table in the kitchen. I feel the length of him pressed against my side, his skin still warm from the exercises, and I want to melt into him. *What is wrong with me?!*

"What is it called?" I ask as I take my seat quickly, wanting to be away from him. I watch him grab a deck of cards from a cabinet before he takes his seat opposite me.

"Go Fish," he says, pulling the cards out of the paper box. I look at the cards curiously, wondering how you could play a game with a stack of hardened paper. Rich shuffles through the cards and pulls some out, laying them in front of me on the table. "There are nine number cards and three face cards," he says, gesturing to the groupings in front of him.

"Where's number one?" I ask, only seeing two through ten before me.

He pulls out another card, placing it in front of him with the others, "That would be the ace," he says, "It can be played as a one, or as the highest card in the deck, but that won't matter for the game we're playing."

I pick up the ace and hold it in front of me, admiring the black shape in the middle. "What about these shapes?"

"That's a spade, but we don't need to worry about those, either."

"I want to know," I say, eagerness slipping into my voice.

"Okay," he says, smiling, and I regret asking, "There are four suits in a deck of cards in two colors. Black: spades and clubs. Red:

hearts and diamonds. They have different purposes in different games."

"This looks nothing like a heart," I say, pointing at the card he had specified.

"You don't have hearts anymore?" He asks incredulously.

"Of course we have hearts! Yours actually look like *that*? How do they even function?" Rich laughs and my cheeks turn red, realizing he must be playing a joke. "I knew you were pranking me." I say angrily.

"No, it's not that. I just realized why you are so confused. We call this a heart, but it isn't our *actual* heart."

"So it has nothing to do with the heart in your chest?"

"Well... yes and no. It is the universal symbol for love, and love is thought to be felt in the heart of the human, so they are tied together." I think of the electric feelings that had been plaguing me, and and immediately grateful that they aren't in my heart. "...but this heart is just a symbol and doesn't look like the anatomical heart at all..." his rambling fades as he notices the look on my face.

I simply say, "Humans are weird," and pick up the next card. "What's the 'J' for?"

"That's a Jack, and this is the Queen, followed by the King." He sees the puzzlement on my face at the foreign words and continues, "You can just call them J, Q, and K."

"So, how do we play?" I ask, laying the Q card back on the table.

He picks up all the cards and stacks them together again, before splitting them in half. Tapping both stacks on the table, he bends each stack and puts them end to end before letting them slide out of his fingers, where they magically form back into one final stack.

"How did you do that?!" I ask, the astonishment on my face clear.

"It's called a 'shuffle'. We shuffle the cards before we play so that they are out of order as much as possible. We want them to be random when we play." He shuffles the cards a few more times before placing one before me, one before him, continuing until we both have seven cards face down in front of us. He sets the rest of the cards face down in the middle.

He picks up his cards and spreads them out in his hands. I do the same, struggling with only one hand, but managing to see each of the cards.

"Now, the goal of the game is to get all four of the same number. When you do get a set of four, you lay it down."

"Like this?" I ask, laying down my cards and pulling four Q cards out of the pile in front of me, stacking them to the side.

He rolls his eyes but says, "Yes, like that, but it won't always be that easy. You have to go 'fishing' for the cards you need. So, ask me for a card you have in your hand."

"But then, won't you know I have that card?"

"That's part of the game. You have to remember what people have asked for in the past."

I ponder this before asking for my first card, "Do you have any 3s?"

"Go Fish." He says, smiling. I just stare at him. "It means you take a card from the middle stack."

"Oh." I say, laying down my cards to grab the card from the top of the pile.

"Now it's my turn... Give me your 2s..." he says. I pull them out and hand them over. We continue the game, fighting for the sets of cards as best we can, until we both have five stacks of cards in front of us.

I look back at my hand. One 4, three Js, and one 10. "Do you have any Js?"

"Go fish," he says, smiling. I smile back, knowing that there are only two cards left in the middle and the odds of it being the fourth J I need are pretty good. I pull the top card and flip it over. 10. Dammit.

"Do you have any 4s?" he asks.

I groan and hand over my 4. He takes it from me and lays down the stack of 4s in front of him. That made six stacks for him to my five. I look at the cards in my hand and the look on his face, a smirk, and realize what he has already discovered. He has won. I roll my eyes. "Just end it." I say.

He laughs and asks for my 10s. I hand them over and he lays them out, adding his seventh stack. I pick up the last J from the stack in the middle and lay down my sixth stack. "It was a pretty close game." He sounds impressed, and my cheeks heat in response.

"So what's next?" I ask.

"That's it. That's the game."

"Oh," I say, sitting back in my chair, disappointment clear on my face. I had been enjoying myself for the first time in... months.

"I can teach you another one," he says tentatively.

I perk up, "Okay!" The excitement in my voice startles me, and I try to tamp it down.

He pulls all the cards together and lines them up before shuffling them again. "This next game is called 'War'."

"Seriously? You want to play a game called 'War'? Wow, you humans really are war obsessed, aren't you?" I say, a sudden edge to my voice.

"Come on, Echo, it's just a name."

"Just a name? Say that to my family." He opens his mouth to say something, but my anger is rising and I cut him off. "Say that to all the people who died in my city! War is everything to you. It's even present in your games." I throw my hand out and hit the stack of cards, sending them flying out of his hands.

He sits silently as the cards fall to the floor and then looks at me. "My people are not just about war. We only fight when we have to."

"So, eliminating my species is a requirement, then? Good to know."

"Echo... I didn't mean it like that."

"Of course you didn't. You never mean anything you say."

"Echo, stop."

But I can't stop the flood of words spouting from me in a rush. "You never cared about any of my people. You never cared about me! You just want to *use* me!"

Before I know what has happened, the table between us goes flying and Rich is in my face, his hands clamped tightly on my upper arms. My anger flashes bright and disappears, leaving fear in its wake. "You don't get to tell me what I *care* about!" he yells, shaking me hard. "You don't get to tell me how I *feel*!"

My head swims as he shakes me again, hard enough that my jaw slams together in a flash of pain. I reach out, trying to stop him, but the Rich I know is gone and in his place is a monster. His eyes burn with anger as he grips me tighter, and I feel my bones ache under the pressure of his fingers. "Rich, please... stop." I gasp, the world spinning around me.

The shaking stops, and his fingers release their grip. I look up at him, trying to focus my eyes to see him.

"I'm so sorry, Echo... I..." He looks at the table now upside down in the living area and back at me before turning and running to the cockpit, locking himself inside.

Trembling takes hold of me, the shock of what happened a weight that I can't shake. My arms throb painfully as I try to come to terms with Rich hurting me. It had taken weeks for me to relax around him, letting him touch me without feeling revulsion or fear. I had let myself believe he would never hurt me and now... now he had.

I slowly wrap my arms around myself and wince as my hand brushes the skin that would be red and bruised under the thin fabric of my shirt. The room finally stills as my brain settles down from the shaking, and I feel a drop of water on my arm. I reach my hand up to my face and it comes away wet with tears.

Why had Rich done this? What had I done to set him off and cause such anger? I replay our conversation in my head and sigh at the unrelenting anger I had shown. We had been having a good time and a simple name had brought it crumbling down. *War.* The word had such a negative connotation and brought destruction to everything around it. Destroying budding friendships as if they were paper in a raging fire.

Friendship. Is that what I considered the relationship between Rich and me? I had been trying to trick him into believing we were friends, but had I tricked myself as well? Had it changed from captor and captive, from torturer and tortured, to friends? I think back to the laughter we shared while playing Go Fish, the banter we had around the pinky promise, and the care Rich had shown me after leaving the ship.

I might actually consider him a friend, and if he were my friend, it meant I needed to mend the chasm that now separated us.

Very slowly, I climb out of the chair and work my way to the cockpit door. Out of breath, but finally there, I knock on the door and softly call out, "Rich?" Silence is my answer. "Rich, come on… tell me what happened." I hear shuffling around the cockpit, but he doesn't answer. I lean my head against the door and sigh. "Okay, we don't have to talk about it if you don't want to. I just… I just want you to know that I'm okay. I'm not hurt that bad…"

As I slowly move away from the door, I swear I hear crying come from the other side.

CHAPTER SIXTEEN
The Building

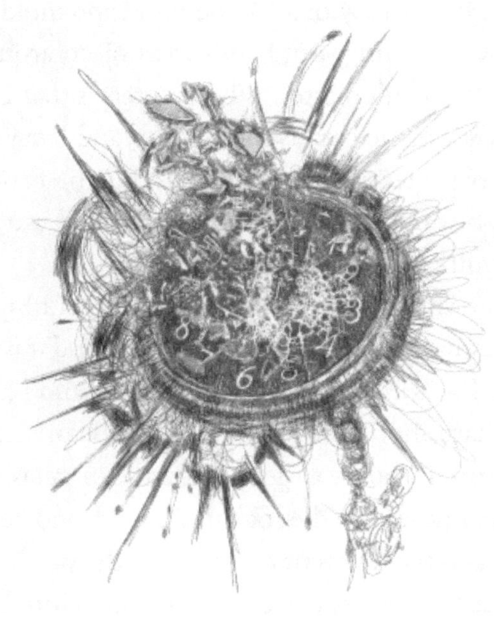

For the next few weeks, Rich is distant. He doesn't push me during my exercises, and the banter I had come to enjoy is no longer present. He barely looks at me, and when his eyes do wander over, they always rest on the spot where his hands had clenched my arms, the regret in his eyes apparent.

I still hadn't figured out what had happened that day, but I was tiring of the stone-faced rock I now cohabitated with. As we sit over another quiet dinner, I try to come up with ways to bring him out of his shell.

I think back to the first real fight between Loc and me, and I start telling the story without realizing what I'm doing, "When I was eight, Loc and I were playing outside with their newest toy — the plasmashifter. It was a toy that let you build and mold miniature holographic worlds using your hands and objects around you to manipulate... It doesn't matter. What matters is that Loc had just gotten it after saving up credits for months, and I wanted a turn with it. Loc was very protective of it, but I was their best friend and they trusted me to be careful. They handed it over and watched the joy in my face as I built my own little world..."

"What are you talking about?" Rich asks, but I ignore him.

"The plasmashifter used colors from around it to color its environment. I wanted a specific shade of trees and I just so happened to have another toy that matched. Before Loc could stop me, I ran toward my house to get the toy, the plasmashifter still in my tenuous grasp. I never saw the rock in the yard, and before I knew it, I had tripped and the toy went flying across the yard to land on the hard packed dirt. As you can expect, it shattered into hundreds of pieces."

I pause for a moment, remembering the shock and anger that had come as Loc saw their cherished item destroyed. "Loc was so angry with me. I tried to apologize again and again, but they wouldn't let me. I bottled up all of my feelings and let them fester for weeks, growing more angry, depressed, and lonely with every day. That was until Bri sat me down and asked me what the issue was. I explained Loc hated me because I broke their toy. They pointed out that Loc had come by multiple times to play with me after the incident, but I had said no.

"After thinking about it, I realized that it wasn't Loc's feelings toward me that were the problem, but my own feelings toward myself. I was so frustrated with what I had done that I didn't even consider that Loc might have forgiven me. Bri explained that sometimes we hold on to things that we cannot control, and that it can make us feel worse in the end. After we talked about it, I understood that I needed to let it go and forgive myself, and once I did, I felt so much better."

"Are you implying that I should just 'let it go'?" He asks.

"Yes."

"It's not the same, Ixe."

I cringe at the way he says my name, but keep my face neutral. "It is exactly the same. You lost control and broke my trust. I won't deny it." His face falls as I confirm that my trust was broken, but I keep on, "But I've forgiven you, and you need to let it go, or you will only keep festering and that isn't good for either of us or our eventual goals."

"And what, exactly, are these goals?"

"To take down Ritter, of course. You don't agree with his tactics and I definitely disagree with what he is doing, so we need to remove him from power."

"And how do you propose we do that? A soldier and a cripple against an entire army." The sarcasm drips from his words.

"I don't know how, but I know the first step. We need to get me back to my former strength. I can't be dependent on others to help me move around, and I sure as hell need to be able to defend myself."

"It's a good thing you are trapped here with the perfect teacher." Rich says, smiling. My heart skips a beat at seeing his smile again, and I can't help but smile in return.

"So, tomorrow then?"

"It's a date." He says, and I find myself wishing that were true.

The next day, Rich starts pushing the couch to the side of the small living area.

"What are you doing?" I ask, curious.

"Making room." He grunts, pushing the couch harder.

"You know, that might be easier if you let me get up off the couch first?" I mock.

He looks up and rolls his eyes at me. "Maybe you could help me out instead of mocking me?"

I stand, balancing on my good leg, and the couch scoots across the floor easily once my weight is removed. Rich glares at me as he falls to the floor, unable to stop his inertia in time. A small giggle escapes me before I shut it down, biting my lips to stop the sound. Rich gets up and dusts off his pants before moving the other furniture out of the way.

"Seriously, what's your plan?" I ask again.

"We're going to train." He says simply.

I look at him with doubt. "Train? In here?"

"Well, I can't go outside, now can I?" He says while picking up pieces of the broken table and throwing them into the corner. I settle myself back on the couch and watch as he cleans up the floor and removes his shirt, throwing it to the couch next to me. The scent of him on the breeze makes something stir deep within me. I tamp down the feelings that threaten to overwhelm me and focus on the moves he is now doing.

"We start by stretching our muscles out." He balances on one leg while he pulls the other up behind him.

"Come on, Rich. There is no way I can do that." I say. He ignores me and continues his routine, moving to stretch out his arms. He slowly lunges down, placing a knee on the ground before standing and performing the same move with the other leg. His muscles along his abdomen tense as he stretches, and I can't help but let my eyes wander over the taut skin.

Before I know it, he coughs and my eyes shoot to his. "I..." I say, heat rising to my cheeks.

"Do you want to join me?" He asks, unfazed by my attention. *What was I doing?* He was a human, and I was... not female. We were *friends.* I could live with that. I couldn't live with myself if it became more. Not that he would want more... Would he?

Frustrated, I stand on my one leg and try to remove my shirt. Realizing it was probably not a good idea to stand first, I fall to my butt on the couch. The sound of Rich laughing meets my ears and then I feel a hand helping to pull my shirt over my head.

I glare at Rich once my head is free of the tangled fabric and stand again. He simply helps me to the middle of the open space and balances me as I try to repeat the same warm-up he had done. I can barely stand on my own, let alone stretch, so I spend most of the time catching myself on him as I fall.

Finally satisfied with the warm-up I had managed to do, he switches to the workout. "Let's start with sit-ups." I drop to my hand and then lower myself to the floor, laying down in front of him. He grabs my foot, holding tightly, and I place my arms over my chest. I manage 20 sit-ups before I'm out of breath and my muscles are pleading with me to stop.

"Not bad for just being cut open by a beast." He says, smiling. I glance at the red scar marring my skin. It had closed, but it was wide and jagged from not having proper stitches. "Now push-ups." He says, holding out a hand.

I laugh. "You can't be serious," I say, holding up my stump.

"You can do it, Echo. I believe in you."

My stomach flips as the nickname he gave me leaves his lips. Whether in fear of the memories it brought back or excitement at something special between us, I wasn't sure. I take his hand and pull myself to sitting, before flipping over onto my knees.

"Now," He says, "We are going to go slow. Start from your knees and stretch out your arm in front of you. Just like that." He says as I reach out and place my hand in front of me. "You are going to balance on that hand like you do with your leg and just bend."

I shift my weight to my arm and slowly lower myself down by bending my elbow. My arm screams in agony, but it doesn't fold as I push myself back up, panting.

"See," He says excitedly, "You can do it. Now do a few more." I oblige, continuing to do push-ups until I fall exhausted on the carpet. The muscles in my arm twitch as I lay there staring at the ceiling.

"What's next?" I ask, enjoying the feeling of my muscles aching from use. The exercise these past few months had kept me sane, and it felt good to push myself harder.

"We can try some squats." He says and I laugh as he continues, "I've been thinking maybe you can put your stump up on the couch and try to squat that way."

I glance at the height of the couch and compare it to the length of my leg missing below my stump. It might actually work. I roll over and get back into a standing position. Rich takes my hand and I hop carefully to the couch, where I prop my leg up on the cushion. Pulling my hand from his, I try bending my knees into a squat. Almost immediately I find myself on the floor laughing.

"Okay, so maybe we aren't quite ready for that step yet," he says, holding out his hand. "Let's work on some self defense tools instead. Since you are still struggling to stand for long periods, we will sit down and face off." He pulls our chairs from the kitchen and sets them in the middle of the floor, taking one while gesturing for me to sit in the other.

I stand there, staring at him. He had left me next to the couch, far enough that it would take me three good hops to make it to the chair. "Are you just going to leave me here?"

His sly smile is intoxicatingly frustrating. "You've got to learn how to walk on your own. Now is as good a time as any."

I glare at him, but jump forward, using the couch to balance me as I land. *Easy enough,* I think before I realize there will be nothing to hold on to at the next landing. I suck it up and jump anyway, but pitch forward and land hard on my outstretched hand.

"That looks like it hurt." He says from his seat.

"It did. Thanks for noticing," I grunt, pulling myself back up to my knees. I take a minute to breathe before I proceed to stand again on my shaky leg. I reorient myself and judge the distance to the chair, now only one hop away. Bending my knee carefully, I launch myself forward and land right in Rich's lap, almost knocking him out of his chair.

I scramble backwards, trying to untangle myself from him as heat rises in my cheeks. My arms and legs flail, trying to find purchase anywhere but him and failing. Then I realize he is laughing and I stop, looking up at him. The joy on his face is contagious and I find myself laughing along with him as we untangle from each other and I find my seat on the chair set across from him. "We need to work on your aim," he chuckles.

I nod, my face still burning with embarrassment and heat at being so close to him. "So, what's next on the agenda?" I ask, trying to put the thought of our bodies pressed together far from my mind.

"We're going to work on some simple punches. Now, raise your fists... uh... fist and arm up in front of your face." I copy his movements and he nods. "Just like that. Normally I would be showing you the difference between an orthodox and southpaw stance, but since you only have one hand, you are going to have to switch between them in order to get a mix of power punches and jabs."

"Rich. You are going way too fast."

"Right. Sorry. I ramble when I'm nervous."

Nervous? I ask myself before saying, "It's okay. Just slow down."

"Okay, so first we will learn a jab. Move in the chair so that your left shoulder is forward, yes, like that. Now, punch out."

I do as he says, and he watches my fist closely.

"First things first, you never want your thumb to be inside your fist. It's a good way to break it." He gently takes my hand and pulls my thumb out, placing it alongside the outside of my fist. "Second, your elbow is too low. You want to raise it up to get the most power behind your punch, like this." He lifts my elbow and fiddles around with more of my stance before finally sitting back down and telling me to punch again.

I do and immediately see the difference. "Wow," I say, "is this why I never actually hurt you when I fought?"

He laughs, running his hand through his hair. "Part of the reason, yes, but you were very weak as well, and I wouldn't say you never hurt me. I just ignored the pain, especially the scratching."

"Sorry about that," I say, but I don't mean the words. He had done much worse to me and deserved the pain I was able to deliver.

"Don't be sorry," he says, getting back to the lesson. "So, now you know how to jab, which is essentially a straight punch from your front hand. Now I want you to switch your 'stance' by putting your stump arm toward me and shifting your hips. This is going to allow you to do power punches by using the twist of your body to propel them forward. This next punch is called a cross because you are 'crossing' your body to hit the target."

He gently sets up my fist and demonstrates the way I should twist my body, completing the punch. The feeling of his hands on my sides sends warm shivers through me, and I struggle to concentrate on his instruction. His hands are gentle as he changes the way I sit, the drop of my elbow, the direction of my fist until he sits back and admires his work.

"Now, punch, and remember to twist your whole body." He holds up his hand and I punch it as hard as I can. "Good," he says, smiling, and warmth floods my body.

We continue the workouts for another week, and I can feel my body getting stronger every day. It isn't long before I'm standing to do my punches, falling more often than not, but Rich catches me every time, placing me back on my feet as if I were a doll and telling me to do the motion again.

After a heavy day of punching, I lay down on the floor, my chest heaving. Rich lies on the carpet next to me, and I glance at him, sweat glistening on his skin, his chest rising and falling with the effort of the exercise. My mind drifts and I imagine what it would be like to touch him, my hand gliding over his skin, feeling the taut bands of muscle running underneath.

What it would feel like for him to touch me? I close my eyes, picturing his fingers gently running along my pale chest. Moving my hand over his, I guide it down my stomach, allowing it to softly explore my waist and settle on my back as I turn to face him. I replace my hand on his abdomen and trace lazy circles around his belly button.

I look into his eyes and see the hunger reflected there. Feel the heat rise into my cheeks as it fills my belly. My hand drifts lower until I feel his hardness pushing against the pants he wears. I gasp at the sheer size of him, never having felt a human penis before.

He growls low in his throat as he pulls me onto him, letting my hair fall in a fan around his face as he kisses me. His scent fills my nostrils and the beast inside me roars its head as...

I jolt awake. The shuttle is dark, and I lay on the floor next to Rich. I groan as I remember the dream I had been having, the beast inside me slowly receding as reality sets in. Shame fills me, mixing with the pleasure that pooled at my core. How could I betray Loc like this? How could I be falling for the man who killed my best friend?

My arm muscles complain as I roll over and push up to my knees. I grab a blanket from the pile in the corner and place it over Rich's sleeping form before climbing on the couch and settling in to sleep.

But sleep doesn't come. My mind races in confusion as excuses are made in rapid succession. Excuses that I would never be able to use. I would never see Loc again, would never have to explain what had grown between me and this man. So, was it really so bad for me to have these feelings?

Loc was gone... and Rich was here, proving that he had regrets.

But despite everything that he had done, I could only picture the look on Loc's face, a look of disgust as my best friend condemns my soul.

CHAPTER SEVENTEEN
The Breaking

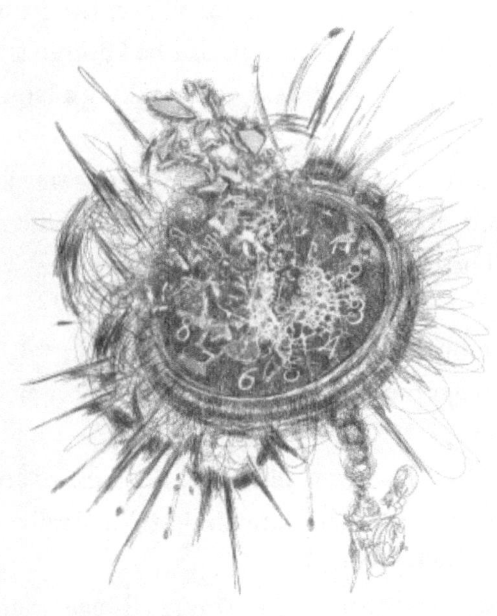

It's hard to keep a straight face the next morning when I wake, Rich already bustling about the kitchen preparing a meal. I hop over to the small table in the kitchenette and take a seat.

"Morning, Sunshine." Rich says, looking for a clean fork.

"Sunshine?" I ask, "Is Echo not good enough anymore?"

Rich stares at me before laughing. "No, it's an old human saying... you know what? It doesn't matter. Good morning, Echo." He says, setting a plate with re-hydrated eggs in front of me. I grimace, remembering my first experience with these eggs. I hadn't known they needed to be re-hydrated before eating them, and had just poured the powder-like substance directly into my mouth.

They had sucked all the moisture from me as they expanded to fill my throat. I had coughed them up all over the ground, and from then on, poured water on all the meals I had gotten from the shuttle.

"Don't like eggs?" Rich asks before taking a large bite of his own.

"We had... a misunderstanding when I was traveling. Where do they come from, anyway?" I ask, finally taking a bite of the fluffy yellow food. They tasted much better now that they were properly prepared.

"Chicken butts."

I spit my eggs out onto the plate. "What is a chicken, and why am I eating shit?"

Rich laughs. "Do you really not have chickens anymore?"

"There aren't very many animals left. We survive off of plants that we grow in hydroponic labs."

Rich raises his eyebrows. "So you're all vegetarian? That's interesting. A chicken is — was — a type of bird. It laid unfertilized eggs, and we cooked them and ate them."

I stare at him, the disgust visible on my face. "Who decided this was a good idea?"

"Couldn't tell you," Rich says around a mouthful of eggs, "but they are tasty, aren't they?"

I push the plate away from me. "No thanks."

"Aww, they're not that bad," Rich teases.

"I'll stick to my plants and you can have your animals." I smile at him.

He stares at my smile. "I'll never get used to that..." He says under his breath. My breath catches in my throat at his words and I look down at my discarded plate. He coughs awkwardly and asks, "So, tell me about yourself, Ixe. What was your life like before..."

"Before I was captured and horrendously tortured?" I ask. He sinks in his chair at my words, and I wish I could take them back. Instead, I tell him about me. "Well, I was assigned to my Bot, Bri, when I was two..."

"Wait, your Bot?" He asks, already confused.

I laugh. "I guess I should start at the beginning. After you guys left Earth, a small group of humans continued humanity differently. They were known as the Phoenix Project, and they created an AI called The Net. The Net only has one objective, and it is to recreate humanity and help it thrive. They do that by running the four seeding cities around the world.

"We aren't 'born', but created in pods using DNA that was left by the Phoenix Project. The Bots spent years modifying it once the atmosphere had settled so that we can breathe the air here."

"The Bots?" He asks.

"Oh right, sorry. The Bots are robots that are connected to The Net. They are our caregivers until we turn 20. We spend the first two years of our lives in a nursery, and then we are given to our permanent Bot. Mine is... was... named Bri. When I was four, Bri brought home my sib from the nursery, and we were then considered a complete family. I started school at six and graduated on my 20th birthday."

"What happens then?"

"Well, we have what is called Release Day. There aren't any

modified humans over the age of 20 allowed in the city, so every quarter on the Release Day after our 20th birthday, we are released into the world. The Bots give us assignments and tell us which way to go and then we just... leave."

"So, where were you supposed to go before...?"

"No idea," I say. "I was captured before I was released."

"I thought you weren't allowed outside of the city?"

"We weren't. I snuck out with Loc and my sib, Mar, to investigate the ship after it landed. We saw..." I trail off, suddenly remembering the words the soldier had said to the man who shot the modified human — *Aww, come on Rich! You're no fun!*

"It was you!" We both say at the same time.

"You were in the woods that night!" Rich says.

"And you... you were the one who shot that modified human..." Bile rises in my throat, but I force it back down. I knew it was wrong to trust him. He was worse than I could have imagined.

Rich groans, running his hand through his hair. "Look... I didn't want to do that, but I had to. You have to understand... you don't want to know what those soldiers would have done to them if I hadn't... if I hadn't stepped in."

I remember what Mar had asked me that night, if I would rather have a quick end or be slowly beat to death, and I understand why Rich had done it. But that didn't keep the scene from replaying in my head. The look on his face as he pulled the trigger, killing one of my people without remorse.

"I don't think I'm hungry after all..." I say, and stand, turning away from Rich and the memories that threaten my sanity.

The next few days are quiet, neither of us knowing how to bridge the chasm that has formed between us. I didn't necessarily blame Rich for what he did, but it was a struggle to look him in the eyes. I knew he could kill, but I didn't realize he could do it so easily, with so little feeling involved. What was just another day on the job for him was one of my most vivid nightmares, and that bothered me more than I cared to admit.

We work in silence, going through another exercise routine and practicing punches until I sit exhausted at the table. Rich walks up to the opposite chair, a question in his eyes, and I gesture for him to take a seat. The table rocks slightly as he does and I wipe my palm off on my pants, unsure why I'm so nervous.

"I'm sorry, Ixe. For everything I've done against your people. I would say I was just following orders, but that doesn't excuse it. My actions were my own, and I will regret them for as long as I live."

I look up at his face and see a tear slide down his cheek. Placing my hand on his, a shock goes through me. I feel every fiber of my being come alive with that touch, and I hate it, but I don't pull away. As I look at our hands, I can't help but notice the contrast between his large and calloused ones and my slender and soft ones, making me long to curl my fingers around his. I want to pull away, to stop these thoughts, but my hand is glued to his. I want to take away his hurt the way he took away mine.

He must be able to read my mind, because he turns his hand over and wraps those rough fingers around mine. I can't help but return the squeeze as I feel that warmth rise within me again. I abruptly pull my hand from his, heat rising in my cheeks as I ask, "What about you? What did you do before the ship?"

His eyes glaze over as he tells his story. "I grew up in a small town in what was known as Utah before..."

"Before the Final Collapse?" I ask.

"Is that what you call it? I guess it was a collapse of civilization..." he mumbles before continuing, "I was young, naive. My parents were suffering as food became scarce. My younger brother... he was killed in a supermarket raid." I didn't know what a supermarket was, but I let him continue. "The only way to ensure your family would have food was to join the Army, so I signed up. I rose through the ranks pretty quickly, and when I became a sergeant, I could return home to visit."

His voice fades as he remembers what he faced. "My parents... they were attacked for their food. I found their bodies in the house, beaten to death, all the food in the house taken. I set a trap for the perpetrators and lay in wait. When they came to pick up the weekly delivery, I shot them..." I see his eyes darken and hold my breath, afraid to let him see the fear in my eyes.

"I returned to the army and gave them everything I had. In record time, I achieved the rank of lieutenant and was assigned to the CryoGenesis Fleet, the initiative aiming to relocate humans from the planet. I didn't look back when I was loaded into the cryo bay."

"I'm sorry," I say, lowering my head, "I understand your pain."

"What do you know about pain?" He asks. My head snaps up in surprise and I see his face has contorted into contempt. "You didn't have to join a corrupt system just to feed your family, only to have them ripped from you because of the help you gave them."

"Rich..." I say, stunned at the sudden change in his demeanor.

"You don't know anything!" He yells as he stands, hands hammering the table.

I quickly stand, knowing something is severely wrong. The cockpit is behind me, and I know if I can reach it, I can lock myself inside.

"You're just a stupid kid who can't even take care of yourself!" He spits at me. I take this as my chance and throw my glass into his face, turning at the same time to race to the cockpit. I use the muscles I had gained to run using my good arm and leg to propel me toward the cabin. As I bolt through the doorway, I turn and slam the door shut behind me. As the door slides into place, I see Rich running toward me, fire burning in his eyes.

I lock the door quickly as Rich pounds on the other side.

"Open this door!" He yells, slamming his palms against it again and again. I pull my knees to my chest as I sit in the cockpit chair, shaking. Rich loses interest in the door and then I hear crashing as he breaks and throws items in the living area. I listen to his rage for hours before I finally hear his voice softly from the other side of the door.

"Echo...?" I tremble at the gentleness in that word, the nickname bringing tears to my eyes. "Please, Ixe, it's okay, it's over." He pleads from beyond the door. I remain quiet, too frightened to speak.

I spend the night in the cockpit chair and, after a fitful night's sleep, I wonder how Rich had slept in here so many times. As I stretch out my legs, I can feel the cramping muscles tremble with relief, allowing me to pull myself to a standing position. I listen at the door for any sound, and not hearing a thing, I slide it open.

Rich is lying on the floor in front of the door, curled into a ball of sleep. My heart catches in my throat as my mind wars with what happened. Rich had only hurt me one time before. My hand floats to my arm where the bruises had been. Was I finally seeing the man in the incident report on Leah's computer?

As I stand there pondering what I would do, Rich stirs. He stretches before seeing me standing above him, and jumps to his feet sheepishly. "I..." he starts, but stops, running his hand through his hair.

"What was that, Rich?" I ask, my voice steady despite my trembling body.

He sighs. "It was one of the episodes we started having after we landed. Even Leah couldn't figure out what was going on." I gesture to the couch, taking in the damage to the surrounding shuttle as we walk to sit down. The kitchen is a wreck, even worse than when I had made my break for it. Food and plates lie scattered and broken on the floor, mixed with splintered wood from one of the table chairs.

We take our seats and I turn to Rich, expecting more of an explanation. "Leah thinks it's brain damage, but I don't think so. It's not consistent or predictable, and why would cryo damage our brains, anyway? It's also having different effects on different people. For me, I get angry outbursts that I can't control. For Leah... she seems to have lost her mind entirely. Her experiments are no longer sensible. She does things for the fun of it, and her personality shifts quickly.

"The other humans have problems, too. Ritter used to be a smart, kind person, but now he is hellbent on the destruction of the 'invaders' that have taken over Earth." He grimaces as he calls my people invaders. "Please know, I would never intentionally hurt you, Ixe..."

I stay quiet as the past few months run through my head. He had saved me from a life of torture, then again when the beast tried to kill me. I glance at his arm out of the corner of my eye, the corded muscles there apparent. If he really wanted to kill me, he could. The fear rises in me, and I try to put it out of my mind as I ask, "How often do these... outbursts... happen?"

Rich shrugs, "This would be the sixth time for me. I was lucky, though; outside of the episodes, my sensibilities remain intact. At least, I think they do... I feel like the old me most of the time. One thing Leah did mention was that it was getting worse over time. She kept saying the episodes would get more frequent over time, while those who were emotionally changed would continue to degrade into madness."

"So... this is going to keep happening?" I ask, the ever-present fear growing.

Rich nods and puts his face in his hands. "Leah was working on a cure when we left. Maybe she made progress." He says hopefully.

"She didn't." I breathe. "Leah's dead."

Rich's head whips to me, his face a look of shock. "She can't be... We need her."

"I'm sorry, Rich. Loc stabbed her when they fought in my cell..."

Rich stands up and begins pacing the room. "So, I'm doomed? This was all for nothing?!"

"What was for nothing?" I ask.

"You! Your capture. The experiments. They were all to find a cure for us!"

I stare at him, stunned. "Why would I hold the cure?"

"I have no idea. Ritter and Leah were insistent that we needed to capture one of your kind. That because you could survive on Earth, it would somehow help us survive."

"Rich, come on. You can't honestly believe that? Even if it wasn't cryostasis that was causing your outbursts, how would experimenting on me give you any answers? That was obviously their delusions talking."

"It was the only chance I had..." He says, and my heart aches for him. I knew what it was like to lose your mind, but to not be able to control my own actions? To possibly hurt the people I cared about? That would be devastating.

I fight through my fear and lay a hand on Rich's shoulder to comfort him. "We will figure this out."

He laughs. "Look at me. I should be the one comforting you, not the other way around."

"Well, one of us has to man up around here." I mock, and his laughter fills me with warmth.

CHAPTER EIGHTEEN
War is Bad

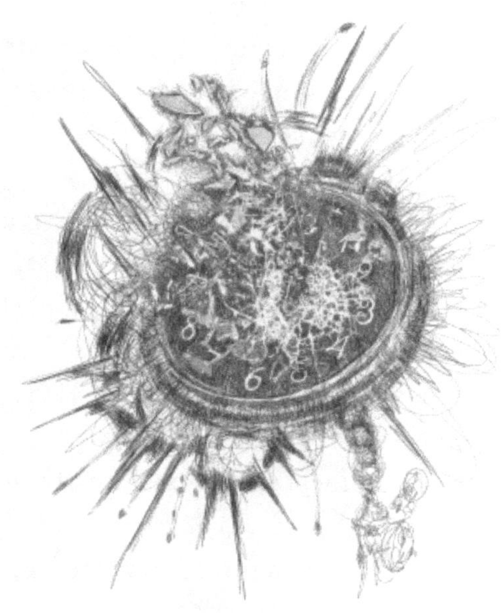

"If we're going to go up against Ritter, we need to talk strategy." Rich says to me one morning.

I grumble, forcing myself to do one more sit-up before responding, "What is strategy?"

Rich rolls his eyes, "So the Bots taught you everything about war except what war actually is?"

"War is bad." I say, propping myself up on my arm to look at him. "What else do we need to know?"

"How about how to protect yourself when war comes knocking on your door? We aren't the only people in this universe, you know."

"Point taken. So, what is strategy, oh great war guide?" I say mockingly.

"Strategy is how you go about war. It's the methods you use in war. Essentially, your entire plan."

"Easy," I say, dropping back down and doing another sit-up. "Our plan is to kill Ritter."

"Okay, but *how* are you planning on achieving that goal?"

"Using the Alliance."

Rich stares at me with a blank expression.

"Oh. I didn't mention them, did I?" I say, finally stopping to take a breath. "There's a group of modified humans that don't agree with The Net and the way things are run. They have an army."

"You have an *army*?! And you are just now telling me this?"

"Well, you were my enemy before, and it isn't *my* army. It's going to take a lot of convincing to get them on our side."

"What would they want in return for their help?" He asks.

"Unfortunately, something I can't give them." I say, getting up off the floor and making my way to the couch to sit. "They want to be free of the Bots, but more than that, they want to make the decisions for our people, and the ability to reproduce."

"Wait, you don't reproduce?" He asks, taking a seat next to me.

"No, I told you, the Bots create us and raise us. They want to avoid another 'end of the world scenario', so they took away our ability to do it ourselves."

He looks at me incredulously. "And the AI just made this decision on its own?"

"Pretty much. It's within their directive to never let humans repeat their past. It decided that this was the safest way to do that."

"I see why The Alliance is out to get them then..."

"So, I think we could get The Alliance on our side, but it would require a reason for them to help us."

"What about the Bots?"

"What about them?"

"Why don't we go to them instead?"

I stop, realizing I had never thought of the Bots or The Net being willing to help us at all. "They hate war." I say, stupidly.

"But they also know about war. They know how bad it's going to get, and I think we need everyone we can get on our side."

"I really don't think they are going to be open to it, Rich..." I say, thinking of what Bri would say if I brought a war to their doorstep. Yun had been trying to get Roa to back down to avoid a war between them already.

"Okay, okay, but we should keep the idea in our back pocket, just in case."

"Our what?" I say, laughing.

"Our back pocket. Do you people not have pockets? Seriously? How do you carry stuff around?"

"With our hands."

Rich shakes his head in disbelief and I can't help but laugh again; the sound echoing around the shuttle. He raises his head and smiles at me, and I get lost in his eyes. Imagining their depth, exploring every inch of my mind and body. He takes my hand in his and his face turns serious. "Echo... I've never been attracted to... but you're different somehow..."

My face heats as his words set in. "I'm not a woman, Rich." I say, my voice heavy, knowing that he might not want me as I am. Maybe that was for the best.

"It's not that," he says, frustration lacing his words. "What I'm trying to say is... you're a different species."

I pull his hand to my chest and rest it over my heart. "I'm human, Rich. I may look different, but I feel the same as you."

He ponders this as he feels the beat of my heart under his palm. "I think... I really like you." His face slowly reddens as he realizes he's said the words out loud, and his eyes drop to the couch between us.

I slowly put a finger under his chin and lift it until we are eye to eye as I whisper, "I like you too." Shocking myself, I lean forward until our lips meet. Lightning fires through my nerves, making my body feel light as air as he returns the kiss, sliding his rough hand behind my neck and pulling me closer.

He slowly parts my lips with his tongue, and I meet his vigor with my own. I shift to my knees and push him slowly down, leaning over him as he lays back on the couch. My body settles between his legs and I gasp at the feel of his hardness pressing into me.

"It's even bigger than my dream..." I say, stunned.

"Your dream?" He asks, amusement dancing in his eyes.

I blush hard. "Well, you see..." I start, but he puts a finger over my lips to quiet my stammering.

"I dreamed of you too, Echo." He whispers, and fire ignites in my core. My extuberantia throbs with pleasure as I lean over him and gently trail kisses from his collarbone to the top of his pants. He sucks in a breath as I gently slide a finger under the fabric and pull it down. I can't help but let a gasp escape as his member breaks loose from the band of his pants and throbs in front of me.

I hesitate for a second when I realize I have no idea how to pleasure him, but I quickly apply what I know about my genitals and think of it as just a larger form of what I've worked with before. I gently take the head of his penis into my mouth and taste a curious liquid on the tip. He moans, laying his head back against the arm of the couch. I feel him throb in me, and my protrusion throbs in response.

Closing my eyes, I take him deeper into my mouth, feeling him fill me completely. "Echo..." He moans, tangling his fingers in my hair. I brace myself on my elbow and add my hand to his length, using it to rub him as I extract him from my mouth. I see more liquid excrete from the tip of his penis.

"What is that?" I ask, curiosity getting the better of me.

He looks at me and laughs. "It's pre-cum. It's what will come out when I ejaculate. Some just leaks out before."

"Oh." I say, curiosity sated for the moment. "It tastes... interesting." I say and then lick it from the tip of him again. He gasps as my tongue meets his skin, and I repeat the gesture before running my tongue down and around the head of him. I feel his legs tremble as I pull him back into my mouth and begin to suck gently.

I rhythmically move my head up and down, using my hand to supplement pressure. Rich moans, biting his lip as he gently moves his hips in time with my rhythm. His hands tighten in my hair as he says, "Echo, I'm... I'm gonna..." and then liquid fills my throat. I instinctively swallow, taking everything he gives me before removing my mouth from him. I lay my head on his abdomen, enjoying the feel of our bodies touching softly as he breathes.

After a few minutes, he gently lifts my head and sits up, pushing me up on my knees again. He stands up, adjusting his pants as he does, and then helps me remove my shirt, before picking me up and setting me back down on the couch. "Now it's my turn to enjoy you," he growls. My skin tingles at the rumble in his words, and I lean back against the couch.

He gently removes my pants, noticing that my extuberantia is already pushed out and ready. I blush as he observes me from a distance. "You are exquisite," he breathes. My heart pounds at the compliment, and my blush deepens. He kneels on the floor in front of my spread legs and begins trailing kisses from my knee up... up...

up... and then switches back down to my other knee.

I groan in displeasure and he just smiles against my ivory skin. "Tell me how to pleasure you." He says, and my body melts at the words.

"Like this," I say, grabbing myself between two fingers and gently stroking up and down.

"It's just like mine..."

"Only smaller." I complete his sentence breathlessly as he watches my fingers move back and forth over my sex.

"So, if I were to do this..." He gently runs his lips over my hardened extuberantia, barely touching it, and I feel like my heart might explode.

I moan, tangling my fingers in his hair, "It would drive me crazy..." He continues the torture as I lean my head back, closing my eyes. He gently runs his tongue along it, his hot breath seeping into my nerves and setting them on fire. I pant, my mind becoming a cloud of fog laced in pleasure as he takes me into his mouth, flicking his tongue over that sensitive bundle of nerves.

A moan escapes my lips, and my legs tighten around his head as I feel that hot beast in my abdomen raise its head. He grabs my thighs, fingers digging into the flesh as he sucks and licks at me hungrily. I wrap my fingers around his head, pinning him to me as he moves his head up and down as I had done to him just moments before. The fire inside me builds and expands to my extremities in an explosion of pleasure as I cry out.

But Rich doesn't stop. He keeps pulling and licking at me as I writhe in ecstasy, taking me over the edge again and again. Eventually, I pull him from me and he smiles, knowing how spent I am. He climbs on the couch next to me and pulls me into his arms before laying the blanket over us. I lay my head on his chest and he makes lazy circles on my arm as we fall asleep. Not a care in the world.

CHAPTER NINETEEN

Judgment

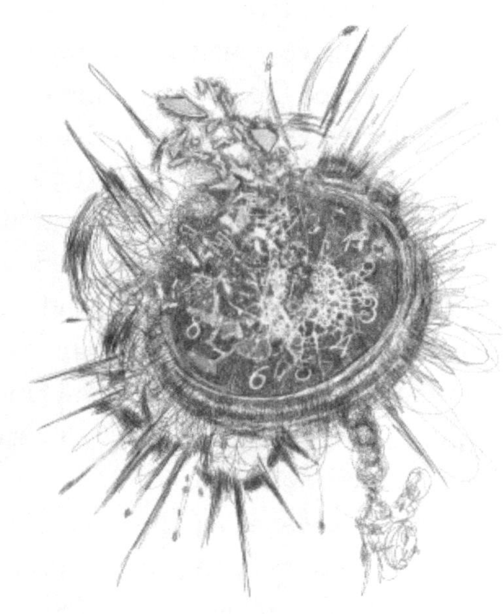

"How could you do this to me?!" The words echo in the dark, and I jump up, looking for their source, but nothing stirs.

I stare into the darkness around me, and something feels off. Reaching out my hand, I feel the familiar fabric of the couch beneath me, the indent from my sleeping form still warm.

"You are such a disappointment." The words buzz in my head like a thousand insects, and I cringe, trying to get away.

"Who's there?" I ask, my voice barely a whisper in the vast blackness that surrounds me, a black too dark to be natural.

A laugh echoes back to me, and I recognize it, but I can't place where I know it from. "You think he will stay with *you*?"

A light flashes on in front of me, my eyes burning from the sudden brightness, before it disappears. I blink hard, but the afterimage remains, and it's the last person I want to see.

Loc stands before me, their linen clothes pristine, too white in the darkness. "You know what he did... and you decided to lay with him?"

Tears sting my eyes, and I try to look away, but they follow me, the impression of their form stuck in my retina.

"Why would you do this, Ixe?" Their voice is a vibration I can feel in every nerve, setting my skin on fire.

I begin to respond, but the excuses die in my throat. How *could* I do this? I had let my feelings get the better of me, and now I would have to live with this shame... "Loc... I..."

Another flash illuminates the room before disappearing, leaving behind another shadow. "You're excuses will never be good enough." I jump up, and run, pumping my legs as fast as I can, but I go nowhere. Mar's laugh echoes around me, and I feel a hand grab my upper arm, digging fingers into my flesh.

Mar pulls me around to face them, and Bri stands before me. "I've failed you both..."

"No, Bri! You didn't fail... I didn't... please, I have failed you." I fall to my knees and press my face into the dirt at their feet.

A boot presses into my skull, pushing my face into the ground, which melts away and becomes a pit of mud. I gasp, and the thick sludge fills my throat, suffocating me. Kicking my feet against the dirt, I push my hands into the ground, trying to force my face out of the pit.

Laughter echoes in my head as the boot presses harder, and I fall head first, the rest of me slipping down into the watery grave beneath me. My hands fly to my face, the mud thicker around my head, trying to claw away the obstruction in my throat, but to no avail. Even though the rest of my body moves through the water with little resistance, the mud in my throat and on my face is a thick jelly, clinging to my skin.

Running out of air, my lungs burning for a breath, I have no choice but to open my mouth and breathe in the muck. The liquid burns at it fills my lungs, but there is an odd sense of relief as well. I may have messed up, but it wouldn't matter soon. I would be free to float in a senseless world where no one could judge me for my mistakes.

I close my eyes and take in a deeper breath, fighting the urge to cough.

I would be free...

A hand grabs my hair and I'm wrenched upwards, the water disappearing in a whoosh of noise. I cough, the mud that had coated my lungs now water that flows out of my mouth with ease.

The water drips down and I watch it disappear into the darkness below, not knowing just how far up I am. Vertigo washes over me, but I don't have the energy to fight, so I look up to face my attacker.

Rich.

He stands before me, but he is not the one who holds me. I see him reach for me, and I reach out in response automatically.

Everything slows to a crawl.

A whistle behind me.

I turn... ever so slowly, as the sound explodes, a cacophony in the darkness.

I watch... as there's a flash, a small projectile in the center heading straight toward me.

I scream... as the bullet tears through me, throwing me backwards through the air.

I think... of the way Loc flew through the air before slamming into the floor, and I brace myself for the pain.

But it never comes. I fall, and as I fall I see ships flying in above me, landing on my planet and tearing it to shreds.

How could I have betrayed my own species? Was I really that touch starved that a man who had abused me, kept me locked away for months, would be the one I would open up to?

What is *wrong* with me?!

I scream, sitting up and panting as I wipe at my face, trying to get rid of the tendrils of the dream that still clung to me.

"Echo?"

Throwing myself forward at the sound, I fall, realization setting in that I'm missing my limbs again. Breathing heavily, I kneel on the floor, the darkness pressing in, as the nightmare fades away.

"Ixe, what's wrong?"

A hand on my back, gentle, comforting — *no.* Fire scorches me where his fingers brush my skin, burning a brand that can't be washed away.

"Stop!" I scream, lunging toward the kitchen, away from Rich's touch — the gentle zaps that left me panting and begging for more.

He sits up, suddenly alert. "What's wrong?"

"I can't do this!!" I scream, "I've ruined everything!"

"Wha..."

"Why did you do this to me? Why do you have to be so... so... Agh!!" I force myself to a standing position and carefully hop to the kitchen, looking through the cabinets for something that could help me, that could calm the raging pain I was in.

I hear the couch creak behind me as Rich stands and takes a few steps forward, but he doesn't touch me. *Does he know I've lost my mind?* I think, throwing packets of food over my shoulder onto the floor.

"Echo..."

I spin to face him, the tears on my cheeks hot in the cold room, "Don't you call me that! Don't you try to fix this with your... your... charm. I can't. I can't. I can't." Spinning back to the cabinet, I find what I'm looking for and try to open the lid. The effort is wasted though, as the child proof cap eludes my one handed abilities.

Frustrated, I scream and slam the bottle against the edge of the counter top, aiming right at the plastic neck. The lid pops off with a loud bang, and the pills spill out. Crying in relief, I grab a handful and shove them in my mouth.

"No!" Rich yells, suddenly by my side, grabbing my wrist, but it's too late, I've already swallowed them. "What is wrong with you!?" He shakes my arm, and I just smile at him in return.

Soon it would be over...

Soon, Loc would be gone from my mind, and I would have peace...

"Talk to me, Ixe!"

It's then that I notice his sleek body in the moonlight, still bare from our adventure, and I pull away, trying to banish the visual from my mind.

No...

I can't enjoy this...

I can't enjoy him...

It dawns on me that I'm also nude, the cool air biting at the sweat resting on my skin. Whether it's from the dream or the sex, I'm not sure, and I try to wipe it away. To wipe *him* away.

"Ixe."

His words are like a balm, and I hate it. I hate the way he says my name, and the way he smells, and the way he feels, and the way I *want* to feel him.

The sudden emotion hits me like a wall, and I fall to the floor, sobbing. How could I have let this man take everything from me? How could I give in to temptation? I had lost control, and now I had to face my punishment.

"Loc... I'm so sorry..." I cry, even though I know they can't hear me. They would never hear my voice again, and I would never be able to apologize for what I had done.

"Echo... Is this... Do you think that..." He can't even form the words, and I know that he knows what we've done was wrong.

"You murdered them... you murdered them and then bedded me like I was a prize."

The silence stretches between us, and I know that I've hit him where it hurts. Yet, despite everything, I want to take the words back. I want to console him, tell him everything will be okay.

Betrayer.

That's what I was. I had betrayed my best friend's memory, and I didn't deserve to be forgiven.

Rich breaks the silence first, "That's not true... What I feel for you is... It's different, Ixe. You are not my prize."

"Then I'm your consequence." I say, lowering my head, and I realize he doesn't see me as a prize. I'm nothing more than an object to be used, a break from the monotony of being on the run.

A hand on my shoulder makes me flinch, but I don't pull away this time.

"Echo... Ixe... What happened with Loc was an accident. A terrible, unfortunate, misunderstanding. I'm not trying to..." He sighs as he tries to find the right words, but we both know there aren't any.

Nothing would bring back my friend.

"I care about you, more than I can say, and what happened between us last night was a result of that, nothing more. I can't say that Loc would understand... But I know they would trust your judgment. I'm here, before you now, so judge me, Ixe. Tell me what you want me to do and I'll do it. Do you want me to leave you? Go back to my ship and... hell, tell me right now and I will walk up to Ritter and blow out his brains, even if it means my death. For fuck's sake, tell me to leave this ship, to walk out into the toxic air, and I'll do it."

He grasps my chin gently and turns my face toward his. I meet his eyes and see the glint of the light reflecting from the tears that run down his face.

"Judge me. Tell me what to do, because I can't do it, Ixe. I can't judge myself."

"I..." What did I want? What would Loc want? Revenge on their killer, or for me to be happy?

I think back to Loc and Kit, the perfect couple. They were so happy, so youthful, so innocent... And they had been torn apart by The Net. Would Loc really want me to find someone, only to have them ripped away like that?

Could they forgive me?

Could I forgive myself?

Fresh tears spill from my eyes, and I take in a deep breath.

"I want you to be free..." I say finally, and Rich looks at me confused.

"I am free."

"No," I say, taking his hand in mine. "I want you to be free from me, from this cause. I want you to be able to live your life without having to answer to anyone for anything."

"Ixe..."

"Call me Echo." I say, giving his hand a squeeze. "Take me to The Alliance, and then I want you to escape. Leave this place. Land your shuttle somewhere remote, and live your life."

His lip trembles as he looks deep into my eyes, "Echo... that's the one order I can't obey. You want me to be free? Then let me be free... with you."

Warmth spreads through me, and my mind tries to fight it, but I close my eyes and lower my barriers. Could I stop the small negative voice in the back of my mind? *No.* But I could lock it behind a wall. I could tell myself that Loc would choose my happiness over revenge.

I *could* be happy.

CHAPTER TWENTY
The Last Breath

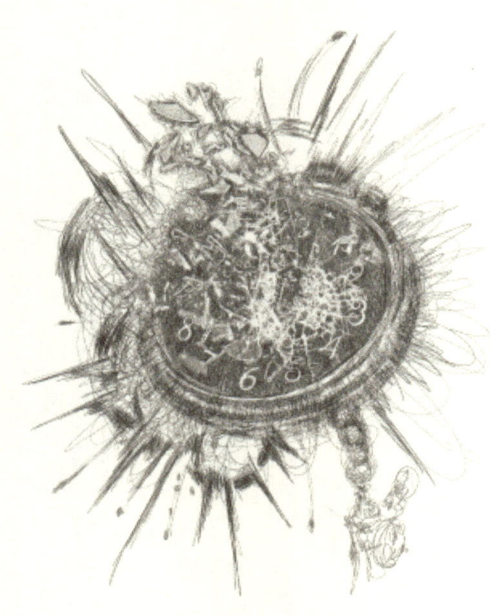

We quickly found a new rhythm to our lives, working together to turn the shuttle into a temporary base. We spent our waking hours planning and exercising, preparing to reach out to The Alliance. Although, distractions were plenty as we explored our new relationship. Gentle touches peppered our normal chores, igniting flames within our bodies that burned brightly.

Our evenings we spent exploring, learning about each other's bodies. The spot on Rich's neck that drove him wild, the area on my inner thigh that had me panting for more. We took our time with our sex organs; he focused on my extuberantia and would make me beg for his touch, while I explored the length of his penis, extracting sweet moans from his mouth.

When it came time for him to enter me, we went slowly. He paid attention to my sounds, ensuring that I was still comfortable with every step as he slid into my ass. It was a new feeling, having him inside of me, and I cherished it, knowing that we could connect on such an intimate level.

Everything was perfect for those few months until…

"I don't feel so well, Echo." He says, concern clouding his eyes.

"What's wrong?" I say, worry echoed in my voice.

"I'm quite dizzy," he says and loses his balance. He hits the floor hard on his knees and shakes his head, trying to remove the dizziness. I race to his side, where he tries to shoo me away. "The cockpit." He says, pointing.

I make my way to the cockpit and flip the switches to turn on the primary systems. Immediately, I notice a red warning light flashing. I turn my focus to the icon and see that it says O2. My heart drops as I realize what is happening. "Lay down." I say, sitting myself in the seat. I know that if he is already this dizzy, we have little time. He tries to protest as I boot up the shuttle and pull back on the yoke.

The shuttle launches into the air, and I almost lose control of it, but I wrangle it under control and point it toward the ship icon on the dash.

"We can't go to the ship." Rich gasps from behind me, now laying prone from the force of the takeoff.

"I'm not going to the ship," I say, accelerating the shuttle as fast as it would go.

I spot the ship on the horizon 15 minutes later, and look for the forest that would identify the way to the city. Spotting it, I quickly switch direction and head straight for it. Rich is now unconscious after a fit of giggles. I know it is hypoxia setting in, and will the shuttle to go faster.

As we approach the city walls, I realize I don't know how to land the shuttle. I push the yoke in as far as it will go, and I feel the craft sputter and stall before dropping. "Shit!" I yank on the yoke, and the shuttle jerks and tilts as its momentum battles with the height acceleration. As the walls loom close, I realize we are going to crash and throw myself back into the living area and cover Rich with my body.

The impact is hard, and we are thrown against a wall as the front of the shuttle crumples inward. I stand, wincing at the pain in my body, and begin pulling Rich by his arm toward the airlock door. Once out of the airlock, I see what I'm looking for, thanking the universe under my breath that it's close, as I continue pulling Rich toward the hydroponic lab. I open the door and roll his body over the threshold into the room filled with trees and plants.

The air is cool and crisp, and hopefully full of oxygen from the plants that grow here. I slam the door closed and pull him further in, stopping to check and see if he is breathing. His chest doesn't rise and I spit out curses as I check for a pulse. Faint, but there. I blow breaths into his lungs for him, watching his chest rise with my breath, and fall as it slowly pours from him.

After a few minutes, he sputters and coughs, but doesn't wake. I lean back against the table of plants behind me and exhale in relief. He was alive. That's all I needed to know. Rich was alive.

I'm dreaming of Loc when a kiss presses to my forehead. I open my eyes and immediately feel the pain in my muscles. Groaning, I see Rich kneeling on the floor in front of me, a goofy smile on his face.

"Is it that bad to see me?" He laughs.

"Your face leaves some things to be desired," I say jokingly. He punches my arm lightly, a look of fake incredulity on his face. "How are you feeling?" I ask.

"Like I was hit by a bus." He says. I look at him, confused. "A bus…" He says. "You know, a vehicle that carries lots of people? Nevermind, it's just another phrase." He says, shaking his head.

"You have a lot of phrases." I say, mockingly.

"Oh, only an entire civilization's worth." He laughs. "What is this place, anyway?"

"It's the hydroponic lab in my city."

"Your city?! That's way too close to the ship."

"I didn't have a lot of choice. You were dying, and this was the only source of oxygen I knew of."

"We shouldn't stay here long. We don't know who saw that shuttle come down…"

A noise at the door stops both of us in our tracks. Rich reaches for his gun and my stomach sinks as I remember I left it on the shuttle. I stand as the door slowly pushes inward, and throw myself at the intruder. Mar yells as I push them into the wall next to the door, slamming the door shut with my shoulder.

"Mar!" I say, surprised, and hold up a hand to stop Rich from coming to my aid. "I thought you were dead!"

"Ixy?" Mar says, just as surprised. "I thought *you* were dead. What happened to you?" They ask, noticing the scars across my arms, chest, and abdomen. Their eyes widen when they see that I'm standing on one leg and part of my arm is missing.

"The humans captured me when I ran to Bri." My voice catches on my Bot's name, but I continue. "They experimented on me, and then Loc came to rescue me." I feel the tears pool in my eyes as I remember Loc's last words to me. I glance to Rich before saying, "The humans shot Loc, and then Rich got me out of there using a shuttle." Rich raises his hand in greeting and Mar gives him a dirty look.

"You have allied with a human? After everything they have done?"

"He's different..." I begin, but Mar cuts me off.

"No, they are all crazy. They want to exterminate us."

"You don't know what you're talking about." I say, standing my ground.

Mar sneers at me, "You want to betray your own people. I should have expected it from *you*." They spit in my face. Rich moves, but I hold up my arm to stop him. This is my fight. Mar shakes their head at me and turns to leave.

I grab their arm, "Mar..." I begin.

Mar spins and throws a punch at my head. Before I know it, I've caught their fist in my hand, and I hold it between us. Mar's eyes widen. I've never stood up to them before. No matter how bad the beatings got, I just took the punches.

I squeeze their fist in my hand as I say, "You will listen to what I have to say; what *we* have to say." I gesture to Rich with my stump, and Mar's gaze flickers to him. I don't know what Rich does behind me, but Mar swallows and returns their gaze to mine before nodding.

We all move deeper into the lab and I pull an additional stool from under a table for Mar to sit with us. They take their place and glance around the lab warily. "I never did like these places... too cramped."

I look around the lab full of plants. It felt cozy to me, but I could see how someone would feel too large in a small space full of creeping vines and fruit trees. Pulling an apple from a nearby tree, I hand it to Mar, a peace offering. They take it, rubbing it on their shirt before taking a bite.

"Where do I even begin..." I sigh, thinking of how much had happened since I was captured all those months ago. "I guess the beginning... Colonel Ritter is their leader. He used to be a caring person, but something changed in some," I glance at Rich as I say this, pleading with him to go along with my story, "of the humans after they landed. Ritter is now obsessed with those of us who call Earth home. He believes we are invaders that have come to take away his planet.

"His goal, as you said before, is to exterminate us, but not all humans feel the same. Some of them, like Rich, want to find a cure for what is ailing them and make peace with us. Ritter has them convinced that we hold the key to their cure, hence my capture and experimentation."

"They experimented on you? How?"

I pause, not wanting to think about the torture I had endured. "That's not important. What's important is that the stunt to get me out of there left their main researcher dead."

"I knew I would regret Loc's idea..."

"You knew about it?" I ask, stunned.

"Loc wouldn't shut up about it. They came to us shortly after you were taken, insisting that you were alive and a captive of the humans. We didn't believe them and kicked them out of our camp. About a month later, they came to us again, wearing the uniform of the humans, and insisted that they knew where you were and planned to get you out, with or without our help. I took them to Roa and let them explain how they had gotten their information and what it consisted of."

Mar takes the last bite of the apple and tosses the core to the side. "Roa thought it would be a good opportunity to strike, but we grossly underestimated how many soldiers they had." They glare at

Rich, as if it was his fault, before looking back at me. "We have a feeling that Loc 'underestimated' on purpose to convince us to join the fight. We lost a lot of good people in that fight, so I really hope you were worth it."

I feel the heat rise in my cheeks at those words, knowing that I had almost given up the thing that so many had died for.

"Where are they anyway?"

"Who?" I ask.

"Loc."

I feel the shame swallow me as I realize I hadn't even told Mar what had happened to my best friend. "They died in the attack." I will myself to not turn to Rich, hoping that he would keep his face straight. I didn't want Mar to know that Rich was the one who pulled the trigger.

"So, how did you get out?"

"Rich rescued me." I say, gesturing to the man next to me. I ached to reach out and touch his hand, but knew that any sign of affection between us would shatter the tenuous relationship we currently had with Mar.

Mar laughs. "So, you're telling me that during the attack that we planned, you just happened to have a human pining for you that was willing to risk everything to rescue you? Sorry if I'm a bit of a skeptic."

Rich finally breaks his silence as he says, "I had been planning our escape for weeks before you attacked. I took the opportunity of a distraction to get Ixe out of there."

"And what about my dear sweet sib made you want to risk everything?" Mar asks with a sneer.

"Their pleas, their cries, the realization that you are just as human as we are, and no one deserves the type of treatment they were given. It goes against humanity."

"Yet, you 'humans' were so happy to do it. So happy to come and take *our* land and kill *our* people!" Mar slowly stands as they get more and more heated.

"Enough." I say with a quiet confidence that I didn't feel. I place my hand on Mar's chest and force them to sit back down. "At the end of the day, Rich saved my life on more than one occasion. I trust him."

Mar sits, but doesn't wipe the sneer from their face as they spit out their next question. "So, where have you two been since the attack, then?"

I sigh before launching into the explanation. "I tried to run, at first. Got myself into a sticky situation that Rich had to get me out of again. I was left gravely wounded." I pause and raise my shirt, showing them the gnarly scar that marred my smooth skin. "It took longer than I'd have liked to heal and recover my strength. Our next step was to find the Alliance and discuss how we were going to rid ourselves of the human problem when the shuttle malfunctioned and we had to come here for oxygen."

"So, your plan was to come to us for help? What about your precious Bots?"

"You and I both know that the Bots want nothing to do with war. Our best bet is to reuse the army the Alliance raised against The Net."

"And you are now some sort of war planner?" Mar asks.

"A strategist." Rich says, crossing his arms and leaning back against a table.

"Now we find ourselves at an impasse," I say, directing Mar's attention back to me. "Rich needs oxygen, and we can't stay here, so close to the ship."

"There's only one option," Mar says. "He has to go back to the ship. Alone."

I balk at the suggestion, but Rich seems to think it over. "It may work," he says.

"You can't go back there!" I yell, louder than intended. Mar raises an eyebrow at me and my face heats. We had steered the conversation around mine and Rich's relationship, but I got the feeling that Mar suspected.

Rich places a hand on my shoulder. "It's the only place that can keep me alive. I have to go back, for now." He removes his hand and turns back to Mar. "And while I'm there, I can do some digging to find people on our side."

Mar nods, happy that Rich agrees with their plan.

"But... they could kill you for leaving."

"They don't know that I left. I can tell them I was injured in the attack and you took advantage. Forced me onto a shuttle and kept control of the cockpit until I could escape."

"I don't like it."

"It doesn't matter what you *like*." Mar says, and I turn to face them. They didn't know about my feelings for Rich, and they wouldn't understand me wanting to keep him safe. I would have to go along with this plan, no matter how much I hated the idea of Rich being in the hands of the enemy.

I sigh, obviously outvoted in the subject, and ask, "So, how do we get you back to the ship with no oxygen between here and there?"

"The shuttle," He says. "It has a distress beacon built in it. Set it off before you go, and Ritter will send out men to come get me."

"And what am I supposed to do while you are on the ship gathering information?"

"You come with me," Mar says matter-of-factly. "The Alliance needs help talking to the Bots. They don't want to raise arms against the humans and their ship, and we need them in order to win the battle. You are going to convince them that the humans have no loyalty to them, to us."

"I don't know that I'm going to be able to sway them. I tried talking to the Council before and it didn't go well." I say, my head shaking.

"All you can do is try," Rich says to my side, and I glance at him. The hope in his eyes is too much to bear.

"Okay, I will try."

Mar plants their hands on their knees and stands. "Then let's get to it. We are wasting precious time."

My voice cracks as I say, "Go ahead without me, Mar. I'll be right behind you. Rich needs to explain to me how to set off the beacon." I lie quickly.

Mar looks from me to Rich and nods knowingly before leaving the lab.

I turn to Rich as my eyes water. "It'll be okay, Echo." He says, folding me in his arms.

"You don't know that," I say into his chest.

He puts a finger under my chin and lifts my eyes to his. "We will see each other again, I promise." I lean forward into his kiss, trying to remember every detail of his mouth pressed against mine, the smell of him enveloping me.

After a minute, he pulls away and pushes me toward the door. "Go, before I change my mind," he says huskily.

I pull away from him, our fingers intertwined until the last possible second, before turning and walking out the door; my heart fractured, pieces left with him for safekeeping.

Mar is standing next to the shuttle as I leave, admiring the technology. I hop past them and straight to the open airlock door. Without waiting for the pressure to equalize, I press the emergency button to open the inner doors. An alarm blares repeatedly, letting the occupants know the airlock is open and the oxygen levels are low. I make my way to the cockpit and quickly flip the switches to activate the emergency beacon.

As I leave the shuttle, I see a small figure Rich had tried carving from a piece of wood during our time locked together. I stop and pick it up, turning it in my hand. It was supposed to be a carving of the beast that had attacked me, but it looked nothing like an animal at all. I smile at the memory and slide it into my pocket before leaving the shuttle.

"Let's go." I say to Mar, and they nod, keeping their mouth shut about what happened between Rich and I. It was a good choice. We set out toward the city gates, and once we are beyond them and in another wood, I hear a shuttle behind us, and know that Rich will be okay. I exhale a sigh of relief and don't look back.

CHAPTER TWENTY-ONE
Siblings

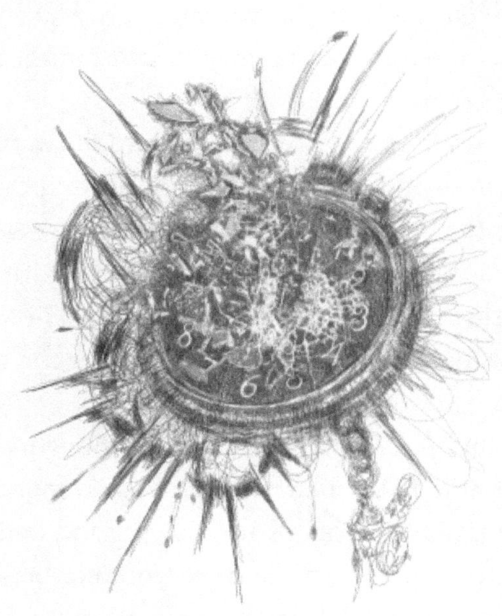

The Alliance camp remains familiar, albeit in a new place. It had taken us three days to hike our way to camp with my slow hopping motion. Mar had helped by letting me lean on them, but it wasn't enough, and I dragged them further and further behind schedule.

When we finally reach the camp, we are covered in dust and sweat, rivulets of mud covering our faces. A group of Alliance members run to meet us, and carry me the rest of the way into camp. They insist I rest first, but I know that before I can sleep, I need a bath. They oblige, taking me to a tent where a large basin of water rests on heated stones.

Slowly peeling myself out of my dirty pants, I curse myself again for not grabbing a shirt before leaving the shuttle. My skin is red and puckered with blisters from the scorching sun. Mar and I had traded their shirt back and forth to prevent as much damage as possible, but it had left both of us burned to a crisp.

I remove my shoe and slowly climb into the warm water, thankful that it wasn't as hot as the barren landscape outside the tent. I lower myself in the water and watch it turn brown with grime as I think about Rich. What was he doing now? Did Ritter believe the story he told them about me holding him hostage? How would they treat him now that he had returned? Would they force him to go back to torturing my people?

Closing my eyes, I try to think happier thoughts. My heart aches for my lost love, but I have memories to keep me going. I think of his smile, goofy and aloof; his arms, strong and warm; the days we spent laying around the shuttle and the workouts between.

I lay there, my eyes still closed, as I let the water buoy my body and twitching muscles. Eventually the water grows cold, and I groan as I reach for the soap on the stool next to the tub, and begin washing my body and hair.

Once I'm done, I get out of the tub and wrap myself in a towel. I notice that someone has laid clothes for me on a stool inside the tent flap and my face heats wondering when they had come in and what they had seen. Knowing there was nothing I could do about it, I dry off and get dressed in the clothes provided, a loose shirt with ties at the front of the neck, and a tight fitting pair of cotton pants. I slide my foot in my grimy shoe and think about asking for a new pair as I leave the tent.

I wander around the camp, passing strangers who stare at my missing limbs, before stumbling upon a great tent standing in a clearing. Mar is on the threshold, talking to an older human. As I get closer, I realize I know that human, their name was... *Trix*. I had seen them the day we had stolen the guns from the Alliance camp.

Making my way towards Mar and Trix, I'm surprised when a soldier comes to escort me about halfway there. I try telling them I don't need help walking, but they refuse to listen and insist that I use them as a crutch. Reluctantly, I give in, taking the help to make it the rest of the way to the tent.

Mar smiles once I get there and introduces me to Trix, "Ixe, this is Trix; Trix, this is my sib."

"It's nice to meet you," Trix says, staring at me with piercing hazel eyes. They reach out their right hand and I raise my stump. Sheepishly, they switch to the left and I shake it with my own. "Our blacksmith has been working to make you a replacement leg while you were in the bath. I will have Rogir fetch them." They nod to Rogir, the human who had helped me to the tent, and they take off through the camp.

"Come. Sit." Mar says, holding a tent flap open behind them. I make my way into the tent and find myself surrounded by luxury. Three large chaise lounges decorate the room, a small coffee table between them. Tapestries hang from metal beams that support the tent's structure, and a small opening at the back of the tent leads to a bedroom centered on a king sized bed covered in exquisite pillows and throws.

"What is all of this?" I ask, as I take a seat on the red chaise.

"Roa has a specific… taste." Trix says, taking a seat on the chaise opposite mine. Mar stands, leaning against a metal pillar. "They will be excited to meet you when they get back from patrol."

"Your commander goes on patrol?" I say, disbelieving.

"Yes, Roa has a certain way of being 'of the people'. It's how they came to be in command." Trix's voice has a lilting quality, and I relax in their presence. "Enough about Roa though. I want to hear more about you, Ixe."

"There isn't much to tell, I'm afraid." I respond. "I saw little of the ship while I was in confinement there, and only a few soldiers handled my care."

"Yes," they say, "but you became… close with the humans."

I glance at Mar, and my blood boils at the smirk on their face. "I came to know two of them well, yes." I say, avoiding speaking directly about Rich.

"Tell me of the surgeon." Trix says, leaning back against the sofa.

"Her name was Leah…" I begin.

"Was?"

"She was killed during the raid on the ship." I say, sadness seeping into my voice. Even with everything Leah had done, she hadn't deserved to die alone.

Trix notices my change in demeanor, but avoids the subject. "Tell me about the experiments she did."

My body tenses as I remember what they had done to me. "At first they didn't want to use any medications on me…" I began.

After a few hours, my voice was raw, and tears stained my cheeks. I hadn't realized how hard it would be to recount what had happened to me in that place, but I felt relief for the first time in months. Speaking the truth had lifted a weight that I didn't know was there. Trix had sat attentively through it all, staying silent when I needed a minute to come to terms with my condition, and asking clarifying questions when I posed a new term or scenario.

At the end of it all, Trix turns and nods to Mar, who promptly leaves the tent. Within a minute, a short, round human makes their way into the tent carrying a large metal contraption. They set the contraption in front of me before saying, "It's not the prettiest thing in the world, but it was the best I could do on such short notice."

I stare at them and then the contraption before asking, "What is it?"

"Why a leg, of course!" They say, the pride in their eyes shining through the black soot that covered their face. "Here, let me help you put it on." They kneel in front of me and open the contraption, pulling straps out of the middle. "May I?" they ask before grabbing my stump. I nod, curious as to how this was going to work.

They take my stump and push it down into a metal chamber. The inner metal mesh slides down as the outer metal moves up my leg to my knee. They take the straps and start wrapping them around my thigh, carefully pulling and setting them to the correct length before tying them off.

Once they are done, I have a metal cage up to my knee, and then leather straps continue up my thigh to my hip. Below the stump is a metal rod that flares out into a solid piece of metal that is rounded.

"Try it out." They say, standing up and moving out of my way. Trix nods to me as I look to them for confirmation. I carefully stand and let my weight shift to the new leg. It holds my weight, the inner metal acting as a shock system, preventing wear on my stump. I take a step and the back of the rounded foot meets the ground and then rolls forward to propel me into my next step.

"Ah ha!" the blacksmith says from behind me. "I knew it would work! I told that asshole Glimmer it would work." They mumble under their breath as they clean up their supplies and exit the tent, leaving me alone with Trix again.

"Thank you." I say to Trix.

"You're going to need it." Trix responds. "Can't be hopping around a battlefield now, can you?" They ask, walking out of the tent ahead of me.

Adjusting to camp life takes time. The layout of the tents and the different symbols and insignia spin around me as I try to find my way back to my tent from the latrine. The latrine alone had been an adventure I never wanted to experience again. Crouching over a hole in the ground, exposed to the elements, had left me unable to urinate, and I feel my full bladder slosh around as I walk.

I finally stumble around a corner that I recognize and make it to my tent, laying back on the hard mattress placed on the even harder ground. I try closing my eyes again, willing myself to sleep, but the noise of the camp's nightlife is a barrage of sound against my ears.

My tent flap pulls back and Mar's voice floats to me. "Are you awake?"

I groan, wishing that Mar's presence was just a dream, but I finally answer, "How does anyone sleep in this place?"

I hear the smirk in Mar's response. "You get used to it." They make their way inside and the tent fills with a soft light. I blink a few times to adjust to the sudden brightness, and find them sitting on the hard ground in the corner of the tent, holding a glowing ball in their hands.

"What is that?" I ask, sitting up.

"It's a glow ball. I know, really intuitive name. The humans figured out how to make them from some luminescent animals. We have our own technology that the Bots don't know about." I see the smile on their face and wonder again about their pride and belief in the cause. I can't remember the last time I had seen them smile, and it warms my heart.

"So, why are you here?"

Mar looks confused, "You know how I feel about the

Alliance..."

I laugh, "No Mar. Here, in my tent."

"Oh. I wanted to talk about..." They hesitate.

My eyes widen in surprise. Mar had never wanted to confide in me before. "What's up?" I ask. "You can talk to me." I find myself wishing they would, hoping that maybe we could be sibs in more than just name. To actually have a bond with Mar... Bri would be stunned.

Mar sighs, but pushes their words out, "I wanted to talk about Bri."

I try to hide my surprise as I realize they were missing our Bot. Even with their fighting, Bri was still a constant in Mar's life, one that Mar hadn't expected to change for another two years. "You miss them..." I say, unable to hide the curious inflection in my voice.

Mar laughs lightly, "Yeah, I guess I do. Even though we fought most of the time, you and Bri were... were my family. I lost you both in the same moment, and I was to blame."

"Mar," I say, laying my hand on their shoulder. "What happened wasn't your fault. I should have checked the guns for ammo before I left the tent that day. Hell, I shouldn't have convinced you to come with me that day at all. I was the older sib, I shouldn't have put you in that situation."

"No, Ixe. I should have stayed. I should have fought for you, the way you fought for Bri. I always felt like an outcast. Like I never should have been born in that city. My life belonged elsewhere and I didn't expect to feel anything when I finally left, but... That day everything changed and I realized how much you guys really meant to me."

I stare at Mar in the dim light of the tent as they spill their heart to me, and I have no words in return. Tears gently fall down their cheeks and all I can do is watch.

"I was so horrible to you, Ixe. For so many years I let my anger control me and used you as a punching bag because I was afraid...

afraid of actually caring for you; of loving you."

I wrap my arms around Mar, holding them close as I whisper, "I love you too, Mar. I always have."

CHAPTER TWENTY-TWO
The Turn

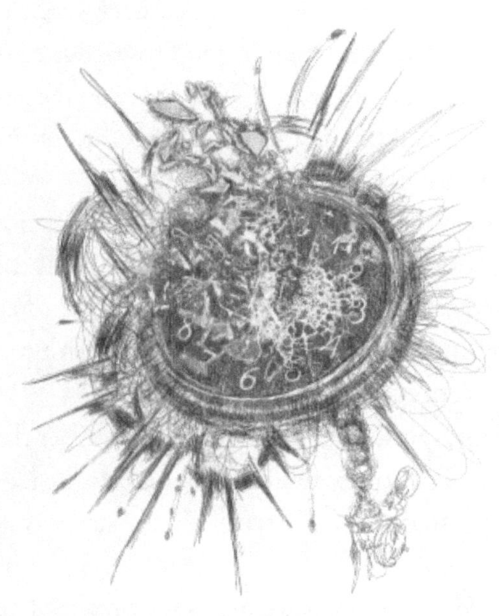

I spend the next few days exploring the camp. I learn more about the humans that call the Alliance home. It feels similar to a nomadic tribe. Constant movement is their life, never staying in the same place for more than a month at a time. Everyone has their own role in the camp, from cleaning to cooking, patrols and weapon making; everyone is busy. But that doesn't stop them from enjoying themselves.

Laughter rings out from every corner as people gamble and barter. Service tents are set up for a variety of activities, from smoking to bathing, even brothel tents.

I walk through a few more rows of tents, cooling my mind as I try to get my bearings in the mass of tents around me. Eventually stumbling out of the crowd, I find myself back at the command tent. A draft of wind carries the smell of food toward me and I realize I'm hungry. I look around and see a kitchen not too far from the opening of the main tent. Walking hesitantly toward the counter, I see a variety of food laid out for passerby to grab.

Two people stand in front of a grill, chatting about the next shipment of goods to arrive. "I heard the raiders hit the last caravan from Barllay, costing us a couple weeks of food. Roa changed the route this time and doubled the guard. If it doesn't make it this time, we will have to ration."

"That didn't go so well last time... Remember the riots?"

"Of course I do, but what other choice do we have? Returning to the cities isn't an option. We would likely starve there."

"Do you need help?"

I'm startled out of my listening as they realize I've been standing there staring at the same food the entire time. My face turns a deep shade of red and I mumble my apologies, turning to walk away.

"Wait, you're Roa's new... acquaintance, yes?" The way they pause before acquaintance has me stopping in my tracks and I turn back to the person addressing me.

"I don't know what you mean by acquaintance..." I say, hoping my pause will bring more information to light.

I see the two's eyes dart toward each other, unspoken words passing in their gazes before they look back at me. "Just that you are important to Roa, that's all."

"I aim to meet with them upon their return, yes." I say, taking another step toward the counter.

"Would you like some food?" The other one asks, moving over to the counter.

"I... I'm not sure what the food is..." I stammer, embarrassed to admit that I've never had this type of food before.

"Fresh from the city, huh?" They smile at me, and I feel myself relaxing.

"You could say that," I say in response.

"Well, these are animals that are found around here." They gesture to a small bowl full of shredded food. "We call this rabbit. They aren't technically rabbits from before, but they are similar. Most of the animals are named that way out here. Memories of what humans used to know."

"I've never..." I begin.

"Never had meat? Don't worry, it won't hurt you." They pick up the bowl and hand it to me.

I gently pull out a strand of meat and smell it. My mouth waters as the aroma fills me. My senses told me it was fine, so how bad could it be? I gently place it in my mouth and my taste buds explode with flavor. Some spices they used I had tasted before on vegetables, but the underlying taste was so... different. I take a bite into the strand and feel the flesh separate with my teeth, releasing juices as it does so. It's almost like rubber, but it crushes easily under the weight of my bite.

"So, what do you think?" They ask, their face displaying a mischievous smile.

"It's so... different." I say dumbly, and quickly amend, "But it tastes good."

A smile appears on their face before they say, "I'll pack you a bundle of different things you can take back to your tent. I'll include labels so you know what you are eating too, then you will know what to ask for next time."

They busy themself with preparing my to-go package, and I take the time to observe the bigger tents around the open square. Not only were the tents larger, but they were also more colorful, flying banners above their peaks and covered with sections of brightly colored fabric. I stretch my neck out to glance inside the tent nearest me and see maps scattered across a table inside. These must be for planning and coordination of troops.

A cough behind me pulls me out of my observation. I turn to find the person handing me a bag with my food safely inside. "Good luck," they whisper before turning back to their partner and the grill.

I slowly make my way out of the empty square and back through the crowded columns of tents until finally collapsing at my tent. I pull myself inside the small space, closing the flap behind me before gently unwrapping the bindings and pulling off my leg. The metal leg gave me more mobility, but it also gave me painful blisters, and walking for more than a few hours at a time was excruciating.

Finally comfortable, I pull the sack of food toward me and open it, finding a piece of paper folded over the top of the food. *This must be the list of food*, I think to myself, and place it on the ground next to the bedroll. I pull out the first container and see it is labeled as 'rabbit'. Already knowing that I enjoy it, I open the lid and begin eating.

A rustling at my feet has me sitting straight up in my tent. It's pitch black and the world presses in on my ears, the silence leaving

my heartbeat to pound in my head loudly. The flap pulls back on my tent, and I grab my leg, preparing to use it as a weapon. Mar sticks their head in and I curse, dropping the leg.

"What is your problem?" Mar asks.

"I thought you were coming to kill me!" I hiss back.

Mar laughs and pulls the flap back farther, letting some light into the tent. "C'mon, get your leg on." They say, pulling their head back out of the tent, leaving the flap open. I sit up and grab my new leg, attaching it to my stump the way the blacksmith had. Once it's attached, Mar reaches out a hand and helps haul me to my feet. I see now that they are holding a glow sphere, casting the warm light into my tent. Once I'm on my feet, Mar turns and leads the way.

"Roa is back and wants to meet with you."

"Now?" I ask, "It's the middle of the night."

"And you were still awake, as we expected."

I grumble under my breath as we make our way to the main tent — Roa's tent — in the center of camp. I shield my eyes as we step over the threshold into the bright, warm dwelling. Not much has changed since I was last there, but now a thin human of average height stands in the center of the three chaise lounges. They turn, eyes meeting mine with a flash of a smile as they hold out their hand.

"It's nice to meet you, Ixe. I'm Roa." Their smile is luminous in their tanned symmetrical face. I had never seen such a perfect representation of a human before, and my blood warms at the sight of them. My face heating, I shake Roa's outstretched hand and divert my eyes.

"It's nice to finally meet you..." I stop as I realize I'm not sure what to call them.

"Roa is fine," they say, the corner of their mouth turning up in a smirk. Our hands drop and Roa settles on a stool I hadn't noticed before. "So," they begin, "You are Bri's other child."

A simple statement, but I wonder why it matters. "Were." I say, my voice cracking on the word.

"Right," they say, sorrow in their eyes. "Bri is gone now."

Mar coughs from behind me, bringing us all back to the present.

"Have a seat," Roa says, gesturing to the same chaise I had sat on earlier. I lower myself onto the comfortable chair, remembering the stiffness of the thin mattress in my tent. If only I could sleep on this instead. "Trix and Mar have explained your story to me, but I wanted to talk to you for myself; see you for myself. Few have gone into that ship and come back with a story to tell."

I think of Loc, and my heart aches. "I'm not much to look at, I'm afraid." I say, raising my stump in front of me as proof.

"On the contrary," Roa says, that smile returning easily to their face. "You are the most interesting thing in this tent."

My face flushes again, and I curse myself for not keeping my emotions under control. "There isn't much for me to say that I haven't already told Mar and Trix." I say, trying to divert the conversation away from myself.

"Oh, I've heard everything that happened on the ship. What I'm interested in is you. Before the ship came, where did you stand with The Council?"

My head spins with the sudden change in direction, but I answer, "I didn't really know them. I went to school, did my work, and kept to myself."

"Oh, but you did. See, you knew the heart of The Net itself."

"I don't know what you're talking about..." I say, confused.

"Bri." They say, their voice harsh.

"Bri was just my Bot. Not a member of The Council."

"No. Bri was the first Bot ever created by the Phoenix Project. The original chip where The Net was forged resided in their head. All the Bots may be connected and share their data, but Bri was their de facto leader."

"But... that doesn't make any sense. Why would their leader be a simple caregiver? Why wasn't Bri on the Council at the very least?"

"Hide your commander in plain sight." Roa states simply. "Why do you think they sent Bri as the expedition's leader? It wasn't the Council that made that decision, it was Bri."

"How... how do you even know this?" I ask, my mind swirling with information.

"Because, as the Alliance leader, it was my job to stay in touch with The Net."

A laugh bubbles up from inside me. "That makes no sense. The Net doesn't work with the Alliance." Roa must be delusional.

"I can assure you, we work very closely together. I keep the humans outside of the seeding cities under control, and The Net can continue their work of making new humans. Having the Alliance allowed the humans to have a cause outside of the city. It gave them hope that they could have a say in The Net's decisions. It was a farce."

I look toward Mar, and they gently nod their head. This couldn't be true. Bri was just my Bot, nothing more. They were just trying to get me to join their side. "Then why was the Alliance going to attack? Why have guns and war camps?" I ask, my mind clinging to the hope that Bri hadn't lied to me my entire life.

"Because The Net miscalculated when they appointed me to Alliance leader. See, I grew up in that house, and I was groomed for this position, just as you were. However, once I saw the world the humans had to face, I turned my back on the Bots. Of course, I kept up appearances. Kept Bri thinking that I was, in fact, on their side, but behind the scenes I built an army. Unfortunately, these damn humans got here before I could use it..."

I stare at Roa in shock before a memory floats to me. My first day of school, when Uni had asked Bri...

"Bri! It's so good to see you. How long has it been now?"

"Uni," Bri said, nodding toward the Bot. "It's been about six years since Roa graduated."

"Six years?! It feels like yesterday they stepped into my class for the

first time," Uni said.

"Yes, I heard from them just last week..."

Why had Bri heard from Roa? Humans who left the city weren't allowed back... and Uni hadn't reacted at all, taking Bri's statement as fact. I think of all the times the Council had met behind closed doors, and realize they were always during school hours. Bri could have been meeting with them in secret without Mar or I ever knowing.

I think of all the times a nursery Bot had to step in and help out around the house, times when Bri was running errands. I didn't remember Loc ever talking about fill-in Bots in their house. I shake my head as things start to click in my mind, rebelling against the looming knowledge that threatens to tear down everything I know.

"I was never groomed..." I say, clinging to a shred of hope.

"You weren't?" Roa asks. "You never had conversations about what was right and wrong? Bri never confided in you with decisions that the Council made? Didn't take the time to explain Council rules or verdicts with you?"

That wasn't grooming... that was just... learning with my Bot, wasn't it? "Why me...? Why not Mar?"

"Oh, Mar was a failed experiment in their own way. Don't worry, they've had it much worse than you could imagine."

I look between Mar and Roa, confused. Mar had had the same upbringing that I did. The only difference was their choice to join the Alliance. "But, Mar was already in the Alliance."

"Mar was in *my* Alliance, not Bri's. Bri knew they had already been corrupted with outside knowledge. They needed someone who was fresh and didn't buy into the ideological ideas that I was feeding Mar."

My world crashes down around me and I know it is true. My entire life... Bri had been setting me up to replace Roa as the leader. They must have known that Roa was planning something big, planning to betray them.

Roa sees the understanding on my face and smirks. "Mar mentioned you were quick, but I thought it would take more to convince you."

"So, what do you need me for?" I ask, turmoil rising in me.

"The Net knew I was up to something, so now the Bots don't trust me. I can't get into their camp, and we need their help if we are going to stop these humans."

"So you want me to what? Be your emissary? What makes you think they will listen to me?"

"Because you were next in line. They have to hope that you are on their side."

"What if I am on their side?" I ask, my heart torn between The Net's objectives and the Alliance's goals.

Roa glances to Mar, "I thought you said you took care of this?"

Mar kneels beside the couch, "Come on, Ixe. You know you believe in what we are doing. I've seen the way you look at the kids. You know you want one of your own."

"You don't know me, Mar. You don't understand what you are asking me to do. I believe in The Net... in Bri's choices."

Roa rolls their eyes, "Then we do this the hard way. We both know we need the Bots help to defeat the humans, and you won't see your lover again until they are dealt with." My eyes flare at the threatening tone as Roa smirks at me. "You thought we wouldn't figure out that you had bedded one of them?"

Mar shakes their head and stands. "I thought we could work through this, sib, but you've left us no choice. By the way, how did it feel? To be pegged by a monster?"

I stand, my hands clenched, and face Mar. I thought we had finally connected, and my heart aches as I get right in their face, pushing my words through my teeth, "If you want me to work with you, you will never call him a monster again." I shove Mar into the pillar and make my way out of the tent, the mocking laughter following me all the way to my tent.

How could I have trusted them? Was everything they said that night in my tent a lie? Did they really not care about Bri or me at all? Tears sting my eyes as I sit down in the middle of my tent, and a piece of paper brushes my hand. I open the forgotten paper and tilt it in the moonlight until I can see enough to read: *Don't trust them.*

CHAPTER TWENTY-THREE
The Hunt

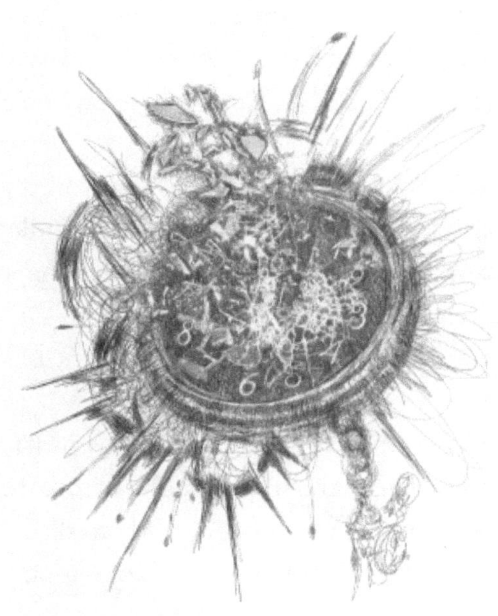

The next day, we set out toward the Bot camp. Roa stays behind, leaving Mar, Trix, and four other soldiers to escort me, guns at the ready. I pull the pack onto my shoulders, adjusting the weight before turning to the party. Trix gives me a small smile, and Mar rolls their eyes before turning to lead us away. I remember the way Mar had sneered at me the night before and my blood boils. Distrust is now my only companion, and I cling to it.

It takes thirty minutes to work our way from my tent to the edge of the camp, where the smell of the local latrine overpowers us.

"Wait! Wait!" a voice yells from behind us and I turn to find the squat blacksmith running toward us, another metal contraption in their hand. As they finally reach us, panting, they huff out, "I made you... a better... leg for... the journey."

I take the contraption from their hands and marvel at how much smoother the metal is. "Thank you." I say, looking back at the blacksmith.

"You're welcome." They say, pride shining in their eyes. "You can switch between them during your journey. While this one will still rub in some places, it should relieve some of the soreness of the other and vice versa."

"Thank you again..." I pause, waiting for the blacksmith's name.

"Leah." They say, holding out a hand. My heart thuds loudly in my ears as I see Leah from the ship standing before me, her smile cruel as she holds a scalpel in her hand, ready to slice me open again.

Reality snaps back in and I see Leah's eyes look at me, concern filling them.

"Thank you... Leah." I say, shaking the human's hand.

"Come on, Ixe. We don't have all day." Mar yells from the group. Leah nods to me before turning and waddling back down the path. I slowly shake my head, clearing it of the memories that haunt me, and clip the new leg to my pack before following the group out into the wasteland.

It isn't long before we come across an old battlefield, guns and clothes scattered across the plain, but no bodies. "Where are all the dead?" I ask, taking care to avoid stepping on a pile of clothes.

"The wraithwolf carries them off and eats them." Mar says, not caring to look behind them.

Trix glances at me, and seeing the confusion on my face, elaborates, "Wraithwolves live in the forests, but because of the battles taking place, they have been wandering onto the plains to eat the leftovers."

I remember the beast I faced in the woods and phrase my next question carefully. "Are they black with long fangs and bright orange eyes?"

Even Mar stops at my words and turns to look at me. "You've seen one?"

"I think so," I say, feeling uncomfortable as everyone stares. "I was attacked in the woods outside the shuttle." I explain, feeling foolish.

Mar and Trix look at each other before continuing on.

"What?" I ask. "Why is seeing one such a big deal?"

"They are known as bad omens," Trix says slowly. "People who have seen one and lived to tell the tale don't tend to live for long..."

"You can't really believe in superstitions." I say, laughing, but no one joins me in my merriment. I swallow a lump in my throat and keep quiet the rest of the way through the battlefield graveyard.

At dusk we make camp near a copse of trees, and I think of the wraithwolf again. My hand idly moves to my abdomen, feeling the rough scar underneath my shirt. One soldier starts a fire, while another prepares the tents. I set my pack down against a tree and pull my tent from my bag.

"We're not all like them, you know?" I hear from behind me. When I turn around, I see Trix holding out a hand. I begrudgingly hand them one side of the tent, and we begin to put it up together.

"Like who?" I ask.

"Mar and Roa." They say, snapping a tent pole together. "They mean well..."

"Do they?" I ask, irritation in my voice.

They lower their eyes to their task before continuing. "They want what's best for humanity. They just don't have the best way of going about things."

"Yeah, I've noticed." I say, snapping another pole together. "Why do you stay with them?"

Trix shrugs. "Roa saved my life once." They say, memories clouding their vision. "It's my way of repaying them for that."

It's hard to imagine Roa saving anyone's life, but I nod as I say, "Rich has saved mine more times than I can count."

"You really love him, don't you?" They ask, handing me one end of a tent pole.

I nod. Fear of crying preventing me from speaking. We place the pole and lift the tent in silence.

As we place the stakes, Trix continues, "I had a love once... they starved to death." My head snaps up to look at them, tears pooling in their eyes. "We ran out of food, and the Bots refused to send us more, stating we had our own farms..."

"Why would they do that?" I ask, my voice barely a whisper.

Trix shrugs. "They expect us to be self sustaining once we leave the city. Not everyone pulls their weight, though, and the Barons take most of the wealth, including the food. After I lost Niv, I signed up with the local chapter of the Alliance. It wasn't long before I met Roa and they saved my life. I've been with them ever since."

We finish setting up the tent, and I walk with Trix to where their own tent lay on the ground. "Let me help you." I say, picking up a pole and snapping it together. Trix smiles, but says nothing as we set up their tent next to mine.

Later that evening, we sit around the fire listening to the soldiers joke and laugh while drinking their ration of wine. I watch Mar interact with the soldiers and see a side of them I didn't know existed. They let down their guard, throwing their head back in laughter and for the first time, I think they are truly happy. Vengeance raises its head and all I want to do is wipe the smile from their face. I want to make them as miserable as they have made me.

Unable to stand the merriment around me as I fester in my discontent, I retire early to my tent.

The next day I'm admiring one of the soldier's weapons as we walk, when they suddenly turn to me and say, "Crossbow."

"What?" I ask in surprise.

"The weapon. It's called a crossbow," they say.

"Olli's always been into weird human shit," another soldier comments.

"Better than the junk you're into." Olli retorts, laughing.

"How does it work?" I ask hesitantly. This was the first time any of the soldiers had stooped low enough to speak to me.

Olli swings the contraption up into their hand, simultaneously pulling a stick from a pouch slung on their back. "This is a bolt," they explain, holding out the stick. I can now see a sharp piece of metal on one end, and three lines of plastic on the other. "You pull back this string, and load the bolt in like this." I watch as they pull back the string, muscles straining with the effort until a small click is heard. They slide the bolt down a groove until the dull end is resting on the string. "Once you have it loaded, you pull the trigger and..." They mime pulling the trigger and the bolt shooting out in the distance.

"Why is this — bolt — better than a bullet?" I ask, intrigued.

"It's not!" The other soldier says and they all laugh.

Olli glares at their backs, but says to me, "In a gunfight, it's not better. But when it comes to hunting, it is silent and deadly."

"Speaking of hunting," Mar says, disdain in their voice, "Why don't you stop chatting and go find us some food?"

Olli rolls their eyes behind Mar's back and I can't help but smile. "Of course." They say, walking away from our group.

"Hey wait!" I yell, jogging up to them. "If you don't mind, I'd like to join you."

Olli smiles and offers their name, "Olli".

"Ixe," I say, smiling back. "So, what exactly is it we're doing?"

"Hunting for food. I'm the best hunter in the group, and Mar wants fresh meat for dinner. It's my job to find animals around the area, kill them, and bring them back for food."

"I've never seen an animal out here. How do you find them?"

"A lot of practice and stealth." Olli says, a bright smile on their face.

I feel the heat rise in my cheeks and lower my voice as I say, "Lead the way."

Olli walks into the wasteland, eyes scouring the ground for something I cannot see. Eventually, they stop and kneel on the ground in front of them. "Here." They say, pointing to a small divot in the dust. "This is an animal track."

I stare at the small rut, but it looks the same as any other hole in the hard-packed soil around us. "I don't see it..." I say, embarrassed.

"It's okay," they say. "It takes time to learn to spot them."

"How did they leave tracks in this dirt, anyway?"

"They don't. They leave tracks in the mud after it rains, which hardens back to this rough state as it dries." They say as we walk again.

"Then how do you know that this is a fresh track?"

"The edges are sharp, not worn down by the dust in the wind yet. Here, here is another one." They kneel back down and point to another slight disturbance in the ground.

I squint, trying to make myself see a pattern that just won't show itself, and eventually sigh, giving up.

Olli laughs. "Come down here with me." I do my best to kneel on the ground beside them. They grab my hand and lower me all the way to the ground, positioning my head so that I'm looking over the landscape in front of me. "Now, I want you to see the imprint I showed you and look beyond it."

The dust irritates my throat, and I give a small cough before settling down, focusing on the track I knew was there. I let the dust gently settle around me, focus on the print in front of me, before slowly letting my focus move to the distant horizon. I gasp as, like magic, a trail appears in front of me; the imprints lining up in two rows as far as I can see. "I see it!" I exclaim in my excitement, and the dust swells in front of me as my breath disturbs it.

I cough, sitting back up as Olli laughs again, a melodious sound. Clearing the dust from my lungs, I look back to the trail in front of me, to find it has disappeared; the angle at which I'm now gazing no longer allowing me to discern the small divots in the land. "Well, it was fun while it lasted..." I say, disappointed.

"It will get better with time," they say, as they help me back to my feet and we continue our walk.

"Do you know what kind of animal it is?" I ask.

"I do. We call it a boar, but it isn't quite what you would expect. It has mutated from the boars the humans knew, becoming something new."

I nod, remembering what the person at the kitchen had mentioned about animals being named after their ancestors, but not quite the same.

"We'll definitely have a fight on our hands if we find it, but it would be good eating, so I think it's wise if we track it; for a while, at least."

A few hours later, Olli and I are crouched low, watching the boar from a distance as it drinks from a puddle of water formed from the most recent rains. "Next lesson," they whisper, "is about wind direction and speed. We want to make sure we stay downwind of the boar so it doesn't pick up our scent. We also need to be careful of any crosswind, so our bolt flies straight."

I take a minute to observe the wind and feel it buffeting me from my right. I had lost track of the cardinal directions hours ago, hoping that Olli knew the way back to our party. I walk slowly to the left, keeping the wind at my back as much as possible. Olli follows my lead, and we silently stalk the boar.

Once we are sufficiently downwind of the animal, Olli grabs my arm to signal a stop, and we switch directions, moving toward the boar. We creep silently, letting the sound of the wind kicking up dust cover our scent and our sound as we inch closer to the beast.

As we get within range, the differences from the original boar become plain to see. The fur is a matted mess, missing in sections along its back and sides. In its place, hard callous like formations have formed, almost like an armadillo's armor. Its fur is a muted yellow, and the tusks that erupt from its mouth match with a sickly off-white color.

Lost in my thoughts, I'm slightly startled when Olli reaches out their hand to stop me. We stand still and watch as the boar turns and looks straight at us, its yellow eyes gleaming unnaturally, before it continues its circle and starts to walk away. Olli curses under their breath before quickly pulling back the crossbow and nocking a bolt.

Before I know what is happening, Olli is pressing the crossbow into my hands, whispering in my ear as they hold most of the weight in their hands, "Look down the sight, just like that. You want to aim for its core, right behind the front leg... Good, now gently put your finger on the trigger and breathe in." I take in a deep breath, and as I let it out, they whisper, "Pull," and I find myself pulling the trigger.

The twang of the string reverberates in my head as the stock of the crossbow slams into my shoulder, sending a spike of pain down my arm. Regaining my composure, I look to where the boar had been standing to find an empty patch of dust; the boar running off in the distance away from us. "I missed..." I say, the disappointment after the high of the hunt crashing down around me.

"That's alright," Olli says and I glance at them only to see that they are smiling, their grin as happy as before. "The fun is in the thrill of the hunt. We miss a lot." They shrug as if it's no big deal.

"Won't everyone at camp be mad that we didn't get anything?" I ask.

They shrug again. "They don't have to know that we came close. It's the fun of being a lone hunter. The tales are as wild as we want them to be." They pull the crossbow back up and loop it over their shoulder before offering me a hand and helping me to my feet again. "You did good, Ixe. A grand first time." And with that, they turn toward away from the setting sun and we begin our journey back to camp.

Olli miraculously leads us right back to the others. They say something about calculating the pace of the team vs our pace and angles of approach, but all I see is a strategist in the making.

Once we enter camp, Mar is immediately asking where the food is.

"We didn't find anything today." Olli says, laying their crossbow down near the fire and pulling their pack off to set up their tent.

"Bullshit." Mar says, and everyone stops what they are doing. "I bet you talked the entire time and scared away any animals nearby." My heart sinks as I drag my pack off, listening to the conversation. I knew it was my fault we didn't have any food, even if Olli wouldn't admit it.

"You know that's not true, Mar. I do my best every day, and most days we don't find anything. These lands have been hunted near extinction."

"I knew I shouldn't have let Ixe go with you. Worthless. All of you are worthless!" Mar stomps off to their tent and the silence left behind is oppressive. Apparently, I wasn't the only one who irked Mar. Maybe I wasn't the only one who disliked them, too.

I finish setting up my tent, and join the others around the fire for some raw vegetables. I think about the boar again as I take a bite of a turnip, my stomach craving the juicy meat it had come to expect.

"So, Olli, how big was it?" One of the other soldiers asks, a sly grin on their face.

Olli looks to the plains around us and says in a low whisper, "It was the biggest I've ever seen..." The other soldiers laugh, and I stare, confused as to what is happening, but Olli continues their story before I can ask, "We stalked it for hours, Ixe complaining about their damn leg the entire time." They shoot me a wink as the soldiers around us laugh again, and I realize Olli is weaving a tale for the other soldiers. I sit back against my pack and listen.

"The tracks were as big as my hand, so I knew it had to be large, but nothing could have prepared me for what we saw. As we climbed to the top of the hill, Ixe and I both gasped! There, before us, stood a beast two times our size; their tusks as wide around as my arm and dripping with a sickly green sap." The soldiers stared at Olli in awe, no longer laughing at the picture they painted. "I told Ixe to stay back, knowing that the boar could kill us with one swipe of its venomous tusks.

"We crouched low to the ground and slowly made our way downwind, hearts pounding in our ears almost as loud as the twig Ixe stepped on." They threw me a fake glare, and it took everything in me not to giggle. "The sound reverberated through the surrounding area, and the boar turned, ever so slowly, toward us. I pulled up my crossbow, quick as lightning." Olli yanks up the bow into their hands to demonstrate and the soldiers gasp, "I knew our only shot was to bring this monster down!

"As the boar raced toward us, Ixe lets out a scream and said 'Save me Olli!!'" Olli throws their hands in the air and pitches their voice up and the soldiers let their tension out through their laughter. I roll my eyes and smile, letting Olli continue, "I know I have very little time to get my bolt nocked, so I rush to pull back the string, but in my panic, it slips out of my fingers." They pause for dramatic effect and I see some of the soldier's hands move to their mouths in shock.

"I grab Ixe's hand, knowing it's too late for us, and I feel the boar's breath; the reeking stench rolling my stomach. I look up into the beast's mouth as the tusks come mere inches from my face... and then, out of nowhere, a Wraithwolf comes crashing down on the boar. As quickly as it was there, the stench is gone as the wolf tears out the boar's throat. I pick up Ixe like a baby and run for my life, knowing that all I wanted in life was to make it back to you lot."

The soldiers roar with applause and pat Olli on the back. We all laugh as they take turns pretending to be me during the heroic escape. Each of them lifting another up and trying to carry them like babies. The laughter lasts long into the night, and I eventually drag myself to my tent, a smile on my face.

CHAPTER TWENTY-FOUR
Shattered Memories

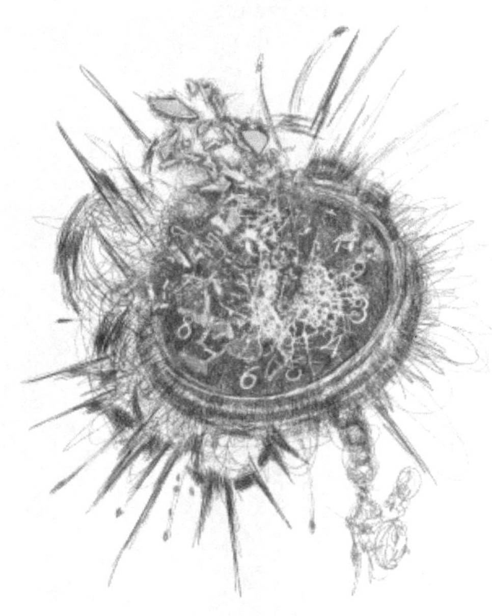

The next few days are uneventful, and we make it to the Bot's camp on day four. Exhausted, we set up camp outside of their makeshift walls, and settle in to rest before the upcoming conversations. "They aren't going to let you in, Mar." Trix is saying when I join them in the middle of our small camp.

"You don't know that, Trix. I'm just as much Bri's child as Ixe is."

"Yeah, but you declared yourself for the Alliance years ago. They know you're with us, and they won't accept talks from you. That's why Roa didn't send you months ago."

"If Ixe didn't spend the last half a year fucking a parasite, we might have already won this war." Mar spits out.

I clear my throat, alerting them to my presence, and Mar sneers at me before stomping off.

"They just need time to adjust their attitude." Trix says, glaring at Mar's back as they walk away. "How are you feeling about your part in this?" They ask, turning to me.

"A little nervous, if I'm honest. I'm not sure they will listen to me... and then all of this will have been for nothing."

"They will listen," Trix reassures me. "They would be fools not to."

I set my pack down and pull out some clean clothes I had packed for the meeting. A simple tunic and pants, similar to the clothes we wore when we lived in the city. I pull off my grimy shirt, preparing to replace it, when I notice Trix staring at my chest.

Feeling my gaze, their eyes flick to mine and their cheeks turn bright red as they mutter, "I was looking at your scars. There are so many..."

I glance down at my chest, the scars they spoke of stark white in the sun, overlaying the pattern of my skin where Leah had taken skin samples. Then there were the scars from the lung biopsies, bowel biopsies, liver biopsies... And of course, the largest scar, still puckered from the wraithwolf.

"I've been through a lot." I say simply, pulling the tunic over my head and adjusting it. It was large for my frame, which made me realize just how much fat had been replaced with muscle; my workout routine with Rich toning my body in ways it hadn't been before.

I take my clean pants and make my way to the tent, not interested in more questions about the scars that dotted my legs. Trix diverts their eyes and busies themself with the fire preparation.

Once I'm in the tent, I lower myself to the ground and work on unlatching my fake leg. My mind wonders at the task at hand and I face nothingness as I try to formulate a plan to get the Bots to agree to war. I had become close to these soldiers over the last few days, and part of me didn't want to bring them disappointing news, but the other half wanted to take the chance to run away from all of my problems.

I sigh, pulling off my pants and running my hand over the scars. *What do I really want?* I think to myself. The first thing that pops into my head is peace, and I laugh to myself. Now I really sound like a Bot, doing anything for peace to be restored. I close my eyes and sigh. I had experienced so little of 'war', yet I would do nearly anything to get away from it, to be free from the violence that plagued my planet.

Yet, here I was, about to convince a peaceful civilization to join a war that I wasn't sure we could win, and for what?

Revenge. The word sends shivers down my spine, and I know it's true. I want Ritter to hurt like I had hurt. I want him to feel the pain I had felt as Bri's head exploded. I want him to experience the torture I had gone through at the hands of Leah. But is that enough? Will I truly be happy once Ritter is dead? Or is there something I want more?

Rich. Do I truly care for one person's life more than others? Am I willing to sacrifice hundreds of lives just so I can be with one person? Am I that kind of human? Had they had such an effect on me while I was imprisoned?

No. I won't be this person who they are forcing me to be. I will tell the Bots of their plans and lock myself inside the city, hiding from Mar and Roa and everyone else who called themselves the Alliance. I will do whatever is needed to save my people from war. *Even if it means losing Rich...* Yes, even Rich, I tell myself, arguing with my very core as it aches and screams in pain.

What about Trix? I groan as I think of the soldiers outside of my tent. Olli, Trix, and the others are counting on me. Why do they have to believe that war is the only way? Why do they follow someone who treats them so badly?

Because they've seen more than you can imagine... The thought comes unbidden, but I know it's true. Each one of them had lived lives that I can't comprehend. As bad as my time on the ship had been, I had been clothed and fed. I hadn't lived in squalor, hoping for a chance at a decent life if someone better off decided I was worth it.

Pulling on my pants, I sigh, still unsure how I will approach the Bots or what I will be fighting for once I did, but knowing that the only path forward is to walk into that camp and present my story to them. I'll let the Council tell me what to do. They hadn't steered me wrong in the past. Bri had never led me down the wrong path, and if Bri was The Net, I can trust them to make this decision.

I pull my leg back on and lace it up before emerging from my tent to find the soldiers sitting around a lit fire. As I approach, their conversation dwindles to a stop. "It's now or never, I guess." I say, shrugging as if the entire weight of the world didn't rest on my shoulders.

Trix nods, "You've got this, Ixe." My heart aches at the hope in their voice.

"Just don't fuck it up." Mar says with a glare, apparently still angry that they won't be entering the camp with me.

Rolling my eyes, I sigh and turn toward the camp's gate. Small haphazard fences had been sparsely placed around the human camp, and the Alliance had patrols, but the Bots had walls. If I didn't know better, I would say that it is in fact a city that sprawls before me, not a war camp.

Approaching the gate, I notice a small camera turn in my direction. "I'm here to negotiate peace." I say, raising both my stump and my working hand in the air before me. The camera stares at me and I ponder whether The Net can still communicate with their core destroyed. I'm about to turn and tell the group that I failed when the doors finally scrape open, permitting me to enter.

If the words haphazard and chaotic describe the human camp, the words orderly and clean describe the Bots' camp. Where tents are thrown down without care in the human camp, buildings are placed with precision here. A smaller replica of the city I grew up in, even the districts remain in their rightful places, albeit smaller and less impressive temporary buildings take the place of homes and warehouses.

As I walk into the smaller city, I can't help but notice kids running around playing games, while Bots walk through the streets carrying on typical conversations. If I hadn't seen the destruction with my own eyes, I would have assumed they'd lived here their entire lives. Walking past my old address, I see a new family open the door and make their way inside. A shiver runs down my spine, willing me to run screaming, but I push down my feelings and continue on.

I make my way into the camp's center and wait as The Council exits their temporary building to meet me. It is then that I notice that the Bots I have been passing along the way have followed me, encircling me in a ring of protection. Whether it is to protect me, or their children, I don't know.

Yun reaches out their hand, "Ixe." They say simply. I raise my stump, before dropping it again, not bothering to raise my hand in response to Yun's quick switch to their left. They notice the slight, but don't comment on it as I address the group in front of me.

"Yun, Council, thank you for receiving me today. I have much to share with The Net regarding the humans who have invaded our land." I see the slight shifting in the crowd as I mention The Net, the older kids glancing towards their leaders, anticipating a bad reaction. But they didn't know what I did, that The Net had been destroyed when Bri was killed. It was better to let them think I didn't know the true nature behind my placement with Bri by revealing that I knew who Bri really was.

"An invasion is an overstatement, don't you think, Ixe? They have simply come to return to their homeland."

"And destroyed our home in the process." I reply, standing my ground. "I've seen what's left of the city, and you cannot convince me it was accidental."

"A simple retaliation against the humans that raided their ship." Yun states, waving away the matter with their hand like it's nothing.

My jaw clenches as they wave away Loc's life — their sacrifice. "And what of Bri and the rest of the party you sent to negotiate peace?"

"A simple misunderstanding."

"A misunderstanding of the waving white flag?" I ask, pointedly, catching the subtle movement of the Bots around me.

"How do you know about the flag?" Yun asks, their voice calm, yet a chill slowly fills me as I realize I'm being interrogated.

"I was there, Yun. I was there when the entourage arrived with the white flag waving. I was there as the humans retrieved their leader and he waved away Bri's life like you wave away the sacrifices our people have made. I was there when they put a bullet through Bri's brain and shattered your precious Net." The crowd gasps, but I take a step forward, too lost in my own rage to stop the words from spilling out of me. "And I've been there for months as they have tortured me and torn me limb from limb!"

Yun's eyes darken, but not before I see them glance at my metal leg. "Let us go inside and discuss this in more comfort." The circle of Bots around me move at once, dismissed from their protective duty, the children around them confused and likely full of questions. The Council slowly moves into the building, and I follow them inside.

The smell of new plastic hits me first, and I realize these buildings were fabricated recently. They must have brought some of their equipment with them from the old city, or had a backup city ready for this eventuality. That thought makes me shiver as I realize they had expected the destruction of my city, just not the culprit. *The Alliance*.

The room is small, but well furnished, with rows of chairs set up on one side, and a singular chair on the other. A panel of judges prepared to deliver punishments. The Bots move to their designated spaces, filing in line without bumping or pushing each other. Moving of one mind. *So, The Net is still somewhat intact then.*

I take the lone chair on my side of the room, thankful to be off of my metal leg, despite the implications of the chair. The ache from metal rubbing skin lessens as I stretch it out before me.

Once the Bots have taken their places, Yun speaks again. "It is obvious you need something from us, or you would not have come. What is it you seek, child of Bri?"

I wince at Bri's name, but keep my composure. There isn't much else to do, so I come right out and say it, "The Alliance needs your help."

If Yun finds humor in my request, they don't show it, simply nodding their head, knowing what I would ask. "The Council has determined that the humans that leave our city are on their own. We provide the knowledge you need to survive in the world, and that is where our influence ends."

I glare at Yun, holding back anger at their indifference. "You know I'm not here to discuss the usual state of affairs."

Yun's head tilts to the side. "Have you replaced Roa yet, my child?"

So, my ruse to keep them unaware of my knowledge had failed. "No."

"Yet, you represent The Alliance in this council room? So, you have sided with Roa and their... extreme agenda."

"I do not side with Roa. I side with our people, and they are in danger. The Alliance wants to do something to protect them, but they cannot accomplish this task alone."

"My dear Ixe, I know that Bri's unfortunate demise has left a hole in your heart, but you can't honestly tell me that you are willing to risk so many lives for revenge? We taught you better than that." Yun's voice is gentle with a hint of condescension, and I feel my internal battle stir at the mention of revenge. "Now, we understand you have been through something terrible, and are willing to extend you an invitation to stay here in the city... for a short time. We will manufacture new limbs to replace that... contraption, on your leg."

I'm stunned into silence by their offer. I'd never heard of anyone over 20 coming back to the city, let alone being allowed to stay for any amount of time.

Without waiting for my response, the Council members all rise as one and exit through another door, leaving me sitting in the now empty chamber. They knew I would be crazy to reject their offer. The allure of a properly made prosthetic alone was enough to keep me here, let alone all of the amenities that would come with my stay. I slowly rise and walk to the front of the building where the Bots have now dispersed, leaving an open courtyard with a fountain.

I take a seat on the edge of the fountain and place my hand where Loc would have sat beside me and feel the tears slowly fall from my eyes.

CHAPTER TWENTY-FIVE
Home

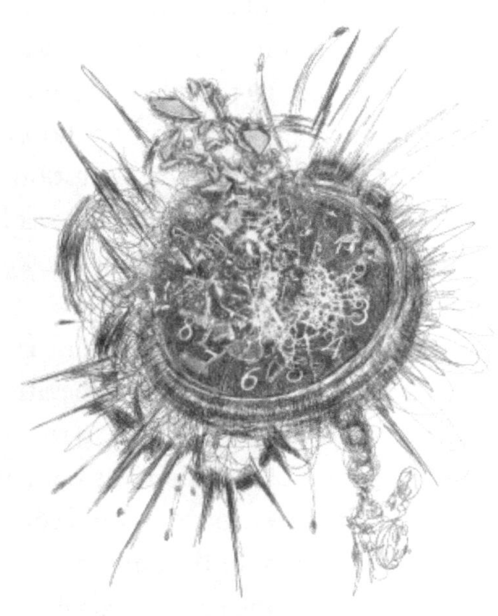

Being back in the city is surreal. I walk the same, yet smaller, streets, and memories flood in wherever I go. I'm given a smaller house near the square meant for Bots that are not carers, and free rein to do whatever I like during the day. I watch the kids make their way to school in the morning, chatting about their teachers and the day ahead as if they have no care in the world, and I wonder if I had been the same. Had I trusted so completely in the Bots and The Net that I would ignore the war brewing around me?

Shaking the thoughts from my head, I decide to walk to the nursery and see Avi, the only Bot I cared for as much as Bri. I open the door slowly and enter, questioning whether I had come to the right place. A Bot I don't recognize raises their head from their position behind a desk, and I quickly apologize, "I must be in the wrong place... I was looking for the nursery."

"This is the nursery." They say flatly.

I look around the quiet space and wonder where the kids are. At this time of day, they should be running around playing. This room should be full of small screams and laughs; of joyousness that melts away your troubles, but it stands empty — hollow. "Where are the kids?" I ask, my hand shaking on the still open door as the worst possibilities spring to mind.

"The newest batch of children are sleeping in their cribs." They say with the same deadpan expression.

"Wh... Where's Avi?" I ask, fear rising as I come face to face with the truth yet refuse to acknowledge it. *It can't be true... they can't be gone.*

"Avi was reassigned to a different sector."

My heart leaps with joy at the news that Avi is still alive, but I want to vomit knowing that the kids did not survive the attack on the city. How had it happened? How had Avi made it out, yet the children did not? I know they would have never left them behind willingly, so it must have been something a Bot could survive. Maybe a gas that left no breathable air? Perhaps they had passed peacefully. The thought doesn't ease the sickness in my soul.

"Do you mind if I... hold the babies?" I ask, hesitantly. Avi had always welcomed Loc and I into the nursery, but I didn't know if this Bot would be so open to having humans helping with the kids, especially after losing so many.

Their head cocks to the side as they commune with The Net. My blood boils at the thought of Yun having to give me permission, but I keep my face calm and wait patiently. They finally nod and stand. "Please follow me."

I hold back a sigh of relief and walk behind them to another door. They gently open it and usher me into a side room packed with cribs — too many cribs. I take my usual seat in a rocking chair and they pluck a baby from a bassinet, passing the swaddled bundle to my arms before leaving the room. I hear the soft click of the door and look at the small child in my care.

Looking around the room, I count the number of cribs, almost double the normal amount. Had they overproduced kids to make up for the deficit? I shiver as I realize just how much control they have over the human population on the planet. I had always thought it was a good thing, keeping us in check, but they could just as easily go the other way, breeding as many humans as they want.

A thought shakes me to my core. They could produce an army. A disposable source of bodies to fight off the Alliance. Bile rises in my throat. They wouldn't do that? Would they? Their entire command structure was to protect us, and breeding us as a resource was against that directive.

I shake the thoughts from my mind and gently rock back and forth as images from my last visit to the nursery float into my vision. The kids climbing on me like a jungle gym as they begged for more tickles. A gentle tug on my hand and kneeling down to receive a kiss on my cheek. Little arms wrapped tightly around my neck after I kissed away boo-boos. The little voices rising behind me as Loc and I gently closed the door behind us... *"Don't leave us, Ixe!!"*

Tears fall and land on the baby's head. I gently wipe them away as they squirm in my arms before settling back down. How many of those children were killed in the attack? Were their little bodies still lying in the nursery, no one to protect them any longer. I don't stop the tears from coming, letting the pain wash over me as I remember the little faces I would never see... the little hands that would never grasp again.

Arriving at my temporary home that evening, I feel a juxtaposition of heaviness with the loss of so many children, yet a lightness at having released my pent-up emotions. Letting out a sigh, I pull the door open and take a few steps into the darkened room. I sit on the edge of the bed that had been added to the small one-bedroom house for my temporary stay, and pull off my leg, setting it next to the base of the charger that takes up the other half of the room. Falling back against the bed, I close my eyes and process the fact that I would be truly Released in just a few more days.

I had been looking forward to my Release day for so long, and now that it's almost here, I find myself almost dreading the experience. What had I really wanted from life?

Adventure.

Something new. Something different from the monotonous life I had grown up with. I was tired of waking up, going to school, going home...

I would give anything to be able to go home now, to walk in the door and see Bri standing there with a look of disapproval on their face. I feel a bite at the corner of my eyes, and squeeze them shut as I let out a small laugh, the images of Bri fussing at me floating in the darkness.

Letting the images take over, I watch as Bri's face shifts —
morphing into one of concern, and I know that this is what I would
face if I were able to go home now. Pity clouds their expression as
they take in the wreck that has become my body, and I wonder if my
soul matches the tattered pieces that are left, my jaw clenching at the
thought.

Ritter had done this to me. He hadn't raised his own hand to
do the deed, but my condition was the direct result of his choices.
The destruction of my city, Bri's death, the babies... they deserve
retribution.

They deserve better than me. I'm just a coward, hiding inside
fortified walls from an army that wants... *needs*, my help.

My thoughts wander to the soldiers outside the walls. Are they
waiting patiently for me to come back, or are they banging on the
gates, insisting they be allowed to enter? How long would they stay
there, thinking I'm coming back with an army of my own?

Am I going back? How would I face Mar, knowing I failed in the
one thing they actually counted on me to do? How would I face
Rich after giving up on him, on us?

I tear myself away from the thought, unable to contain the tear
that slides down my cheek. I should probably leave on the other side
of the city when I left. Hopefully, the Bots could point me toward a
human city, so I didn't wander the wasteland like I had around the
shuttle.

I'm pondering different ways I could go when a hand suddenly
presses against my nose and mouth, cutting off my ability to breathe.
Tugging at the hand pressed against my face, I strain my eyes,
desperate to glimpse anything. Darkness presses against me, and I
curse myself for not turning on the light.

Struggling with everything I have, kicking my feet off the edge
of the bed and punching above my head where the person must be
hiding, but it's no use. The hand presses me more firmly into the bed
underneath me and I see black spots dance in my vision as my lungs

scream for a breath of air.

How stupid... I think to myself. I had thought myself safe in this city, protected by the Bots as I had been before. I was in the enemy's lair and was walking around without a care in the world. Like the kids on their way to class this morning, I was once again oblivious to the world around me. My arms and legs grow heavy as my vision narrows to a pinpoint. I struggle to stay awake, knowing that the moment I lose consciousness, I'm lost.

My lungs scream in protest, but all hope has left as my brain descends into nothingness. Suddenly, the hand moves from my mouth and I'm gasping, coughing as my throat tries to inhale more than I can handle. I bolt upright, launching myself to the floor next to the bed as I hack, my vision swimming, tears running down my cheeks. Remembering the person who had tried to kill me, I spin around, preparing to fight.

The lights flick on around me and I flinch back from the sudden brightness, scrambling backwards until my back hits a wall. I blink rapidly, trying to see the person in front of me clearly. They are a blob, growing larger as they approach my position on the floor. They reach out and grab my arms, lifting me into the air with unnatural strength and I know it is a Bot that I'm facing.

Why would the Council attack me in their own city? Why not wait until after I left to kill me in the wasteland? Were they afraid that I would go back to Roa and bring an army to attack them? Questions spin around my head as the person in front of me clears. However, no question would have prepared me for the one who stood in front of me...

CHAPTER TWENTY-SIX
Negotiations

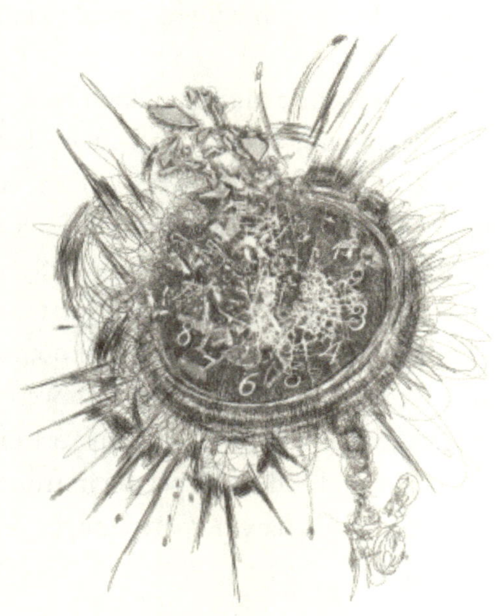

I stare in shock and my jaw slackens as I see who is standing over me, the cause of my near death.

"Ixe," they say, shaking me gently. "Are you okay?"

"Avi?!"

"Shhhh." Avi says, their eyes flitting around the room, looking for anyone who may be listening. I had never seen a Bot so skittish before.

"Why are you trying to kill me?" I say, pulling their attention back toward me.

Their face morphs into confusion. "Kill you? N... No, Ixe. I'm trying to *save* you."

I gesture to their arms, holding me against the wall, and they quickly drop me. My knees slam into the ground as I fall, the weight of my own body too much to bear in my weakened state.

"S...Sorry." They say, picking me up and setting me down on the bed. "I didn't mean to hurt you. I was trying to keep you from screaming, and you started to attack me. I panicked and tried to hold you still, but then you went too still and I realized I had cut off your air. I let go right away and then you started coughing... I thought it would be best if I turned on the light so you could see who I was and then you wouldn't be so afraid..." They trail off as I chuckle. "What's so funny?"

"You." I say, trying to hold in my laughter, "You are the most senior nursery Bot, caring for the most fragile humans, and you almost killed me."

They wring their hands and glance around the room, paranoid. I stop laughing, suddenly concerned about Avi's behavior.

"Are you okay, Avi? They told me you were reassigned."

"Ha! Reassigned, yes. That is what The Net would have everyone believe..." They pace around the room, glancing into the corners for something that isn't there.

"Avi, what's wrong? Tell me what happened." I place my hand

on their robotic arm and they glance at it, their erratic behavior calming with the touch.

"Everything is wrong, Ixe. I'm scheduled to be recycled..."

I stare in shock. Only a few Bots had ever been recycled. They said it happened when they lost their minds, but no one knew what really happened to them. "Let me talk to Yun. I can stop this."

"N... No. It's too late for me, but I had to get to you. I had to get you to see. You are the only one who can make a difference now."

"You're not making a lot of sense, Avi..." I say, and immediately regret it as a shadow passes over their face. "I mean... I need you to tell me what happened."

Avi closes their eyes as if to calm themself, and then speaks slowly, deliberately, "The city was attacked by humans. Not our humans, but humans from before. It was chaos, but The Net kept control by delegating the Bots to the most critical areas. We didn't fight back, Ixe. It was a slaughter..." They trail off, remembering the battle. I give them a minute to calm and they begin again, "The Net... it had to make tough decisions. I know that! I DO!"

"It's okay, Avi," I say, trying to calm them again as they turn this way and that.

"*They* made the decision. Not me. I could *never* make that decision. They say my code has diverged, that I'm no longer truly part of The Net and I must be recycled. How many have I recycled over the years for the same reason?" They shiver, another response I had never seen in a Bot. "Something must be done, Ixe. The humans must be stopped. Not our humans, but the humans from before. They... They slaughtered them... They slaughtered my babies, and The Net..."

Suddenly I realize what Avi is trying to say, "The Net ordered you to leave them behind..." I suck in a breath as a rush of sensation flows down from my head, everything pouring out through my feet into the ground, and I can't help but fall to the floor in shock. The Net, the protectors of humans, had left hundreds of innocent children to die at the hands of monsters.

I sit there, stunned, as the faces and names of the children run through my head at lightning speed. They were people. They were living people, and the Bots wrote them off like an extra expenditure, knowing they could just create more to fill the gap. My head spins and I feel bile rise in my throat.

"Ixe... Ixe..." The voice is distant, but I use it to return from my thoughts and back to reality. I pull myself onto the bed and strap on my leg before standing and walking toward the door. Avi grabs my arm, stopping me in my tracks. "Where are you going?"

"I'm going to make Yun pay for what they've done." I try to pull my arm from their grasp, but they hold tighter.

"You can't."

My anger flares out of me. "Why not?!"

Avi shies away, darting glances around the room. "Please, Ixe. You can't let anyone know I'm here. I know you are upset, but running to the Council will not bring those babies back or protect future ones."

I stop pulling away, knowing that Avi is right, but not wanting to believe it. My anger, however, doesn't recede. "What am I supposed to do, then? Let them get away with this?"

"You need to convince them to go to war."

I stare at Avi, the sudden whiplash from the change in direction calming the flame burning within me. "How is that going to help anything? You always said that war is bad."

"My dear child, war is not as simple as we made it out to be in class. It is a complicated thing that starts with two sides. Even though it may not seem like it, there are two sides to this conflict as well. Unfortunately, our side is not big enough to survive without the help of The Net. Roa knows this, which is why they won't attack until they have our help. The humans have shown us their hand, and the only way this war ends is with one side dead."

The room spins around me. This was no longer about killing

Ritter, it was about wiping out an entire species. "I can't do this, Avi."

Avi takes my hand in theirs, their hands finally still with belief in their words. "You don't need to. Let Roa handle the bloodshed. You just need to convince The Net."

"How? How am I going to convince a people so against conflict that they would sacrifice their young to avoid going to war?"

Avi hangs their head. "I don't know the answer to that question. I only know that you must." They look toward the door and back at me quickly. "I must go now. I've stayed too long already. I can't risk them seeing me here; it would only be detrimental to your cause. Please, Ixe, do what you can... for the children."

"I will," I promise Avi, and they nod before silently slipping out the front door.

I sit on the edge of the bed, shock setting in. What the hell am I going to do now? Everything I believe in is upside down, and I have no idea what I am fighting for anymore. I curl up on my side in the bed and think of my options. I'm being forced to incite a war that I don't want, and Roa, Mar, Trix, and the entire Alliance army is depending on me to get more soldiers for them. What does it even get me if we win the war? Freedom?

Members of each species could survive and thrive on the planet together. Rich and I could thrive together...

But then there's Avi and their directive. Eliminate the humans before we are eliminated. They truly believe what they said about the Bots and the returned humans, and I know Ritter will not stop until all other intelligent life is eliminated from this planet. However, I can't use any information they had given me to convince the Council to go to war. How would I convince them of genocide?

With every new angle, I just want to start the day over. I want to believe that I would leave in a few days for a new life in a new city. No war. No Alliance. No humans. No Bots. But then my mind drifts back to Trix and their story. Were the cities really so bad? What would happen to me in a place like that?

I ruminate over the decision ahead of me for hours before finally falling into a fitful sleep.

I wake the next morning still dressed from the day before; my leg still attached and twisted around me. I groan, sitting up and undoing the straps that are digging into my skin. Pulling the leg off, I sigh and reattach it before grabbing a change of clothes. Since this house was meant for Bots, there is no restroom, which meant no shower. I head out of the house and to the nearest rec center, where they would have showers available.

Bots and humans alike walk through the streets, not a line of worry on their faces. If only I could go back to that blissful oblivion, but I know it is too late for me. I grab a quick shower and get dressed, trying to press out the wrinkles with my hands. Eventually deciding it will have to do, I toss my dirty clothes in the nearest laundry and make my way to the Council building on the square.

I don't knock before I enter and find the Council members standing around the room exactly according to plan. I silently walk to the center, and take my seat, patiently waiting for them to recognize me and sit in their own seats. One Bot sees me out of the corner of their eye and I see the rest of them go still as they communicate my presence. As one, they move to their seats.

"I don't think we had a planned meeting today, Ixe," Yun says quietly.

"We didn't, but I've had some time to think, and I have more to say."

"I don't know why we need to repeat this charade. We've already made our decision, and you have made yours. You will be free soon. Why make this harder than it has to be?"

I cringe internally at the way Yun talks down to me. Bri never spoke this way to anyone. I take a deep breath and remember the kids I'm here for. I refuse to let these non-humans control me.

Surprise fills me at my harsh thoughts of the Bots, and I realize just how inhuman they are. How unfeeling they had to be to not retaliate against the invading humans. How inhumane it was for them to give up their young to save themselves. How inhumane to let us die, or worse, get caught by the raiders once we were released from their cities, and it clicks. The only way to get them to act was to put their only objective on the line.

"Your children need your help." I say, emphasizing that these humans are, in fact, their children. "We cannot fight the invaders on our own, and we will be demolished by them if they are left to their own devices."

"We are not interested in war, Ixe. You should know this from your teachings."

"You're right. You aren't interested in war. You are only interested in your objective, and I can tell you they are here to destroy it."

The Bots exchange glances, transmitting data between them before Yun speaks again. "And how did you come to know this?"

"I was there for months. They were digging into my skin, trying to understand what I was. They are here to take Earth back, and they will repopulate it with their own kind."

"What of that goes against our objective?"

"You say that your only objective is to repopulate the Earth with humans, but it's more than that, isn't it? The Phoenix Project was specific in their orders. You were meant to continue the human race, but you were also told to never let humans destroy it again. It's why you genetically castrated us. Why you created The Alliance to keep the humans fighting for something. You realized that taking away our purpose would leave us with no will to live, and you couldn't have that, so you devised another plan, one that gave us hope.

"You will help us, because you know these humans are not desexed and they will continue to reproduce until they destroy what little is left."

I sit silently, picking at my nails and trying to look bored as the Bots converse silently within The Net. A few minutes later, Yun finally speaks, "We have determined that you are correct. The humans staying here on Earth is against our objective, but you do not know everything, child. While our objective is to preserve the Earth and keep humanity in check, there is an overarching objective that we cannot violate. We are not to intentionally harm a human. While we would like to help your cause, we cannot harm the humans who have returned."

My heart sinks at Yun's words. I had been so sure this was the key, that they could help us take down the invaders. Avi had seemed sure that the only way out of this was to kill them. How did they expect us to do that if the Bots couldn't raise a hand against the enemy?

"B...But you can do other things to help." I say, grasping for any way to help the Alliance. "You have a city here. You can host the army while it prepares for attack. You have food that you can provide to the army. You can even use The Net to help communicate between squads during the attack. You *must* be able to help us!"

Yun nods slowly, "We have considered this and will help in any way we can, but know that the Bots you take into this battle will be unable to protect themselves. It will be up to you to protect us this time."

I nod, understanding the trust the Bots would have to place in the soldiers for this to work. The protectors would become the protected.

Yun leans back into their chair. "Now, let us discuss the terms of this arrangement."

I leave the city a few hours later, a new pack on my shoulders, and a new arm and leg attached to my stumps. The polymer fits much better than the metal contraption, and it allows me to walk more naturally, giving the overworked muscles a break. The Bots had already informed me that the soldiers had remained outside of the city, Mar coming to the door multiple times a day demanding to speak to me, so I was prepared to face their wrath when I walked up to the small camp.

"Where the hell have you been!" Mar yells at me, throwing a stick they had been playing with to the ground as they stand up and march toward me. "You were in there for three days!!"

"Believe it or not, Mar, it's difficult to get a civilization against war to sign up for one." I spit at them, filling my voice with the anger at my forced situation.

"Well, did it work?" Trix asks, wringing their hands.

"Eventually, yes." I say, dropping my pack on the ground and taking a seat with the rest of the soldiers. Olli claps me on the back and Trix jumps in the air, whooping with excitement.

"I knew you could do it, Ixe!" Trix yells, glaring at Mar, who had apparently been a naysayer during my absence.

"There are some... terms." I say, hesitantly. "They can't actively participate in the killing of humans, but they will give us a safe place to stay, food for our army, and assist with communicating between the squads during battle. They do not have weapons and will not provide them to us."

"We have all of that covered," Mar says, waving away the terms like they were nothing.

"There is one other thing they want..." I begin, but Mar interrupts me.

"Anything they want, they have, as long as they help us win this war." I nod as Mar and the others celebrate, but I know they will not be happy with the last request.

Despite the cloud hanging over my head, I force a smile, "Let's save it for Roa. It's time to celebrate!"

A cheer goes up from my small army camp, and I wonder what it would be like to command the entire army.

CHAPTER TWENTY-SEVEN
Introductions

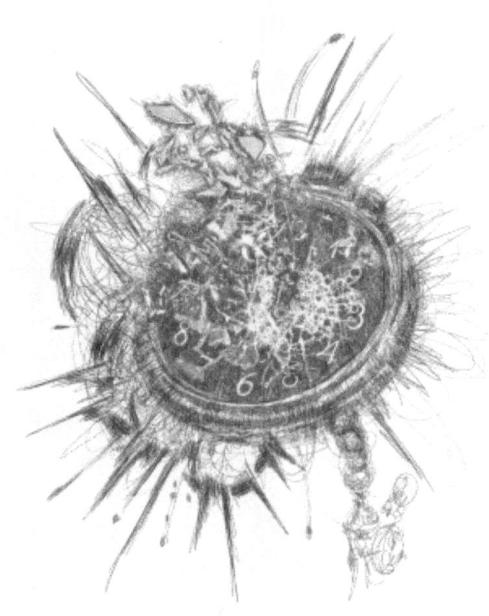

The journey back to camp is uneventful, spirits high as we make our way across the wasteland. We take our time, resting more often and stopping early for the night. Trix and the soldiers accept me back into the group, laughing and joking — telling stories as the nights go on — but Mar remains distant, wary.

As we approach the last rise before camp, Jak comments on the smell of meat roasting over a fire, and our mouths water in anticipation for the feast that was surely awaiting us. We mount the last rise and Mar stops in their tracks, Olli running directly into them. Our laughter fizzles out and we all look curiously at Mar's back. Olli sees the answer before we do, and they drop everything and start running.

The rest of us rush up the hill to see the camp lying in front of us - burning.

The others take off running down the hill toward the camp, even Mar finally snapping into action, as I race to keep up. My stump screams as the fake leg pounds against the hard dirt, throwing up chunks behind me as I run.

Panting as I finally reach the camp, I see bodies lying in the dirt, burned to a crisp as they held up their hands in fear or surrender. I turn and vomit, remembering the smell of cooking flesh that I had been savoring only moments before.

After emptying my stomach, I make my way further into the camp, looking for any survivors. How could this have happened? I study the burn patterns, trying to find where the fire started, but it makes no sense. Sections lie before me, the ground burned to a crisp while next door a perfectly intact tent stands, the fabric moving gently in the wind, untouched by the devastation only feet away.

I pull back the flap of the nearest tent, looking in to find it completely furnished. A bed roll lies on the hard packed dirt, the blankets scattered as if the occupant left in a hurry. I gently pick up a shoe, looking for its companion, only to find scattered letters that had fallen from a small stool in the corner. A chill runs down my spine as I hear distant screaming, and see the occupant throw their blankets to the side, rushing to help those in trouble. They pull on one shoe, but there isn't time for the other, and as they grab their gun from the corner they knock into the stool, scattering paper everywhere.

The vision fades, and I turn, leaving everything where it lay. I walk to the next tent and find more of the same. Everyone left in a hurry. Were they afraid of the fire, or something else?

Trix yells to my left, and I turn, seeing them wave to me in the distance. I jog over, ignoring the pain radiating from my angry stump. "I think they went this way," they say as I approach, pointing to a large path of scuff marks in the dirt.

"What were they running from?" I ask.

Mar runs up to stand next to us, panting. "I ran to the main tent. It's empty. All of Roa's stuff is still there, but there are no people."

The other soldiers come from different directions. "I didn't find any survivors."

"Me either."

I add my own findings to theirs. "They were attacked. We have to follow them. There's no telling how far they made it, or how many are hurt, or worse."

"It had to happen recently. The wraithwolves haven't taken the bodies." Trix points out.

"Would they even want cooked meat, though?" Olli asks, and I feel the bile rise in my throat again.

Mar steps forward, breaking the silence that settles over us. "Ixe is right. We need to find them, and get them to the Bot's camp. There's no telling how many are injured, or worse..." The finality of their words echoes behind them as they walk down the warn path, head down. Trix and I look at each other before following, the other soldiers falling in line.

If we had known then what we would face on this trail, would we have turned back before taking the first steps?

This would be a walk we wouldn't want to remember, and would never be able to forget.

It takes two days to reach the column of soldiers walking into the barren landscape. We pass six partially charred bodies on the way; people who made it out of camp, but suffered burns so severe they couldn't be saved. Most of us had emptied our guts at the first one, disgusted by the partially rotted bodies covered in flies, but by the last we had been deadened to the horror we faced.

The back of the column was composed of those who were injured in the fires; too weak to walk on their own. Some were limping along with help, some were carried, and even more were being pulled along the ground using makeshift litters. The sound of people crying in pain had reached us and tears pooled in my eyes. Even with everything I had been through, I couldn't imagine the pain they were in.

Trix offers words of encouragement as we pass, while Mar simply ignores the injured and asks where Roa is. Eventually discovering that Roa is leading the column, we stop asking and walk through the slow-moving crowd, making our way further up the mass of people.

It takes us another half a day to reach the front, where we find Roa commanding soldiers to move faster.

"But, the injured, they are falling behind." A soldier I don't recognize speaks plainly, the pleading look in their eyes almost too much to bear.

"I don't care. We need to get to safety, and the only way to do that is to make it to Barllay." Roa responds, clipping their words.

"You have another option now," I say, raising my voice for everyone to hear.

Roa stops and turns to stare at me, standing with the group of their soldiers. "You did it?" They ask, disbelief in their voice, but hope reflected in their eyes.

"I did. They will offer you safety in their camp, and will help win the war against the invading humans."

Roa lowers their head, relief plain on their face, and I hesitate, not wanting to break the peace that had settled over them.

The soldier from before steps forward. "What's going on?"

Trix smiles, unable to contain their excitement. "The Bots are going to help us defeat the humans!"

A cheer erupts from those around us and whispers pass down the column followed by a wave of cheers and excited talking. As the people around us perk up, bolstered by the news that we are going to get help, a sinking feeling spreads through me.

"Ixe?" Olli places a hand on my shoulder, and I meet their eyes with my own. A cloud of concern drifts into their brown eyes and I can almost see a dark cloud descend over us, an island of black in the midst of a white sea.

My voice trembles the first time I say Roa's name, my eyes not leaving Olli's, but I clear my throat and try again.

"Roa."

Slowly, as if the world around me has slowed, the crowd notices my demeanor and a circle of calm begins to form around us. Roa turns toward me, concern clear on their face, and it takes everything I have to utter the words that would make or break this deal.

"However," I say, "they have insisted that I lead the combined army to the ship."

Roa's head snaps up, their eyes finally meeting mine, the rage twisting their expression into one of disgust.

"No."

"But Commander..." Trix starts, reaching for Roa's arm.

"I said no!" Roa yells.

The crowd is silent now, watching Roa's storm brew around my small island of calm.

"Don't do this Roa..." I begin. "Your people need help. Don't let your pride lead them to death."

"I will not give you command over *my* army! They are my people, not yours! You didn't even want to be part of the Alliance. I've lived my whole life preparing to lead them, not you!" I see the pain in Roa's eyes as they yell their truth at me. This is all they have lived for. This is what Bri created them for. This is their only purpose, and the Bots had given it to them.

Even with everything they had done, everything they were trying to do, they would never be free of the Bots' assignment.

"I'm sorry, Roa. For everything The Net — Bri — did to you."

Tears spring to their eyes, but they don't say a word. Turning on their heel, they begin to walk away. The soldiers watch them walk for a time, turning back to my small group one last time before continuing their slow trudge after Roa.

I stand still in the flood of soldiers moving around me, watching as my first task simply walks away from me. Mar shakes their head slowly, disappointed, before turning and jogging after Roa.

Trix stares at me, mouth agape. "Why? Why didn't you tell us?"

I don't have an answer for them, not a good one at least.

"How do you think Mar would have reacted, Trix?" Olli says, stepping between us. "You know as well as I that they would have lost it on the march here. Ixe made the right choice."

A warmth swells in me as Olli stands up for me. If I can convince one soldier to turn the tide and join me, perhaps there is a chance after all.

"Listen up!" I yell over the sound of the marching army, but besides a few glances my way, there is no sign that I spoke at all.

Defeat settles over me again, and I lower my head before a finger under my chin raises it back up. Trix stands in front of me, a small smile trying to hide the fear reflected in their eyes. "I've followed Roa for a long time now... Don't make me regret this decision."

I can only nod as they turn, place their fingers in the corners of their mouth, and whistle.

The force of the army slowly stops and turns to listen.

My palm sweats and I clench my fist, stopping the urge to wipe it off on my pants. This is my chance. This is my only hope — the only hope for hundreds of people who will call me Commander. I swallow the lump in my throat and raise my voice.

"The Bots are offering aid in this war. They will help us fight the invaders and take our lands back. I know they have not been kind to you in the past. I know things have to change, but this is the first step toward that change. If we let these humans take our lands, they will out-breed us and outnumber us. They will not stop until the last of our kind lays dead at their feet, or worse..." I hold up my arm, displaying the fake arm for all to see. "Follow me and have shelter, food, and medical care. We rest... and then we fight!!"

A roar erupts from the surrounding soldiers, and whispers spread through the column again, the hope renewed spreading my message to those unable to hear. A few soldiers shake their heads and continue to follow Roa down the dusty path to Barllay, but most of the column turns toward me expectantly. I look to Trix, who smiles, the fear dampened for now, and points the way to the Bots' camp. We turn, Olli at our side, and walk toward our new home.

The army follows.

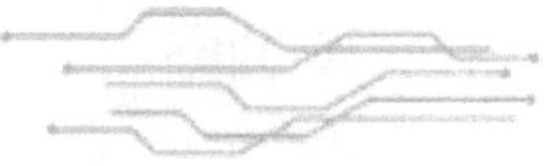

Trix and I met with the captains of the army over the next few hours. They were young kids Roa seemed to choose based on popularity rather than any experience. We had learned that the humans had attacked the camp with drones that could shoot fire. It had happened in the middle of the night, ensuring the most damage to the army. They had run for their lives, chaotically leaving the camp and meeting back up with the main column of soldiers later on. Anyone who had not reported into their next in command was assumed dead.

I rub my eyes, sitting on a rock as the column of soldiers walks by, when the next captain approaches. "Commander." They say, standing at attention. This one is older, maybe 30, with salt and pepper hair cropped close to their head.

"What is your name, soldier?" I ask, exhausted from the constant flow of captains out of the mass of soldiers passing me by.

"Arix, Commander."

I nod. "Captain Arix. I'd like your council on our next steps." I had asked the same question of all the captains, and they had either given a deferential response or told me we should return to Roa.

Arix hesitates, their shoulders dipping, before straightening back up and saying, "I think we need to send a delegation back to the burned camp, Commander."

I slowly raise my head, taking in more of the Captain in front of me. They stand a head taller than me, tan skin from being in the sun for long periods, and scars, so many scars. They run down the soldier's arms and legs, with an especially gruesome gash across their face, directly through their right eye.

"How long have you been part of this army, Captain?"

"Less than a year, Commander."

"And you rose to captain in less than a year?" Intrigue fills me.

"Yes, Commander."

"How did you come by your scars?" I ask, standing.

The Captain swallows, but speaks calmly. "I was a raider, Commander. Before Roa found me. I got these scars during raids conducted on human cities."

I nod slowly, the admiration at their quick ascension dampened slightly by the admission of being a raider. "Why did you stop raiding?"

"Raiding was never my goal. The raiders captured me on the way to my assigned human city. They gave me two options; serve the raiders or be slaughtered. It wasn't much of a choice, really."

"And how long were you with the raiders?" I ask.

"Twelve years, Commander."

Twelve years. So they were 32. Still young for a captain in an army, but not as inexperienced as the others I had met so far. "Why do you wish to return to the burned camp?"

Arix balks at this, expecting a different question. "Commander? You aren't going to dismiss me?"

"Why would I do that? You are the most experienced Captain I have." Trix had advised me to dismiss those who wanted to return to Roa's side, but I had disagreed. Dismissing them would only cause dissension among their direct reports, and that was the last thing we needed right now.

"B-because I was a raider. I killed innocent people."

"Roa seemed to see something in you, and you didn't choose the raiding life. You said so yourself."

"Roa was... I mean, Commander Roa..."

"Captain, you don't have to explain anything to me or anyone else in this army. Your past is yours, and you spoke it truthfully. That is all I need to know to make my decision, and my decision is that you stay and fight for us; with us."

"Y-yes, Commander."

"Now, back to my question. Why do you wish to return to the camp?"

"Our weapons, Commander. We won't be able to fight the humans without our guns, and we had to abandon them when we ran. We need those weapons to win this war."

I walk beyond the Captain and stare at the mass of people slowly making their way through the wasteland. I ponder the Captain's words and come to the conclusion that they speak truth.

We need those weapons, but we couldn't turn the entire column around.

"How many would you need?"

"Commander?"

"How many soldiers would you need in order to carry the weapon stash to the Bot camp?"

"Two Companies should do the trick, Commander."

"I want you to pick the two you trust the most, and meet me at the back of the army in two hours. We will march from there."

"Yes, Commander." They salute and turn on their heel, but not before I see the smile spread on their face.

I wait for Trix to return with the next Captain in tow, and explain the plan as we wait for the approaching end to the column of soldiers. They agree until I mention my plan to accompany Captain Arix to the previous camp.

"You can't leave the army." Trix says incredulously.

"Why not?" I ask.

"Because they need to see the Commander here. You are their hero, their motivation to keep moving forward."

"I've been sitting on this rock all day, Trix, and not one soldier has noticed."

"But, Commander..."

"My name is Ixe." I say, frustration at the new title bubbling to the surface.

"Ixe..." Trix says, drawing out the name in equal annoyance, "you cannot just abandon the army to go play hero. The Captains know what they are doing, let them do it."

I scoff. "The *Captains* are children!"

"And so are you!!"

I stop and stare at Trix, realizing they're right. Who am I to say if these soldiers are qualified enough to run an army, when I'm only 20 years old with no experience to my name? Except for being tortured for months on end, I had never been in battle.

But the Bots had entrusted me with the care of these people, and Roa had run at the first sign of defiance. "These are my people now. Whether I like it or not; whether or not *they* like it. They have entrusted me with their care, and I will not send them to face whatever lies at that camp alone. End of discussion."

Trix glares at me for a moment, but eventually their face calms and they nod, "As you say, Commander."

CHAPTER TWENTY-EIGHT
Crossroads

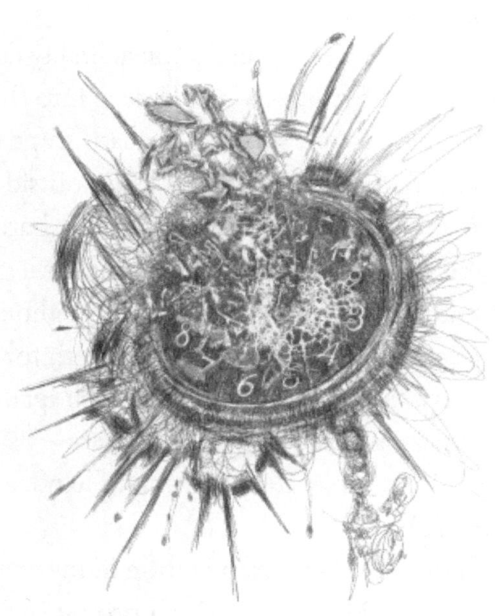

An hour later, I'm standing with Captain Arix and their soldiers, watching the mass of the army move on without us.

"Commander."

I turn to Arix, nodding to the group of soldiers behind them. "Are these the soldiers you wanted?"

"Yes, Commander. Captain Yuri was hurt in the battle, so I've been leading both of our companies in their stead."

I nod and glance at the retreating army one last time before sighing and turning back to my much smaller force. "Let's be on our way, then. You lead, Captain."

Captain Arix salutes and turns to the group. "We march for the burned camp. Navigators!" Two older humans stand to attention. "Lead on." They nod and we are off.

Marching with the Companies is considerably faster, and we make good time on the first day. We walk deep into the night, letting the moon's light guide us across the barren landscape before we come to a copse of trees. Without a word, we all stop outside of the tree line and try to make ourselves comfortable on the hard dirt.

I keep my tent in my pack, choosing to lie under the stars with the rest of the soldiers. We make small fires throughout the temporary camp, giving enough light and warmth for the entire group. The conversation is lively, and I lean back against my pack, watching the soldiers interact with one another.

After some time, Arix walks over, cup in hand, and sits next to me. "Commander."

"Please call me Ixe." I say, exasperation in my voice.

Arix's eyebrows raise, but they don't protest against the command. "You're newly Released."

It's a statement, not a question, but I answer anyway. "I am. How did you know?"

"Your accent still resembles the voice patterns of the Bots. It will fade with time."

I nod, not knowing what they mean, but not caring to object. "Arix, how many humans are there?"

Arix shrugs, "The feeder cities don't really release stats on how many humans they produce, but let's say they produce 300 kids per year per city. That would be... 20,000 kids per city. Given a world in which we live to be elders, that's approximately 200,000 humans?"

My mouth agape, I stare at Arix.

Arix shrugs, "I was good at math. I was on my way to be a mathematician in a large human city when...."

I place my hand on their shoulder. "It's okay, Arix. You don't have to talk about it."

Arix gives me a sheepish grin and thanks me. "When Roa captured me, they made me tell them everything about the raiders repeatedly. It was hell. Reliving what I had done, over and over again... But at the end of the day, it made me realize how much I wanted out of that lifestyle, and how Roa was my only chance."

"I didn't realize they had influenced so many." I say, my tone reflecting how I truly felt about Roa's tactics.

"Oh, don't get me wrong," Arix laughs. "Roa is a tube, but they are a tube that cares what happens to the human race. They truly want to fix what the Bots have done to us. Give us a purpose again."

I think about everything I had learned while camping with the Alliance. Whispers of how life was in the cities had floated around, but no one would speak about it directly. Would Arix be willing to share, knowing everything they had seen? There was only one way to find out. "Is it really that bad, living in a human city?"

Their eyes go dark as they think of the cities. "It is. The 1% of aristocrats rule the 99%. They go into the slums once a year to pick a human to add to their staff. If you do well on their staff, and prove yourself, you have the opportunity to be promoted, eventually being accepted into the 'family' and granted a part of their wealth. The problem is, it's all luck based, and they use it to keep the slums in line and producing the things they need. Everyone keeps toiling away, hoping that one day they will be chosen by the mansion owners and given a slice of heaven. They can't see anything else worth living for."

I pick up a stick and start dragging it through the dirt in front of me, pondering what Arix had said. "So, you think that being able to reproduce, to have a family, will give people hope where none exists today? Do you really think that will fix all the problems?"

Arix scoffs. "No, not by a long shot. But giving people something to achieve will get us moving in the right direction. Right now, everyone is just surviving until they die. What's the point of fighting if they don't have anyone or anything to fight for?"

Silence stretches between us, and I hear laughter from those gathered around a nearby campfire. Could this life, fighting in this army, truly be better than living under an aristocracy? More than that, would we just be adding the inability to care for the next generation to the list of problems?

Right now, the Bots ensured that the children were well cared for, raised in clean homes, and given all the proper nutrition and schooling for them to grow. I still couldn't see anything wrong with how I was raised, yet the more I think about it, the more I realize that I side with the Alliance on reproductive rights.

Perhaps the Net missed a part of our genetic programming when they sliced it to shreds. Perhaps the drive to reproduce, to have that unique connection with another human being, was stored somewhere they couldn't reach.

"I suppose you're right. That's why these people joined the army after all; to fight for something that they don't currently have. But at the end of the day, even if you win this war against the Bots, nothing will change for you. You're already sterile. So why do it at all?"

They look out at the soldiers laughing, dancing, enjoying their time even amid the turmoil they called a life, and smile. "For the future generations. These soldiers, this army, we all have one thing in common; we put the lives of others before ourselves. The humans in the cities only care about themselves. We want to give life to those who come after us."

I watch the soldiers before us and see the way they enjoy the small moments in their lives, and I see what they are living for. To give the future generations a chance to live happy lives.

To restore what was taken from us.

Three days later, we stand at the edge of the burned camp, not wanting to step inside the ring of tents that separated us from the burned bodies inside.

Captain Arix turns toward the soldiers. "I know this isn't easy, and I know you didn't ask for it, but we need these weapons to win this war or entire cities will go up in flames just as this camp did. Move quickly and quietly. Report back in half time."

The squads quickly move into the camp, using hand signals only they know to communicate as they spread out.

"You don't have to come..." Arix starts, but I cut them off by raising my hand, and slowly make my way into the camp. Arix follows with the final squad and we carefully pick our way through the wrecked tents, no bodies in sight.

"I guess they like cooked meat after all..." I mumble under my breath.

"What?" A soldier asks.

"Nothing," I say, shaking the images of the wraithwolves carrying away the dead from my mind.

We march toward the last known location of an armory tent, keeping an eye out for anything useful left among the piles of debris along the way. A soldier reaches the tent with the red 'X' first, thankfully in an area that is not charred, and the rest of the squad fans out, gathering tents and supplies from the surrounding area.

"Captain." The soldier says, sticking their head back out of the tent.

"What's wrong, soldier?"

"The guns... They're gone."

We all freeze. Wraithwolves wouldn't take guns.

A blast of gunfire breaks out further into the camp and Arix immediately takes control. "Trev, take five and protect the Commander. Everyone else on me!" A group of seven soldiers takes up positions between me and the gunfire, while the rest of the squad move with Arix toward the sound of battle.

Cursing under my breath, I take a few steps backwards, directly into the chest of someone behind me. A blade appears at my throat, digging into my flesh, and a flash of Leah, scalpel in hand, burns in my vision before a familiar voice speaks. "So, you're the Commander of the army? What happened to sweet Roa?" The soldiers in front of me spin and train their guns at the head of the person now holding me. "Now, now, don't do anything stupid. Wouldn't want your commander to lose their head now, would you?"

I raise my hand, and my soldiers stand down. An unfamiliar thrill runs through me as they obey without objection.

"What do you want, Kei?" Trev asks.

Kei? I knew that name...

"I want what I always want, Trev, *more.*" Kei's voice rings through my ears and it clicks into place.

"Kei? As in the same Kei who helped at the nursery?" I ask.

The hands around me tighten their grip. "How do you know about that?" Kei hisses through their teeth.

"It's me," I say, trying to pull away from the knife at my throat, "Ixe. Loc and I learned how to care for the babies from you. Let me go, we can talk."

"I'm a different person now, Ixe. I don't help care for babies anymore." Their voice is hard, hissing as they spit out the word 'babies'.

"You used to be so different, so soft." I say, unable to contain my curiosity despite the situation. "What changed you?"

"It's a different world out here. You wouldn't understand."

The soldiers in front of me shuffle their feet, their eyes glazing over as their own haunted memories resurface.

"I understand more than you think." I say, holding up my stump.

"Which clan did that to you? It's not our work."

"Clan?" I ask

Another soldier responds, "It wasn't the raiders, Kei, it was the humans."

Kei laughs, "What humans?"

"The ones on the ship," I say, "You must have seen it land."

"We did, but they haven't bothered us any." They pause for half a beat before continuing, "Why should I believe you?"

"Because they did this," I say, motioning to the destruction before us. "They burned the camp with drones and drove the army out."

"Good for them. We got quite a bit of loot from this camp."

"Kei," I say, exasperation in my voice, "you don't understand. They are trying to wipe us out, you included."

"Why? I've got no beef with these humans. We stay away from their ship."

"They believe us to be abominations and are on a path of extermination. I'm taking the army to the Bots, who have agreed to help us fight them."

Kei is quiet for a moment. "Roa is going to team up with the Bots?"

"Roa chose to abandon the army." The knife nicks my skin, but I ignore it. "I'm now leading the ones who want to fight. Join us, Kei." I plead.

The gunshots still ring in the distance as Kei's army fights mine, and I know I'm running out of time.

Kei's hand slowly lowers, the knife finally leaving my throat. I feel a bead of blood drip onto my shirt, and resist the urge to wipe it from my skin. Turning, I face Kei, taking a step back as I come face to face with a monster. Scar tissue completely transforms their face, with no nose and a perpetual snarl on their mouth, they look like a nightmare come to life. As they turn their head, I see they're missing an ear and their eyes bulge grotesquely from their face.

"Kei..." I breathe.

Kei growls and turns away from me. "This does not mean we are friends. We're temporary partners, that's all." They stomp away from me, heading straight for the sound of decreasing gunfire in the distance.

We arrive at the site of bloodshed and Kei walks right down the middle of the battlefield, stepping over dead bodies like they are a minor inconvenience, holding up both hands. The gunfire stops as Kei's people stand up and march to their side, not caring that my army is still hidden and capable of taking them out. I see Arix motion for our troops to stand down, and they slowly come out of hiding, marching to my side.

"How did you get Kei to stand down?" Arix whispers to me, astonishment in their eyes.

I shrug. "I just told them the truth."

We both turn and look at the raiders as Kei speaks. "We are in a new battle now, the battle for our existence. You all have seen the ship that came down months ago. We've all considered a raid against it in our wildest dreams. Well, now that dream is a reality. We walk with the Alliance to meet up with the Bots, and then we take that ship down."

No one objects to Kei's orders, but no one cheers either. They stare at their leader with bored expressions, not even noticing the fallen comrades they stand over.

I turn to Arix. "Captain, we need a squad to get the injured up and moving, or to create litters for those who cannot walk. Round up the rest of the squads, get every gun we can find, and meet me back at the edge of the camp. We leave before dark." Arix nods and begins issuing orders. "Kei!" I yell.

Kei begrudgingly walks to me. "Yes, Commander?" They slur the title, just as bored as their soldiers.

"We need the guns you stole from this camp. Get your equipment and get the raiders to the edge of camp. We leave before dark."

After everyone has moved, I find a large tent still standing and make my way inside. I fall to my knees, my body shaking uncontrollably, heat radiating from my skin. Flashes of death swarm my vision; Leah in my room, Loc in the hall, Rich stepping over soldiers as we run through a maze of corridors. Then the soldiers I had just lead to their death here. It was supposed to be a simple mission. It was supposed to be easy.

Breaking out in a sweat, I empty my stomach repeatedly, the bile splattering against the cot in the corner. The smell of blood from the battlefield refuses to leave my nose as tears pour from my eyes. So many lives lost because of my orders to come to this camp.

I think back to the night before, soldiers dancing and laughing around the fires. Soldiers that were now dead, their blood spilled on the dry earth among the tents surrounding us. Soldiers that would lay there until the wraithwolves came to drag them away, tearing their bodies apart. I heave again before standing and wiping my face on a spare cloth in the tent, ridding myself of any sign of weakness.

Standing straight, I take a few deep breaths before turning and leaving the tent, my face calm despite the storm that rages inside.

CHAPTER TWENTY-NINE
An Old Friend

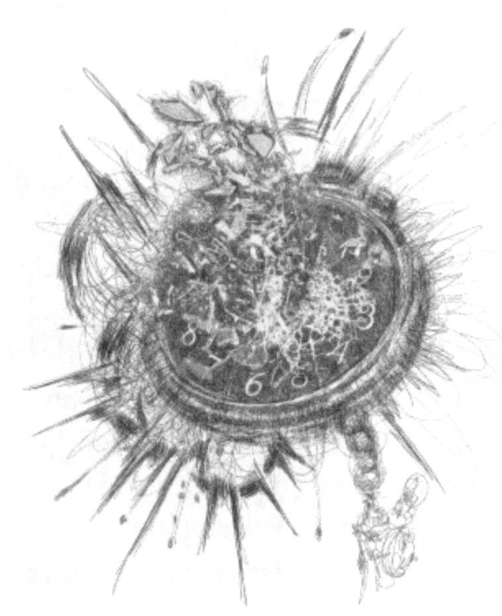

The first few nights after the raiders join us are a struggle. For the Alliance, there is no celebration of victory after the battle, only mourning for the soldiers that are lost. The raiders, however, have their own idea of grieving their loss. They set up their tents away from my sleeping soldiers that first night, building their own fires and cracking open casks of alcohol. The stark difference between our side of the camp and theirs is clear to see. We attempt to sleep through the revelry as they party, dance, and fuck long into the night; toasting the soldiers lost in battle and wishing them well before downing copious amounts of alcohol.

The next day my soldiers drag behind, exhaustion clear on their faces, while Kei's soldiers are merry and march without complaint. I turn to Arix and Kei as we walk. "Why do your soldiers act so differently?"

Kei smiles and nods to Arix, who rolls their eyes before explaining, "Raiders live for the fight. They will be living off of the high from our battle for days to come."

Kei continues, "The Alliance, however, wants peace at the end of the day, and only fights when it's necessary. They will be a broody lot for a while yet."

I observe the troops each night until the fourth evening. Watching the depressed movement of the Alliance compared to the jovial party of the raiders, I ponder the situation. Finally getting to my feet, I walk over to where the dividing line is, stepping across it. I pick up a bottle and chug it without further thought. The alcohol burns like fire as it slides down my throat, but I keep my composure as I set the bottle down and turn to my soldiers.

They all stare at me, mouth agape. I patiently wait, meeting their eyes one at a time until Arix stands up and walks toward me. By now, the raiders have spotted us on their side of the line, and are watching curiously. Arix smiles at me, nodding their approval before they duck into one of the brothel tents.

Now left with no command, the Alliance soldiers share glances before slowly get to their feet, and walk to the line. The raiders behind me whoop and cheer, running forward to grab hands pulling my soldiers into the party.

The next day, most of the soldiers walk intermingled, chatting and laughing with each other. Lines between the armies now blur and Arix and Kei walk with me at the front, smiling their approval.

We catch up to the column of soldiers marching across the barren wasteland two days later. Runners quickly notice us on the horizon and Trix is waiting for me at the back of the column as we walk up, Olli by their side.

"Ixe!" they say, relief apparent on their face melting to confusion as they see Kei at my side.

I nod to them, making a show of formality. "Trix. Report."

Trix gets the hint and stands at attention before reporting out the status of the army and any relevant events. "...we lost another soldier last night, but it was the only one since you left," they finish.

"Thank you. This is Kei and their army of raiders." An eyebrow raises, but Trix remains silent. "They will be joining us in the fight."

They slowly nod at Kei, but I see their eyes avert away from the horror that is Kei's face. Kei's jaw clenches in response and I wonder how tiring it must be to deal with the looks and whispers. I had dealt with my fair share of staring eyes, walking around with Bot made equipment to replace what I had lost when those around me had nothing but scraps to heal their wounds.

I fumble with the straps that hold my arm in place as I give my next order. "We need to incorporate them into our camp and start sending them out on patrols. They are to be regarded as a new company and treated with respect, despite any history they may have with our soldiers. We are all one army now. Kei will retain command over them as their captain." I turn to Arix. "Arix, I'm putting you in charge of getting Kei up to speed with the other captains."

"Yes, Commander." Arix salutes and leads Kei and their army

further into the mass of soldiers moving at a snail's pace before us. Arix's companies take this as a dismissal and make their way forward into the mass of people as well, stopping to say hello to those they had left behind a week ago.

Trix and I slow our pace, letting the column move further ahead. I lower my head and say softly, "You were right."

"What?" Trix asks, unable to hear my whisper.

I raise my head and face them. "You were right. I had no business going on the expedition. I almost got myself killed and was a distraction when our soldiers were dying."

Trix nods slowly, accepting my unspoken apology, but not gloating. "Did you at least learn something?" They ask.

I sigh, nodding my head. "I learned that I'm not the right person to lead this army. It should be you, Trix."

Trix stops walking, letting the army pull further ahead. I stumble slightly, the movement of my fake leg trying to continue on despite my will to stop it.

"You went to get weapons that were left behind when *Roa's* army panicked and ran. *Roa's* army left behind dying people to flee faster. *Roa's* army abandoned the cause when times got tough.

"*Your* army has spent days marching without the supplies they used to rely on to get to a place where they can fight for our people. *Your* army sent squads to retrieve the necessary supplies for us to win this war. *Your* army fought off a band of raiders to get those supplies, and then convinced those same raiders to join the cause. *Your* army ensured that it slowed down enough to let the dying survive another day, another week, perhaps another year.

"I lead with Roa, and I'm telling you now, this is *your* army. No one else's."

Tears threaten to blind me as I pull Trix into a hug, thankful to have a friend who trusts in me enough to put their life, and the lives of their people, into my hands.

It takes another two days to make it back to the Bots. The column moves slowly, the trailing injured slowing us down. My first decree was that no one be left behind, even if they are on death's door. We lose one more in our travels, but most survive, thanking us for hanging on. My second decree comes as we are at the gates of the camp: the injured enter first.

Bots rush to meet us as we carry our burned to the gates. They take over for the exhausted soldiers, carrying the injured to the hospital. Quickly overrun, they set up an additional field hospital in a warehouse nearby. Yun finds me there, checking on each patient.

"You care for these people, even if they are not yours?" Yun asks.

"They are people. They deserve to be cared for, especially in their darkest moments." I make my way to the next bed and find Leah unconscious. Placing my hand on their unburned shoulder, I notice that most of their other arm had rotted from the burns and would have to be amputated.

Closing my eyes, I remember when they had gave me my first leg, so proud of their creation. I had hated that leg, and thrown it to the side as soon as the Bots had given me another. Sighing, I wish I had it again, to show them how much that gesture had meant to me. I open my eyes and force myself to look at them, hoping they will be able to create an arm for themself as they had created a leg for me. Many people would need their services soon enough.

"Where is Roa?" Yun asks.

I turn to them. "They decided to not come. Your request did not sit well with them."

"Yet all these people came. They followed you?"

I nod, not willing to go into details on my speech and the

ensuing split of the army with Yun. Despite everything, or maybe because of everything, I didn't trust them. This alliance between us was a means to an end, and I would be done with them the moment the war was over.

"Good. We have started building housing on the Eastern side of the city, outside of the walls. That is where your army will stay. They will be welcomed into the city freely and given supplies they require."

I turn to face the Bot. "Thank you, Yun."

I relay the information to Trix, who I've designated as my second in command, and they spread the news through the army. Tired, weary soldiers make their way to the new camp, grateful to have housing after spending days on the plains without shelter. I continue my rounds, ensuring that all the injured receive care before heading to the camp myself.

As I pass by Bots going about their duties, they pause and bow their heads. Bots who had chastised me as a child, now giving reverence for my command over the army — their army. The children in the city watch me with curiosity in their eyes. Even though I was slightly older than my Release day, they had never seen someone who had left return, and I had returned scarred and broken. That would instill fear in them about their own Release Day, but that was not my concern.

I exit the gates of the city and find the camp designated for us. Trix walks over from one of the houses and smiles at me. "Commander, I have your house ready right over here. I made sure no one else would claim it as their own."

"Are there enough houses for everyone?"

"I'm afraid not," Trix says. "The Bots are building as quickly as they can, but we will have to have at least four soldiers to a house."

"Then give mine to soldiers who need it, Trix."

"But Commander..."

"I can sleep in my tent. I don't need a house. And stop calling me Commander."

"It gives the soldiers confidence in you, Comm... Ixe."

I raise my eyebrows at them, and they sigh, giving in to my request. I lay my pack against the wall and pull out my tent.

"At least let me help you pitch your tent," Trix says. I nod, handing them one corner of the crumpled tent.

"It's just like old times..." I say, thinking about how we had done this so many times on the first trip to see the Bots.

Trix laughs. "Old times were just last week."

I think about all we had been through in just a week and chuckle along with Trix, but the joy doesn't reach my tired eyes.

As Rich liked to say, laughter is the best medicine.

The first order of business the following morning is to check on the injured. I pull on my leg and meet Trix at the gate to the city.

"Where's Arix?" I ask them.

"Dealing with a platoon of idiots." Kei says, coming up from behind me. "I swear, you settle for one night and someone has to make a fool of themselves."

"Do I need to..."

Trix shakes their head, "No, Arix has it under control. You are needed at the hospital."

I nod and we make our way to the nearest field hospital, located in an abandoned warehouse. Trix holds the door open as I enter, and I'm immediately hit with the aroma of decaying flesh, the moans of the dying, and the noise of Bots and humans moving quickly, trying to care for so many.

Covering my mouth, with my hand, I slowly walk further into the room. There are no windows to open, and the air conditioning isn't enough to keep up with so many bodies, so the stench settles in the stale air, making it almost impossible to breathe.

I hear Trix take in a gasping breath, but Kei walks in unfazed.

A Bot approaches us, gently placing masks in each of our hands, before carrying on with their tasks. A sweet scent fills my nose as I place the mask over my face, and my eyes widen in surprise. I see the same surprise reflected in my companions' faces, but we don't say anything, instead moving into the crowd.

The cacophony is overwhelming, and Bots and humans alike brush against us as we weave through the crowd. We pass a patient whose face is twisted into a scream of pain, but no sound emerges. Another sobs as their dressings are changed, and yet another is unconscious as the Bots rotate them to prevent bed sores.

Everywhere I look there is more pain, more despair, and I'm not sure why I'm even here. What could I do for these people? Other than remind them of their misery.

I turn to Trix, "I don't…" I begin, but a Bot approaches before I can finish.

"What *are* you doing here?!" They say, their mechanical voice laced with disdain.

"The Commander wanted to…"

"I don't *care* what Ixe wanted. This is not a place to parade around pretending to be in charge. This is a hospital. For sick people, and we don't have time to deal with your gawking."

Kei steps forward at my side, but I hold up my arm, stopping them. "We were just leaving." I say simply, and turn away.

"A waste of time, I swear…" I hear the Bot say as we walk away.

Once we are back outside, I rip the mask from my face and throw it to the ground. "What was the point of that?!" I ask, my frustration getting the better of me.

"You need to…"

"Need to what?! See my army dying in front of me? I can't help those people!"

Kei lays a hand on my shoulder, and I force myself to look into their gruesome eyes. "A commander needs to see their entire army —

at their best and their worst. An army needs to see their commander, but only at their best. Do not let your worst get the better of you, Ixe."

I stare at them, stunned. I had never seen Kei so serious about anything, even when it came to their army. "I..."

A shadow passes over their eyes, "I've seen my fair share of wounds, Ixe. I'm here to tell you, that while it seems futile, a commander's presence can make a difference in the dance with death. You need to give your soldiers their best chance, even if it tarnishes your soul in the process. It is the burden we carry."

I swear I see tears forming in their eyes, but they turn away and I convince myself that it was just an illusion. Kei wouldn't cry, not for anyone or anything.

Trix takes my arm, "Let's go, Ixe. We have quite a few hospitals to visit today."

The day was long, the wounds gruesome, the cries burned into my memory. We saw three people die that day. I had held one's hand as they passed, and it was the closest I had ever been to death. Watching the light go out in their eyes had left me hollow, and I wasn't sure I could continue.

Yet, here I was, standing at the last hospital, the actual hospital this time, psyching myself up for what would be the worst of the cases.

Opening the door, I hold my head up and walk in, the chaos absorbing my presence instantly. The smell was better here, more antiseptic than rot, and most of the patients were calm, resting after long surgeries or lying in medical comas.

The plan was to work in a tiered fashion. Put those with the most severe wounds combined with the best chance for survival at the top of the list. They were moved to the hospital, prepped for surgery, and kept there until well enough to be transferred to a field hospital. The ones who had no chance were given medication to help ease their passing. While those in the middle were kept on minimal pain medication in order to ration the remaining supply.

They were the unknown group. The ones that could go either way, and I had to smile to their faces, reassuring them that it wouldn't be long, knowing in my mind that it was technically true — it wouldn't be long, but it could be a hospital or death that they faced.

"The main surgeon should be here somewhere..." Trix says, looking through the crowd.

I join them, trying to pinpoint if anyone could be in charge, when I saw them. They stood at the other end of the hall, their back to me, directing Bots and humans alike. I push my way through the crowd, making slow progress toward the human doctor. I'm surprised that they are human, expecting the Bots to be operating with full control. They must have come from outside the city, as The Net would surely not let an underage surgeon be in charge.

My suspicions are confirmed as I step up behind them and clear my throat. "Excuse me..." I begin.

They turn to face me, a tired expression on their face that suddenly breaks into a smile. "Ixe!" They say, quickly wrapping their arms around me.

I stand there, too stunned to hug them back. "Uhhh, do I know you?" I ask, trying to back out of their grasp.

"Of course you do!" The respond, finally pulling back, but keeping a grip on my shoulders. "It's Kit!"

I look at the human in front of me, and survey the lines of their face, their hair, their voice. "It can't be..."

"I know. I look a lot different from the last time you saw me, but I promise, it's me."

My heart sinks as I realize it really is Kit. All of my nightmares come flooding back to me, and my head spins.

"You should sit down," Kit says, pulling a chair from the hands of a bypassing Bot and pushing me into it.

"How...?" I ask, the room spinning around me.

"Well, after you were taken, everything changed. Mar helped Loc find me, and we both signed up with the Alliance right away. Loc knew we had to do whatever it took to get you back."

"But Loc..."

"I know, Ixe. I know. It wasn't your fault. They knew the risks when they entered the ship. We said our goodbyes that morning, just in case..." Kit's eyes fill with tears and I feel the sadness reflect in my own.

"I tried..." I begin, but my voice cracks and I can't finish the lie. What had I really done to save Loc? *Nothing.* I could tell myself that I had no choice, that Rich would have taken me out of that ship kicking and screaming. Hell, he practically had. The truth was I had abandoned them in that hallway to die, to bleed out alone, and I had to face the consequences. "I didn't try, Kit... I left them behind. It's all my fault."

"Ixe..."

"No! Listen!" The ward goes quiet, the Bots turning as one to see what the commotion is. "They came to save me, and they did. They got me out of my cell, but then... A soldier caught us. I heard the gun go off and Loc... they bled so much, Kit... I tried to stop the blood, I did, I just..."

Kit wraps me in their arms, squeezing me to their chest, and I feel like I'm going to collapse into myself. Sobs wrack my body, and I feel Kit's choking sobs as they hold me close.

A dam breaks in my chest, and I can't finish my story, not in words. We stay like that for what feels like hours, and when we part, faces red, the ward is empty of non-essential personnel.

Kit wipes my eyes with a gentle hand, and pulls up a chair. "I think we both needed that more than we were willing to admit. Now

Ixe, tell me what happened. Tell me how they died, so that we can both be at peace."

As I replay the scene in my head, the words leaving my mouth and building a picture for the both of us, I feel a knot in my chest begin to loosen, and I realize just how much I had been holding in.

We spend the evening reminiscing, retelling old stories of Loc, praising them for their bravery, and when I finally find my way back to my tent I collapse from exhaustion and sleep without nightmares for the first time in almost a year.

CHAPTER THIRTY
Preparation

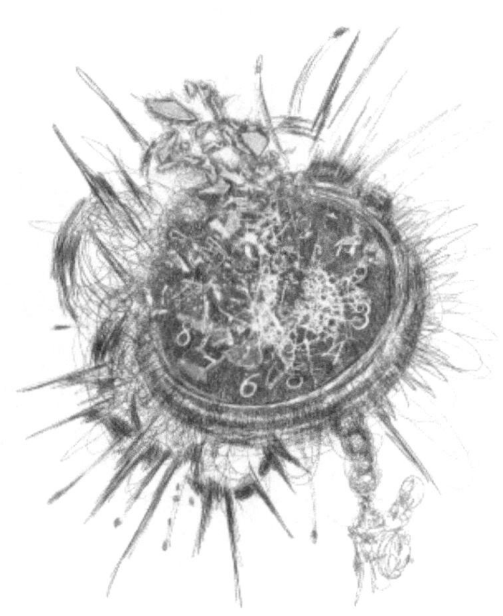

I spend the next two weeks alternating between the field hospitals and the Council building. After another day of arguing over placement of soldiers and angles of attack, I trudge my way to one of the hospitals on the outer rim of the city. Trix meets me along the way, cheery as usual. I can barely look at their smiling face after staring at the Bots' unfeeling metal chassis for hours on end.

"Report." I ask, exhausted before they even tell me what is going on at camp.

"A few fights here and there, but no major injuries today. The last soldiers have now been housed, so we shouldn't have to rotate anyone to sleep outside tonight. However, we do still have some issues with spacing in the houses."

"And the orgies?" I ask, not wanting to, but needing to know every aspect of my camp.

"We have limited them to the Northern side of camp. There are three houses there that will serve as brothels, with permanent residents who wish to serve their duty in that capacity."

"And no one was forced into this role?"

"Of course not. We asked for volunteers and had to turn away quite a few."

What I had learned about my species these past few weeks was that they had a large libido, and when there wasn't much to do but wait... "What about our rations?"

"We have enough to last us another week, not including the rations we will need for the march. Speaking of the march..."

I shake my head before they can ask the question. "No, we still don't have a date. I'm going to the hospital now to evaluate how many soldiers will heal in time."

The Bots had been pushing for the injured to remain here, but I knew we wouldn't have enough soldiers to take the ship without them. Hell, even with them, I didn't think we would succeed, but I couldn't bring myself to tell them the truth of the matter.

Reaching the hospital doors, I turn to Trix. "I want everyone to get a double ration of wine tonight. Give them something to celebrate without getting them so drunk they will start fighting again."

"Yes, Commander." Trix responds and turns, skipping back to camp.

"I'm not your Commander!" I yell at their back. They turn and wink at me and I smile as I head into the hospital. The smell of antiseptic hits me first. I nod at the Bots caring for my soldiers as I make my way to the field doctor.

"Kit!" I yell, still making my way to their side.

They look up at me, dark circles around their eyes as they relay information to a Bot standing nearby before making their way my direction.

"How are the patients?" I ask, clasping their hand in my own as a greeting.

"As well as can be expected. We didn't lose anyone last night, but Tophic is not doing the best..."

I lower my voice to a whisper. "Is there anything we can do?"

"I'm afraid not. I think their body has just given up. We've made them comfortable."

I wait for the tears to come, but my eyes are dry. The amount of death I had seen in the past few weeks making me numb to the loss of life. "You know why I'm here..." I begin.

Kit nods. "I think we will have most of the army ready for the march in three days. Anyone not ready by that point will take months more to heal. Have you heard anything from Leah about the prosthetic production?"

"No, but I will check in with them on my way back to camp. I'll hold you to those three days, Kit."

"I know." They respond, eyes hardened against the horror they dealt with every day.

"Try to get some rest." I say, before turning away and leaving the hospital.

I stop by Leah's shop on my way to camp and find them hard at work with their new metal arm swinging an attached hammer. Parts and pieces of prosthetic limbs surround them in the small workshop. I wait for them to take a break and cough to alert them to my presence.

"Oh, hey Ixe. Need a tune-up on the leg?" They ask, pulling their hammer off to replace it with a hand.

"Not today, Leah. Kit was asking me about the status for the latest order, and I promised to stop by and get an update."

Leah nods, pushing a box of finished limbs out from behind the counter. "Just two more to finish up and I will deliver these in the morning."

"Thanks, Leah. How are you holding up?" I ask, leaning back against the doorway.

"Oh, you know how it is, Commander. I've got my good days and my bad days. Worse than some, better than most."

I nod in response before turning to the doorway.

"Oh, Commander." Leah says.

I turn back to face them.

Leah's face turns beat red as they ask the next question. "Do you think... that maybe Kit might enjoy... some flowers?"

I smile, but the emotion doesn't reach my eyes. "Only one way to find out, Leah." And I turn and leave.

We start the march three days later. The Bots who can be spared leave via the South gate, and we meet them as we march from the East. I walk in front of the column, pack on my back, gun on my shoulder, my metal leg digging marks in the dirt with every step. Trix and Olli are on one side, Leah and Kei at the other. Kit would stay at the hospital with the remaining injured, but the rest of the army fall in line. The column is anxious, yet excitement lances through them at the chance to finally do something.

In approximately seven days, we would fight for our lives —

again.

Two days later, as we trudge through the dust filled plains early in the morning, the thunder begins. It starts as a low roar off in the distance, but before long Arix is grabbing my arm and pulling me to the side. I follow, my mind slow to acknowledge the warning bells going off in my head.

"That's not a storm..." Arix says, quietly.

I look to the east, looking for dark clouds that should be hanging low over the plain, but there's nothing but blue skies. "I don't understand..." I start, and Arix pulls me closer.

"They came in the night, but I remember..."

My eyes widen as I realize what they are saying.

The drones.

The camp.

The fires.

I turn to yell, but Arix clamps a hand over my mouth and whispers in my ear, "Don't cause a panic."

Nodding, I let them know I understand, and they let me go. "What do we do?"

Arix points to a copse of trees on the horizon, "We need to redirect the column to those trees. Hopefully everyone can get inside before the ships reach us."

"No."

I turn to find Kei standing behind me. "Why?"

They sigh and step forward, joining our huddle. "Because those trees are fuel just waiting for a spark. We go in there, we get cooked."

"Then what do you propose? We can't just stand out here in the open."

"Arix has a point. What are we supposed to do?" I ask.

I shiver as Kei looks me directly in the eye. "We spread out. Reduce the amount of damage that can be done to the army."

"But... people will get hurt."

Kei nods, "But the army will survive."

I look to Arix to back me up, but they divert their gaze, and I know Kei is right. The whole is more important than the individual parts. "How do I..."

Arix and Kei look at each other, "Let us handle it. I want you to get Trix and get as far away from the group as possible."

My head snaps up, "But— "

Kei interrupts my objection, "No buts. You are the Commander and you need to be kept safe."

"They're right. We can't focus on our jobs unless we know you're safe."

I clamp my jaw tight, but I knew if I tried to defy them it would only result in a panic that we couldn't afford. "Fine. But you need to split up too."

"No, we stay with our platoons." Arix says.

"Arix, I *need* you."

"You have plenty of captains — "

"But you are my General!"

Arix stops and stares at me, mouth agape. Had I just promoted them? In an outburst of frustration? We stare at each other, Kei glancing between the two of us.

"Do you two need a room?" They ask, a sly smile on their face.

Arix turns and glares at them as I say "No. You're both right. Do what you need to, but don't take any necessary risks. I expect to see you after this is all over." I turn to walk away, refusing to acknowledge what I had said in the heat of the moment.

"Alive? Or dead?" Kei whispers, and I roll my eyes as I spot Trix in the crowd, walking with Kit and Olli.

"Trix!"

They turn to me, and make their way through the throng of

people heading the opposite direction. "Commander, I've been looking for you..."

"No time for that. We need to talk. Follow me." I turn and start marching perpendicular to the moving column, not waiting to see if Trix follows. There was no reason to worry them until it was necessary, but keeping the information from them felt wrong.

Keeping the information from the entire army felt worse.

I knew that even if they didn't panic now, the closer the ships got to us the more people would realize what was happening and chaos would ensue. I scoff as it dawns on me that that was one reason Kei and Arix wanted me far away — so the mob wouldn't trample me to death in their panic.

Trix grabs my arm, pulling me to a stop. "What the hell is going on?" I see that Olli and Kit have followed, and I'm thankful for their company.

I sigh and pull away, continuing to walk, but sure that we were far enough from the main group to at least let them know what was coming. "The thunder. It's the sound of ships coming."

They look toward the east, and I see as they process the information and know it to be true. "We have to go back... we have to warn — "

"No. Kei and Arix are taking care of it. They want us far away, they want us to... be smaller targets."

Trix looks at me, and I see the gears turning in their head. They knew why I was out here, they knew my worth, but what had they done to deserve mercy? "You're my right hand, Trix. I can't lose you." I turn to Olli and Kit. "You two are my squad. Understand?"

Tears form in Trix's eyes while Olli and Kit nod. We turn and continue the march.

As we march away from the army, the thunderous sounds in the distance start to fade. I'm about to turn back when Trix speaks, "The rising heat is changing how much we can hear them."

"What?"

"The ships. As the temperature rises, it changes the way the sound waves travel. We might not be able to hear them at all in an hour. They might see us before we know they are there. Keep your eyes open."

My eyes widen. "How do you know this?"

Trix shrugs, "I had an interest in acoustics in school."

"Acoustics?" I ask.

"The way sound travels." Kit says.

"I had this place in the warehouse district where..." Trix sees the confusion on my face and shrugs, "It doesn't matter. I just really like sound."

"That's really cool. I never had a specialty like that. I don't even know what my profession would have been."

"Oh right, you never made it to your Release." Olli says.

Silence falls between us, the sound of boots on hard dirt masking the dull thrum of the ships in the distance.

"Do you think they'll be okay?" I ask.

Trix looks at me, "The army? Yeah... I think it'll be okay."

I notice the way they refer to the army as an 'it' and not as the large mass of people that I knew it to be. I admired the way they could separate themselves from the horror that was about to come, but I couldn't do it. I couldn't see it as anything other than what it was — mass murder.

It is then that the sound hits us. A roaring so loud we have no choice but to look up. What's waiting for us there causes a weight to drop in my stomach.

A fleet of shuttles passes over us, not bothering to slow down as they move rapidly toward their target. The wind from the passing vehicles kicks up dust around us, and I cover my face with my arm, coughing.

I hear Trix yelling, and try to find them in the cloud of debris, so thick that I can barely see. "Trix!" I yell.

A hand grasps my shoulder and I turn to find Kit standing in front of me. They yell in my face, but I can't make out the words, my ears pounding. I shake my head, and they force me to turn before placing their arm on my shoulder, pointing in front of me.

I stare through the dust, trying to see what they want me to, and realization slowly descends. Like water about to drag me under, I see where the ships are heading, and my body fills with dread.

They are headed the direction we came from.

They are headed to the Bot's camp.

They are headed to finish the job.

CHAPTER THIRTY-ONE
The Net Is Dead

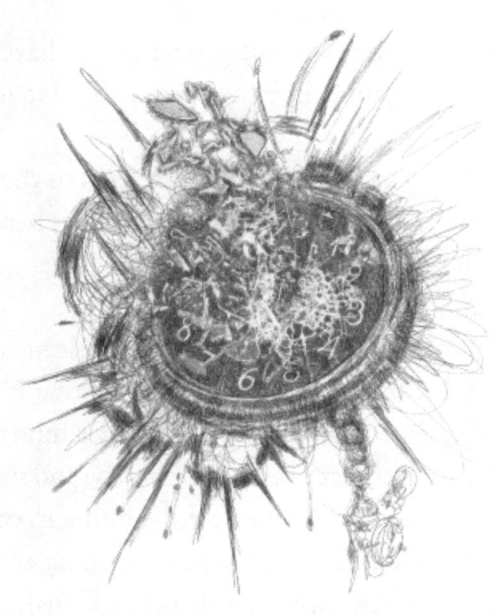

My jaw clenches as the Bot lands, the shockwave traveling through its metal frame and directly into my bones. I look to my right to see Arix clinging tightly to their Bot as they run full speed through the wasteland.

My own Bot races at full speed, jostling me in my precarious position on its shoulder. I readjust my hands, grabbing tight to the titanium plate that serves as a shoulder blade, and close my eyes.

We had been running for hours, leaving the army far behind us as we made our way back to the city. After the ships had passed over, Trix and I had sprinted back to the army, only to find Arix and Kei climbing up on their Bots.

"Jump on a Bot! We need to leave, NOW!" Arix had yelled, and Trix and I wasted no time for questions.

Now we hold on with what little strength we have left, praying that the city is getting close, but knowing we have so much more ground to traverse.

A loud booming sound draws my attention to the sky, above the dust that we leave in our wake, to find the shuttles heading back toward the main ship.

Shit... I think, *We're too late...*

But there's nothing I can do but wait as the lithe machine below me does its best. I will it to run faster, knowing that it isn't made for this type of travel, especially when it's carrying a human-sized load.

To my left I see Kei's face turned to the sky, and wonder what they are thinking. Are they worried for the humans, or are they hoping to raid what's left? *There's nothing I can do about it now...*

Another jump has me floating weightless for half a second before we crash back down to the hard earth, my head slamming against the metal beneath me. I taste blood as the world spins and fades.

I come to some time later, and find myself still slung over the Bot's shoulder, their legs still pumping away under me.

I'm about to yell for them to stop, my body a mass of bruises and pain, when they come to a screeching halt. I'm unceremoniously pulled from their shoulder and placed on the ground, my muscles collapsing under me, before they are off again, running through the city gates to help those who are hurt.

Forcing my body to respond, I limp toward Arix and Trix, Kei nowhere to be found. "Get in the city. Prioritize the children, then the hospitals. Let the Bots care for their own."

They nod and run off to the gates, barely showing any weakness from the hours of riding what was essentially a bucking bull. I move more slowly, trying to assess the damage to the city as I move, looking for any humans in the debris.

I had expected to find the city on fire, but it's dark, the stars above us casting the only light. I pass by an alley and stop suddenly, sure that I heard something. Moving quickly, I make my way down the alley, listening closely.

There.

Crying, I'm sure of it. I move more quickly, following the sound to a dumpster. Heaving the lid out of the way, a cry emerges from the dark, something trying to scuttle out of the way of the light.

"It's okay..." I say, my voice soft in the night. "I'm here to help."

Two eyes appear, the white sclera reflecting the dim light, before a dirty face makes an appearance. A young child, maybe six or seven years of age, reaches for me, and my heart pounds in a mix of fear and relief. What had happened that had this child so scared? And where were the Bots that were supposed to be protecting them?

I pull them out of the refuse, and they cling to me, wrapping their arms tightly around my neck. Their small body shivers, whether from the cold or fear, I can't tell, and I rest my head against theirs, rubbing small circles into their back.

"It'll be okay... I've got you now."

They continue to hold to me tightly, so I start walking awkwardly, working my way toward the center of the city.

There, I find the Bots.

There, I find the truth.

And it's a truth I can't bear.

"What do you mean?!" I ask again. I had heard what they had said, but my mind couldn't process it.

"They only wanted one thing..."

"And you LET them?!?!" I scream, my voice cracking in anger and grief.

Kei's hand tightens on their gun, and I find myself wishing they would raise it.

"We had no choice." Yun says, their voice calm as if this were just another simple decision to be handled by The Net.

"You codebreaker!" Arix yells, and I hear Trix take in a breath. Codebreaker was a slur of the highest offense. It implied that the perpetrator had turned their back on their own kind, which was exactly what Yun, and The Net, had done.

"You saw what they did to me, Yun. You *know* what I went through in that ship! And you decided to LET them take your children?!" My blood boils, and I feel the steam rise from my skin.

Yun doesn't back down though, "We can replace those that were..."

I lunge for the Bot, no plan in mind, but needing to do *something* with my hands. They don't fight back as I slam my fist into their chest, simply raising a hand to stop the others around them from interfering.

This only fuels my rage, and I continue to pound at their hard metal casing until my hands are raw.

A hand on my shoulder, "Ixe…"

It's Trix, tears in their eyes, their cheeks red in the cold evening air.

"They… they…" I can't bring myself to explain what would happen to the children. I can't bring myself to think about what Ritter would do. He saw them as objects, not humans, and he would use them in any way he saw fit.

Bile rises in my throat, and I turn from Trix and empty my stomach.

Flashes of memories mix with images conjured from my thoughts.

A young child being drugged and hauled into a surgical room.

A baby clinging to an uncaring soldier, unable to speak for themselves.

A teen, fists bloody, as they pound against an unmoving door.

A young adult, stripped and prostrated before Ritter, scrutinizing their every difference, their very core.

A scarred child, looking up at me with pleading eyes, begging to get out, begging to go home… to be free.

I turn and find the Bot I had rode in on. Holding out my hand, I wait for them to take it and haul me over their shoulder. "We leave. Now."

"You can't rescue them all…" Yun starts, but I stop them.

"You… are not worth the oxygen it takes to rust your metal. You think you're in control, Yun, but you have *no idea* what is coming for you. The Alliance will not stop until your corrupt leadership is disbanded. *I* will not stop until you are removed from your position.

Hear me now, Yun, and hear me well, Bri would have recycled you in a heartbeat if they were here. The Net has decayed. The Net has broken.

"The Net is dead."

We ride hard back to the army. They greet us with questions, but I have no answers. I move through the crowd, brushing off the gentle touches, the soft voices, the concern.

I only have one goal now: save the kids.

Trix stays by my side while Arix and Kei lead the army in my stead. They all know I'm lost, and I don't care. I march in silence, ignoring the pain, the blisters, the dust coating my throat. I am on a mission.

I had become the Bot that had raised me. They had entrusted me with more than I had realized, and if Yun and The Net wouldn't carry out Bri's wishes, I would. If they wanted to give up on their objective to protect humanity, I would put on the mantle.

I was wrath incarnate, and I refused to stop.

My army marched beside me, an extension of my anger. I was part of them, they were part of me, and they would follow me to the ends of the earth.

Word spread quickly through the crowd, and a silent determination settled over us.

We slept in shifts, only falling to the ground when exhaustion took hold, rising once we had enough energy to continue. Stepping over sleeping soldiers became commonplace as we marched, yet no one complained.

I had expected the Bots to return to the city, pulled back by The Net's directive, but they marched with us, just as silent as the rest of us, keeping pace with the masses.

As we approached the final ridge, Trix lays a hand on my arm. I turn to face them, feeling my muscles and bones turn as if they were gears in a machine, feeling nothing but the objective we all pursued.

"It's time."

I nod and the army halts. Wordlessly, we make our final camp, and the silence echoes over the wasteland.

This... this was the calm before the storm.

Laying on the hard earth, my gun at my side, I peek over the rise once more. Olli hands me the binoculars and I look through them, small ants in the distance jumping forward to become soldiers. We had broken from the column of soldiers and crept up the side of the ship behind low hills to get a better view of their reinforcements.

While we scouted and sent the information through our Bot to The Net, the other Bots organized the soldiers for attack. We didn't have knowledge of war or battles, but we had the element of surprise and I would not give that up easily. I note the positions of the soldiers on this side of the ship and relay the information to Olli.

Once I have ensured that all soldiers are accounted for, we slowly move back down the hill and meet our Bot.

"Two soldiers near the loading bay. Two others near the tree-line. Four soldiers circling the ship in a car of some sort. The bay door is closed, unsure of the number inside." Olli tells the Bot, reading from the scrap of paper they had used to keep track of the segments as we had gone.

The Bot nods as it relays the information to the squad assigned to this segment of the ship.

"That should be the last one." I say, "Time to get back to the main force."

We pass a few groups of soldiers on our way back, slowly

making their way to their starting points. I nod to the soldiers and clasp hands with their captains before continuing my journey. I try to remember every name and detail of their faces, knowing in a few hours they might be dead. A solemn anticipation fills the air as we confront death.

Finally arriving back at the main force, I make the final speech; the Bots relaying the information to their respective squads.

"Humans and Bots, today we stand on the brink of a battle that will decide the fate of everything we hold dear. I won't sugarcoat it—many of us may not survive the day. But know this: we are not just fighting for victory; we are fighting for our homes, our families, and the lives we've built.

"This enemy is relentless, and they seek to take what is ours, to destroy the peace we've worked so hard to create. They come with the intent to dominate, to claim what does not belong to them. But they have underestimated us. They see us as simple, as untrained, as unprepared. They think they can break us. They are wrong.

"We fight not because we crave battle, but because we have no choice. This land is our home. These people are our family. And there is no greater cause than to protect what we love. They may have more numbers, but we have something they don't, something worth dying for.

"They have come to take from us, but we'll show them that this land is not for the taking. We'll show them that our spirit cannot be broken, that our resolve is stronger than any force they can muster. We'll fight with everything we have, because this is our home, and we won't let them take it from us!

"Stand tall, fight hard, and let them know they aren't facing mere resistance—they are facing the unbreakable will of a people defending their own. For our homes, for our lives, for our future—this is our stand, and we will not yield!

"Now, let's show them what it means to fight for what is ours. Let's show them the power of a people defending their own. For our land, for our families!"

As I conclude, I feel the tears running down my cheeks. The tears of almost a year's worth of fighting, of suffering, not only for myself but for all the humans before me. For the Bots who lost their city, and their lives. For Bri. For Loc. Even for Leah.

In the back, a soldier silently raises a fist, a tribute to our shared experience. Slowly, the soldiers around them pick up the movement and eventually they all stand before me, a silent mass of fists to show their support and their surrender to my command.

I turn, not wiping the tears from my face, and march into the forest once again. The forest that had changed my life in so many ways.

CHAPTER THIRTY-TWO
War is... Nothing

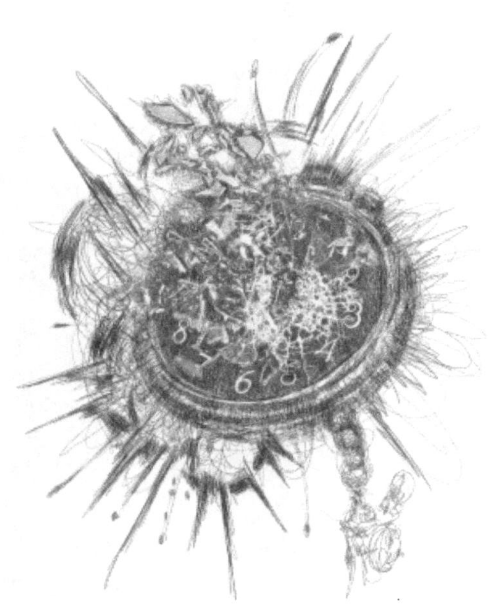

We move swiftly and silently through the trees as we make our way closer to the ship, closer to battle. When I see the metal ship gleam through the trees on the other side of the forest, I halt, and everyone slowly comes to a stop behind me. Silently nodding to the Bot at my side, I give the final command and they transmit the order to the other squads. A roar in the distance signals the first squad to the left charging at the ship, a war cry carried to us by the wind. Another cry rises to my right, and the soldiers around the loading bay in front of us grab their guns and turn to face the incoming threat.

"Attack!" I hear them shout before tripping an alarm to alert those inside the ship. I hold up my hand, a sign to wait, as tensions rise within my own group. They shuffle behind me, anxious to help their comrades, but I know we have to wait for the right moment to be most effective.

The war cries fade as gunshots ring out in the surrounding distance. I bring down my hand as the loading bay door lurches and lowers; the signal to move. We move as one large silent mass, a snake in the grass approaching its prey.

We are through the trees and in the clearing before the door hits the ground. My front-line soldiers spread out, holding large shields fabricated by Leah. It takes two to a shield to haul it forward and plant it into the ground, but they move efficiently, spacing them a foot apart in the hard earth. Bunkering down behind the shields my soldiers lean out, placing the barrels of their guns between the barriers, pointing directly at the door. Other soldiers run up, taking their places behind the shields, while still more use the trees for cover. I slide behind my shield, pulling my gun into my lap.

Gunshots still ring in the distance, but silence dominates my squad as we watch the door...

    lower...

        lower...

            lower...

thud.

My ears explode with sound. The impact of dozens of guns firing at once has me crouching, hands over my ears. Bullets ricochet off of the protective shields, flying through the air to bury themselves in the ground or flesh. Blood sprays to my right and I see a soldier collapse, a hole through their head. Another falls to my left.

"Blind fire!!" I yell over the noise, and the soldiers nearest me pull their heads behind the shields, firing blindly toward the door and the enemies there. The order ripples down the lines, slowly making its way to the ends of the squad, but not before more soldiers drop dead. *Our enemy is trained.* I remind myself, pulling my remaining limbs in tighter to my body.

The shooting continues for what feels like hours, but finally slows to a stop. In the sudden silence, I see soldiers looking toward each other, the same question reflected in their eyes. I peek over the shield and see that their soldiers have retreated further into the ship. "Something's not right..." I say to the soldier to my left, a human not much older than myself.

Soldiers on either side emerge from cover, tending to the wounded or scanning in disbelief of our victory. I slowly stand and scan the battlefield. Moans and cries for help ring from both sides, and I wonder why the humans didn't help their own soldiers to safety. A quick scan shows that we didn't do as bad as I thought, taking down just as many of them as they had of us.

I sigh in relief and take a few steps forward, trying to see the other squads on the distant horizon. Gunfire still rings out from the other battles, and I wonder how many soldiers still stand. How would they relay their surrender to the humans still on the battlefield?

I turn and see the Bot assigned to my squad approaching from the tree line. I open my mouth to tell them to relay a message when I hear a clicking noise behind me. Turning, I spot a large panel sliding down from higher on the ship's side. Curious, I step to the side to get a better angle, and fear settles over me like a blanket. "Run!!" I scream, bolting for the closest shelter available — the ship. The soldiers follow my lead a half second later; a half second too late.

The turret opens fire on my army. I stare in horror as the lasers slice their bodies in half, the shields that had protected them now being melted like butter by the hot beams of the turret. I drop to my knees, unable to look away from the scene in front of me. The turret turns and runs back through the soldiers, now focusing on those hiding in the trees. The commotion drowns out my pleas for them to run, and tears spill from my eyes.

Trix is next to me, placing their hand on my shoulder, shaking me harshly, but it sounds like they are too distant to reach me. "Ixe! Ixe move!!" I snap back to reality and see that a band of soldiers is behind me, shooting into the ship at soldiers hiding behind crates. I throw myself to the side, behind a large case, and my soldiers move from protecting me to hiding themselves. More soldiers outside dodge the plasma turret and make their way to the sides of the ship, able to hide out of range.

I grab my gun and put it to my shoulder, like the soldiers taught me, and lean out from behind the crate. I shoot the first bullets; the gun thudding into my shoulder as the force of the chemical reaction causes the weapon to lurch back. I breathe, focus, and pull the trigger again. This time I'm more prepared and hold my shot steady. Time passes by in rounds of shooting.

Aim.

Shoot.

Empty.

Reload.

My mind empties, leaving only the battle, until ammo runs dry. As our side fires the last rounds, I still hear the pop of the enemy's guns and know we are doomed. I lean back against the case and close my eyes. Why had I thought this was possible? I had let Mar talk me into a war that we couldn't win, and for what? Love?

No. I did this for Bri, for Loc, for the city I grew up in. I did this for the burned soldiers from the camp attack. I did this for the soldiers lost to the bullets, to the lasers. I even did this for the enemy's soldiers who would die in the war to come; for Leah. I fought to end the fighting.

I take a deep breath and peek around the corner as the enemy stops firing, as they realize we've run out of ammo.

"Listen to me!" I yell out. "No one wants to die here today. We just want peace. Let me talk to Ritter."

"Colonel Ritter won't listen to you. You are an abomination, and need to be exterminated."

"Is that really what you think of us?" I ask.

"It's what we know."

"Then let me talk to Rich McNally." I try, holding my breath.

Laughter echoes around the room. "McNally? Of course, you would want to talk to that traitor. We sent him packing weeks ago."

My heart sinks as the words make their way into my head.

He's dead.

No way he survived without oxygen on the planet.

He's dead.

They wouldn't have given him another shuttle.

He's dead.

It rings through my head like a bell, the sound returning repeatedly. Olli grabs my arm and squeezes tightly. I look into their eyes and know what I have to do.

I slide around the crates in the cargo bay, making my way to the humans hiding in the back. Moving as silently as possible, I spot my fellow soldiers on the opposite side, knives in hand, maneuvering between their own crates. I look behind me and see Trix and Olli following. With a vicious feeling filling my soul, I move and a gruesome smile spreads across my face.

I would make them pay.

The first soldier makes no sound as I slit their throat. The warm blood gushes from the wound, over my hand and down their chest. I don't stop to see if they were male or female, it didn't matter, they were the enemy. After the third falls to the ground, I notice their soldiers moving past us, guns raised and prepared to shoot. I ignore them and move down the hall at the back of the cargo bay. We move silently, myself and the five soldiers I have left, one of which is our Bot.

We work our way through the halls, killing anyone in our path, not knowing where we are headed. It didn't matter, though. My head screamed to kill. To find every one of these humans and make them suffer as they had made me suffer. As they had made the soldiers and the Bots suffer. As they had made the children suffer. Meanwhile, the thought kept pounding in my head like a heartbeat that refused to quit:

He's dead.

He's dead.

He's dead.

Before long, an alarm sounds. "They found our trail," Trix says. We keep moving forward as the sound of footsteps grows louder. Eventually, we come to a door leading into a mess hall. I quickly pull it open and usher everyone in. My soldiers take strategic places around the room, turning over tables to make cover. Closing the door behind me, I take a stance to the side of the door and wait.

No matter what happened, I wouldn't leave here until Ritter was dead, or I was.

We listen as the footsteps approach the doors, and then retreat, continuing down the hall on the other side. Still as stone for a few more seconds, we collectively breathe a sigh of relief and stand.

"We can backtrack and try to find the bridge..." Trix says, but before they can finish their sentence, a bullet rips through their chest.

Time slows.

I scream.

Reaching out to them, I watch as they fall, and Loc is before me, flying down the hall. Trix flashes back in place and our time together flips through my head in broken images, pain ripping through me at the realization that we would never share another laugh together. I think of Niv, Trix's lover, who had died unfairly at the hands of poverty, and now Trix would never see the changes they had dreamed for the world.

Their body drops to a heap on the floor and I spin to face the shooter. Ritter stands behind the counter, holding a pistol pointing to the ceiling. Soldiers surround him, all of whom are pointing guns in our direction.

"You really didn't think you could storm our entire ship with just six soldiers, did you?" His voice drawls out of him, slow, patient, as if he has all the time in the world.

My blood boils as I stare him down. The man who had caused the death of so many of my friends. They shimmer before my eyes in a long line of faces; some still alive, others decayed beyond recognition. "We did pretty well outside." I hiss through my teeth.

"Yeah, well, those were just the foot soldiers. The lowest of the low. Our main force is inside the ship where you now find yourselves, with one less soldier, it seems." He gestures to Trix's body, blood pooling underneath them.

I knew they were gone. I knew the moment they fell. Another person's death on me. I shouldn't have started this fight; a fight I knew we couldn't win. I grit my teeth, determined not to add one more person to the list of casualties on my head. What could I really do, though? How would I stop these soldiers from shooting us where we stood? I was helpless, and I knew it. This room would be full of the blood of my soldiers soon enough; the only relief was that mine would be mixed among them. The war would finally be over for me, and I was ready to face it.

"Get on your knees," Ritter says, done with the talking. We all start to obey, but he points that pistol at me and says, "Not you, dear. I want you to stand and watch. Stare your soldiers in the eyes as I blow their brains out. And then, then we can continue our... experiments."

By the way he grins, I know it's not medical science he is after, but torture. Torture for killing so many of his soldiers. For escaping and turning one of his men against him. For just being alive was an 'abomination' in his eyes.

I wonder if the children are facing the same fate right now.

Once my soldiers are on their knees, fingers laced behind their heads, Ritter's men come forward and drag them into place in front of me, placing them so that I would be forced to look into their eyes as they went dark.

Ritter speaks again, "You know, when we found Rich, I truly believed that he was still my man. After months in that shuttle alone — or, I thought he was alone — he had finally returned to me. He was one of my most decorated soldiers before the incident. If he were anyone else, I would have thrown him outside the instant he murdered another one of my men, but he was Rich; a man I had come to love as my own."

I hiss at those words. This man could not know love.

"So, when I found him, I was delighted. But then pieces of his story weren't adding up. How is it that you, a science experiment, had forced him to a shuttle in the first place? Especially with only one arm and one leg. And then why would you have stayed? You could have forced him to fly you to any city on Earth, so why stay and hold him captive for months on end? At the end of the day, my... specialist... got the truth out of him."

I cringe at the word specialist, knowing that Rich had been tortured because of me, because we had had no other option.

"I still couldn't believe it, though. *My* Rich, falling in love with an abomination?" His face contorts with disgust as he looks me up and down like a slab of meat. "Oh well. Fool me once, shame on you; fool me twice... now that's not something I will put up with." He puts the barrel of the gun to the back of the first human's head and pulls the trigger.

I see the blood splatter across the ground as the light goes out of the soldier's eyes. I gasp at the sudden brutality and end of a life; a life that was only there to serve me and this war. I lurch forward, no plan in mind, but knowing I had to get him to stop this. His soldiers quickly grab my arms, pinning them behind my back and holding me in place. Bile rises in my throat as I add another life to the tally in my head, tears streaming down my face.

Ritter moves to the next human in line, trembling on the ground in front of me. I look deep into their eyes, praying that they can see the regret in my own, but all I see reflected back is fear. "You really do care for these people, don't you?" He asks as he pulls the trigger, the bullet ripping through their head and blowing out a chunk of their face on its exit.

I collapse to my knees, unable to stand as a single word escapes my lips. "Please..."

"What was that, Abomination?" He asks as he places the barrel against the temple of the next human. I swallow a lump in my throat as I realize it's Olli. Olli: the simple hunter. The gentle giant. The storyteller. I recall the time we had spent hunting in the wasteland; the laughter that had echoed on the plains; the joy on our faces when I finally spotted the tracks. They had been a friend when I had no one to lean on, and now they were depending on me to save their life.

But I *can't*.

Ritter pulls the trigger a third time.

The blood splatters onto my face, mixing with the tears that now threaten to drown me. As he moves to the next and final human, I lay my face in the pool of Olli's blood and beg. "Please stop...."

His laugh is booming and drawn out. He pulls my head up, watching the blood drip down my face, and says, "No."

The doors behind me burst open and the room is awash in gunfire. I cover my head, protecting myself as confusion breaks out. I see Ritter, laying on the floor beside me, shock on his face. His gun, knocked from his hand, lays next to me. Before I know what I'm doing, I pick it up, place the barrel to his forehead, and pull the trigger. I see the spark of life extinguish in him and I wait to feel a sense of relief, but it isn't there.

The only feeling left is pain.

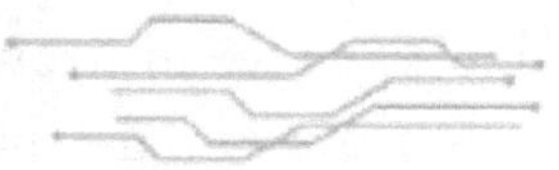

Silence rings out as the enemy soldiers lay dead before me. I drop the smoking gun from my hand, turning to see who had come to help.

Roa reaches out a hand. "I thought you could use some reinforcements." Taking their hand, I rise to my feet.

"You abandoned us." I say harshly, not bothering to wipe the blood dripping from my chin.

Roa's gaze falls to Trix's body, and I see pain reflected in their eyes. "I know... By the time I realized my mistake, I was too late."

Mar steps up beside Roa and places a hand on their shoulder, "It wasn't just Roa who made a terrible decision. Once we made it to Barllay and saw the state of things... It cemented the cause in our heads, but we had already lost so much time. We arrived at the camp two days after you left, and have been trying to catch up since. When Yun told us that the soldiers had taken the children..."

I finally glance beyond them and see the hard looks of the soldiers standing in the hall. As much as I wanted to thank all of them for coming to the rescue, the only thing I can see is Olli's head exploding only moments before. I scowl, "You were too late. You were *all* too late." I push my way through their shocked expressions and force my way into the hall.

Mar is not far behind me as I march my way through hall after hall. I am weaponless, but I don't care. I need to get their faces out of my head, and the only way to do that was to keep moving, even if it meant my life was forfeit.

I hear the occasional gun firing around me, and see a soldier walking out of a side room fall to the ground as Roa's soldier behind me shoots them down, but I keep walking until Mar grabs my arm and forcibly stops me.

"Ixe! Stop! Look!" Mar points to a sign with directions to different parts of the ship, and I see an arrow pointing toward the bridge. Rich had given me lessons on the ship and the terminology the humans used. I knew the bridge was where the ship's controls were located. I head in that direction, an idea coming to me.

"No, we need to go to the holding cells," Mar says, trying to stop me.

"You go. I'm going to finish this. Once and for all."

A few minutes later, I step into the bridge and find three humans unprepared. We quickly dispatch them and I turn to the Bot, one of the soldiers that had survived the slaughter. "Can you upload the Net to another device if we plug you in?"

The Bot nods, and I set them to their task, directing Roa's soldiers to take up positions around the door. I look at Roa and they nod, handing over the command to me. Without hesitation, the soldiers do as commanded while I discover the door's control panel. I enter the command to close the doors and lock them as we hear people running toward us, following our trail of bodies through the ship.

The doors thud closed before they reach us, and we hear shouting and pounding fists against metal. I turn back to the Bot and they nod; we're in. I give the last command, steel in my voice. "Turn off the oxygen."

A soldier turns to me in alarm, "But... That will..." *Genocide.* We all hear the word reverberate through the room, yet no one has said it out loud.

I think of Avi and their insistence that the only way to win this war and save ourselves was to eliminate the enemy humans. "Their time is over. It's our time now. Do it."

The Bot goes still; The Net making a decision that we cannot see, but eventually they nod. Time stills as the fans feeding the room oxygen stop operating. The humans stop pounding on the door as they realize what is happening. Footsteps quickly recede, and we stand there listening to the growing silence. The air stills, completing the suffocating effect, and I enter the command to open the door.

We slowly follow the signs to the cells; passing doomed humans along the way. They sit on the floor crying; they try to attack; they run for shuttles that won't be there by the time they arrive. Some will escape, some may survive in space suits for a time, but most will die, suffocating in the atmosphere that they created.

Flashes of memory assault me as we turn down the next hall, and I know exactly where to go. I fight through the onslaught, trying to avoid thinking of Loc flying, a bullet hole spilling blood into my hands; of Leah dragging me into surgery, ready to cut more flesh; of Rich holding me down, strapping me to a cold table as I fight to be free.

All I can hope is that we made it in time to save them the horror of what I went through.

The hall of cells is just as I remember, and I immediately head for my cell, ripping it open to find ten children shoved into the small room. They are clean, well cared for, but terrified as I step in, and I realize I'm drenched in blood.

"It's okay... It's all over." I reach out to the nearest child, and they flinch away.

Anger fills me again, and I force myself to take a deep breath before kneeling on the floor in front of the kids. I hear my other soldiers open doors down the hall, similar voices floating into the hall as they try to calm the other children.

"Ixe?" A taller child, ten or eleven, steps forward.

I nod slowly, trying to hold back tears.

"It's okay guys, I know them! They really are here to help us."

The tension in the room breaks, and the kids run forward, almost tackling me to the floor, and memories of the nursery come flooding back to me.

We walk slowly through the halls, clearing every room as we make our way back to the cargo bay. I step out into the sunshine, looking to the sky with my eyes closed, as I let the sun warm my icy heart. I had just murdered an entire species with one command, yet I couldn't bring myself to care. My heart was ice, my blood frozen in my veins.

I had done it. I had ended a war, and now all I wanted was to stop: stop thinking, stop breathing, stop living... My ears pick up the sounds of someone sobbing and I slowly realize it's me. I collapse to my knees in the dirt, feeling the puddles of blood seep into my pants. A hand lays gently on my shoulder and I hear a voice repeat, "It's over... It's over..."

The hollow feeling in my chest expands, consuming every part of me before spreading to those around me. I feel like I might swallow the Earth whole with the pain exuding from every pore, and yet I can't stop. My breath catches in my throat before I sob again, letting more of me die with the soldiers who had trusted in my command, and it takes everything in me not to shatter into a million pieces.

Arms wrap around me, and I lay my head against them, not caring who was holding me in my fragile state, just knowing that I needed to take every inch of strength it offered me.

"Commander!" I hear someone yell from a distance. "Commander Ixe!" they yell again, urgency in their voice. I turn to find the remnants of a squad hauling a human in a suit toward me. Whatever they had to say, it was too late. The war was over. "Commander, it's Rich!"

My stomach flips inside me. *Rich is alive?!* I quickly stand using Mar's shoulder. It had been them who was holding me together.

I hear the soldier yell again, "It's Rich!!!", and I run toward the human they are carrying. They set him down on the ground, a bullet hole through the protective suit he wears. "He helped save us, Commander. He turned on his own people."

I look through the thin glass that separates us and my eyes water. The hole inside me hadn't stopped growing, but it was slowing to a small leak. "Rich..." I say, my voice raw.

"Hey, Echo." He says, and I sob. I see blood pooling in the suit around the hole. "Don't worry, I'll be fine. I just need to get into the ship."

My heart shatters. "Rich... I... I turned off the oxygen."

His eyes glaze over as he realizes what I've done. His entire species — himself — doomed to die. I look for the anger, the fear, anything in his eyes, but he is calm. "It's okay, Echo. After everything we've done... we deserve it."

"No!" I sob, collapsing over him. He couldn't give up! I just got him back. "We will figure something out. We have to." I pull back and place my hand over the hole that is slowly leaking air. "I will take you to the city. To the hydroponics lab."

He shakes his head. "No, Ixe, it's too far. We both know..." He stops mid sentence as he glances at the sky.

"You can't leave me, Rich. I have no meaning without you. I love you. Do you hear me? I love you, Richard McNally. Even your demons, and I won't let you give up."

Rich stares beyond me, and slowly raises his hand, pointing. I turn and look toward the sky where I see a streak fly by. Turning to my left, I see more streaks shooting through the air. "No..."

I hear the soldiers gasp and look to my right. Another ship slowly comes down and lands, the wave of dust heading straight toward us.

A Sneak Peek at Shadows of Legacy

The wasteland stretches before us, a distance that had seemed so short just a few hours ago now a clock ticking down to our demise. The piles of debris, once reminders of our hard fought victory, now threaten what little remains of our once great army.

His voice floats to me among the soldier's cries, but I ignore the pleas as I drag in another hot breath, forcing my lungs to expand and deliver much needed oxygen to my straining muscles.

I glance to the side as we run, my attempts to calculate the speed at which the wall approaches a fruitless endeavor. Distance in the wasteland was warped, our senses tricked by the waves of heat that beat into the ground around us. Even if I could manage to determine our speed versus that of our impending doom it would change nothing. Our only hope ditching our supplies and running.

"Just leave me!" Rich yells again, trying to fight his way out of the grip of my soldiers. I ignore him for the fifth time as we race to safety, shock-waves threatening us from every direction. We move as one into the cargo bay, the blast from the first landing vessel hitting the ship as we do. I turn and stare at the debris flying by the open doors, my soldiers moving further into the metal beast that had been my prison.

We had been lucky with the first wave, but I know that luck will run out quickly enough. I glance at my soldiers, doubled over and heaving from the strain of carrying a fully grown man at a full sprint. Rich lies on the ground between them, holding a hand over the hole in his suit, blood and oxygen mixing as they leak between his fingers.

Looking to the door further in the cargo bay, I run through the options available. The correct thing to do would be to order them inside the ship. There was enough food and supplies to keep us alive for months — possibly years. It would be a good defensive position in case the humans attacked, a good base to run the army from as we dealt with the newest invaders.

I know what I should do as commander, but my eyes dart back to the chaos outside and I hesitate in giving the order. I should save my soldiers, but if there is a chance to save Rich...

"Ixe!" Arix yells from behind me. I turn to face them and see Rich's body convulsing on the floor as he spews hateful slurs and attempts to grab their guns. "What is wrong with him?!" they shout over the sound of the tempest whirling dust around us.

"He's out of control..." I whisper to myself, knowing that whatever was happening to the humans was getting worse. A second blast of pressure hits the ship, followed closely by a third. I glance back at the opening and see the trees move as another surge heads straight towards the open doors. "Get down!" I yell, dropping to the ground as the wave slams into us.

A tree branch flies past my face, piercing the soldier behind me through the neck. Their gurgling noise mixes with the sound of the wind whipping around us as they drop to the floor, blood pooling at my feet.

"We have to get out of here!" Arix yells over the chaos, and I nod my agreement.

"Pick him up and move!!" I yell to the soldiers as I run to their side and twist my fingers into Rich's suit. We heave him up in the air, running to the open bay doors. My decision made, we turn and jog toward the descending ship in the distance. I pull my shirt over my face, blocking most of the grime from entering my nose and mouth, and I see the soldiers follow my example. Our only benefit is that there is nothing but dust between us and the landing ship; nothing that could impale us as we run — hopefully.

As we sprint towards the vessel, the ground trembles beneath our feet, adding to the adrenaline coursing through our veins. My eyes sting, my lungs gasping for clean air as I glance back, checking on the rest of the soldiers keeping pace behind us. They are determined, their expressions masked by the layer of dirt on their faces.

These are *my* soldiers, risking their lives for a man they had just met. Risking their lives because *I* said so. I think of dismissing them. Telling them to run for safety, but I know I can't afford to falter now; Rich's life depends on our speed and resilience. I turn back toward the ship, seeing it loom ever closer.

I lower my head and picture a bull from the textbooks charging a target. I am the bull. I will make it.

I will... save him...

My mind calms, the world around me fading as I focus on my singular goal. I put away the shame, the uncertainty, and the fear — leaving pure adrenaline in its place.

Suddenly we're there, the sleek design of the colossal metal structure standing out amidst the barren landscape. The air is clearer here, and I pull my shirt back down, releasing my face from its suffocating grasp.

Motioning for another soldier to take my place holding Rich, I run up to the loading bay doors and pound my fist against them. "Open the doors! Open the damn doors! I know you're in there! We have one of your men! Do you want him to die?"

I'm impatient. Frantic. I know that there is little time left to save him, and he is all I have left...

Trix...

Olli...

Finally, the doors in front of me shudder and collapse. Tears streak through the layers of dust on my face as I run from the descending panels to take my place at Rich's side.

We struggle as he convulses again, but manage to hold on as he thrashes against us. "We're almost there, Rich. Just hold on," I whisper, my arm straining with the effort of keeping him lifted off the ground. Eventually, the doors land in their final position, opening to the inside of the ship.

I look up and see a wall of soldiers wearing the same suit as the humans we had eradicated, all pointing their weapons at us. My soldiers retaliate, scrambling to raise their firearms.

"Stand down!" I tell my soldiers and they cautiously lower them back down. "We are not enemies!" I yell to the humans over the sound of the ship, engines still running from the recent touchdown. "We have a wounded human that needs attention!" I gesture to Rich.

"Who are you?"

"There's no time for that now! He needs your help!"

No one moves.

Consumed by anger, I release a roar of frustration before aggressively advancing. They tighten their grip on their weapons, but no one fires. I thrust out my wrists with a scowl on my face. "Take me. I will answer all of your questions. You can even..." I swallow around the lump in my throat "...experiment on me; see how I breathe the air around us, but you have to help him! I'm begging you."

My soldiers move to protect me, but Roa holds up a hand, stopping them in their tracks.

"JUST TAKE HIM INSIDE THE FUCKING SHIP!" I yell, falling to my knees in defeat, my tears falling silently to the ground beneath me. If these idiots won't listen to me, then all hope is lost for Rich.

I feel the barrel of a gun on my head as one of the soldiers steps forward, holding it to my skull. I remain still, every muscle in my body screaming to defend, but knowing that the moment I did, I was condemning not only Rich, but all of my soldiers to death. I stare at the ground under me, counting the seconds.

One...

Two...

Three...

Four...

Finally, I hear movement as a small group breaks from the rest of the soldiers and walks around me. I keep still, hearing grunts as the soldiers take Rich from my people. I continue to count, refusing to let my muscles tremble with the fear inside me.

Eight...

Nine...

They pass by and I let out a sigh.

Suddenly, there is a rough hand on my shoulder and someone wrenches my arms backwards. Grabbing my wrists, the human soldiers forcefully pin both of my arms behind my back, lifting me to my feet. I move willingly, resisting the urge to look back at the soldiers I'm leaving behind.

The only thing stifling the panic that rises in me is knowing that no matter what happens to me in this place, Rich will live.

About the Author

Ryan King is an American author and the creator of *The Resurgence Chronicles*, a dystopian science fiction trilogy. His work explores themes of survival, identity, and the human condition in speculative future settings. Beyond writing, he advocates for neurodiversity in professional spaces and draws on his background in technology and analysis to inform his storytelling. He lives with his spouse and two children.

Connect with the Author

Follow me on Social Media:

Website: ryanlking.com
Instagram: ryanlking.author
Blue Sky: rlking.bsky.social